THE EMPIRE OF EMPTY WARS

SERPENTS AND KINGS
BOOK THREE

S.M. GAITHER

THE EMPIRE OF EMPTY WARS

S. M. GAITHER

A BRIEF GLOSSARY OF THE LOCATIONS, DEITIES, AND CLANS OF THE SUNDOLIAN EMPIRE

Kingdom of Valin

Capital: Rykarra

Ruled by: High-Rook-King Emrys

Provinces: Cobos, Tera, Sievos, Nyres

Served by Middle-Gods/Goddesses: Kerse (Bone Clan), Taiga (Ice Clan), Moto (Fire Clan)

Formerly Served by: Mairu (Serpent Clan)

Significant Landmarks/Cities: Village of Vanish, Antiek Jungle, Northern Sinhara Mountains, Greybank Peninsula, Cobos Desert

Kingdom of Lumeria

Capital: Idalia

Ruled by: Sun-Queen Eliana and Sun-King Levant

Provinces: Naquad, Permarn, Kyros

Served by Middle-Gods/Goddesses: Cepheid (Star

Clan), Indre (Sky Clan), Nephele (Storm Clan), Inya (Moon Clan)

Significant Landmarks/Cities: Verlore Forest, Nephele Dustfields, Indres River, Southern Sinhara Mountains, Vespera (the village of Stars), The Siran Caverns

Kingdom of Galasea

Capital: Eriden

Ruled by: Stone-King Cederic and Stone-King Erik

Provinces: Eshnur, Kemar, Calah

Served by Middle-Gods/Goddesses: Namu (Oak Clan), Intaba (Mountain Clan), Santi (Sand Clan), Amanzi (Sea Clan)

Significant Landmarks/Cities: Kemarian Mines, The Bay of Sinking Souls

CLANS OF THE  Sundolian Empire

Rook

ICE

BONE

SERPENT

FIRE

Sun

STAR

MOON

SKY

STORM

Stone

OAK

MTN.

SAND

OCEAN

CHAPTER 1

THE PRISON CHAMBERS OF THE PALACE OF THE SUN WERE blindingly bright, which made it impossible for Alaya to properly see her tormentors.

Her eyes watered. She kept them fixed on the gritty stone floor, watching as it glittered in the sunlight. Magic sparked around her, an electric current of it circling her body—not quite touching, but buzzing close enough that the hairs on her arms and along the back of her neck had prickled to attention. Her heart was racing, tingling with that electric energy, hammering a little faster with every pulse of it.

The Storm-kind responsible for that magic stood in one corner of her prison.

Sylven Adler, the man responsible for bringing that Storm-kind to her, stood in another.

And the King of the Sun, as always, watched the spectacle from a platform high above, his body a lanky silhouette with a crown of sharply twisted spires on its head.

Above him were the windows that surrounded the entire room, fitted with special shades that were almost constantly being adjusted by servants. Those windows were designed with a purpose—cut and angled in such a way that throughout the entire day, the sun's rays were forever being siphoned through them and made to shine directly onto the spot where Alaya was shackled to the wall.

A minor annoyance, really, compared to the other things she had endured during her time in this place. But they were likely hoping that she was only one minor annoyance away from breaking completely.

They were hoping in vain.

She would not be broken.

The sunlight grew bolder, suddenly, as if in punishment for her rebellious thoughts. Alaya imagined Solatis, the upper-goddess of the Sun and the patron deity of Lumeria, breaking through the clouds with her sword of light, stabbing through the windows and spotlighting her prisoner.

Alaya closed her watering eyes. Focused on the bit of warmth that the blast of sun had at least brought with it. Moments later, she heard Sylven walking closer to her.

She had memorized it now, after days of this: The particular sound of his steps against the stone. His gait was distinct. He tended to favor his right leg; hardly noticeable unless one was paying attention.

But she was always paying attention. Paying attention to those small sounds, to the feel of the gritty stone under her palms, to whatever small warmths she could imagine washing over her skin. All of the things keeping her grounded. Keeping her from breaking...

And taking her focus away from the restless, dangerous power simmering inside of her.

She heard Sylven crouching down beside her.

She wanted to turn her body away from him, but she kept still. It wasn't as though she could go far, anyhow; the shackles confining her were attached to chains so short that she couldn't even properly stand. Even worse, they seemed to tighten every time she moved.

"You can stop this, if only you use your magic," said Sylven. "I know you can take hold of the Storm magic encircling you. That you could crush it, or simply throw it back at the one creating it. I've seen you do it." His voice lowered to a near whisper. "Why not show the Sun King what you're capable of? Make certain that any thoughts he might be having of abandoning our alliance are demolished? Make him *fear* you, as he should?"

Alaya lifted her head, the movement causing a bit of that magic still twisting around her to brush her elbow. She winced at the sting it caused, and at the memory of the day's torture and the torture of all the days before that —the collective pain of it all burned across her skin, ached in her head, thrummed deep in her bones.

"Why suffer when you could fight?"

She blinked her eyes open. "Because I am not a fool."

"Most certainly not," he agreed. "But you also aren't immune to pain, and everyone has their limits to what they can withstand. There's no point in dragging this pain out when we both know that you're only going to give in eventually."

"No," she said. "I am *not*."

Because time would heal bruises and aches, along with whatever additional scars the looming Storm-kind might leave on her body. Hopefully.

But it *wouldn't* heal the side-effects of her own power, should she choose to use it.

Only another Serpent-kind could do that.

The use of the more intense forms of her magic—such as when she controlled *other* people's magic—scrambled her thoughts and drained her life force, opening up a kind of void inside of her. Others born with the mark of the Serpent could sacrifice their own energy to her, and she could take it and recover by it...

But when another Serpent-kind's energy filled in that void, it carried other pieces of them in with it.

And whether those pieces were malicious or benevolent, they *all* altered her in some fashion. In minor, temporary ways, usually; she was far more powerful than most Serpent-kind, and so she could shed most of their influences as surely as a snake twisting free of its old skin.

The only one she hadn't managed to entirely twist free of was Sylven.

His energy was dangerously invigorating. More powerful than any other Serpent-kind's she'd encountered—but then, so too was the influence he worked over her in return.

In the few instances when she'd let him in, his controlling magic had come along with his healing, bending her thoughts to his liking, distorting them so completely that she now found it difficult to trust even the simplest fact in her own mind.

She *knew* he was doing it.

He had made no secret of it. But she had no choice but to rely on him—because nothing else she'd found could bring her back from the dangerous edges that her magic carried her to.

It had been only weeks ago when she'd last faced a deathly edge. Weeks since she and her magic had finally faced off against the magic of Haben, the High King of the Sundolian Empire.

She remembered trying to control the breath from the king's lungs, the beat from his heart.

She remembered falling from the roof of his palace.

She remembered the ground rising up to meet her, but not the impact of it. And then she had awakened—barely —in a camp in the northern, mountainous parts of the Lumerian Kingdom.

At first, she hadn't known what day it was.

Where she was.

Who she was, nor who the faces flashing in her mind were—and once she *did* remember them, she had no idea how many days had passed since she'd last seen Emrys or Sade or Rue, nor what had happened to them in those days since she'd apparently been carried away from the city of Rykarra.

And there in those mountains of Northern Lumeria, she had begged for death.

She had received healing instead, and because she had been too far gone to realize what she was doing, she hadn't pushed Sylven away as she should have; she had instead grasped his hand.

More of his magic had siphoned its way into her, poisoning her mind further.

When she fully woke, she had been told that she'd killed the High King of the Sundolian Empire. And she believed it—her memories of that battle with him were not spotless, not entirely untwisted, but they were certainly *there*.

Her body had ached badly enough that it was easy to believe she had performed devastatingly powerful magic, too.

Magic that should have killed her. That *would* have killed her—as Sylven had already reminded her, multiple times—if he had not chosen to save her and bring her back to the Sun Palace, just as he had once before.

He had been trying to work his magic over her, to convince her to serve alongside him and strengthen their alliance with the Sun King, Levant, ever since.

She had resisted.

Even with Sylven's poisonous magic pressing through her thoughts, she was aware enough to know that she needed to *continue* resisting.

Which was why the Sun King had declared her a potential danger to both himself and his kingdom, and demanded she be locked up in a cell.

If she cannot be controlled, she will be contained.

If she can not be contained, she will be killed.

Sylven, however, did not intend to let her die.

She knew this. She was too powerful, too potentially useful to him.

His expression now was one of mild contempt; the closest he usually came to letting his frustrations with her show.

She was in no position to gloat, but she couldn't help the smug satisfaction she felt over knowing that, at least for the moment, she was winning their battle of wills.

She lowered her voice to the same covert tone he'd used and asked, "Is it killing you, not being able to get what you want for once?"

He shrugged. "I'm a patient man."

"All the patience in the world is not going to break me, just so you know. If anyone is dragging things out unnecessarily, it's *you.* You could just let me go and save yourself a lot of trouble."

"I'm not concerned with a little trouble. And I've broken far more powerful people than you." The words were so perfectly calm that they were unnerving, but Alaya kept her voice steady and fought off the shiver trying to rip through her.

"Then why is it taking you so long to deal with *me*?" she asked.

He didn't reply for a long moment.

Then his hand reached forward and snatched her by the chin.

She tried to jerk out of his grasp.

He only gripped her more tightly.

Suddenly, the shackles around her wrists and ankles were tightening along with his grip, just as she had imagined them doing earlier—only, this time, it was not from her own movements.

It was magic.

Serpent magic.

His magic.

Sylven's lips were mouthing silent words, and she felt a shifting in the energies of the room; ever since she had taken the fire-soul into her body, she had been able to *see* those differently-colored energies around most things if she focused on them.

She couldn't see Sylven's energy, for some reason.

She had never been able to.

It was strange, and yet another facet of her powers she didn't understand, but it didn't matter at the moment; what mattered was that she could still *feel* the energy of Sylven and his magic—and she felt that magic wrapping around her metal bonds and squeezing them closer to her skin. They squeezed so tightly that, within seconds, her hands and feet had turned numb, while a sharp, stabbing agony shot through the veins of her wrists and ankles.

A single, pained gasp rushed out of her.

And she hated herself for several fiery seconds after it escaped her. *Hated* the way it made Sylven's lips curl into a knowing little smile, the way his quiet voice was filled with mocking concern as he asked, "Does that hurt?"

She forced the word out through teeth gritting involuntarily with more pain: "No."

He laughed. His blue eyes danced in the light of the Storm-kind's still-hovering magic. "If you don't want to give in to *me*, then perhaps I'll let my friend step in and have a turn."

"Go ahead. He doesn't frighten me any more than you do."

Sylven turned away, still laughing quietly to himself as he glanced first to the king above—as if to make certain he was paying attention—and then to the Storm-kind.

"Go ahead," he told the Storm-kind.

Alaya dropped her gaze to a hairline crack in the stone floor. She unclenched her jaw and focused on deep, calming breaths. Dragged herself back against the wall. Tried to brace herself. But her shackles were still too tight, her hands and feet too numb; she couldn't feel enough of that floor or wall to truly make use of its solid support. She felt as if she were gripping sand, feeling it rush through her fingertips and fall, piling around her, threatening to bury her...

Then the first bolt of Storm-kind magic hit.

It struck her chest and stole away her breath. Her mouth snapped shut. Her body convulsed. Her face scraped the wall, ripping a stinging wound across her cheek. She felt heat and blood welling up. Some of that blood trickled down toward her closed lips, mixing with the frothy spit leaking from the corner of her mouth. Her vision blurred, but she fought through it, blinking back into awareness over and over again while pushing the back of her head firmly against the wall in order to keep it from lolling about.

At least a minute passed.

Perhaps longer.

Finally, the Storm-kind lowered his hands and braced them against his knees, pausing to catch his breath while keeping his eyes fixed on Alaya.

Her body still hummed with electricity. She kept her eyes open and her head lifted so that she could see it: The white aura of that Storm-kind, shining more brightly from the use of his magic.

Her own magic writhed, curling and uncurling inside of her, and the Serpent mark on her hand seemed to burn, as if to remind her it was there. That it was there, and that it would be so easy to *use* it. So, so easy to take hold of the Storm-kind's energy and twist it into her own magic. Into her command.

That part was *always* easy, here lately—the power and the violence.

It was the aftermath that troubled her.

Could her power and violence kill Sylven, too?

Because if it couldn't, then she would have succeeded

only in making herself a drained shell for him to infect and then wield however he saw fit.

The Storm-kind straightened up and closed the space between them once more.

Alaya's body went rigid even before he whispered the first of the clan-specific words that brought his magic back to the surface. She fought the urge to close her eyes. Swallowed every gasp, every whimper that tried to escape as electric magic pulsed through her again.

It was hellish, every nerve ending in her body burning with its own personal fire. The room darkened and spun. Faster, faster, *faster*—

Until finally it stopped, abruptly, as the Storm-kind groaned in exhaustion and dropped to one knee.

Her burning went on, though.

Sylven was looming over her a moment later. "Fight back."

She looked away.

"*Fight back.*"

She *was* fighting back. By not giving in. By not letting him control her in any possible way—and she could tell it was driving him insane, which was its own kind of victory.

"You will die here if you don't *fight*."

Now it was her turn to smile. She had to spit out a mouthful of that foaming saliva and blood first, but then she managed it: a wide, reckless grin that would have made her best friend Sade proud. "You won't kill me," she said, matter-of-factly, as she cut her eyes back toward Sylven. "I'm too valuable."

He took a step back. Studied her bleeding face for a moment.

She glared right back, her lips still drawn into a fierce, imprudent smile.

He lunged forward, hooked a hand around her throat and slammed her head back against the wall. The shackles around her wrists and ankles began to tighten once more, crushing so completely that she dully thought there was a chance he might be trying to sever her hands and feet from her body. Was that even possible? It seemed like it to her dazed mind, and so she braced herself for the potential, sickening *pops* and the gushing of blood as those shackles tightened further.

Instead, they eased abruptly.

"Actually…" Sylven began, his voice swimming somewhere high above her, "you're right. I'm not going to kill you. Because again: I know you will give in before it comes to that."

"I wouldn't count on it."

His hand cupped her chin, more gently this time, and he tilted her eyes up toward his. "You will beg for death, soon. But I won't give it to you. And when that moment of begging comes, you will realize that the only way to make this stop is to do as I tell you to do."

She tried, again, to jerk her head from his grasp, but she was too dazed and he was too strong, and she succeeded only in painfully jostling her burned and broken body even more.

She said nothing to Sylven's threats. She only continued to breathe in deeply through her pain, and then moved on to calmly studying her surroundings, darting her eyes around as best she could without being able to actually move her head.

The king had already walked away.

The Storm-kind had collapsed in his corner, spent from the inordinate amount of magic Sylven had forced him to use.

It had been an obscene amount of magic, really—but Alaya had withstood it, and she intended to *keep* withstanding it, regardless of any other magic that might be thrown at her. She would be strong enough to withstand it.

She *had* to be strong enough.

Sylven's grip on her was still ruthless. Blood and saliva were building in her mouth once more, foaming up from both the electricity still tumbling through her and the threat of vomit rising in the back of her throat. She felt the need to spit, and so she did—

Directly into Sylven's face.

He threw her head against the wall one last time, sending fresh pain ringing through her skull and cascading down her spine. Then he stepped away. She slumped halfway down the wall before she managed to catch herself and remain standing.

"I am going to give you one more night to *think* about

the choices I've given you," he seethed, swiping the spit from his face with a large, scarred hand. "Tomorrow, I will begin to take this more seriously."

"I'm not afraid of tomorrow," she hissed back. *"Or of any of the days after that."*

He had already turned away from her. He walked over and snatched the Storm-kind by the arm, yanked him to his feet, and then shoved him toward the door. He followed the stumbling magic user out of the prison cell without another glance or word spoken toward Alaya.

She waited until she was certain he wasn't coming back before she allowed herself to collapse fully to the floor.

Her breaths came in between painful shudders. Her body trembled from the current of electricity pulsing in her blood. And perhaps because of that current, her heartbeat refused to slow, pounding an exhausting, erratic rhythm in her chest.

She closed her eyes and searched her mind for memories, for faces, for something that would give her the strength to ignore her pain. Opening them again, her gaze fell on the feather-shaped scarring across her arm. The symbol of her childhood friend, Kian. His face was easy to picture, as were the hundreds of memories that came with it.

But he was gone, now.

Next came thoughts of Sade, the one who had accidentally killed him. They had reached an understanding over that killing, if not quite a forgiveness, and Alaya knew that Sade was strong, and reckless—but was she strong and reckless enough to storm the Sun Palace to save her?

Reckless enough, maybe, Alaya thought with a frown.

But she hoped not.

Her thoughts landed last on an image of a beautiful young man with forest-green eyes. Last, because she had been trying her hardest not to think of him at all.

He was the most difficult to make sense of. The most painful. Her memories of him had been tainted, she knew, by Sylven's magic, and by her own fears and uncertainties that had been running wild during her time spent in this cell.

And yet, there were plenty of things that remained clear.

Images of his smile, of his laugh, of the feel of his arms wrapping around her and the whisper of his voice, so close to her ear as they'd lain together with hardly any space to breathe between them...

But now he was the high king.

He had the power to save her, perhaps—but would he try to? And if so, what could he possibly do that wouldn't ignite an all-out war between the three kingdoms he was supposed to be in charge of uniting?

She sighed. She didn't want anyone starting—or escalating—any wars over her. She didn't want anything happening to Sade during any reckless rescue missions, either.

So, as far as she was concerned, all of her friends were gone now.

Their faces stayed with her, at least, easing her toward rest on a bed of memories and softer things. She curled into herself as best she could with the shackles restricting her. The sunlight was finally fading, and the guards walking the platforms high above had stopped adjusting the curtains that guided it in. It was nice not to have the glaring irritation of sunbeams directed onto her face, but in their absence, the shift in temperature felt brutal. Her silent tears burned terribly hot against her rapidly-freezing face.

She allowed those tears to fall freely now that no one was around to see them.

But when she woke, she would stop crying, and she would find a way out of this mess.

And she would do it alone if she had to.

CHAPTER 2

ALAYA AWOKE IN A DARKNESS TINTED WITH MOONLIGHT.

She was not alone.

A figure knelt at her side, dressed in robes of midnight blue, with a hood and scarf hiding everything aside from her violet eyes and the dark circles beneath them. The sight of her alarmed Alaya at first, but that alarm passed quickly.

This woman had been here before, after all.

Alaya watched her for a moment. Held her breath. Tried not to wince at the sting of an ointment-drenched cloth being pressed against the bloody scratches on her cheek. And then, just as she had the last time they'd been alone in the dark like this, she asked, "Why are you helping me?"

And just like last time, the Sun Queen did not reply. She had hardly spoken at all during any of these treatment sessions, as though afraid the very walls might overhear them.

Alaya was almost certain the king did not know his wife was here.

Which explained the cloak, and the way the queen kept glancing to the platforms above them, as if expecting to see someone spying on them. But there were no guards where there had been earlier; had Queen Eliana ordered them all away? Secured their silence somehow?

Alaya's gaze drifted down from those platforms and back to the queen. If not for her striking, oddly-colored eyes and the distinct white jewels accenting them, Alaya might not have recognized the Sun matriarch underneath the layers of fabric she'd wrapped around herself.

She had now risked tending to Alaya three times. And Alaya was grateful for it, but she was also thoroughly confused by it—and somewhat suspicious of it. The past months had changed her; she was now automatically suspicious of *any* person acting as though they wanted to help her.

"Couldn't you send a servant to do this?" she pressed, trying to sit upright.

Queen Eliana breathed in deeply through her nose and placed a firm but gentle grip on Alaya's arm, holding her in place. There was a nasty-looking burn on that arm, and Alaya's movement had threatened to undo the bandages that Eliana had started to secure over it.

The queen still did not speak, but her narrowed gaze said enough—*Be still. I'm trying to help you.*

Alaya remained tense, but she no longer tried to twist away from the queen's touches or ask any questions. As suspicious as she was, she also desperately needed an ally within this prison.

They had formed something of a relationship before these past few days, at least; the queen had been kind and welcoming, if somewhat aloof, when Alaya had first landed on her doorstep, weeks ago. Alaya had been injured then, as well, and Eliana had seen to it that she was cared for by the best doctors available in Idalia.

They ultimately had to go elsewhere—to the Bay of Sinking Souls—to seek out answers to Alaya's complicated condition that no Idalian doctor could have dreamt of. But the queen's hospitality had not ended after that; once their business on that western coast was finished, she had welcomed them into the Sun Palace a second time, tending to the needs of Alaya and her companions as they prepared for their final battle against High King Haben.

She had declined to take part in any of that battle planning, but she had once again given Alaya the finest of rooms and clothing, and supplied her with countless servants and other luxuries. They had enjoyed a handful of private chats, too, and Eliana had even entrusted her with several articles of jewelry and other personal artifacts.

So Alaya wanted to believe that, for whatever reason, the Sun Queen at least *liked* her well enough.

But how much would Eliana be willing to risk to

help her?

"Thank you for this," Alaya said quietly, trying to make her voice softer and less suspicious than before.

The queen nodded. She looked lost in thought for a few moments more before she cautiously pulled the scarf from her face and said, "You will have to fight back. Sylven will not show mercy for much longer."

"He's hardly showing it now."

"It could be worse. It *will* get worse, if you continue to be stubborn."

Alaya stiffened, her suspicions rising once more.

Had Sylven told the queen to say these things?

"I can endure whatever pain he causes," Alaya said, flatly.

"It isn't simply about who can endure the longest."

"He won't kill me."

"Perhaps not. But my husband will."

Alaya's lips parted, then slowly closed again. She swallowed hard.

"Levant grows...impatient." The queen absently threaded her fingers through the hair framing Alaya's face, breaking up the strands that had grown stiff with dried blood. "Impatient and frightened. He wants to believe that Sylven can control you because he thinks Sylven is his ally, his greatest hope of more completely— and *easily*—overthrowing Rook rule and taking a greater control of this empire for himself."

"Greater control?"

"He aided in the assassination of Haben because it has

put a younger, far less experienced king on the Rook throne. One that he has already gone to the Council of Fifteen about, to express his 'concerns' about that highest throne now being held by such young blood."

"The Council of Fifteen..."

"Yes. You've heard of them, I presume?"

It took her a moment to recall it, but yes; she had. Even in the small, tucked-away village of Vanish—where she'd spent most of her childhood—she remembered overhearing occasional mentions of this council.

They were a group of elders, one from each of the fifteen most important of their empire's clans. Fifteen differently marked men and women. Those marks, of course, represented one of each of the three upper-gods— the Moraki—as well as the twelve Marr that had served under the greater three since long before their empire had been formed.

The council had once held much greater power, but their influence over the empire had weakened somewhat after Haben started his destructive, all-consuming rule. It was also technically only a council of fourteen these days; there were no Serpent-kind represented anymore, as far as Alaya knew—not since that clan had been banished beyond the edges of the three kingdoms.

These were only the most basic of facts about the council; what they did, or *had* done, during their meetings was cloaked in shadows that few in the empire were permitted to explore.

"I've heard of them in passing, at least," Alaya told the

queen.

The creak of an opening door came from somewhere above them.

Both women froze in place, moving only their eyes to scan the platforms overlooking Alaya's cell.

A tense moment passed. When no one appeared, the queen slowly lowered her gaze back to Alaya's. She started several explanations regarding that council, then seemed to decide that a passing knowledge of it would have to do for the moment.

"They will be relieved to be rid of Haben and the instability he has caused our empire for decades," she continued in a hushed tone, "and they won't need much convincing to support a shift in power. 'It is time for another of the Moraki's descendants to hold the highest throne in Sundolia'—that is the line my husband will be feeding them, no doubt. He will insist that the Sun-kind are due to rule."

"Why does there have to be a high throne at all? Wouldn't it be more logical to spread the power amongst *all* the kingdoms and clans?"

"There is nothing *logical* about these political games, my dear." She tucked a few strands of that blood-stiffened hair behind Alaya's ear. "Everyone wants their chance at the height of all things. The Rook had their turn. Now, many of the Sun clan, and the ones who serve it, have convinced themselves that it is only fair that they also have a turn. And thus the cycle of war continues unto infinity."

Alaya felt as if her body was sinking into the cold stone beneath her, weighed down by the depressing scenarios the queen's words painted in her mind.

Was there really no end to all of this?

No; she refused to believe that.

"High King Levant..." she muttered. It sounded no better than *High King Haben* to her ears.

"Yes," said the queen. "And his first act of greater power will be to appoint Sylven to the throne in Rykarra —a deal I believe they agreed on before Sylven helped lead that attack on the Valinesian capital a week ago."

"The Council of Fifteen will oppose a Serpent-kind on *any* throne, won't they?"

"Perhaps. Which is why Levant and Sylven hope to use you to finish dealing with Haben's line, and to clear a path to that throne and make the need for a supplanter more dire—they will convince all that will listen that an empty throne would be more dangerous than even a Serpent-held one. But if you continue to resist Sylven's attempts at controlling you..."

"I fully intend to continue to resist him," Alaya spat.

The queen nodded, and Alaya thought she might have seen the beginnings of a smile curling on the older woman's lips.

"Then you must get out of this palace."

Alaya summoned strength from somewhere deep inside, and she managed to push through her pain, to rise up and maneuver herself into a more proper sitting position.

"And I want to help you escape," Eliana concluded, her violet eyes watching closely as her patient slumped against the wall.

"But *why*?" Alaya huffed, the question breathless as another burst of pain burned through her.

The queen considered the question for a long moment. Her fingers reached for the pendant that hung around her neck—a white, translucent stone with nicked edges. The *Tear of Solatis*, she'd informed Alaya weeks ago; a precious heirloom that had been passed down to the oldest children of Sun-kind royalty for generations.

"Because I want you to live, for starters," the queen finally whispered, squeezing that stone more tightly.

Eliana had no children of her own to pass the heirloom down to, not anymore; her daughter had died years ago of a mysterious illness. Her passing had driven the Sun Queen mad with grief, the stories said. And she was *still* mad from that grief, according to some of the rumors still circulating in the Lumerian Kingdom.

The woman before her did not seem of unsound mind at all to Alaya. But the tired lines that her grief had carved into her face were still clear, as clear as the feather Alaya had scarred into her own skin, because grief was not a thing that was easily wiped away.

And perhaps, she thought, *grief and madness look similar to people who have never truly experienced the first of those.*

Alaya watched her clench the stone, close her eyes,

and take several deep breaths, and she wondered if Eliana was thinking of her daughter in that moment.

But she had not been bold enough to bring up the dead princess during their last conversation regarding that jewel, and she would not bring her up now, either.

Instead, she asked, "What exactly did you mean before, by *clear a path?*"

The queen let the stone drop back to her tawny, age-spotted skin. "You have already killed one Rook King. And High Queen Zahra is dead as well. If King Emrys is killed, then the Valinesian throne will, at the very least, need a steward; Sylven will manage to take that much control easily enough. And from there..."

If King Emrys is killed...

If they could control *her* into killing him.

That was their plan.

It was the answer Alaya had expected, and yet it still sent a shiver rippling through her. She leaned against the wall and closed her eyes.

"Part of you still believes it might be safer if you stayed a prisoner, doesn't it?"

Alaya opened her eyes, only to instantly avert them from the queen's pressing gaze. "I need my full power to fight against Sylven. But that full power will *also* make me more vulnerable to *his* full power. It's another endless cycle of war."

The queen rose to her feet, tugging the sleeves of her cloak down and pulling its hood more securely into place. "You must find a way to break that cycle."

"Yes, well, I'm open to any suggestions you might have as to *how* I should do that." It was difficult for Alaya to keep the bitterness from her voice—but she attempted to, at least.

And she had been *trying* to find ways to break that cycle, of course. To better withstand her power, and to gradually push the limits of it further and further without consequence, so that she wouldn't need healing from Sylven or any other Serpent-kind.

She had obtained the fire-soul already, too—that piece of magic stolen from Mairu, the middle-goddess who guided the Serpent clan—and now it resided inside of her, merged with her own soul. A soul that was partially-divine, because her mother had been a heavenly shade of that same goddess.

The fire-soul had made Alaya more powerful—and somewhat more stable—but it was not enough. Or *she* was not enough to make full use of it. Or perhaps she was too much of something. Who could say? She was a puzzling creature, neither fully divine nor fully human, and it felt as if pieces of her were still missing...or, at the very least, out of order.

"Endure this prison for one more day," said the queen, taking hold of her concealing scarf and preparing to lift it back into place. "I am moving plans into motion now—other people and other things that can help you escape. I only need a little more time to finish arranging it all."

Sylven's warning echoed in Alaya's mind.

Tomorrow, I will begin to take this more seriously.

Another shiver crawled through her. But the Sun Queen looked as though she really did have a plan, and Alaya was curious about what it could possibly be; so she nodded.

"You need to be less stubborn tomorrow, I think," said the queen.

"What do you mean?"

"No spitting in anyone's face."

Alaya snorted. "We'll see."

"You can't let them torture you to the point you're at now, where you can hardly move; you'll need more strength than that if you want to successfully escape this city. I can only help you so far."

Alaya wanted to object, but the queen had a point; it seemed like every part of her ached in some way. The thought of outrunning Sylven and the rest of the palace in her current condition was daunting, at best.

"Let them think they've broken you, long before they actually *have*. And play it convincingly enough that I have cause to intervene."

"You want me to pretend I've fainted or something?" Alaya asked, still dubious.

"Convince them that you are hanging on to your life by a thread, however you need to do it. And then trust that I can convince my husband to *spare* that life, at least for a moment. Then you will rest, and tomorrow night, I —or one of my associates—will show you the way out."

"And you think Levant will listen to you?"

"He has strayed a great distance away from the man

he was when we married. But I am still his wife. He is still loyal enough that he will stop if I ask him to stop."

"What about once I'm gone? What if he realizes you tricked him?"

She knelt and reached for one of Alaya's hands, carefully sliding up the shackle on its wrist and inspecting the bruised skin underneath it one last time. "You let me worry about that."

Another creak of steel sounded from above. Then came the sound of doors slamming and feet shuffling, and suddenly the queen's eyes were wide, her quiet voice more urgent: "Can you do this?"

The memory of those shackles squeezing her wrists made Alaya's lungs feel like they were filling with lead. She could still feel phantom spasms of the pain Sylven had caused her. Tomorrow would be worse. Tomorrow would...

No, it doesn't matter.

She nodded.

She had withstood worse. She would not be afraid. She would survive this. And after that, she would figure out her next step. The war was not over yet, perhaps, but it was not endless; she would not let herself believe that death and terror had to be this world's constant.

"One more day, and the path out will be ready for you to take," the queen promised, as if she could still see all of the fears and doubts that Alaya was refusing to let herself feel. "One more day," she repeated. "*Endure.*"

"I will."

She gave Alaya's hand a light squeeze, lifted the scarf back over her face, and then she was gone.

CHAPTER 3

Rykarra, City of Rooks, Capital of the Kingdom of Valin

THE MOMENT SHE WALKED INTO THE ROOM, EMRYS COULD TELL that Sade's mission had been unsuccessful.

She had a tendency to wear her emotions in plain sight, this one; and if the scowl on her face had not given her away, then the way she slammed her quiver and bow to the table and then flopped dejectedly into the chair opposite him certainly would have.

"Another useless lead," she sighed, slumping deeper into that chair and pulling her dark red hair over her shoulder. "I'm beginning to suspect that Levant is purposefully planting these leads in hope of distracting us from coming farther south and properly investigating him and his palace."

She spoke as freely as she scowled, as if the two of

them were the only ones in the grand study where Emrys had spent most of his afternoon.

But they were not alone.

Emrys was rarely alone anymore. He was constantly surrounded by prattling advisors, fawning nobles, and by members of his personal guard. Or by who was *left* of all of these people, at least, after they had culled the ones that had refused to denounce the former high king's rule —and the ones they suspected of still longing for that rule, despite their claiming otherwise.

Dozens upon dozens had been dismissed. Some had been imprisoned. They had done what they could to sort through the wreckage and rebuild a formidable, functioning palace as quickly and efficiently as possible.

But Haben's rule had been long, and his poisons ran deep.

It had already been an exhausting undertaking, trying to sift those poisoned weeds from the people with truly healthy, noble roots and intentions, and it was far from over with; it would be a very long time before Emrys felt safe walking the halls of his own palace, he suspected.

Assuming that day ever came.

And yet, he was still surrounded by several familiar faces that he somewhat trusted; Captain Grim Helder, for example, was a Rook-kind who had been personally looking after Emrys for most of the past decade. He was now the head of Emrys's personal guard, as well as a decorated leader in the Valinesian Army.

Lady Isoni of the Bone clan, his mother's longtime friend and advisor, remained in the palace as well.

And both of these people now stood with their soon-to-be-crowned king, wearing identical, icy expressions as they watched Sade help herself to the basket of flat breads and fruits that one of the servants had recently delivered.

Sade still didn't seem to notice them—or more likely didn't care, he suspected. "I would be willing to bet my soul that Alaya is being held prisoner in the Sun Palace." She paused long enough to rip off a chunk of bread and chew it with a furious amount of force. "And that Levant is scheming something terrible involving her and those Serpent-kind he's tangled himself up with."

Captain Helder cleared his throat, and he thawed his gaze enough to let it shift onto Emrys. "Your Highness, King Levant withdrew all of his forces from our kingdom after your father's death. His quarrel was with Haben, not you; he has pledged nothing but support for your forthcoming rule, and he has adamantly denied these allegations regarding that girl, and—"

"Well, of course he's *denied* them," muttered Sade, which drew a huff of indignation from Helder and a sigh from Lady Isoni. "What do you really expect he's going to do? Stitch himself a banner that says *I'm a villain!* and then come wave it around in our courtyards?"

The captain's jaw clenched. His gaze flickered between Sade and his young monarch, clearly expecting Emrys to offer some sort of reprimand.

Emrys, however, said nothing.

In fact, he had been considering appointing Sade as an official member of that personal guard of his—at least partly because he wanted to see the look on Helder's face when he did it.

He had his misgivings about Sade, it was true, and their past was not particularly smooth. But she had worked tirelessly in the past days to track down any and all leads regarding Alaya. And he was fairly certain she hadn't slept more than a few hours, nor paused her hunting long enough to have even a proper meal during any of those days.

Sade wanted Alaya back as much as he did—and that was saying something.

She also had the ability to move much more freely through the kingdom compared to himself at the moment, as every move that *she* made was not being relentlessly scrutinized and endlessly fretted over.

But he had refrained from giving her any sort of title just yet—one earth-shattering event per week would suffice, he supposed, and it had scarcely been a full week since High King Haben's lifeless body had been thrown from the rooftops of this very palace—but he couldn't bring himself to so much as glare in Sade's direction, as Captain Helder was still doing.

Because he and Sade were allies now, whether they liked it or not.

"But does he really *need* a banner to declare such things," Sade continued, "when we know for a fact that he has been working alongside the likes of Sylven Adler?"

"We can hardly fault the Sun King for seeking the council of Serpent-kind, can we?" replied Helder, stiffly. "Not when our own crown prince is rumored to have been laying with the most dangerous of those who carry that Serpent mark. If we would like to—"

Emrys lifted a hand from the gilded armrest of his chair. "Your point is made. You can stop talking."

The captain held up his own hands in a gesture of peace-keeping. "I am only speaking the truth."

"Go speak it elsewhere," Emrys said, rising to his feet and gesturing toward the door. "I believe we've chatted enough for one afternoon, besides."

A muscle worked in Helder's clean-shaven jaw, but he didn't disagree. The two of them had been wrapped in conversation for the past hour, after all, in what had felt like an endless discussion regarding the best way to secure the trading posts along Valin's southern borders.

"Don't you have some new recruits you should be preparing to train, anyhow?" Emrys suggested, by way of softening the dismissal. "There has been enough turmoil and turnover within our ranks as of late that you should have no trouble finding a more productive way to spend your time."

After one last cold glance in Sade's direction, Helder acquiesced with a bow. "Of course. As you wish."

The other guards accompanying him—who had been watching the conversation in attentive silence—peeled away from the wall and followed him out. A few of them stationed themselves just outside the door.

Emrys walked over and closed that door. There would be no getting rid of those guards on the other side of it, and he didn't bother trying; Helder had insisted on tripling the security that shadowed his crown prince, and it was the one point that he refused to budge on.

As annoying as it was to allow it, Emrys knew the captain had a point about this; Rykarra had been relatively calm in the days following his father's death, but it would be foolish to assume that no one was plotting to finish off the highest royal family in Sundolia and continue dismantling its reign. Levant was not the only enemy of the Rook-kind and their rule.

Far from it.

The late afternoon sun streamed through the tall windows, cheerful and bright, tempting Emrys with reminders of how unseasonably warm the past few days had been. He longed to be outside in that warmth, away from these meetings and expectations. Away from this room and the scent of dusty books and ink.

He used to relish those scents. This had once been his mother's favorite place in the entire palace, and as a child, he had spent hours sprawled out on the shaggy rug in front of the bookshelves that lined its back wall, looking for any excuse to stay close to her.

She had passed her time in here by reading every book on those shelves at least twice; by trying her hand at painting and sketching; by writing everything from stories to detailed accounts of the palace's day-to-day happenings to long, thoughtful letters for her many acquaintances throughout all three kingdoms.

He had spent that time studying, focusing mainly on the history of this empire and on Sundolia's dozens upon dozens of languages—in-between listening to his mother read her writings and perusing whatever other interesting things she'd plopped in front of him.

He had official tutors responsible for teaching him things like history and language, of course; but it was different, studying it from these ancient, primary texts. The feel of the yellowed and crinkling pages, the weight of their bindings, the sight of hand-written notes and smudges in the margins... There was a bright sort of magic in those old books that the droning voices of his teachers could not replicate.

But the bright, blissful days full of that magic felt like they were from another lifetime.

Now, the acrid scent of ink only reminded him of how many letters he himself had written that morning. Letters to various leaders throughout the Sundolian Empire, explaining the events of the past week and extending an invitation to his upcoming coronation.

So many things were riding on those words he had wrestled with since long before the sun came up.

Had he chosen the right ones?

His attention had drifted, his gaze locking onto the window, and his eyes began to water from the brightness filtering in.

He blinked back into awareness.

And he briefly considered flinging open that window and leaping to the gardens below. It was only a second-floor room; he could survive the jump. And from there, he could grab his horse and set off. Or perhaps convince Rue —the dragon who was currently roosting in the old stables by the forest—to carry him far beyond the edges of this city.

By dragon-flight, they could be at the Lumerian border by nightfall.

He could find Alaya himself, and personally cut down anyone who stood in the way of getting her back.

And let this kingdom and empire fend for themselves in the meantime?

His burning gaze found the crown on his desk, resting next to several pieces of discarded parchment; parchment that held the failed beginnings of his first attempts to write to those other leaders in his empire.

He walked back to that desk, suddenly acutely aware of the silence that had overtaken the room—and the stares that followed each of his heavy steps. Only himself, Sade, Lady Isoni, and one of his senior magic advisors—Lord Tomas Feran—remained in the study now, but it still felt like the entire empire was watching him from the windows.

Predictably, Isoni was the first among them to break the silence.

Also predictably, she was quick to offer him more unsolicited advice.

"With all due respect, Your Highness, I hope you

aren't actually considering confronting Levant about this. Attacking him would be a ridiculous move. A grievous misstep in your young, and might I add, still *precarious* reign. A reign that hasn't even *officially* begun yet—"

Emrys stopped her with a curt look.

She inhaled and exhaled a breath through her nose, but she held her tongue for a moment, watching him as he settled back into the velvety cushions of his chair.

Sade's gaze darted between the two of them, clearly sensing an impending eruption and watching with interest. Lord Feran looked as though he wished he'd left with Captain Helder.

"Levant would consider it an act of war," Isoni insisted. "And rightfully so."

"They stole her from me," Emrys snarled. "There is your act of *war*."

"An act of war against *you*. But against your subjects? Your allies? Do you think they care about what happens to that girl?"

He didn't answer; he only yanked open the bottom drawer of the desk and pulled out more parchment. He had no real plans for it—no letters left to write—he only wanted something to occupy his hands with.

"They do not," Isoni continued, answering her own question. "In fact, most of them would likely agree that it's better if Levant keeps her and...*deals* with her."

He reached for a bottle of ink, and then the pen that was resting beside those letters he'd discarded earlier.

Isoni braced her hands against the desk, leaning

forward and glaring at him until he cut his gaze up toward her. "You have less than two weeks until your official coronation," she snapped. "I suggest you start thinking of something *other* than that Serpent girl and whatever's become of her. Something such as this kingdom that you are now responsible for, and the greater good of the complete empire. If your mother was here, she would—"

Emrys stood up so abruptly that the parchment scattered and Isoni actually took a step back, looking alarmed —which was a strange expression on her normally cold and collected face.

She opened her mouth only to close it again, as if even *she* realized that she had gone too far this time.

"She is not here," Emrys said, his voice low. "*I* am. And I would also remind you that you were *her* most trusted advisor, not mine. And if you suggest leaving Alaya to her fate to me one more time, you may go ahead and consider yourself relieved of your counseling duties."

The room felt as if it was darkening, shrinking, spinning around him. He braced a hand against the edge of the desk and kept his breathing steady, his gaze leveled on hers.

While the two of them remained locked in their glaring, Lord Feran moved in silence, walking to the desk and placing a wrapped object before Emrys.

That object, and the note attached to it, were the reason Feran had interrupted Emrys's meeting with Captain Helder earlier—the only reason he was in this room in the first place. He had been sent on a mission, just as Sade had, and it looked as though *his* mission hadn't been entirely fruitless.

"I'll be back later, and we can discuss this in a calmer, more private setting," the advisor suggested.

Emrys nodded. He was curious about what that wrapped object might have been, but he didn't look at it. Out of the corner of his eye, he watched Lord Feran bow and then leave the room, but he never let his focus shift completely from Isoni.

"You're dismissed as well," he told her.

She glared at him for a moment longer, before lifting her chin and tilting her head in the slightest of nods. She turned on her heel and stalked toward the door.

He waited until she was halfway across the room before he called after her: "You've forgotten something."

She drew to a stop. Turned stiffly back to face him, and unhinged her clenched jaw. "My apologies," she said, before offering the deep bow that was customary after dismissal by a king. She avoided looking at him as she rose back to her feet.

She slammed the door on her way out.

Sade stared at that closed door for a moment before speaking. "Can't you demote her to like...a scullery maid or something?"

Emrys gave her a cross look—though, admittedly, he had entertained similar thoughts in the past.

Sade shrugged and reached for the bowl of fruit sitting next to that bread she had been helping herself to.

She plucked a few bright purple berries from it and shook them around in her hand, picking away the stray leaves and twigs clinging to them.

Emrys settled back into his chair once more, leaning heavily on the armrest and pressing fingertips to his temple. "She had a point, unfortunately. As did Captain Helder."

It was the reason he hadn't permanently dismissed either of them, as he had done with so many others; because they spoke the truth to him—whether he wanted to hear it or not—and truth was a rare, precious commodity in this palace.

Sade popped one of those berries into her mouth and chewed it slowly and without comment, though the thoughtful gleam in her eye prompted him to keep talking.

"Just over a week from now, nobles from every province will be descending for the coronation," Emrys told her, "and every single one of them is going to come with an agenda. With demands. With a desire to make *connections*, agreements..."

"And a desire to wed their noble daughters to you?"

He grimaced. "You've heard the same rumors I have, then."

"The city has been very talkative these past few days," she said with another shrug. "Congratulations: You are the most sought-after bachelor in all of Sundolia."

He scowled.

"Please tell me you aren't considering securing any alliances in that manner?"

"Of course I'm not considering it." He could hardly put enough indignation into the words.

Of all the stupid questions...

Why did nobody in this palace seem to understand that he had no desire for any queen other than Alaya?

Sade popped another berry into her mouth. "What's our plan, then?"

"...Plan?"

"I know you don't intend to follow Isoni's advice about forgetting Alaya. It's what...twelve days until your coronation?"

"Yes."

"At which point things in this palace will get even *more* complicated and nightmarish. So, what are we doing in the meantime?"

He hesitated. Truth be told, he was still working on figuring that out. All he knew for certain was that Sade was right: He wasn't going to leave Alaya to her fate.

"I'm not leaving until we come up with a plan," Sade informed him. "Preferably one that involves storming the Sun Palace and letting Rue eat Sylven and the king and every one of the slimy cohorts they've managed to collect."

His brow furrowed at the thought. He reached for the decanter of wine next to that food she was helping herself to, poured them both a glass, and sipped his in silence for several minutes.

Without any conscious thought, his gaze ended up trailing toward the object that Lord Feran had left.

"What is that?" Sade asked, her eyes following his as she leaned up in her seat and nodded toward the bundle of cloth.

He took the wrapped object and tossed it into the top drawer, where it landed beside two other things that he kept close and secret—a letter his mother had written long ago and a frayed red ribbon.

"It's a last resort," he told Sade.

"A magic-related one?"

He sighed, but he could hardly deny it; she was one of the few people with definitive knowledge of his recent descent into a dangerous, questionable brand of magic.

Even Alaya wasn't aware of that magic—though she likely had suspicions.

He had planned to tell her the truth about it all. About that, and about his true feelings for her, and countless other things. But then...

He pushed the drawer shut. "I don't need magic to deal with this. There are plenty of Valinesian troops stationed in the foothills of the Sinharas, less than a day's ride from Idalia. I am going to send an order to move some of them farther south, into that capital city. A covert operation—at least to begin with. Some can blend in as civilians, others will infiltrate the Sun Palace and look for evidence of whatever Levant and Sylven are up to, and then report that evidence to me. Then we'll decide how best to act." His gaze drifted toward the door.

"I don't intend to tell any of my advisors about this plan."

She nodded.

"So do you think you can manage *not* to run your mouth for once, and to keep it between us?"

She gave him a slightly over-exaggerated bow. "I'll do my best, my most-esteemed Royal Pain in the Highness."

"Good."

"I still would prefer we just storm the Sun Palace and let the dragon eat everybody."

"Fine. Let's do that." He calmly reached for his quail-feathered pen, carefully writing the day's date at the top of a fresh piece of parchment before adding, "And then I will put you in charge of burying the dead that such an attack will ultimately result in."

Sade pursed her lips. "Fine. I see your point. Covert operation it is. For now."

"For now," he agreed.

A pause, and then: "What if they find her, but they aren't able to help her? How long do we wait?"

He didn't want to think about all of the *what ifs*.

But Sade's gaze was insistent.

"I can't leave this palace until after the coronation." The words made his stomach twist painfully. "The invitations are sent, the guests will start arriving within days, and if they find that I've headed off to potentially start a fight with the Sun King...well, that isn't going to do much to secure my rule."

Sade's frown deepened, but she didn't disagree.

"But after that, if Alaya is not here, if she is not found and safe, then my first official act as king will be to pay Levant a little *diplomatic* visit."

Sade hugged her arms against herself and nodded, her eyes glazing over with thought once more.

Emrys mirrored that thoughtfulness for a few moments before he cleared his throat and said, "So, we have a plan."

"We do."

"And now you can leave."

"I did say I would, didn't I?"

"There's the door," he said with a sweep of his hand.

She grinned. "If you end up being terrible at everything else as a king, at least we know you're good at dismissing people with just the right touch of angry authority."

"Out," he insisted.

She gave him another of those exaggerated bows. Then she turned to leave, snatching more bread and a shiny pink apple from the tray as she went.

"But one more thing, Sade."

"Yes?"

"If Rue will cooperate, keep scouring as much of the kingdoms as you can. Leave nothing unturned. No person unquestioned."

This time, the bow of her head was more genuine. "We'll find her soon."

"We will," he agreed. But neither of them said what

he was certain they were both thinking: They *had* to find her soon.

Before it was too late.

He drained the rest of his wine. Sade closed the door behind her. He was finally alone, and the first thing he did was pour himself another glass of wine. Then he wandered toward the windows. The sky was deepening toward early evening, stretching into shades of deep reds and purples that weren't as blinding as they had been earlier.

Another day passing, right before his eyes.

Before it's too late...

Was he *already* too late?

The gods only knew what Sylven had done to Alaya after he'd taken her. The amount of magic she'd used to kill the high king had been unprecedented, and, as strong as she was, excessive use of that magic left her vulnerable. Weak in precisely the way that Sylven could take advantage of...

Emrys glanced down at the glass in his hand.

Already empty again.

He fought the urge to smash that glass against the floor. Instead, he clenched it tightly in his fist as he pressed his forehead against the warm window and closed his eyes for a moment.

If only there was a way I could see her, a way to know for certain where she is...

A sudden chill shot down his spine.

He stepped away from the window. Looked back to

his desk, his heart suddenly racing at the thought of what he had tossed into the top drawer of that desk.

The wine buzzed away any hesitations he might have had. He was across the room in an instant, yanking open that drawer once again and retrieving the bundle of cloth, unraveling it so quickly that he ended up flinging its contents to the floor.

A key thudded to a stop at his feet—a tarnished silver key with an ornate top that resembled flames.

He bent to pick it up, along with the letter that had been wrapped up with it.

There was an address at the top of the letter, along with a series of symbols; the latter seemed to be a code, and perhaps part of another step in unlocking that address.

A Fire-kind had written this letter, he knew. But aside from the coded symbols, all of the other words had been messily scribbled in the language of his own Rook clan— out of respect toward him, he supposed. Beneath those symbols were four short sentences:

It would be my honor. Stop by whenever you like. Bring a stained blade. Make it fresh.

Such a simple message. Vague enough that anyone who intercepted it would be unlikely to understand precisely what it meant. But Emrys understood it.

Rook-kind had no innate magic; like the Sun and the

Stone clans that commanded the kingdoms of Lumeria and Galasea, they ruled by strength of numbers.

But there were dozens of other, smaller clans in this empire—and they *did* have magic. The Marr clans, and the lesser-spirit clans...and that clan-specific magic could be taken and used, even by one of the Rooks, if one knew the proper way of doing it.

He was no expert in this manner of magic. Not yet. But he knew enough to be dangerous.

And he had thousands of subjects now. Plenty of detractors, yes, but then there were others that were eager to align themselves on the right side of his rule. Eager to sacrifice whatever he asked in order to prove their worth and allegiance to their new high king.

It was far too easy to think of ways he could ask his subjects to prove themselves.

So easy that it was...*frightening*.

Yet he was still thinking of it. Because he knew there was magic in this empire that could allow him to see Alaya. To find her. Perhaps even *go* to her. And there was magic that could make him strong enough to, as Sade had put it, *storm the Sun Palace*. They wouldn't need a dragon to deal with Levant or Sylven; he could become a monster capable of doing it himself.

The magic to do so existed.

He would only have to take it from others.

And if they offered it freely, in order to prove their devotion to him...

The sound of voices outside his door jarred him from his thoughts. He gave his head a hard shake.

What was he thinking?

He wrapped the key and its letter back up, shoved them out of sight, and instead took out that red ribbon that the key had been sharing the drawer with.

It was Alaya's. She'd accidentally left it behind weeks ago, after paying a late-night visit to his room. He wasn't sure why he'd kept it. It had struck him as an odd thing to do, even as he'd tucked it away for safe-keeping, but perhaps....

Perhaps he'd kept it because it was proof that she had come back to him, in spite of all of the things trying to keep them apart.

She would come back to him again. Or he would go to her. Either way, they were not finished. He knew she was still alive. Still fighting. He would get her back, even if he had to do it while balancing the weight of his new crown.

"We don't end like this," he muttered aloud to no one.

And then he poured himself another glass of wine, and he drank until he believed that was true.

CHAPTER 4

Idalia, City of the Sun, Capital of the Kingdom of Lumeria

"Good morning, Goddess."

Alaya automatically lifted her head at the sound of Sylven's voice. But she said nothing, keeping her eyes on the same place they had been focused on for most of the past hour: a symbol of the Sun-clan that was carved into the space above a nearby door. She watched its pointed edges, the tip of each one inset with a white jewel, glittering in the early sun's rays.

The servants weren't directing that sunlight onto her. Not yet. The room was not blinding, nor sweltering or suffocating. It was...peaceful, almost. Quiet. Otherworldly, with its tiny specks of dust floating in the warm light, with its damp air that swallowed up most sound, with its smell of rust and old dirt and other lost, ancient things.

And Sylven came to her, as he always did, with equally quiet steps and an equally peaceful tone of voice.

"Shall we practice your magic this morning?" he asked, in that pleasant, fake voice he always used to start these "practice" sessions.

One, two, three...eight. There were eight points on that Sun-clan symbol. Over and over, Alaya counted them, still avoiding looking in Sylven's direction.

The soft thud of more footsteps drew her attention downward. Two women had entered through the door beneath the symbol. They were dressed in simple, yet elegant clothing, with jewels affixed to their faces in the way that was common among the courtiers and high-ranked guests of this palace.

Alaya's gaze darted toward their hands, their wrists, those places where a clan-mark would usually be visible, but she couldn't see anything from where she slumped.

"Fire and Ice," Sylven answered for her, sounding as pleased as ever.

So here is today's brand of torture.

Well, she could withstand it. The Storm-kind magic had been almost unbearable, because it had made her body feel as if it was convulsing beyond her control, and losing control of herself remained one of her greatest fears.

But the burning flames of Fire-kind magic and the

burning bite of Ice-kind magic, she convinced herself, were things she could endure.

She wasn't afraid to burn.

She repeated those words silently to herself as Sylven crouched down beside her.

I am not afraid to burn.

"You could control them, if you'd like to try," Sylven told her.

I am not afraid to burn.

"Go on, use your magic." His voice lowered. "They won't resist you. They won't attack."

I am not afraid to—

"Let me remind you: I am not going to be *patient* today."

She cut her eyes slowly toward him.

"This is your first and last chance to cooperate."

Wordlessly, she slid her gaze back to the two women.

They were staring at her. Waiting, like lionesses poised and ready to spring. She could see their energy around them. Hazy shades of red and powdery blue, respectively; colors that occasionally sparked into something brighter, into bold strands that twisted in mesmerizing patterns around their bodies.

She could break those bodies if she wanted to.

Take hold of those bright strands and rip them in whatever direction she chose. She had ripped a king from his palace—quite literally—and choked the life from him in a similar manner. So of course she could fling these two back through the door, or up onto those platforms above, or out one of the countless windows...

Or she could control whatever magic they tried to throw at her. Catch it and throw it back at them, or at Sylven.

None of these things were part of that hasty plan she had made with Eliana, but it was impossible not to think about doing them.

Her hand twitched. She pulled it as far forward as she could in her bindings, enough that she could peer down at the Serpent mark in her palm. At the coils of its body shimmering with her waking fury, reminding her of her power.

She could feel Sylven watching her. Likely smiling that pleased, slight smile that he reserved specifically for her in those moments when she showed any sort of weakness.

She didn't care.

Let him smile.

She could rip that from his face as easily as she could rip the air from the lungs of those women who were watching her so intently. She could...

Wait.

King Levant stepped into the room—on her level, this time, instead of glaring down from those platforms above —and an image of his wife's face, creased with concern, floated to the front of Alaya's mind.

Endure.

She closed her fist, hiding her Serpent mark, and braced it back against the wall.

There would be a time to fight. Right now, she only had to survive. To get out of this palace. To get back into the free air where she could think clearly again and determine her next steps.

"I don't want to control people," she told Sylven. "I don't need to. I am not as weak as you."

His tall frame shook with mirth as he rose back to his full height. He gave a small, almost lazy wave of his hand.

It was the only warning she received.

The women had clearly been told to strike fast and without mercy.

Alaya did not even think of swallowing the cry that ripped out of her; it came so quickly she didn't realize it was happening, didn't realize the inhuman noise was coming from *her* until she happened to catch sight of Sylven's face. Of the slight upturn of his lips. Of the hint of amusement and triumph in his dark eyes.

The heat had exploded first in her chest. Now it snaked to her shackles. Bit by agonizing bit, the metal around her wrists and ankles grew hotter, branding her, filling the air with the acrid scent of her burning flesh.

Endure.

She curled back against the wall. The fire followed her. Sweat dripped from her forehead. Trailed into her eyes and mouth. She closed them both, squeezing them as tightly as she could and focused on the feeling of them pressing together. She would keep pressing through this. This wouldn't last forever. It never did.

He wasn't going to kill her—

But this time, Sylven did not command his servants to stop.

He had always stopped them before. A bit of torture, but then always a pause so that he could ridicule Alaya and try to make her give in to his demands, so that he could drag out her suffering and try to make her more susceptible to his mind games.

She curled deeper and deeper into herself, still waiting for the moment when she could breathe again.

No pause came.

The fire burned without ceasing around and within her. Her skin blistered and bubbled up along her arms. It looked as if the flames had seeped underneath her skin— leapt from her shackles and seared deeper—and now they were burning her from the inside out.

Every time she thought those flames might dissipate, every time the Fire-kind would stop to catch her breath, a jolt of Ice magic would move in to take the Fire's place, and Alaya would have to fight the urge to scream again.

Soon, she felt her lips moving, trying to betray her, trying to form the word *please*.

Please stop.

She swallowed the words down, knowing he would show her no mercy unless she did as he asked. She wouldn't beg for it, either way. She would just continue to endure.

With a soft, delirious laugh that only she could hear, she recalled the question she had asked Eliana—if the queen had wanted her to *pretend to faint*.

Another minute of this, and Alaya wouldn't have to *pretend* anything.

She tried to find that symbol above the door again, but failed.

The sunlight streamed in through one of the windows above her, suddenly siphoned directly into her face. And though she had sworn it wouldn't happen this way, that brilliant, infuriating light was the very thing that made the hold she had on all of her plans and power...*slip*.

She was tired of suffering.

She was going to kill every single person in this room, and she was going to enjoy doing it.

Her chains began to rattle, though no part of her had actually moved. A metallic *ping* echoed loudly in her ears. The first link of those chains, coming apart. She let her head fall toward her chest. Blinked her eyes and focused until she saw the faint grey shimmer around those chains. Inanimate objects never glowed as brightly as people.

But she could still see that muted energy.

She could grab it. She could—

"ENOUGH!"

Through her heavy-lidded, blurred vision, Alaya saw Levant look to his wife, to where the queen stood in the doorway, and then hold up his hand.

The Fire and Ice-kind both stopped. They bowed to

their king, and then they backed toward the walls as Eliana entered the room.

Sylven started toward Levant in protest, but the queen was closer. She cut him off. After a brief standoff, Sylven followed the Fire and Ice-kind's example, bowing low, before slowly backing away from the king and queen.

Alaya tried to reposition herself so she could see the scene unfolding more clearly. The movement caused her blistered skin to pull taut, sending fresh pain splintering through her. She was forced to close her eyes once more, to keep the room from spinning and her stomach from heaving up what little contents it contained.

She breathed in a deep, shuddering breath. She kept her eyes closed, but managed to focus through her pain, to quiet her seething power and simply listen for a moment.

The queen's voice floated toward her, soft but clear and brimming with power. "If you are going to kill her, then do it mercifully. Not like this. Since when does the Palace of the Sun employ this sort of torture? We are above this, Levant. Kill her cleanly, or not at all."

Kill her...

Why would the queen even *suggest* that he do that?

The question skipped through her mind, but Alaya hardly had the strength to protest, or to guess at the full meaning behind anything anyone was saying. Her eyes fluttered open again. She watched as the king cleared his throat and turned to Sylven.

"My queen is right. The prisoner is not complying, so

she is of no use to me—and these torture sessions *are* growing tiresome. You've had your fun. But I believe an execution is in the best interest of my kingdom and our goals, now."

"Your Majesty, if I may—"

It brought a fuzzy, faint satisfaction to Alaya's battered body and soul, to watch the king hold up his hand and silence Sylven. The Serpent-kind started to argue, but Levant continued to ignore him, summoning the Fire-kind woman to his side.

"Deliver a message to Master Holland for me," he ordered. "Tell him to prepare for an evening execution."

The Fire-kind bowed her head, and her mouth opened to reply—

But the queen spoke before she could, her glare leveled on her husband. "Today is the Eve of the Spring Sun."

Levant studied her for a long moment. An entire, unspoken conversation seemed to pass between the two of them until the king's elvish features twisted, ever so briefly, into what looked like pain, before settling back into an unreadable mask. "So it is," he said.

"You will not take anyone's life today." Eliana's voice was so quiet that Alaya could scarcely hear it. "This date is black enough as it is."

The Fire and Ice-kind both bowed their heads, and Sylven scowled and averted his eyes out of what might have been begrudging respect, or at least recognition. Alaya's thoughts still churned in a sea of pain and exhaustion, and she couldn't think of what this date might have signified to the Sun-kind.

But the king clearly understood; he had only to consider his wife's words for another moment before he nodded and said, "Tomorrow evening, then."

"Thank you." The queen's eyes shimmered with what looked like real tears.

She plays a convincing role, Alaya thought dimly.

The king nodded, turning to leave and beckoning Sylven to follow him.

Sylven's gaze lingered on Alaya, even as he turned to obey the king's command. He said nothing. He mirrored Levant's expressionless mask, but the meaning in that long, emotionless look was still clear enough.

We are not finished.

Her eyes sought the more comforting face of Eliana.

But the Sun Queen was already leaving, and she did not look back.

So Alaya closed her eyes, leaned back against the wall, and waited for the pain to stop.

CHAPTER 5

At some point, Alaya had fallen asleep, and when she awoke, it was dark once more.

And once again, she was not alone.

But it was not the queen who crouched next to her. It was a girl—younger looking than Alaya herself—with dark skin and darker hair that crisscrossed her head in intricately braided patterns. The girl's hazel-green eyes glistened with fierce determination in the faint moonlight. Her lanky body was tense as she crouched down beside Alaya, looking prepared to spring across the room and out of sight at the slightest sign of trouble.

Alaya tried to sit up. She didn't feel as weak as she had the night before, but that wasn't saying much, honestly.

"Who are you?" she demanded, much too loudly.

The girl held a long finger to her lips, eyes casting about for any eavesdroppers. There was a symbol on her wrist—a curved line serving as the base for three more wavy lines. It made Alaya think of steam rising off a lake.

Mist-kind?

Alaya tried to focus through those dull aches that seemed to permeate every inch of her body. She thought she remembered Sade reading from a book about this clan; they were lesser servants of the Moon-kind, who in turn followed Inya, a middle-goddess of the Sun Court whose magic involved revealing directions, finding paths, unlocking things.

"My name is Hacari," whispered the girl, once it seemed no one was around to overhear them. "Her Majesty sent me to help lead you out of the palace. There are others helping, too; they've lured the guards away from us, and away from the path I'm planning to take you on."

Before Alaya had a chance to question any of this, Hacari pressed her hand against the rough stone walls, whispered a few words in what must have been the Mist-kind language—

And then stepped back as that wall began to glow.

It was a shimmering, white imprint of Hacari's bony fingers at first, but as she whispered more of her clan's words, that glowing pattern shifted and lengthened, spun into a small circle that soon expanded outward, opening a hole in the wall as it went.

Alaya stared, lips parting slightly as she tried to make sense of what she was seeing. The wall continued to fade away, and soon, she could clearly see another room on the other end of the opening portal.

"You'll have to take care of your shackles by yourself," Hacari told her. "My magic is limited in what it can open—and those shackles are enchanted with some sort of spell, I believe?"

"...They tighten whenever I try struggling against them," Alaya confirmed, wincing a bit at the memory of the metal digging into her wrists. The skin along her wrists was burned now, too—branded by that Fire-kind earlier—and even the slightest movement that shifted those shackles across the blistered skin made her eyes sting with tears.

"The queen seemed to believe you could break free without much struggle," said Hacari, her focus still on the wall she was opening. "It's what comes *after* breaking them that's going to be difficult. But that's why she sent me to help."

Hacari stood up a little straighter at the mention of her mission, her lips quirking with a slightly smug confidence. The expression reminded Alaya of some of the older girls in the orphanage back in Vanish; once they were old enough that Ma trusted them with more elaborate duties, those girls became insufferable, really. Reckless with newfound confidence and a smug sense of having risen above their fellow orphans. It was a rite of passage; Alaya and Sade had been those girls, once upon a time—and perhaps that was why Alaya suddenly found herself liking and trusting this Mist-kind girl a bit more.

Hacari's eyes fluttered for a moment, then squinted in concentration as she pushed through and finished her spell. The passage was complete; where before there had been only dirt and stone, now a short hallway awaited them, its edges smooth and its top curved as if it had been woven into the palace's original layout. Alaya could clearly make out a table in that room on the other end, along with a dimly-burning lantern that sat in the center of it.

"Hurry up," Hacari urged. "My spell isn't indefinite, and the guards outside this cell won't stay distracted forever."

Alaya nodded. She had no way of knowing if this girl could be fully trusted, but this still seemed like the best chance she had of escaping.

She wasn't going to waste it.

She braced herself for movement. Worked her way up onto her knees, let the waves of pain roll through her while she gritted her teeth for a moment, and then she found her focus and shifted her vision until she saw it: the grey color weaving around her restraints. Still faint, as with most inanimate objects—until she tried to move, at which point darker sparks of magical energy swirled into sight.

Black sparks.

She had seen this shade of energy before, hadn't she? The details were vague, scattered by whatever atrocities Sylven had committed against her mind after that battle with Haben had left her unconscious, but...

She remembered the high king using the same energy. *Mountain-kind energy.*

And somehow, knowing the type of magic she faced always made it easier to control it. She clenched her fists. Imagined those sparks of black magic being crushed against her palms. The cuffs around her wrists stretched and groaned in response.

There came a metallic *pop,* followed by a series of *clink*s, and then the first of her shackles fell away. The second followed quickly after, her magic making it writhe on the ground like a newly beheaded snake for several seconds before it stilled.

The bonds around her ankles were broken with only slightly more effort.

She stood—too quickly—and the room tilted and spun around her. It was the first time she had been able to properly stand in days, and her muscles tightened and burned with protest.

Hacari didn't wait for her; she sprinted through the opening she had created without looking back.

Alaya wobbled after her for a few steps, then managed a weak jog to catch up. That other room, and the table within it, seemed to slide farther away from her with every step she took—until finally, she reached that table and practically fell against it.

Stupid, wobbly muscles. She felt like a newborn foal, all spindly, uncertain legs with no hint of grace.

Beneath that table she leaned against was a bag. Hacari grabbed it and quickly rifled through its contents, eventually pulling out a small vial of brown liquid.

"Drink this."

Alaya took the vial and gave it a questioning sniff.

Hacari made an impatient noise deep in her throat. "Why would I break you out just to poison you?"

Still frowning with uncertainty, Alaya lifted the vial to her lips.

"It's *matago*," Hacari informed her. "An old Oak-kind remedy with a hint of their magic in it. It will revive your own magical energy and dull your pains temporarily. You'll feel *terrible* once it wears off—even worse than now —but the hope is that you'll be a hundred miles away from this palace before then." Without waiting for a reply, the Mist girl ducked back under the table and then reappeared with a fine traveling cloak and a sturdy pair of boots. "And once you're done drinking that, put these on. There are letters from the queen hidden in the inside pockets of the cloak; once you're safe, you can read them. They will help you find your way."

As she spoke, the wall she had opened slowly closed with a noise like leaves being softly rustled by a breeze.

"That was an incredible amount of power for someone of a lesser-spirit clan," Alaya remarked, after downing the first half of the vial. It tasted better than she expected—like tart berries—but the jarring, instant jolt of magic that soon followed the sip could only be described as unpleasant. The power of it continued to thrum through her, making her teeth chatter and her fingers and toes curl, as Hacari shrugged off the compliment.

"I'm actually less talented than I *should* be," Hacari said, "but Her Majesty insists on keeping me around, all the same."

"What do you mean?"

The girl hesitated, as though she didn't think the details were important just then. But after a moment, she answered the curious look on Alaya's face by saying, "My father was Moon-kind. My mother, Mist-kind. And it's rare for the lesser mark to present itself, you know? So I should have carried a mark of the Marr, but instead I'm a lesser-spirit." Her gaze drifted back to that now-closed wall for a moment of thought. "Yet, I still seem to have more of that Moon Goddess's strength than most Mist-kind."

Alaya nodded along with this assessment, and then steeled herself for the second gulp of the Oak-kind concoction. She was better prepared for the rush of magic this time. It was a *cleansing* fire, after all; a pleasant sort of tingling that was burning away all the torture of her past days.

She licked the few drops still clinging to her lips, puckering a bit at the tanginess, and then held the empty vial out, marveling for an instant over how *light* and pain-free her movements suddenly felt.

"That's..." She couldn't think of a word to capture her amazement. "*Potent*," she finally said.

"Glad it's working," Hacari said offhandedly. She was

on the other side of the room, quietly cracking open a door just enough to peer outside. "Because it's only going to get more difficult from here."

Alaya pulled on the cloak and boots, and then she crept a few steps closer to Hacari, listening for the dangers that no doubt awaited on the other side of that door.

"From this room, it's a relatively straight path to outside," Hacari explained in a whisper. "I'll lead you as far as the outer walls of the garden; they're low enough to scale, and on the other side you'll see the Moraki Road —follow that north, past the towers made of gold and glass. It's the quickest way out of the city and into the foothills. You'll find a few small farms in those foothills, including one that will provide you with a horse and with some more supplies; the information you need to find them is all included within those letters tucked into your cloak."

She gave all of these instructions without pausing for breath. Her eyes never left the hallway on the other side of that door.

Alaya opened her mouth to ask for clarification, but a sudden flash of torchlight distracted her.

"There's the signal that we're safe to move," Hacari hissed. "Come on!"

Together, they raced as quietly as they could through the eerily dark and empty hallways. Their surroundings blurred together. Alaya focused only on following the relentlessly quick pounding of Hacari's feet, until suddenly, she felt cold air whipping across her face, and she slowed for half a step to deeply breathe it in.

Outside.

She was finally breathing fresh air again, and it rejuvenated her almost as much as the liquid in that vial had.

They sprinted along cobblestone paths. Swiped aside hanging branches. Darted wildly away from the occasional sound of conversations that floated over them, and careened around corners to avoid encountering people.

Finally, they reached a low stretch of that outer wall Hacari had mentioned. The Mist girl hurried into a pool of shadows being cast by a massive grey tree, beckoning Alaya to follow.

"This is where we part ways," she said.

"You've been an incredible help to me, I—"

"Don't worry about thanking me." Hacari's eyes stayed on the path that had brought them to this corner, watching for followers. "Just get back to your Rook King. Warn him of the monster Levant is becoming. The Army of the Sun will march north soon, and the Valinesian throne must not fall to him. It *cannot fall to him.* Not if we want any hope of lasting peace in this empire."

Peace.

The word fell like a taunt to Alaya's ears. She wanted to nod in agreement. To remind both Hacari and herself that peace had been the objective all along, and that she would not rest until it had been achieved.

But she was already thinking about what a long ride it was going to be to Rykarra.

Could she make it back there in time?

Would it really matter so much if she did?

Hacari somehow seemed to understand her hesitation, all those unasked questions; her eyes finally stopped darting over the path behind them. She tilted her head toward Alaya and her lips pulled into a slight smile. "You had several conversations with Eliana the last time you stayed here, didn't you?"

"...Yes."

"Her Majesty is a very good judge of character. Don't believe the things you've heard about her; she is not mad. She chose to help you for a perfectly sane reason."

Alaya focused on taking a deep breath, silencing those doubts rolling through her mind.

"And don't believe all of the things people have said about *you*, either," Hacari added. "There are plenty of people who are grateful to you for killing Haben, and who believe that there is a way forward for this empire—and that this way involves *you* and the new Rook King. People like Her Majesty, for example."

"And like you?"

"Yes. And lots of others."

Before Alaya could respond to this, a sudden shout in the distance made Hacari's eyes widen.

"That sounded like Captain Tarathiel," she said, shoving Alaya toward the wall before turning to run. "*Go,*" she called over her shoulder. "I'll divert them!"

Fear seized Alaya's heart at the thought of what her new friend might be running off to intercept. But she forced herself to keep moving, convincing herself that Eliana must have had some sort of plan to keep the Mist-kind girl safe.

She looked to the tree towering over her. Narrowed in on the brown-tinted energy floating around it, and then she wrapped her control over that energy and bent several large branches down to her level. She hopped quickly from one branch to the next, until she was high enough to vault over the wall with ease.

She landed deftly on the other side. A road stretched before her, heading north past towering buildings of gold-trimmed glass—all of it was just as Hacari had told her, so far.

It felt almost...*too easy.*

Pulling the hood of her cloak tightly around her head, Alaya started off at a brisk pace.

She had walked for perhaps a mile when the silent night was suddenly interrupted by the barking and howling of hounds. A large host of them, from the sound of it.

Were they hunting for her?

She ducked into an alley between two shops, pressed against the cold stone of one of the buildings and tried to make herself smaller. She held her breath and listened closer, attempting to pick up the sound of any humans that might have been accompanying those dogs.

A sudden, excited baying of one of the beasts made her pulse quicken.

It's caught the scent of something.

Was it of her? She breathed out several curses before deciding to keep moving. It was likely only a pack of stray dogs, scavenging the city for scraps, catching the scent of rats scurrying in another alley somewhere...

Except, they sounded as if they were getting closer.

People were coming out of their houses now, throwing open their windows in half-asleep stupors and demanding to know what the noise was all about.

Alaya broke into a run.

The sound of howls seemed to be growing more distant, and she thought she might be able to outrun the dogs—

Until she rounded a corner and found herself face-to-face with an entire pack of them.

And her body went rigid with terror as she realized: *These were not normal dogs.*

These were the *surma*. The infamous hunting beasts of the Sun Kingdom. There was a legend that the first surma had been a gift to the Sun Goddess; that the middle-goddess Inya had bathed wolf pups in moonlight, turning their fur silvery white and their bodies supernaturally powerful, and then she had given them to Solatis— who had in turn gifted their offspring to the kings and queens who ruled Lumeria in her honor.

Only the royal leaders of the Sun were allowed to own these beasts.

Which meant that Levant already knew his prisoner had escaped.

"So much for things being *too easy*," she muttered.

A chorus of growls answered her. At least a dozen pairs of burning red eyes followed her every movement. They had no master in sight, but the surma stalked toward her with no need for spoken commands, their muscles rippling beneath their moonlight fur, their lizard-like tails whipping excitedly back and forth. A yellowish-green aura surrounded each of them, its sickly color like pus from an infected wound.

The first beast lunged, black claws aiming for her throat.

CHAPTER 6

Alaya swiftly took hold of the energy surrounding the beast lunging at her, and she threw it aside, sending the creature hurtling in the same direction. It struck a pile of firewood with a yelp and was swiftly buried by an avalanche of falling logs.

Alaya's gaze hesitated on those logs for a moment.

It would be much easier to lift those into her control than to try and control this entire pack of living, sentient creatures...

Two more broke away from that pack and raced toward her.

Alaya yanked several of those logs into her control, and she began to throw them. She struck the closest beast in the head. The growl in its throat crescendoed into a startled, painful bark that died abruptly as it collapsed to the ground.

The second darted out of the path of Alaya's next

throw, only to be thumped in the side by a follow-up throw. It rolled across the ground. Slammed into the wheel of a parked wagon. It staggered back to its feet an instant later, shaking the dust from its fur and fixing its wild, fiery eyes on her once more.

She lifted her hand, and another piece of wood with it, preparing to hit it again—

Only to be overtaken by a third beast she hadn't seen coming.

It had gotten behind her, somehow. Its paws struck her back. Claws sank in between her shoulder blades. She cried out in pain and tried to twist away, but ultimately crumpled underneath the weight of the massive creature.

She scrambled the instant she touched the ground, and she managed to slide partially out from underneath the beast. But half of its body on top of hers was still enough to keep her from moving any farther than that. She wriggled, managed to turn around and look up—

Just in time to see its teeth snapping toward her face.

She caught it with an outstretched hand, a panic-stricken plea to the Serpent Goddess flying from her lips and freezing the creature in mid-bite.

But it wouldn't be moved completely. Something was pushing back against her control, suddenly. Something strange, something that felt different than the surma's distinct energy.

That 'something' kept knocking her magic aside every time she felt like she had managed to take hold of the surma with any real, precise command.

She couldn't force the creature to move with her magic, but she kept it still and unbalanced enough that she managed the strength to kick it off. While it swayed away from her, she fought her way up to her hands and knees.

But the rest of the pack had converged on her fallen form. Several were already crouched, muscles coiling, preparing to throw themselves at her.

Heaving for breath, she stared down the surma closest to her and slammed her hand into the earth. Whispered another plea, and in the corners of her vision, she watched as the energy steaming up from the dirt brightened into spirals of brilliant reddish brown.

Once it was bright enough, she tore her focus away from the surma and fixed it fully over that rust-colored energy.

With a few twists of her wrists, the ground parted, separating her from the surma with a chasm that ran all the way across the wide street.

The beasts paced the edge of the opening, heads tilting as if sizing up the space. But buildings edged either end of the chasm, and its length was too much for even these supernatural creatures to jump.

Wasn't it?

She didn't wait to see; she turned and started to run.

A shriek of terror slowed her down.

Keep running, she commanded herself. *Keep running. This might be your only chance.*

She kept running.

Until she heard another shriek. She stopped and twisted around, expecting to see people screaming over her magic—over the swath of road she had destroyed.

But no; the sound was coming from some distance away from that destruction. The surma had abandoned the edge of the chasm she'd opened. The sound of shattering glass, followed by more screams, reached her. Her frantic gaze found the pack of beasts surrounding a ramshackle building—a tavern, it looked like—that was still bright and bustling with the energy of dozens of people, even in the middle of the night.

Too many people.

Several of the windows were broken. The doors, splintered and caved in. Alaya watched in horror as a surma flung itself through one of the few unbroken windows, shattering it and landing with a thud that echoed through the night before being lost within more screams.

A handful of brave men and women stood in front of those busted doors and broken windows, waving fiery lanterns and brandishing knives and swords to try and drive the beasts away.

A body was already on the ground a short distance from the front of the tavern. Two of the surma were fighting over it, taking turns ripping pieces of it free before tossing them into the air and then snatching them between their jaws and swallowing them whole.

Even from a distance, the sight of it, along with the amount of blood pooling from the kill, turned Alaya's stomach.

Since when do the king's hounds attack his own people?

But she knew the answer even before she asked herself the question.

They hadn't caught their *real* target, so now...

She stumbled back toward the edge she'd created and knelt down beside it. Her gaze lowered away from the tavern and fell instead to the dirt and stones piled far below. She took note of the energies, swirls of grey and red and brown. She could pull some of that debris back into place—enough of it to make a bridge—without breaking a sweat.

Sylven's voice floated over to her before she could move. "The dogs are distracted. Go ahead and run."

"Call them off." She didn't look at him as she spoke.

"I haven't the power, I'm afraid."

"*Liar.*"

He laughed. "Why don't *you* call them off?"

The chorus of howls and blood-curdling screams grew louder.

She lifted her livid gaze and found him watching her from the front steps of a house just across the chasm. "*Call. Them. Off.*"

His lips twisted into a grin. "Run while you can," he suggested again. "You don't need to play hero. You don't owe these people anything. *I* would run."

He *would* have, she had no doubt.

And she was furious with herself for thinking, however briefly, that he had a point. Running made more sense in the grand scheme of it all.

She stood and dusted the dirt from her knees.

"Go on," Sylven called to her, nodding her back toward the escape path she'd turned away from.

She kept her glare fixed on him as she struck a hand out over the opening and lifted a half dozen rocks into her command. She drew them up and suspended them in the air, and then used them as stepping stones. Five calm, quick jumps, and she landed gracefully on the other side.

She strode toward the tavern just as calmly, her arms outstretched, her focus reaching out, her magic seeking those beasts that were wreaking havoc.

Three of them lay dead already, their bodies shot through with arrows or otherwise carved up by the tavern goers.

She caught one of the living beasts as it attempted to launch itself through a broken window. She imagined her magic like a leather whip, wrapping around its body and pulling taut. Then she cracked that whip and released her hold, letting the body fly into another of its nearby pack members. The force of it was enough to send both creatures slamming into the wall of the tavern, knocking loose the jagged edges of glass still edging the window.

Their cries of pain drew the attention of several others. Those others lifted their heads toward Alaya— many of which were dripping with blood and drool—and started to trot in her direction.

She quickly counted nine approaching.

She focused on the closest one. No outside force resisted her this time; it was only her magic wrapping around the aura it carried, only the beast's own energy resisting her attempts to command its body.

It didn't resist for long.

Soon it was crumpling, as if shoved down by an invisible hand between its shoulder blades. Its head thrashed angrily about, revealing a white throat stained with blood.

How many people had it killed?

Sweat dripped between Alaya's eyes. Her body trembled slightly. But with a furious grunt, she pushed through and overcame the last of the creature's resistance. It flattened against the ground, gasping for breath as she took hold of the brightest strands of its aura and suffocated them with her magic. That magic crushed the breath from the surma's lungs; ripped the very life-force from its body.

Within seconds, it had stopped moving.

The two behind it fell to her magic just as quickly, collapsing into awkward heaps of long, twisted legs and twitching muscles.

More plodded out from the inn. A sliver of panic wound through Alaya at the increasing number of them.

She couldn't kill them all.

Taking their lives drained too much of her own life-force. The city was beginning to spin around her as her body grew more and more weightless, disconnected from even the very ground beneath her feet.

She could feel Sylven watching her, waiting for her to fail.

She didn't look back at him.

Instead, she narrowed her gaze on the closest of the surma, and she took hold of one of them; a weaker hold than she'd used to kill the others, but still strong enough that she could control its steps with only a slight beckoning of her fingers.

Once a few were under her command, the others seemed to follow without the need for much additional effort. Whether because of the pack-like nature of the surma, or the overwhelming force of her own power that was still building with her desperation and fury, she didn't know. She didn't care.

All she cared about was the fact that when she turned and ran again, they all followed her this time.

She avoided the crevice she'd made, darting instead down a maze of dark alleyways until she finally came to a part of the city where the houses were farther apart and the yards became wide open fields.

She was no longer thinking of the road Hacari had instructed her to take.

She only wanted to drag these beasts as far away from as many innocent people as possible.

The surma were faster than she was. More than once, they started to overtake her, to circle around her and cut off her route.

She had to keep stopping, taking hold of the energy of whichever surma was closest to her and mercilessly squeezing it out of existence.

Each time, the surma paused long enough to sniff and

lick at their newly-fallen pack member, giving her a chance to regain a lead.

But they never stopped chasing her.

The uncertain whimpers would always cease, and then they would resume their chase like beasts violently repossessed—and they *were* possessed, she guessed, by Sylven's magic. *He* had been the force she'd felt earlier, pushing back against her own forces, and now he was going to push these beasts until they ran her into the ground.

Or he was going to *try* to do that, at least.

She made it to the edge of the city. In the distance, she could see the moonlight rippling off the Orobas River that created part of Idalia's north border.

That river was wide. Deep. Swift.

She was exhausted already; swimming didn't seem like an option. Her magic could part the river, but commanding that river's turbulent energy could very well be the last spell she managed before her body and mind gave out on her.

She halfheartedly swept her gaze along the river, searching for a bridge...

She was not that lucky.

With a hasty glance over her shoulder, she found the surma closing in yet again. Their number seemed to multiply every time she looked back.

But she had succeeded in getting them out of the city, at least.

Her gaze turned to the right, toward a distant

grouping of trees that appeared to grow into a thick forest as they sloped toward the river.

Perhaps I can lose them in that forest.

It wasn't a *good* plan, but she broke into a sprint all the same.

As she reached the edge of those trees, she skidded to a stop and turned around. As quickly as her exhausted body could manage, she created another chasm between her and the approaching beasts. She made it as wide and long as she could—but she didn't have the buildings to help close off the edges, this time; the wide-open space was impossible to close off completely.

They would find a way around.

But it bought her a minute or two, at least. She made the most of these minutes, shooting off into the woods, careening wildly around trunks and leaping over bramble patches, frequently changing directions and carving a quick, winding trail that would hopefully confuse her pursuers.

She reached the river and ran parallel to it for a minute, until she reached a stretch that was considerably more narrow than any part she'd come across thus far.

There was a faint trace of a path beaten along the shoreline, leading down into the waters; it looked as if this might have been an often-used crossing point whenever the river was at a low point.

But it had rained several days this past week, and even though it was relatively narrow here, the Orobas's waters were still too swollen and swift to easily swim.

Still, if she could just catch her breath, perhaps she *could* part that river—and stay conscious after doing it.

Her boots squelched and slipped through the mud, down to the edge of the black water.

She took several deep breaths. Closed her eyes for a moment, then opened them to see pale blue energy drifting along the surface of the river like fog. She narrowed her focus, and the brighter shades of that aura began to emerge.

Then she felt it: powerful energies behind her.

She turned, expecting to see the pack of surma leaping to knock her into the dark river.

Nothing was there.

This section of the shoreline was clearer than most; there were only a few spindly trees—none big enough to hide a beast as big as a surma. She squinted into the darker, thicker clutches of the more distant trees, searching for red eyes between the branches.

She saw none.

It was deathly quiet, save for the rush of the river.

But she could still feel that energy. Individual sparks of it growing bolder—closer—and occasionally crashing together into one terrifyingly powerful wave of it. A pack's worth of energy, falling into sync as they approached their prey.

A moment later, she felt Serpent-kind energy join it.

She managed a steady, calm voice. "I know you're there."

Sylven didn't reply.

"Why don't you fight me yourself?"

A low chorus of growls answered her.

She stepped away from the river, onto less muddy, more stable ground. "Are you so frightened of me that you have to send these dogs to do your bidding? *Coward*."

Four of those dogs rushed out of the darkness and flung themselves at her—

Only to be struck down in mid-air by an invisible hand.

Alaya barely held in her gasp.

Sylven walked into sight, his step unhurried and his expression faintly amused. He didn't glance in the direction of the fallen beasts, three of which had already gone completely still. The fourth was convulsing with pitiful yelps and twitches that soon grew fainter and farther apart.

He had killed four of those beasts without flinching; he wasn't even breathing hard.

How?

A chill momentarily froze her to the spot as she realized: She had no idea how powerful he truly was. How powerful he might be capable of becoming.

And his power still was not there for her to see, no matter how close he came or how hard she tried to focus on it: His aura was invisible. She couldn't control his magic, couldn't suffocate it or crush his life with her power if she couldn't *see* the threads of that magic, that life...

And now she was alone in the woods with him, her body already trembling with exhaustion.

"You really want to fight me?" He paused, tilted his head to the side and studied her as if he was truly giving her a chance to change her mind—or perhaps to beg for mercy.

She did neither.

"Then come on: Let's fight." He causally lifted a hand, muttering something under his breath as he did.

She heard the water behind her swirling, likely rising up to crash over her; she didn't glance back to see.

She didn't think. She didn't have the energy left to think. She gritted her teeth and ran forward, out of the reach of the river. Then she took hold of the tree closest to Sylven. With a jerk of her hand, she uprooted it and flung it.

He caught it with his own magic at the last instant, but still lost his balance under the weight. He was forced down to his knees, where he struggled for a moment beneath the crushing weight of the thick trunk and its countless branches that were clawing, tangling around him.

Alaya took only an instant to catch her breath. Then she was darting closer to Sylven once more, her gaze zeroing in on the ground around him. She started pulling that ground apart. One section after another crumbled, until he stood on an island of unstable earth that continued to crumble and shift as he struggled to gain full control of that tree that was still partially wrapped in Alaya's magic.

Alaya paused on the edge of one of those chasms she'd created, watching her enemy struggle.

Her power hummed. The world was alive with colors —the blue river, the rust-colored earth, the silver-green trees—countless different energies to choose from. Countless different energies to finish crushing Sylven with. She breathed in deeply through her nose and reached for the swirling, rusty light of the earth, preparing to bury him.

He reached a hand toward her.

She paused. She wasn't sure why. Perhaps because it was such a strange sight; it looked almost as if he wanted her to take that hand, to pull him to safety, to spare him. It was a plea. And he was not the pleading type.

It was not a plea she had any intention of answering.

But then that hand twisted, along with his expression.

Suddenly, it felt as if he had taken her head in his hands and tried to crush it. Pain exploded behind her eyes. An uncomfortable tingling crept over her scalp. She dropped to one knee, clutching her temples. She tried to look up, to find the earth's energy once more, but a voice in the back of her mind stopped her. A voice that was not her own, slithering through and leaving questions in its wake—

What am I doing?

Why am I trying to kill him?

Her uncertainty lasted only a few seconds.

But it was all Sylven needed.

The ground beneath him had stabilized. Then came a mighty *crack!*—a piece of the tree splintering from the rest as Sylven hurled the remains of it into the river. That splintered piece was sharply cut, a natural spear that he wasted no time in throwing.

It whistled violently through the air, magic carrying it and nearly driving it into Alaya's still-tingling head; she clumsily rolled aside and just barely managed to avoid being impaled.

She pushed onto her hands and knees and watched as he summoned rocks from deep in the earth, just as she had done earlier, and used them to leap across the fissures she had opened.

She jumped back to her feet. Ripped off the restrictive cloak she wore and rolled up her sleeves. Glanced at her glowing mark for strength, for a reminder of who she was and what she was capable of.

Sylven lunged for her, lifting pieces of the ground and cutting off her escape routes as he came.

She leapt over falling stone, careened around the upheavals of earth, her eyes seeking more objects and energies to weaponize.

They danced up into the forest and then back down along the riverbank, ripping more of the ground apart, lifting trees and boulders and launching them at each other, spinning and darting around the increasingly destroyed landscape with a reckless, supernatural speed and strength.

After several minutes of this, Alaya was heaving for breath. He had backed her toward the river again without her realizing it. She heard it rising once more at his command, felt the drops of cool water splashing against her as the wild waves sloshed and strained against his control.

Sprinting away from that river seemed impossible this time; her legs were burning, already threatening to crumple beneath her.

She caught a flash of steel near Sylven's hip, focusing on it long enough that she noticed the dark blue energy floating around it. She took hold of that energy and pulled. It came into her control so quickly it surprised even her; the short blade ripped from its sheath and swept upward, cutting a diagonal, bloody slash across his chest.

With a roar that was more fury than pain, he countered with a wild swing of his fist that sent a powerful wave crashing into her legs.

She steadied herself, bounced away from his swinging hand, and she again sought the fallen blade. Its steel glinted beneath the waves, the energy around it more difficult to see amongst the increasingly chaotic tangle of the river's aura.

Another wave slammed into her.

She stumbled. A single misstep that left her foot lodged awkwardly in the muddy bottom of the river, and then Sylven's hand was around her shoulder. Then a second hand was around her throat. He didn't bother with the blade. He relied only on his own furious, brute strength.

She was overpowered, shoved backwards into the water. Her head crashed under the waves. The water rushed up her nose, burning and choking her and inciting panic. The roar of the river and her own heartbeat thundered in her ears, blocking out all other sound and dulling all her other senses, but a vague thought still managed to float into her darkening mind: He didn't want to drown her.

He wanted her to part the waters and save herself, knowing that such an act would bring her to the edge of her strength.

He'd seen her do it before. Weeks ago, she had parted a river and walked out of it only to collapse on the shore and wake up days later, dazed and confused and completely vulnerable to his magic—to his control that seemed to latch on more tightly, more irreversibly, every time he used it against her.

This was the ending he had planned all along.

She couldn't play along with it. She wouldn't play along with it. She shouldn't...

But her *lungs*. Gods, how they *burned*.

Was this how she died? Which was the more terrible fate? To be controlled, or to be killed?

Faces swam in her mind. Sade. Emrys. Rue. And finally: Hacari. Then came the conversation they'd had in the garden, the way the brave girl's eyes had pleaded with hers. *There are plenty of people...who believe that there is a way forward for this empire—and that this way involves you.*

If she died, so too did that way forward.

She had to live, regardless of what happened next.

The waters parted slowly. She was so detached from her body, from her pain, that it felt like her magic took no effort at all—though she knew better than to *believe* that feeling. She was draining herself. Opening herself up to attack. To *him.*

But she was also breathing. And her eyes were opening, staring up at a black sky not distorted by water. She felt cold. Heavy. But, somehow, she managed to roll onto her side and expel the water from her lungs and the bile from the back of her throat.

Black dots swarmed her vision.

Stay awake! she commanded herself.

Her hand was shaking. She braced it into the muddy river bed, and her eyes sought her mark once again, hoping to see it flaring with life, with a fire that might reignite her failing strength.

The mark was a strange shade of black, as though the dragon had shriveled and died from that merciless cold that had overtaken her. Alaya tried to lift her hand from the mud. It didn't move. It felt as if invisible ropes were crisscrossing her palm, pulling tight over that mark, chaining her dragon down.

What is going on?

The words formed on her lips, but she couldn't speak them. Again and again she tried and failed, until she was so frustrated that she could feel tears burning in the corners of her eyes. But even the cry cutting up into her throat made no noise.

Sudden warmth caressed her cheek.

She felt her body giving into it. Closed her eyes. Felt her ragged strength unclenching, relieved that it no longer had to hold on. A hand closed over her mark, and the warmth that dove into her veins was so pleasant that her entire body shivered with a sigh of relief.

"Go to sleep, now," said a soothing voice. "You'll feel better when you wake up."

CHAPTER 7

Rykarra, City of Rooks, Capital of the Kingdom of Valin

Ten Days Later

EMRYS SURVEYED THE SCENE BEFORE HIM, WORKING HARD TO keep the curl of disgust from his lips.

He was seated in the grand, marble-tiled receiving room at the front of the palace, flanked on either side by advisors and guards. Before him, servants of Lord Redwald— the ruler of the Calah Province of Galasea— were piling gifts.

More gifts.

Trunks of them, this time, all stuffed full of the fine clothing that the forest cities of Calah were known for. These garments of silk and fur joined the already expansive collection of things Emrys had been given, adding to the hoard of jewels and artwork and sculptures and other countless, ultimately useless objects.

"Only the finest of our work for the soon-to-be highest of our kings," said Lord Redwald with a sweeping bow.

A spindly servant with nervous eyes bounced between the trunks, pulling out select pieces and briefly displaying them as though he thought he were in the marketplace, trying to coax Emrys into buying something. He held up a particularly warm-looking cloak lined in grey fur, and the sight of it made the back of Emrys's neck burn.

Surely, there was someone else in your province who could have used these clothes more than me, he thought, staring at the door behind the servant and silently willing him to hurry up.

Before Emrys could speak any part of his disgust, one of his councilors responded with an uttering of gratitude—spoken in the Oak-kind language, as this was the symbol that graced Lord Redwald's hand. The nervous servant replied in the same language, and then he hastily but carefully refolded the clothing and closed the trunks.

Emrys put a fist to his heart and briefly lowered his head—another customary sign of thankfulness in those northern parts of Calah—before waving the man and his servants away.

Dozens more had come before them, and still more followed. The guests and well-wishers included many of the lords and ladies of Valin and Galasea's combined seven provinces, along with the masters and keepers of individual cities. The Stone Kings of Galasea themselves were due for a visit later in the month; in the meantime, they had sent their eldest daughter, Princess Lorralin, on their behalf.

Sun-King Levant had sent no one.

There were no noblemen or women from any province of Lumeria.

It was possible this troubling fact had gone unnoticed by some, owing to the sheer number of guests who *had* shown up. And perhaps some southerners would make an amicable appearance before it was over with. New groups were marching up to the palace's gates with every passing hour, after all.

So, despite his concerns, Emrys continued to put on a polite face and receive guests and gifts.

The additional guests who filed in as the afternoon wore on turned out to be mostly made up of the elite of Rykarra and other cities that were nearby—though there were also old friends from his mother's desert tribe, and even representatives from the lands beyond that harsh northern desert; Seylas Elassidir, Lord of Silverfall, and his handlers had made the trek down from the Kethran Empire, both to pay respects and to discuss border matters.

Hours after it had begun, the parade of well-wishers and gift-givers finally began to dwindle.

Emrys felt that nervous concern itching in the back of

his mind again. He found himself watching more and more desperately for someone of Lumerian background to walk through his doors. For a messenger with even a short declaration of support, or for some other sort of olive branch that Levant might have decided to extend.

None came.

The more optimistic of his advisors were thrilled at the impressive turnout all the same. Even without a showing from the south, there were plenty of allies to be made and strengthened here, plenty of pieces for a promising future that might fall into place if only they could play them correctly...

And the day's games were only just beginning.

Now, it was on to playing his next part. Another part that he somehow felt ill-prepared for, despite the years he'd spent imagining these scenarios in his mind. But there was no stopping what had been set in motion. No room for second-guessing himself.

So he walked, one foot after the other, toward his personal chambers. Two guards followed in his wake, closely watching for any guest who moved suspiciously, or even too enthusiastically, around their royal charge.

Those guests were milling around in every nook and cranny, chattering about the transformation the palace was undergoing. Most were excited, in awe of the festivities that would soon begin in earnest. Emrys's coronation was to be the grandest party this kingdom had seen in years—because what better way to distract from a building war, his courtiers had insisted, than by throwing a massive party?

We must act as though we haven't missed a step.

One foot after the other, until the empire believes that the high throne of the Sundolian Empire is as stable and as strong as ever.

The Kingdom of the Sun is no threat to us—and we will celebrate to prove it.

They reached the floor where his room was located. Passed a multitude of guards stationed by the stairs, and then stepped into a hall that was quiet enough for him to hear the echoes of their footsteps. His chambers were one of only two currently-occupied places off of this hallway; at the other end was Lady Isoni's room. She had taken up that space at the high queen's request once Emrys had reached boyhood, and she hadn't moved since.

You will stay close, the queen had directed her, *to help keep him out of trouble.*

How well Isoni had managed this task was debatable, of course.

His escorts stopped and bowed as they approached his room. He went alone from there, and it was a short but lonely walk. He was grateful for the complete silence, for a moment to catch his breath in private—and yet it felt eerie to be so alone, too, given how many people were crammed into the rest of the palace, most of whom were vying for a chance to see him and speak with him.

A small army of servants was waiting for him in his room. Despite being surrounded by them, that loneliness from the hallway persisted as they helped him prepare for the evening's banquet. He felt their hands working, making final adjustments to his shirt and the fine, silver-edged coat he wore over it. He heard their voices, reciting the long list of guests who had requested a personal audience with him. He inhaled the scent of kohl and bitter berry-based dyes as they painted the traditional lines and symbols of his rank and clan across his skin.

But he didn't *see* any of these things. Not right away. Because throughout the entire ordeal, he was staring out the window high above his desk, watching the clouds being pummeled along by increasingly high winds. A storm was rolling in from the north, it looked like.

As a circlet settled onto the dark waves of his hair, he forced himself to pay attention to the rest of the room. To thank his servants, and then turn to the mirror in the corner of the room and face his reflection.

Despite having braced himself for that reflection, he still inhaled a bit too sharply at the sight of it.

It was the paint across his eyes that did it, perhaps; the black, bird-shaped mask with wings unfurling up across his temples. The look was traditional. It was the same mask that Haben had worn throughout his rule.

The dark design dulled Emrys's eyes, making it more difficult to see how their green shade had been inherited from his mother. They were not blinded and scarred as Haben's had been, at least; that was one of the more barbaric traditions of Rook culture that he planned to do away with.

But he still looked entirely too much like his dead father.

"Are you alright, Your Highness?"

"Yes," he replied after a pause.

The servants nodded, falling into silence once more. They would not question him further. Their job was done —and he reminded them of this—and most of them began to file out of the room. But one of them hesitated and reached to straighten the circlet on his head.

That circlet was not the high king's crown; it was a ceremonial piece that had been made specifically for this banquet. The silver-wrapped diamonds coordinated well with the two rings another servant offered him a moment later. One of those rings had belonged to his father; it was in the shape of a black bird, its wings twisted and meant to curl around the wearer's finger. The glaring eyes were made of two diamonds that gleamed almost pinkish in some lights, as if blood stained the bases they had been set into.

The other—a more elegant design of silver twisting around a white stone—had been a gift from his mother, given to him on his eleventh birthday. It was the last birthday of his that they had truly celebrated. The last one before Haben's descent into madness had started in earnest, and the queen had stopped doing anything that might draw extra attention to her son.

He put both of them on. Absently spun his mother's ring around for a moment, studying it. It reminded him of tree branches tangled together, allowing only glimpses of a full moon through their embrace—which made him think of the countless nights he and his mother had climbed onto the roof of the library tower, just so they could count the stars and recite wishes in that particular old magic of bright moonlight.

He lost himself in those memories for a moment.

Then he took a deep breath, and he left his room.

When he reemerged, that hallway outside was still empty and quiet—save for a lone figure that was quickly approaching him.

Sade.

He gave her a curious look as she reached him. "What's this? Did you bribe the guards into letting you onto this floor—" he nodded to the knife that was clearly visible in a sheath at her ankle "—weapons and all?"

"Charmed them, more like."

"If they fell for the likes of *you*, then it seems they're even more useless than I suspected."

She smiled a bit at the thinly-veiled jab, and then shrugged. "It's hard to find good help."

"I'm noticing that."

"You look terribly fancy, by the way," she commented, giving him a quick glance-over.

"And you don't," he noted, loosening the cuffs of his jacket and rolling them partially up his forearms. It looked decidedly undignified, but he didn't care; the buttoned-up cuffs felt like shackles. He was tempted to take that coat off altogether, but... Well, that would have looked even *more* undignified.

"You're not joining the party?" he asked Sade.

"I'd rather light myself on fire and go streaking through the city."

"That sounds like a fine alternative, in all honesty."

"Besides, I have more important things to see to."

He had already started to make his way past her, but the tone of her voice made him stop. "...More important things?"

"Mmhmm."

"You have another lead?" Despite weeks of those leads that had amounted to nothing, he still felt a defiant spark of hope at the possibility.

"A promising one," Sade replied. "The word is that she was spotted in Hollowforge last night."

"Hollowforge?" His heart fluttered unsteadily for a few beats. "She's that close?"

"Yes. So I'm leaving, but I'll be back in a few hours. With any luck, I'll find Alaya *and* miss this overblown party entirely, and it'll be a good night."

He nodded. His throat felt unbearably dry, suddenly, and tight with the irritation of knowing that he *couldn't* miss this party. Even if she...if...

Was she really that close?

The thought of not being able to see her, despite their closeness, was nothing short of infuriating.

The frustration on his face must have been obvious, because Sade cleared her throat and attempted to temper it by saying, "It could be another false lead."

"But if it's not..."

"Then I need to intercept her before she crashes tonight's party," Sade finished, kneeling to adjust the sheath at her ankle.

He folded his arms across his chest and lifted his eyes to the ceiling, his mind racing.

"Because it would be foolish for her to approach the palace with all of these extra people swarming around it. Right?"

He didn't look down at her.

"*Right?*" she pressed.

"...Of course."

"I'm usually all *for* making a scene, but even I think it would be foolish to add any more complicated guests to this particular party."

He didn't hesitate. "I'll go to her, then."

Sade frowned as she stood up straight again, but he kept talking anyway.

"If you find her, tell her to wait for me. It might take me a while to manage it, but I *will* find a way to slip away from the palace, at least for a little bit."

Sade looked for a moment like she was considering arguing, but then she simply averted her eyes and nodded.

"I want a report the instant you return, even if you have to pry me away from whomever has me cornered at that particular moment." He thought about it for a moment, then sighed and added, "Actually, *especially* if you have to pry me away from people."

She agreed with a bow. Tilting her head toward him,

her grin was wide—shamelessly amused at his personal miseries. She turned to leave, calling out with a little backwards wave: "Have a great time at the party!"

He scowled after her.

She didn't look back.

CHAPTER 8

Emrys continued on his way, losing himself in his still-racing thoughts, until he reached the stairs and the escorts that were waiting for him there.

Things began to blur together after that: his thoughts; the descent to the grand ballroom; the countless faces they passed on the way; the sound of music and laughter giving way to silence as his name and title were announced to the expectant crowd.

It was dizzying, how quickly that crowd surrounded him. Overwhelming, almost. And he had never been the type to get overwhelmed easily.

People had always gravitated toward him at these kinds of parties before. But in the past, they had done so with a kind of hesitant curiosity. A beckoning of his hand or an intentional smile had been enough to draw anyone he wished to his side—but then he had been able to escape them just as easily. Because he had *controlled* them. Used them and then discarded them without a thought. Any interaction had ultimately been aloof and superficial; he'd believed there was no need for anything more complicated than that.

He could have done the same thing now. The consequences would have been greater, perhaps, but he was still tempted to avoid entangling himself with these people, to carry on his enigmatic reputation and settle into the dark edges of the room.

A long table sat at the back of that room, the chair at its center already reserved for him. He could have reclined in it and let the people come to him if they dared.

And he might have done this, if Lady Isoni had not already been seated to the left of that chair.

Her glare said it all: *No, you may not.*

So he resigned himself to a few hours of mingling amongst the guests instead.

The first of those hours was uneventful enough, at least. Most of those guests only wanted to repeat the same dull, rehearsed lines to him: condolences for the loss of his parents; declarations of their support for his rule; compliments on the food and drinks that were being passed around.

He shook hands and made polite conversation until he believed that he had earned a brief respite. But as soon as he attempted to slip away and take that recess, he felt a hand clasp around his arm. He turned and found himself face-to-face with a man old enough to be his father.

This man's eyes were a steeled shade of blue, the

corners of them wrinkled from what must have been years of glaring impatiently at people. His dark blond hair streaked to silver in places, and his heavily wrinkled brow and the deep sag of his jowls further betrayed his age. But despite that age, his stance was formidable, his posture powerful and unyielding. The symbol of the middle-goddess of Ice and Winter, Taiga, ran across his palm.

Emrys knew this man well. Lord Marius Valaste, ruler of the Nyres Province. The house he'd descended from was one of the oldest, most powerful in the frigid northwestern edge of their empire.

The followers of Lord Marius and his house were a warrior people, always had been, and the infamous army that he presided over—known in the common tongue as the *Sword of Winter*—was one of the empire's deadliest forces. An earlier version of that force had been instrumental in establishing the Rook throne as the highest power in Sundolia—and then in protecting that throne from the Serpent uprising and all the other threats it had seen in the years since.

When Lord Marius had responded to Emrys's invitation, he had assured him that he and his army served the high throne and the Rook clan that ruled it—not solely the king himself. Haben was dead, and so now he would serve Emrys instead.

It was as simple as that, he claimed.

Emrys was not convinced of this loyalty—or of anybody else's, for that matter—but if there was any alliance that needed to be reaffirmed tonight, it was this one.

He abandoned his thoughts of taking a break, and instead turned to fully greet the lord.

"Your Highness," Marius said, pressing a fist to his stomach and bowing low.

"Lord Marius. I'm pleased you were able to make it."

"Walk with me for a moment?"

The other partygoers had given the two of them more space than Emrys had enjoyed all night; Lord Marius was one of the more powerful men in the room, and the combined force of them was apparently enough to give people second thoughts about crowding closer. The only ones who remained somewhat close were Emrys's own personal guards, who were subtly watching for any sign he might give for them to intervene. He lifted his palm to them, freezing them in place, and kept his eyes on Marius's as he said, "Of course."

The two strolled toward the smaller of the grand ballroom's two open spaces, a space pinched off from the larger area by a short hall lined with portraits of influential Rook-kind. Marius stopped just before they reached this hall, studying a tapestry that wrapped around the rounded end of the corridor for a moment before he spoke.

"The reports are that Levant aided you in the assassination of Haben. I told myself I wouldn't believe it until I heard it from a direct, reliable source." He peeled his gaze away from the artwork and gave Emrys a pointed look.

"He played his part," Emrys informed him.

"I see." A pause, and then: "I've also heard that things between your kingdoms have since soured—rather abruptly and dramatically."

Emrys kept his tone noncommittal. "The Sun King has always had a flair for dramatics, hasn't he?"

"Indeed, he has." Marius clasped his hands together behind his back. "But the same could be said of Rook-kind, could it not? I mean no offense, of course."

"None taken."

"But you should know that the dramatics this time could push us into a full-scale war. Skirmishes along the border are increasing. Several hundred dead in the past week, alone, is the word. And thousands are said to be mobilizing across Lumeria, ready to rebel, and the Serpent-kind—"

"The numbers are exaggerated. The rumor monster moves with more power and speed than either of us ever could."

Marius released a slow breath. He made a clear attempt to twist his mouth into a more agreeable expression, and he said nothing else for a long moment. It felt suspiciously like the lord was waiting for Emrys to plead for his help, to admit that he felt overwhelmed and in need of the fabled Sword of Winter to come to his rescue.

It was help that Emrys might need before the end, he could admit that—but not help he intended to grovel for. He was to be the high king, after all. Not a beggar or a coward ready to fall so easily at anyone's feet.

Perhaps Lord Marius needed reminding of that.

"At any rate, I prefer not to discuss work at the same time I'm trying to celebrate," Emrys said.

"The high king should always be aware of his 'work', I believe."

He mirrored that thin smile the Ice-kind was giving him. "Have a drink, Lord Marius." He grabbed a goblet from a tray carried by a nearby servant and offered it to the lord. "You seem edgy."

Marius took the goblet but didn't sip from it.

While the lord continued to study him, Emrys continued to hand out drinks to all the other guests around them. He made a point of not concerning himself with whatever Marius was thinking of him at the moment—whether it was disdain or concern or anything in between—and focused instead on making those other guests laugh and crowd around him.

After a few moments of this, he chanced a look over his shoulder and found Lord Marius watching him still, the bemusement in his expression growing with every additional admirer that Emrys drew to his side.

Finally, the Ice Lord sighed and let his lips relax into a slight smile. "Well, you are more charismatic than your father was; I will grant you that much."

"Given that my father was a murderous tyrant, I'm not sure that makes *me* sound all that impressive," Emrys said, "but I will take it as a thoughtful compliment all the same." He lifted his glass to the lord, and he felt the anxious knot in his stomach unclenching a bit as Marius lifted his in turn.

They drank together, the conversation becoming lighter, easier, and it continued that way until a young woman approached them.

"Ah—my daughter, Lady Korva." The lord took her hand, drew her closer and kissed her cheek. As he released her, she turned to Emrys, lifting the heavy skirts of her emerald dress and dipping into a low curtsy.

The resemblance between her and her father was only slight; she was taller than him, with a birdlike elegance and eyes that were softer, the grey-washed color of a sea settling after a storm. Her hair was a shade paler than her father's, as was her complexion—though that complexion was flushed pink at the moment. Whether from too much wine, or from her sudden proximity to the future high king of the empire, Emrys wasn't sure. But he sincerely hoped it was the former.

In his experience, drunk women were easier to deal with than infatuated ones.

"I believe you've met before?" Lord Marius questioned.

"Once," said his daughter, her grey eyes focusing intently on Emrys, "when we were very young."

"I'll leave the two of you to get better acquainted, then."

Emrys did not object—although this felt, once again, like a bit of far too obvious scheming from Lord Marius. He took another long sip of his drink. Korva procured a goblet for herself as well, and the two meandered from one area of the room to another, caught up in a surprisingly pleasant, if slightly dull, conversation.

She had started to prattle on about something regarding her younger cousin and an unfortunate horseback riding incident, when the lights dimmed, suddenly. The music softened. The vibration of drums shivered through him and prickled his skin, and it became impossible not to think of the last time a party had been thrown in this room—and the woman he'd danced with then. The way the music had changed after she'd taken his hand and pulled him out into the middle of the floor. The way she had moved against his touch. The way she had glared so fiercely at him and demanded that he help her. He'd denied her and let her go, and he'd tried not to get any closer to her after that.

Honestly, he'd tried.

But he'd never stood a chance, really.

Lady Korva's voice pulled him from his sea of memories. "Well, does he?"

"...Pardon?"

She laughed softly at his distracted tone. "I asked if the new high king dances?"

Emrys managed a polite smile. "Not tonight, he doesn't."

She leaned one shoulder against the wall, a hint of a pout on her painted lips. "Why ever not?"

He managed a quick lie: "I'm afraid I sprained my

ankle during a sparring exercise the other day. Must not risk aggravating it, you know."

She moved closer to him, tilting her face toward his. The long curls of her half-updo fell like a curtain, such that he was the only one who could see the slightly mischievous curve of her lips. It made the moment feel uncomfortably intimate. "What a pity," she said.

"It truly is." He took a step away from her, briefly averting his gaze and sweeping it over the rest of the room. "But you're in luck; there seems to be no shortage of able-bodied noblemen here tonight. I'm sure you can find someone worthy of your charms to dance with."

The softness in her eyes disappeared abruptly as her smile became a sharp line. "Fingers crossed for me, then."

"I will say a prayer to the lesser-spirit of Luck on your behalf."

"How generous."

"It is. Do spread the word about the new high king's generosity for me, won't you?"

She laughed at this, a sound that was as sharp as her smile, but not entirely without humor. Much like her father before her, she seemed bemused, unsure of what to make of her new high king.

He was fine with that for the moment; let them keep guessing until he became more sure of things himself.

"If you'll excuse me," he said, politely bowing himself out of the conversation and turning away. He crossed the room without attracting much attention, somehow. A combination of his guests becoming increasingly intoxicated and unaware, perhaps, as well as the distracted look on his face; now that he had started to think of Alaya, the rush of questions and uncertainties he'd been keeping at bay all evening were impossible to push away.

Where was Sade?

What had she found?

Why wasn't she back yet?

He was so caught up in these concerns that he ignored the questioning looks his advisors gave him, moving swiftly to his seat at the head table without comment. He might have forgotten these advisors were surrounding him at all, had Isoni not cleared her throat and spoken a moment later.

"Lady Korva looked rather annoyed when you walked away from her."

"Did she? Poor thing." She struck him as someone who was easily annoyed when she didn't get what she wanted; he assumed she would survive the insult he'd given her.

He poured himself a glass of water, clutched the cup of it tightly in his hand, and sank more deeply into his chair.

He could feel Isoni staring at him.

"Go ahead and speak," he sighed. "Spit out your lecture before you faint from the effort of holding it in."

Isoni kept her voice low. Calm. Calculated. "Lady Korva would make a fine queen. And it would be a *smart* alliance to strengthen. The Ice-kind have served Rooks faithfully since the beginning of our empire; your patron deities are linked, and Lord Marius and his ancestors have proven true to that bond, time and time again. Why not solidify it even more?"

He let himself imagine it, only because he wanted to distract himself: A different life, where he woke to the pale-haired Lady Korva beside him and called her his Queen of Ice.

The vision lasted mere seconds.

That was all the time he needed to know that he didn't want such an alternate life to become a reality.

"There is nothing wrong with her," Isoni pressed. "She is beautiful, intelligent, an accomplished leader of both soldiers and—"

"She's delightful."

"And yet you're not interested."

"Not in the slightest."

Mere minutes had passed before Isoni tried again: "There's Stone-Princess Lorralin to consider, as well. There has been talk of your possible betrothal to her since the day she was born. It would be a safe, expected thing in this empire that could use something safe to hold on to. And she's here tonight for precisely that reason, I suspect; you could at least go dance with her."

"But that would be entirely too predictable and boring, wouldn't it?"

"Petulant child," she muttered.

"Petulant *king*," he corrected with a good-natured grin; he had already had too much wine to care about the rude tone she was taking with him.

"Not until tomorrow," she snapped.

He laughed.

She didn't. "At least sit up straighter, would you? For Moraki's sake, you're slouching like a peasant that's never seen a throne, much less sat on one. And you were *drinking* like a peasant, too, I noticed."

"If you keep trying to play matchmaker for me, I assure you I am going to start drinking far more."

This drew the slightest twitch of a smile to her lips. She turned away before it could form completely, and the sigh she heaved was equal parts tender and exasperated. Without another word to him, she waved several servants over and ordered them to bring food.

Minutes later, several plates were dropped before them, and she said only one last thing: "Eat."

He ate. And he made small talk with Captain Helder, who stood behind him, as he surveyed the crowds below and tried in vain not to think about what might have been taking Sade so long.

An hour passed.

Then another.

The guests were beginning to thin, and he was running through possible escape plans in his mind, wondering if it was too early for him to dismiss himself. And then, if there was some excuse he could come up with to leave the palace, to discreetly go and search for Alaya himself. He wouldn't have to tell his council *what* he was searching for, would he?

He was growing more and more desperate, almost

fully prepared to launch this ill-advised plan, when Sade finally appeared in that crowd below him.

He nearly rose from his seat at the sight of her. The sensation of several gazes turning, following his movement, stopped him. He lowered his gaze slightly to the table in front of him, but he never lost sight of Sade.

And the instant he felt the eyes on him easing up, he lifted his gaze and stared at her again.

She was weaving her way through the crowd, moving stealthily, but still drawing a few odd looks due to her attire. She clearly didn't care about these looks; she was moving as though on a mission, and then her eyes were searching, finding his, and her lips finally formed the words he had been waiting on for what felt like an eternity—

I've found her.

CHAPTER 9

IT WAS SEVERAL FRUSTRATING HOURS BEFORE EMRYS FINALLY managed to find himself alone in his room, and then several more minutes after *that* before the voices outside of his room quieted.

He had given strict orders for his guards not to disturb his sleep. But he still checked and double-checked the locks before changing into the darker, more casual and comfortable clothing that would allow him to move more freely through the city. He quickly packed a bag of extra clothing, along with the food he'd carried up from the banquet—he didn't know how long Alaya had been traveling, or how worse for the wear she might have been from it—and then he scrubbed the paint from his face, took the crown from his head, pulled on his belt and boots, and fastened his daggers against his back.

The last thing he grabbed was a sword. Not his own, but Alaya's; it had been recovered from the scene of her battle with his father. He had been keeping it safe ever since. She was incredibly attached to this curved blade, and he couldn't wait to give it back to her.

Everything was secured. A moment later, he was standing before the fireplace, feeling his way along the grey stones until he found the slightly nicked piece that he was looking for. He pulled that nicked stone down. An iron plate, stamped with a fiercely glaring bird, presented itself to him.

There were multiple ways to get this rook bird to open the path it guarded.

Fire-kind magic had become almost natural to him by this point, so it was fire that he chose to use; he summoned it into his palm and held the small flame next to the iron until the lines of the bird glowed bright red.

The stone on the other side of the hearth opened, revealing a staircase.

It was one of two hidden escape routes that led out of his room. They were meant for emergency use only, and only a handful of people in the palace knew about them.

How wonderfully befitting of a king, to be creeping through the darkness like this, he mused as he wound his way down the roughly carved steps. After descending a hundred feet or so, his pulse slowed enough that he could think more clearly, and he thought to summon more fire so that he could actually *see.* The stone walls glittered around him. He still couldn't see all the way to the bottom, but he could at least pick up his pace.

A few hundred feet more, and he came to the end of the stairs and the beginning of a tunnel.

The walls turned to dirt that pressed close on every side; he frequently had to duck to avoid dangling roots and wriggling insects, and to wipe away the damp bits of earth that he kept accidentally brushing into his hair and clothing.

He halfway expected Isoni to be waiting for him at the other end of this tunnel; it wouldn't have been the first time she had intercepted his attempts to sneak out in the middle of the night.

She wasn't there this time, though. There were no guards, either—because the path only led *out* of the palace, not into it. Once he passed through the wall at the end, which was enchanted with both Mist and Sky-kind magic, there was no turning around.

It meant that slipping back inside unnoticed would be more difficult, of course. But he would deal with that when he came to it. For now, he kept moving, darting in and out of the shadows of trees that edged the outskirts of the palace grounds. He was able to stay in those shadows —and out of sight—until the point where he had to pass through the gates and into the city. He could avoid the main gate, but even the smaller ones were guarded.

Sade was waiting patiently in the shadows closest to one of those smaller side gates. She'd told him she would be during the brief, discreet conversation they'd managed to have in the ballroom, and he was finding that she was reliable about these things.

He wasted no time with greetings. "Where is she?"

Sade's eyes darted toward the guards in the distance. They didn't seem to have noticed anything was amiss, but she still matched his whispered tone when she replied. "Waiting for you at the Shrine of Moto."

"She's alone?"

"Yes."

"The keepers of that shrine..."

"Have been dealt with."

"...Dealt with?"

"We didn't kill them. Relax. They just became incredibly *sleepy* all of a sudden, so Alaya and I tucked them into the storeroom behind the main temple."

He grimaced at this, but he didn't question it further. It was another thing he would simply have to deal with whenever he came to it. "And she's...in one piece?"

Sade nodded, though her eyes were clouded with an emotion he couldn't readily name. "Yes," she finally said.

He arched an eyebrow.

"She looked healthy enough. I just have a bad feeling about tonight, is all." She hugged her arms against herself. "I don't know; it's complicated. Just hurry up and go to her. I hated leaving her there alone."

He pulled the hood of his cloak up. "I'll be back before sunrise."

"I'm coming after you well before then, if you're not back—because I'm not covering for you when people start waking up and wondering where the hell you are. I'm not that good of a liar, sorry."

"Fair enough."

"Take my horse; I tied her behind the ruins of the eastern watchtower for you."

"Thank you."

"Here we go, then," Sade said, taking a deep breath and turning toward the guards at that side gate. "Get ready."

He pulled the cloak more tightly around his shoulders, and he watched as she strode toward the guards. There were only two of them there. They were far enough away that he couldn't hear what she shouted to get their attention, but whatever it was, it succeeded in drawing them away—at least, for the moment.

He moved as quickly as he could while keeping his steps silent. Hoisted himself up and over the iron bars, dropped to the other side, and ran until he was out of sight of the gate.

The ruins Sade had mentioned had just peeked into view when he heard a vaguely familiar voice behind him.

"Moving rather fast on that sprained ankle, aren't we?"

Damn it.

He slowed to a stop and turned to find Lady Korva approaching. He cleared his throat. Lowered his hood, and did his best to appear casual.

As casual as one could be while they were dressed all in black and carrying a suspiciously full bag down an empty road in the middle of the night.

"You're out late," he said.

Unusually late.

Had she been tracking him, somehow?

Had her father put her up to this?

"I've found that a city at night is never the same as it is in the daytime." She folded her arms across her chest and gazed thoughtfully at the starless sky, at the silhouettes of buildings and smoking chimneys rising behind him. "I've never experienced Rykarra at night."

"Perhaps I can arrange a tour for you sometime," he suggested. "But tonight, you really should stick to the safety of the palace."

She didn't react to the offer. Her gaze steeled over as she lowered it back to him. "Where are you going, my prince?"

"I have business in the outer city that needs tending to," he replied coolly.

"You're going alone?"

"I'm alone, aren't I?" He glanced around the empty road. "So the answer is *yes*, obviously."

"Is that wise?" Her tone was not particularly accusatory, but it was dangerously curious.

"I assure you, your soon-to-be king is both generous *and* wise. There's no need to question that wisdom."

"I question it only out of concern for that almost-king's well-being."

Impatience heated his blood. He should have been on Sade's horse, racing across the city by now. He needed to get rid of this Lady Korva. Quickly. And without drawing attention to himself—which meant that setting anything on fire was out of the question, no matter how fiercely his impatience burned.

He moved closer to Lady Korva. Noticed the way her body stiffened, the way her lips parted as if in anticipation, and he knew he could use that to his advantage. He dropped his voice to a low murmur. "Wait up for me, if you're so concerned. I'll stop by your room when I get back, to let you know I've returned safely."

"I..."

It was cruel to do it, but flustering people to get what he needed was an old habit. And this Lady of Ice was clearly flustered by his sudden closeness, so he moved even closer, and he took her chin in his hand and forced her gaze to his.

"But in the meantime, you can keep a secret, I trust?"

The steel in her eyes had melted away, and the pools of grayish-blue were widening slightly. He felt her skin growing hot underneath his touch.

It would be a pain to deal with later, if she actually *did* wait up for him, but all he cared about at the moment was getting away.

She cleared her throat, stepped back, and quickly tilted her face away from his. "I can."

"Good." He gave her a roguish grin before turning away and walking the rest of the way to Sade's horse.

He caught sight of Korva again as he trotted that horse onto the road; she was leaning against a fence, staring absently into the city. Their gazes met. He pressed a finger to his lips.

She nodded slowly before pushing away from the fence and heading back toward the palace.

He was not a fool; he wasn't convinced she would keep any secrets for him after she'd come to her senses. And he regretted not warning Sade about her—or about Lord Marius—now that he thought of it. He hardly breathed as he nudged the horse into a quicker pace; he was waiting for the sounds of someone alerting the guards to his activities.

But none came.

So, she was keeping their secret for the moment, at least.

He inhaled deeply. Readjusted his cloak to better hide his face, and then snapped the reins and raced for the edge of the city.

CHAPTER 10

THAT STORM THAT HAD BEEN ON THE WIND EARLIER WAS STILL threatening. No raindrops had fallen, but the humidity still hung in the air, sheets of it that dampened Emrys's cloak as he pushed through them. A full moon was out tonight. It was hidden behind the heavy clouds, but its light still bled through and washed the city in a milky glow. He could see by that glow, even on the darker stretches of road, and even once he had passed out of the city and into the woods.

He was pushing the horse at a reckless pace, and he knew it. He was trying to outrun any more obstacles that might be waiting to ambush him. It was only a matter of time before something else tried to stand between him and his Dragon; he was convinced of this. He was *waiting* for this, his eyes darting wildly along the path, his body seizing and his pulse racing faster at every sound that seemed even slightly out of the ordinary. Something else was going to try and stop him, something was coming, it was impossible to believe otherwise at this point...

Nothing appeared. There were no more interruptions, no more hesitations this time—and then the Shrine of Moto was rising into view, finally, its curved red roof bright and bold and sudden in the moonlight.

And there was a person sitting on its front steps.

Emrys drew sharply to a stop, his breath and any hope of coherent thought or speech all leaving him in a rush.

Impossible, the dark voice in the back of his mind continued to whisper.

But no; she was real.

She had noticed him, and now she was rising slowly to her feet, wincing a bit as she stepped out from under the temple's overhanging roof and into the rain that had finally started to fall.

He dismounted in a daze. Walked over to her in the same way, though all he really wanted to do was run and wrap her in his arms and never let her go again.

She spoke first, her voice soft: "Hello, Rook."

A thousand things he'd planned to say in this moment...all of them vanished at the sound of that voice.

"Or—sorry—do I have to refer to you as *Your Majesty*, now?"

"That's not official until tomorrow, actually." He returned the slight smile she was giving him, but then his eyes were darting, searching the darker places around them while he held his breath and listened. He wanted to silence his doubts, to stop expecting something to ambush them and rip them apart again.

But godsdamn it, he *couldn't*.

"Are you wondering if I brought the entire Army of the Sun with me?" she asked.

He slowly drew his gaze back to her.

Her.

She was really standing there, her golden eyes really watching him, that familiar half smile on her lips, her dark hair framing her beautiful face...

"A crown has a way of making a man paranoid," he admitted.

She nodded to show she understood, but her voice was even quieter, and maybe slightly pained as she said, "It's just me tonight."

It was foolish to believe her, maybe. He was the high king; he had to be smarter now. More cautious. If anything happened...

He didn't care.

He should have. But he didn't. He wouldn't look away from her again. He couldn't stand another second of not looking at her, of not touching her, of not having her safe in his arms.

He closed the little bit of space remaining between them. His fingers threaded through her hair, gripping her tightly and holding her still as he leaned down to press his lips to hers.

Her response was passionate and quick; she lifted onto her toes and pushed more deeply, more completely into the kiss. They became oblivious to the falling rain, to the dark pressing in around them and whatever that darkness might have held.

They resurfaced from their oblivion minutes later, and only because they needed to properly breathe. He held onto her even then, one hand pressed against her back, the other caressing her rain-slicked cheek. He felt light-headed. Both of them were shivering, though it wasn't especially cold.

"This feels like a dream," he whispered, pushing a few damp, wavy strands of hair from her face.

"We should have dreamed up some better weather," she replied.

He laughed. And then he was kissing her again, tasting the rainwater on her lips, taking one last drink of her before he had to take a proper step back and let the rest of the world come into focus once more.

"It was storming the last time we reunited like this too." She smiled, but her eyes were sad. "Do you think it's just following us? Something about us seems to call the storms, wherever we go—doesn't it?"

He pressed another kiss to her forehead, letting his lips linger against her skin while he closed his eyes and tried to think of a response. Then, unable to resist, he pulled her more tightly against him again, resting his chin on the top of her head, and he breathed her in for several moments more before he finally said, "We have a lot to talk about. A lot of brewing storms..."

She nodded against his chest. Her fists clenched the

front of his shirt, her arms braced for balance. "We should get out of *this* storm, first." She lifted her head away from him and looked toward the shrine, her brow creasing with uncertainty.

He desperately wanted to suggest that they get out of the rain by going back to the comfort of his palace. He wanted to believe that they could ignore all of the other people in that palace and all of the complications that would surely arise if he walked arm-in-arm with her through the front door.

He could keep her safe from whatever complications came, couldn't he?

What sort of king couldn't keep even the people he loved safe?

Almost as if she could hear his troubled, conflicting thoughts, Alaya cleared her throat and said, "I think it's probably better if we stay out of the city. Sade mentioned—"

He shook his head, cutting her off. If not the palace, then he at least wanted an actual room. A warm fireplace, a proper table and food, a proper bed... Somewhere that she could be safe and comfortable until things in the palace calmed down and he figured out what to do next.

"We can go to the edge of the city, at least," he told her. "The inn in Sector Eleven; I know its keeper well; she used to work in the palace, and she was close to my mother. She's trustworthy—and capable of being discreet."

Alaya's frown didn't budge.

"New shrine keepers will be along to relieve the ones you and Sade dealt with," Emrys insisted. "And out here in the open air like this is hardly the place for a long, private conversation."

He reached for her hand. Her gaze was stubbornly fixed on his. She still didn't agree, but she didn't object to the points he'd raised, either, so he tried to be patient. He kept silent. Moved his hand absently over her wrist, losing himself all over again in the realization that she was in front of him once more, and in the impossible feeling of her real, solid skin—

Until he felt something strange.

Something that felt like scars. Scars that he was certain hadn't been there before.

In the darkness, he caught a glimpse of marred skin before she pulled away from him and tucked her hands under her arms. And the Serpent mark that covered her palm...was it a trick of the moonlight, or had it looked strange as well?

All those other storms surrounding them felt distant and irrelevant, suddenly. "Let me see your wrist—and your mark." It came out sounding like a command; he had used that harsh, authoritative tone so much in the past week that it was automatic, even toward her.

Unsurprisingly, she made no move to obey his command. Her chin lifted defiantly. "Not now," she said. "Not here."

An odd, burning combination of fury and concern washed over him.

What had happened to her while they were apart?

What was she keeping from him?

He swallowed the follow-up command that tried to roar its way out of him. "...Fine," he said. "We'll add it to the list of things to discuss. But we are not staying here in the middle of the woods to do it; I'm bringing you to a proper room."

Their stubborn standoff lasted only a few more seconds before she admitted defeat. She exhaled a long breath through her nose, nodded, and then she went deeper into those woods to collect her things. She returned a few minutes later on horseback, distractedly arranging her saddlebags as she trotted over to him.

"Lead the way," she said.

A SHORT TIME LATER, Emrys had quietly explained his situation to the old innkeeper. His purse was several dozen paystones lighter, but he had secured an entire wing of the cozy inn for himself and Alaya. Their horses were stabled, and while Alaya made herself comfortable in a room, he managed to procure several drinks and a tray of stew, along with breads and little cakes—a much warmer and more substantial meal than the food he'd tossed into his bag at the palace. It was terribly late, but the inn's staff had still been eager to help him, which was useful; he just hoped that eagerness didn't lead to gossip that would attract unwanted attention.

He knocked softly before reentering the room they

were staying in. It was empty when he stepped inside, but as he placed the tray on the table beside the fireplace, Alaya emerged from the adjoining washroom. Her face was clean, scrubbed free of the signs of her travels. Her hair was smoothed and neatly braided. She was wearing one of his shirts—one of the items that he'd stuffed in that bag from the palace— and what appeared to be little else. The outline of her body was temptingly visible through the relatively thin fabric, fabric that reached only midway down her thighs, and put the rest of her long, bare legs on full display.

A flicker of white-hot desire skipped through him, but he ignored it for the moment and went to work setting the food out on the table and pouring both of them a drink.

"The innkeeper still hasn't expressed any...*concern* at this arrangement?" Alaya's voice was hushed with uncertainty.

"Not a word of it." He glanced up from the plates he was laying out. "You still don't believe me?"

"She knows who you are, of course. Does she know who *I* am? Who you're with?"

"You make it sound like I'm sneaking around with a harlot that's trying to destroy my reputation."

She shrugged. "I've been called worse things."

He frowned at the thought. "Mistress Kamari knows not to question why I needed to slip away from the palace for a bit. One of the perks of being the high king, and the crown prince before that—"

"Is that people don't get to deny you or question you?"

"I don't think this particular person *wanted* to deny me or question me, for what it's worth. I told you: She's an old friend." He straightened up, stepped away from the table and reached for her hand. "We're safe for a little while. Relax."

She didn't ask how long 'a little while' might turn out to be.

He didn't elaborate on the matter.

Neither of them wanted to think about that particular question, he guessed.

She took his hand and let him lead her over to the table, only to quickly pull that hand away from him again as soon as his touch wandered too close to those new scars on her arm. She tucked those scars out of sight, just as she had outside of the Shrine of Moto.

Still trying to hide something from him.

A muscle worked in his jaw, but he managed to keep his mouth clamped shut for the moment.

He wasn't hungry, but he sat quietly and sipped at the warm cider that was equal turns spicy and sweet, and he let her eat in peace—without bombarding her with the countless questions running through his mind.

"This is strange," she commented after a few minutes.

"How so?"

"It feels like we're playing make-believe, doesn't it? Like children—except that instead of pretending we're kings and queens, like most children do, we're pretending to be commoners in the city."

He twisted the ring his mother had given him around on his finger, thinking. "I didn't spend much time playing make-believe as a child," he said.

"You didn't?"

He tried to make his voice lighter as he added, "Not a lot of other children to play with in the palace, and the servants were rarely up for a game of pretending."

"That sounds...lonely."

He shrugged it off. "So is being a king, it turns out. But one finds a way to manage."

It might be less lonely if I could manage to bring you back to the palace with me, he thought. But before he could find the words to tell her this, she absently lifted her hand to push her braid back over her shoulder. The sleeve of his shirt fell back, and the firelight caught on her newly-exposed skin.

She was too slow in drawing it out of sight; she tried, but this time, he was *certain* he'd caught a glimpse of something disturbing—and now he couldn't hold in his questions any longer. "Your mark, Dragon. And the rest of your arm. I still want to see it."

She froze like a thief caught in the act, her hand closing slowly into a fist, which she then lowered to the table. Her smile was wry. "You are nothing if not persistent."

"I need to know what happened while we were apart."

She moved her chair closer to his. Without further comment, she rolled the sleeves of the shirt up and presented her arm to him.

His eyes found the twisted serpent across her hand first. Its coloring had changed. It had once been the pinkish-red of an old scar, flashing occasionally to the shade of burning embers when she was accessing her magic; now, it was tainted with black. It looked as though dark clouds were swirling against the serpent's scales.

He had never seen anything like it before. His heart skipped oddly in his chest at the sight, but he decided not to comment on it, not yet, and instead he moved to that newly scarred skin above the mark. This strange pattern of burnt, wavy markings, he *did* recognize.

"This was done by Fire-kind magic."

She pulled the sleeve back down. "It was."

"One of my soldiers?" His heart ached a little more, thinking of all the places he had those soldiers stationed, and of all the things she'd likely had to fight her way through to get back to this city. Things she'd had to fight *alone* because he had been so buried in politics that he hadn't been able to go to her...

But she shook her head. "It happened before I left the Palace of the Sun."

"Alaya...who did this to you?"

"We were only training with some Fire-kind; things got out of hand. It wasn't malicious."

"*We?*"

"Sylven and I, we—"

He stood up abruptly, his hand starting toward one of his daggers before he caught himself. The violent motion made Alaya's eyes widen slightly. He brought his hand back to his side just as quickly, his fingers curling and uncurling as he paced for a few steps until he felt calm enough to speak.

"I should have guessed that," he muttered, more to himself than her.

Alaya kept her eyes on the table in front of her. "He helped me," she insisted. "He helped me recover after that battle with your father nearly killed me, and for the past weeks he's been guiding me, trying to—"

"And what did he do to you to make you believe that he's *helping*?"

Her eyes flashed toward him, and he saw it, almost as if on cue: A darkness in her eyes that should not have been there.

It reminded him of the moment, weeks ago, when they had escaped his father and brought down part of the palace dungeons in the process. Or *she'd* brought it down, really. And her magic had nearly overwhelmed her. Her eyes had turned black. Soulless. Lost to her magic, to forces neither of them understood, and for several terrifying moments she had not been herself at all.

This time, that blackness in her eyes was gone within the span of a breath.

He didn't want to believe it had truly been there to begin with. It had been a trick of the firelight, perhaps.

And her mark...maybe the darkness tumbling through it was a mistake of some sort, too.

Gods, how *badly* he wanted to believe that.

"Never mind him." Emrys pinched his fingers against his temples, hard, as if he might squeeze the image of that disgusting Serpent-kind from his memories. He couldn't think of him just then. Not if there was to be any hope of finishing this conversation in a rational manner. "What about the rest of it? You were in the southern kingdom?"

She nodded.

"There have been rumors flying that Levant was holding you there; I'd hoped they weren't true, but apparently I was mistaken."

Her reply was quick, adamant: "Levant is not your enemy."

Emrys braced his hands against the table and hung his head so that she couldn't see the irritation starting to build in his eyes.

"He's afraid of what you might do," Alaya told him. "But I asked them to let me come to you, to talk you into putting an end to this building war—and they let me go in hopes that I could. They *let me go.* Don't you see? They want peace."

"They want me to lower my guard."

"Yes, and then they will lower theirs in turn. That's how peace works."

He fought to keep the anger from his expression as he lifted his eyes back to her—

But he didn't manage it, judging by the way she drew

back and quietly said, "You really don't trust me about any of this."

It wasn't a question. It was a statement. And it cut like a knife in his gut, because it wasn't true. He *did* trust her; or he trusted the woman beneath all of the complications and magic, at least. The problem was that it was impossible to tell how much of that woman was actually speaking to him now—and how many of her words were being twisted and controlled by Sylven's magic.

This was the reason he couldn't bring himself to banish the advisors who doubted their relationship.

This was the reason he couldn't march Alaya into the palace and declare her his queen.

Because she was not safe.

She was the only queen he wanted, but he didn't know how to *make* her safe, or how to keep her that way, and he hated how helpless it all made him feel.

"Your silence speaks volumes, Rook." She turned away and busied herself with cleaning up the food and drink between them, the words flying a little more viciously from her mouth with each dish she stacked onto the tray. "You don't trust me. You don't trust Sylven—or any other Serpent-kind or any king that might align themselves with such kind. There was never any chance that one of *your* kind might truly want to make a queen out of me, whatever lies we tried to tell ourselves. We were *always* playing pretend. You're very good at it, for someone who supposedly never had much practice."

"That isn't true."

"Prove that it isn't."

He wasn't sure what to say.

She finished piling plates onto the tray, and then she moved to crouch next to the fireplace, grabbing its metal poker and stoking it until the glowing embers flared into true flames. Silence stretched between them, lasting several moments, until she tilted her face toward him and said, "That's what I thought."

The words fell from his mouth before he could stop them: "I love you."

She clumsily leaned the poker back against the stone. Stood up. Turned slowly back around, her lips parting but still holding back her reply.

The fire continued to build behind her, its light wrapping around her body and casting long, still shadows across the room.

"I don't really know why you're saying all these ridiculous things," he continued. "But I'm tired, Dragon. I'm tired of going in circles with you. The entire world is against it, apparently, and maybe you are against us, too —I can't tell sometimes—but I love you all the same, and I should have said it before now." He clenched his fists tightly, indifferent to the painful bite of his nails against his palms. "There are too many damn things in the way, is all."

He would have sworn her eyes flickered strangely again; only brighter, this time, instead of darker.

But there was nothing bright about the cold, emotionless voice that she eventually spoke in: "How can you love someone you don't trust?"

He shook his head. "I'm still trying to figure that out," he whispered. "I swear I'm trying."

They stared at each other without speaking for several breaths. The fire began to die as abruptly as it had risen, and soon its glow felt much more intimate, encasing the two of them in a shroud of orange with darkness on either side.

Alaya's face softened a bit in that warm glow, and she looked as if she was searching for softer words, too—at least until she abruptly closed her eyes and reached for her head. Her face contorted in pain. She dropped to one knee.

Emrys was at her side in an instant, taking hold of her arm and trying to help her back to her feet. "Are you alright?"

"I'm fine," she hissed, shoving him away. It felt like there was a flicker of magic behind that shove, her power briefly grabbing him and forcing him to stumble back a few steps.

And he was suddenly too frustrated—and confused—to speak. So he didn't reply. He only drew slowly away from her and watched as she struggled back to an upright position, still holding her head with the hand not grabbing desperately onto the table's edge.

"I'm fine," she repeated, blinking her eyes open and glaring at him.

He had his doubts. But she seemed relatively calm and

stable now, so he backed toward the bed and gave her space for the moment.

He removed his belt and daggers and neatly piled them next to the table between the bed and the window. He briefly considered lying down, but instead, he turned to that window, pushed its curtains aside, and his eyes automatically sought the direction of the palace.

Did they know he was gone, yet?

Fog encased the city outside, as well as the window itself, but he could still see the outline of the palace's tallest towers. The flames that ran across the top of those towers were usually tinted to different shades whenever an alarm was raised. They seemed to be burning their natural reddish-orange color for the moment, but he kept staring at them for a few minutes, fully expecting that to change.

At least five minutes passed before he heard Alaya moving again. The floorboards creaking underneath her feet, the metallic scrape of the fireplace poker being properly sheathed in its holder, and then the sound of glasses clinking and a bottle opening...

Silence followed, and then, "I'm sorry." Her voice was little more than a whisper. "I'm trying to figure this out, too."

He nodded but didn't turn around, even when he heard her coming closer and setting something—the clinking glasses from before, it sounded like—on the table beside the nearby bed.

"You can't take your eyes off it for long, can you?" she asked as her reflection appeared in the window beside his.

"...I wish I could, Dragon."

A moment later, her arms were wrapping around his waist. She pressed the side of her face against his back. Breathed in deeply. Exhaled slowly. The feel of her warm breath, of her chest rising and falling against him, sent a pleasant shiver racing up and down his spine. His gaze stayed fixed on the rain-splattered window, but he took one of her hands and lifted it to his lips. The kiss made little bumps rise up along her skin.

"How much longer before that palace realizes you're gone, I wonder?" Her voice was muffled against the folds of his shirt.

"It's a miracle they haven't already raised the entire city in alarm."

She worked her fingers more completely into the spaces between his. Squeezed. Hesitated for a beat, and then she pulled him around to face her. "Let's keep pretending while we can, shall we?" Without taking her eyes off his, she stepped back and reached for the two glasses she'd placed on the nightstand, offering one to him.

He stared at it for a moment before his lips curved into a crooked smile. "To pretending, then," he agreed, taking the glass and lifting it to hers. They sipped in unison. The wine was equal turns bitter and sweet as it slid down his throat, a taste that felt achingly appropriate for the moment.

He didn't look back to that city outside as he drank it. The palace and its storms could wait. They would *have* to wait. Because he saw only her, now, and the space between them grew less and less, until she was close enough that he could hear—no, *feel*—her heartbeat pounding so clearly that it might as well have been his own.

He cupped her face and tilted her mouth to his, tasting the few drops of that bittersweet nectar that clung to her lips. He closed his eyes for a moment and savored that taste, caressing her cheek with one hand and holding her closer to him with the other. He kept her like this for a moment, his fingers pressing against her back, sliding a bit lower every time their kiss deepened.

He drew away from her only to take her emptied glass and place it, along with his own, on the window sill.

His head was already spinning—the wine had been more potent than he'd realized, apparently—and the world swayed a little more violently as he and Alaya crashed back together. Her arms hooked around his neck, pulling him down, steadying him, drawing him back into their interrupted kiss.

His hands moved to the front of the shirt she wore, undoing the ties across her chest, loosening it enough that one sleeve dropped from her shoulder. He trailed his lips across her newly exposed collarbone, up to the curve of her neck and shoulder.

A soft gasp of pleasure escaped her. Her arms tightened

around his neck, and she guided him the short distance to the bed. As her legs bumped into it, she paused long enough to tug his shirt up over his head. Her hands were against his bare chest a moment later, fingertips skimming down along the lines of his stomach, igniting little fires as they went.

He grabbed her hands, leaned her back over the edge of that bed, and pinned her against the mattress while he captured her lips with his once more.

She was breathless, eager, perfectly arched beneath him as he kissed her.

But the room was still swaying strangely—enough that he was forced to pull away after a moment and find his balance again. He swallowed an irritated grunt and lifted her farther onto the bed, finding equilibrium on the sturdier surface.

They fought and tangled themselves amongst the blankets the way they had been fighting and tangling themselves together since they'd met—neither content to be still, to be pinned for long or outdone in their passion. It was explosive and dangerous, relentless and hungry, beautiful and desperate.

She managed to push him onto his back. She was leaning over him an instant later, her knees pressing against his hips, her face inches from his, loose strands of her braid tickling his cheek.

He could have picked her up, rolled her over and continued their battle easily enough.

He decided to surrender.

"I win." Her mouth was close enough to his that her lips brushed with the words.

"I let you win."

She scoffed. "Since when do you *let* me win anything?"

"Since I foolishly went and fell in love with you, I suppose."

He felt her smiling as her mouth pressed to his again, much softer now that he had admitted defeat. Her lips fell open to let him in, and his tongue eagerly accepted the invitation to explore her softness, her warmth, growing bolder every time a caress made her hips rise and fall in a beautiful rhythm against him. His hands clenched the bottom of her shirt, pulling the fabric up across her smooth skin.

And then she...stopped. Her lips fell back together, forcing him out. The pleasurable sounds she'd been making turned sharper. Pained. She leaned away, pinching the bridge of her nose and squinting her eyes shut.

"What is it?"

"Nothing," she mumbled.

All he wanted to do was grab her, pull her down and go back to kissing her until she forgot about whatever it was that kept causing her pain.

But somehow, he managed to make himself pause. To shutter his desire for the moment, and instead take hold of her hips and gently guide her from his lap and onto the bed beside him. He sat up and, feeling another rush of dizziness threatening, he leaned back against the head-board and simply watched her for a moment, concern furrowing his brow.

She was silent and still for several deep breaths, and then she curled closer to him. Her fingers intertwined with his once more. The fingertips of her other hand traced over his knuckles, outlining the ring his mother had given him, but she seemed distracted and distant as she did it. Her eyes were staring at the door by the window—the one that led to the city outside.

"Already thinking of running away?" He tried to make his voice light and teasing, but he didn't quite manage it.

She drew her gaze away from the door and became fixated on his ring, instead—perhaps to avoid looking at him and truly answering his question.

"...It was a gift," he told her. "The white stone in it came from the Cobos Desert; they say these stones are magic, that you can only find them on nights when at least a thousand stars or more are visible above the sands."

"It's lovely."

He twisted it from his finger and held it between them. "It's yours," he told her. She opened her mouth to protest, but he took her hand and continued before she could: "It's all yours, you know. Everything I have—every-thing in the palace—it's yours. All you have to do is ask."

"Everything..."

He could hear the doubt creeping into her tone, and he knew what caused it. "My advisors will see reason eventually. I will *make* them see reason. After this coronation business tomorrow, my reign will be secured and I *will* have you for my queen."

Again, she started to protest, only to apparently change her mind and keep silent.

He slipped the ring onto her finger. It was far too big for her, but after a moment of staring at it, her eyes narrowed in concentration and she whispered something in the Serpent tongue.

The world was spinning again. He was beginning to think that wine had been somehow spoiled, and he was going to have to have a talk with Mistress Kamari about it. But despite his growing sickness, he managed a lazy smile as he watched the ring being manipulated by Alaya's magic, its silver band contracting until it fit snugly on her finger.

"Yet another useful Dragon trick," he commented.

For some reason, she didn't seem able to return his smile. She silently stared at the ring for a few more minutes, her head resting against his chest. "I'm full of useful tricks," she said, almost more to herself than him.

Then she crawled off him and the bed and staggered away, clutching her arms against her chest and mumbling something to herself.

Concerned, he moved to follow—

And he was instantly struck by a wave of dizziness so powerful that he was forced to grab one of the bed's posts to keep from falling to his knees.

She looked back to him as he struggled, but she said nothing.

The room continued to churn violently. He laid back against the mattress, staring up at the ceiling, trying to make it stop.

That stupid wine.

"Something we drank is apparently not agreeing with me," he muttered. "What about you? Do you feel sick?"

No reply.

The silence was...eerie, almost. A terrible, gut-wrenching possibility occurred to him then, and though he didn't want to, he rolled over onto his side so that he could see Alaya again.

She was still watching him.

Still not speaking.

And earlier...he'd turned his back on her for only a few minutes, but it might have been enough time for her to take those wine glasses and...

No. She couldn't have.

"You're showing more resistance than I thought you would." Her tone was perfectly emotionless. "It's dragging this out for much longer than necessary."

"Oh, Dragon." His eyes fluttered shut. His lips curved with bitter amusement. "What have you done?"

How could he have been so *foolish?*

He heard her footsteps coming closer, and he managed to blink his eyes open. To catch one last glimpse of her as she reached for her sword, for that curved blade he'd brought back to her himself. Her eyes were vacant.

Dead. She withdrew the blade, and he saw the Serpent mark glowing against her palm.

It was black.

"Good-bye, Rook," she whispered.

He closed his eyes.

CHAPTER 11

EMRYS EMERGED OUT OF DIZZYING BLACKNESS AND INTO A VIVID nightmare where he couldn't move.

Alaya was still there. She had redressed, coat and boots and all, and had one of her bags open on the chair beside her. *Preparing to leave?* She didn't look in his direction. She seemed to be purposely avoiding looking toward the bed, even as she continued to gather up things and throw them into that bag.

Another rush of darkness overtook him. When he resurfaced from it, Alaya was closer, staring down at him, her sword twirling restlessly in her hand. Her eyes were so dark they were unrecognizable.

"Why are you still awake?" she asked.

This was not a nightmare.

He was awake. Awake, and though she was twisting that sword closer and closer to his chest, she hadn't killed him yet. It was clear that she had drugged him, that she was waiting for those drugs to take proper hold of him before she tried to...to...

"I want this to end peacefully for you."

He opened his mouth to reply, but the tip of her sword grazed over his lips, cutting him off.

"So don't do anything foolish," she warned.

He did it anyway.

What little bit of focus and strength he had, he managed to concentrate into a kick that he aimed at her side. It caught her off-guard. The sword jerked away from his chest. Fire-kind words hissed out of him, and the blade Alaya held glowed red-hot.

She dropped it with a curse and stumbled back, massaging her burned hand.

He rolled from the bed and landed, catlike, on his hands and feet. Alaya's sword rose into the space in front of him, still glowing faintly with heat—

Of course. She didn't need to *hold* it to control it. She only needed to use her magic. Her hand struck out in his direction, and the blade sliced wildly toward him.

He rolled to the side. The sword snarled itself in blankets instead of his body, and while she tried to rip it free, he crawled as fast as he could with limbs that felt unnaturally heavy and sluggish.

The words she muttered in the Serpent-kind language began to sound more like curses. He thought of summoning more fire, of creating a wall between them that might hide him and hold her off until she came back to her senses. But setting Mistress Kamari's inn ablaze seemed a poor way to repay her for her discretion and kindness.

He needed to get out of this place.

He spied his daggers out of the corner of his eye. Lunged for them and the belt they hung from, snatched it all up against his chest, and then staggered for the door that led outside. It wasn't graceful. He felt as if he were running through thick mud—and then suddenly he was outside and he *was* running through thick mud; it had rained more than he'd realized while they were inside, and it was still drizzling now; the inn yard was slick and full of sloshy, glistening dark puddles that were ankle-deep in some places.

He tripped and stumbled through those puddles, trying to find his bearings, trying to decide which direction to escape to. *Which one had the least amount of people? The least amount of witnesses? The least amount of innocent bystanders—*

The door slammed open against the inn wall.

He heard Alaya splashing across the messy ground, her boots falling with an almost inhuman quickness.

He didn't look back. He only ran faster. He cleared the low fence at the edge of the inn's property; hoisting himself up and over the splintering wooden posts took more effort than it should have. He had no idea what had been in that wine, but its ill effects seemed to be exacerbated by motion. He needed to keep moving, but it felt as if something was taking hold of his muscles and squeezing them every time he tried.

One hand clutched his knee, the other his knives, and he doubled over for a moment, heaving for breath and trying to overcome that tension in his muscles.

He heard those splashing footsteps coming closer, closer...

He pushed upright and turned to run again.

But suddenly, she was right *there*, vaulting over the fence and cutting him off.

He twisted wildly away and sprinted as far as he could in the opposite direction, despite the protests from both his body and mind. He made it to a darker street where the houses began to spread out, and he ran until he'd reached the last of those houses. Beyond that was a stretch of the Red River, banked by thick overgrowth and a steep incline. He paused. Quickly wrapped his belt around him and adjusted the daggers against his back as he scanned the darkness, watching. Waiting.

He couldn't run forward, and to run to either side would bring him back to areas with far too many people. There was no clear path of escape.

But it didn't matter.

Because he couldn't run anymore.

He couldn't outrun Alaya, certainly not in the state he was in, and every step now was only making him weaker and easier to kill.

Kill.

Why was she trying to *kill* him?

She had never been this far gone before. There had been moments of confusion, of forgetting—but always, he could still see her through it. But when she'd loomed over him back in that room, those eyes had not been hers. At all.

And that blackness swirling across her mark...

It all had to be related, didn't it?

Fury lit a heated path along his skin. What had they done to her in the Sun Kingdom? *What the hell had they done?*

He would find out, and then there would be a revenge more swift and brutal than anything this empire had ever seen.

But first, he had to survive the night.

Survive. The word pounded through his brain like some wild thing, determined to be heard over the pain and the confusion swirling together in his mind.

Flames sprang to life against his palms. They rose up taller than himself, and he was staring through them when Alaya finally appeared in the middle of the dark street.

She glared at that tumbling fire as she stalked toward him. "You aren't Fire-kind."

He lowered his hands to his side, but kept the fire burning in one of them.

"You *stole* that magic," she growled. "Precisely like your father used to steal it. Everything they said about you was the truth; the empire is no safer with you on the throne than it was with Haben. All Rooks are the same."

"You don't actually believe that. And besides, I can explain this magic, this—"

"Don't bother."

"This is not how I wanted to tell you that I—"

She rushed forward, sword drawn back.

He tossed the fire from his hand, ducked her swing, and threw an arm into her stomach. He hooked tightly and spun, throwing her to the ground. Her curved blade nearly grazed his cheek as she flew away from him.

He straightened with one of his daggers in hand, his other hand outstretched and drawing the fire on the ground back to a more formidable blaze. He took that blaze and stretched it taller and wider, creating a barrier between them that left only the outline of her body visible, and only when she moved.

She leapt back to her feet. He couldn't clearly see her face, but he could feel her glare, burning hotter than anything he could conjure.

"Wake up," he pleaded.

"I am awake," she snapped before leaping forward. The inferno between them barely even made her pause. She flew recklessly toward him, flying straight through the flames and emerging with her sword drawn.

He barely managed to parry her attack, locking his blade with her larger one, nearly dropping to his knees as he tried to keep her sword from sinking in. His awkward stance offered no leverage. Between that and his weakened state, he couldn't shove her away. The sharp edge of her weapon pressed closer and closer to his chest.

He jerked a knee into her stomach. As she gasped for breath, he wrapped a foot around her ankle and pulled.

She landed on her back, splattering them both with mud. Her sword slipped from her hand. He grabbed it and flung it as far as he could toward the river. It landed in a snarl of brambles and sank slowly for a moment before tipping up and diving out of sight.

A cheap move, followed by another cheap move.

If she ever woke up—if she *remembered* any of this—said moves would likely be the first things she brought up.

For the moment she made her displeasure known only by rising back to a crouch and then springing forward, sweeping her hand across the ground as she came. That ground erupted under her control, sharp upheavals of earth rising beneath Emrys and almost knocking him over. He dove aside, rolled several feet, then staggered several more, before the ground finally began to smooth and settle again.

His dagger had slipped from his hand at some point; he turned around to find it lying amongst the rubble of upturned earth, at least ten feet away.

Alaya was only a step behind him.

She didn't bother to recover her own weapon. Instead, Emrys felt the second of his own blades lifting from the sheath at his back. Her magic brought it deftly into her hand, and its edges glinted in the light of what remained from the fire he'd summoned. She spun it around in her hand, testing its weight for a moment, before lifting and pointing it toward him.

"Wake up," he tried again.

She didn't reply. She only narrowed those too-dark eyes toward him as her lips moved with silent words.

His own eyes darted toward where his weapon lay, but a sudden paralysis struck his legs before he could make any attempt to reach it. Her magic, holding him in place.

And then his dagger returned to him with another flash of that controlling magic.

It flew through the misty air with only a flick of her wrist—and it sank deep into his chest, twisting as she twisted her hand, carving deeper, burning a path through him.

He dropped to one knee. He wanted to collapse completely, but her magic was still cradling him, partially holding him in place. He had to blink away the darkness several times before he managed to look up and find her face.

"*Wake. Up.*" The words were little more than breath this time.

He tried to twist free of her grip, but his aching, drugged body was too weak and too slow, and her magic was too strong.

The second dagger pierced lower than the first, sinking in just above his navel.

She released him, then, and he somehow managed to control his fall enough that he landed on his back—though it likely didn't matter; the blades couldn't be pushed much deeper than her magic had already pushed them.

He tried to keep his eyes open.

Survive, insisted that wild voice inside him, though it was little more than a whisper now. He still tried to listen to it. He kept breathing. His eyes stayed open, wide and darting around for something to anchor him. He kept breathing. In and out, in and out. He kept breathing...

But no, he was already beginning to forget. How he had gotten here, how he'd become so cold, what he was doing, who he was—

Until his darting eyes found her again, standing only a few feet away from him, and suddenly he remembered everything.

Alaya was still just standing there, her head lifted toward the dark sky, rain drops sliding down her face. Her brow was furrowed, her lips pressed in a thin frown. She almost looked as if she were searching for something— something she'd lost amongst those stars that refused to reveal themselves during the rain.

A massive shadow overtook them a moment later.

Emrys thought he had imagined it. That he had finally closed his eyes and given in to the hallucinations that death had brought along with it. He forgot to breathe for a moment. But then a low, almost mournful roar vibrated through him, and he gasped and inhaled deeply once more.

Rue.

The dragon circled above them, her massive body casting shadows that further darkened the already dimly lit road.

Alaya grabbed the sides of her head and dropped to the mud.

It looked like the same, agonized pain that had overcome her back at the inn. But he couldn't go to her this time. He tried, but the smallest motion made those blades in him twist and cut more deeply. It was almost worse than the fire burning through his insides, worse than the pain each breath shot through his chest, to be so close to her but unable to reach out and touch her.

And he almost thought to himself that things couldn't possibly get worse than all of this—but then he heard the sound of hooves pounding along the muddy road. A great host of them, accompanied by the occasional urgent shout.

He couldn't see the Palace of Eyes from where he laid in the mud, but he suspected that the flames along its top were burning a brilliant shade of white.

He managed to cough, to painfully clear his throat and murmur a single word: "Dragon."

Alaya's gaze snapped up. Found him. Her eyes were back to their normal soft, golden-brown shade. And he might have felt relief at this—enough solace that he could have died in peace, even—if not for the horror shining in the golden depths of those eyes.

"What have I done?" she whispered, pulling herself to his side and gingerly touching a hand to his blood-streaked chest.

"It doesn't matter right now," he coughed.

"No."

He gritted his teeth. "...Focus."

"No, no, no, *please no*—"

He snatched her hand and managed to hold it tightly enough to keep her from further exploring the wounds she'd left. Blood and muddy water squished between their fingers, trailing down his palm and over his wrist.

"Listen...to me." His words slurred, but he got them out. "You have to run. You...you can't let anyone...see you here like this."

"I can't just leave you!"

The hooves pounded closer, and now lights were flickering on in houses, and the shouts in the wind were clear enough that he might have recognized who they belonged to if he'd paused to listen.

He squeezed Alaya's hand as tightly as he could. "*You have to go hide.*"

"No." She was still shaking her head—but she was also slowly backing away as she did it, her gaze momentarily darting toward the lights and sounds in the distance before fixing, desperately, back on his face. Her hand stretched toward the briar patch that had swallowed her sword. A span of a deep breath, that was all it took, and then that blade was flying back to her. She caught it without taking her eyes off his.

He tried to force his lips into something that resembled a smile. "You haven't managed...to kill me yet," he muttered. "Don't worry. It will take more than this."

Rue let out another cry; it sounded as if she had flown well past the river.

Alaya stared at Emrys for a few more painful heartbeats, her face twisting with regret and fear. With devastation. But she nodded—there was no other choice if she wanted to live.

She turned and fled.

Emrys watched her figure growing smaller and smaller, until concentrating on the small dot of her made his head feel like it might split into pieces from the pain.

By some favor of the lesser-spirit of Luck, it was Sade who reached him next. He saw her running for him while the rest of the hunting party remained just behind her; it appeared some of that party had stopped to speak with the increasing number of city folk who were opening their doors and stepping uncertainly out into the damp night, clutching their dressing gowns around them.

Sade slid to a stop and fell onto her knees beside Emrys, sloshing more water and mud over him as she came. "What *happened?*"

It was getting harder to stay awake, but he managed to lift a finger in the direction Alaya had disappeared into. "Go...after her. Stop her from leaving the kingdom. But keep her...keep her..."

Damn it.

He felt no more pain, only frustration and annoyance that he couldn't make himself speak more quickly, more clearly.

"You can't...let anybody find her. *Go.*"

Sade went, scrambling so quickly away from him that she nearly tripped on the soggy ground.

The dagger in his stomach had eased its way out. It was resting just beyond his fingertips. He stretched out his hand and cupped it around the gilded handle, little by little, walking it closer to him until he could fully grasp it.

He had a vague thought of: *Cauterize the wound. Stop the bleeding.* He managed to direct enough Fire-kind magic into the blade that it burned bright orange. He took his other hand and tried to feel across his stomach, searching for the edges of that wound. But the amount of wetness he found pooling on his skin was alarming to the point that it disoriented him, nearly making him drop the dagger.

He could no longer tell what was muck and rainwater, and what was his own blood.

He clenched his teeth. Took several ragged breaths. Gripped the dagger more tightly and reinforced the magic that made it glow. He found the line of pierced flesh and pressed that burning steel over it. Pain radiated through him. He bit down hard, catching his tongue and flooding his mouth with a sickly metallic taste. He thought he might faint. Likely *would* have, if not for the voices that distracted him before he could.

It's the prince! Over there!

Seconds later—or was it minutes?—he blinked and then opened his eyes to find himself surrounded by people. Someone was kneeling beside him, saying his name over and over. Someone was applying pressure to his stomach, to his chest, and the sky swirled above him, the raindrops like a thousand tiny shards of glass diving toward him. He closed his eyes, not wanting to see the moment they stabbed his skin.

A hard slap on his cheek jolted him back to awareness.

"Don't you *dare* close your eyes."

He blinked through the burning, blurring pain that came with trying to see, and he grimaced when he realized it was Lady Isoni staring down at him. "I'm...going to be lectured about this, aren't I?" he mumbled.

Her tone was odd as she lifted his head into her lap and pushed the rain-soaked hair from his forehead. "Stay awake, Emrys."

"I believe you mean 'stay awake, *Your Highness*'."

"Open your eyes."

Her voice had grown sharper, but he didn't care, because he was leaving now.

"*Open your eyes!*"

He wasn't certain where he was going, but it was dark and warm and it was not *here*, not drenched in blood and burning with reminders of things he hadn't been able to stop, of people he hadn't been able to save. He could see it when he blinked, a sort of hazy peace that was waiting for him just beyond his last breaths.

And when he closed his eyes this time, that peace welcomed him in, and he surrendered himself to it.

CHAPTER 12

Alaya ran.

She ran until she came to a narrow strip of the river that was mostly shielded from the city's houses. Paused. Parted the water with her magic and then ran even faster across the damp ground, down the hill on the other side, until the city's border wall came into sight. She drew briefly to a stop as she caught sight of the guards strolling along the edge of that wall.

Emrys had commanded them—perhaps bribed them a bit—into looking the other way when they'd passed through here earlier.

Now those guards were distracted by the dragon flying overhead; they didn't notice Alaya as she slid into the shadows underneath the city gate. She still pressed against the stone of the arched passage as she crept through it, trying to make herself as inconspicuous as possible.

She wanted to press even closer, to make herself even smaller.

She wanted to fold up and disappear.

But instead, she made it to the other side, and she kept running.

She ran until she was blind with exhaustion, and then somehow, her legs kept moving on their own, driven by a desperate need to get away from the awful things she'd done. She wasn't even certain what she *had* done. Not entirely. She only knew she needed to get away from it.

It had been Rue's voice in her head—a soft whisper of a voice that sounded more human than dragon—that had woken her up in the city. Now, it was Rue's eyesight sliding over hers, showing her the way once more; when she focused on their connection, Alaya saw a clearing in the center of the forest. The dragon was landing in that clearing. Waiting for her.

That forest seemed to be growing darker and thicker with every step she took through it, but Alaya never slowed. She was close to that clearing, she could feel it—

Something slammed into her side, sending her spinning. She crashed into a tree. Her left arm absorbed most of the jarring impact, and a painful tingling radiated out from her elbow. Cursing, she pushed away from the trunk and reached for her sword.

Her assailant was faster; hands were suddenly around Alaya's wrist, yanking her away from the sword before shoving her back against the tree.

A pair of furious blue eyes glared into hers.

"Sade? What are you—"

"No, what are *you* doing, *you absolute idiot?*"

Alaya wriggled free, elbowing Sade in the stomach as she did, creating enough space between them that she managed to break away and start running again.

Sade was faster. She had *always* been faster. She dove for Alaya's legs and held tightly to them, pulling her down to the ground and knocking the breath from Alaya's lungs.

"Are you out of your mind? Let *go of me!*" Alaya kicked wildly. When that didn't work, she twisted around and clawed for Sade's face.

Sade let go of her legs only to wrap a crushing grip around Alaya's arms. The two of them rolled through the damp undergrowth, clawing and kicking, breaking branches and collecting leaves as they went.

It felt strangely similar to all of the times they'd wrestled together as children. Only now, there was no one here to calm either of them down. Sade's father was gone. So was Kian—and his mother's stern gaze was a thousand miles away, too, unable to guilt them into stopping and stepping away from each other.

So Sade's fury went unchecked, and her fist soon managed to connect with Alaya's jaw, and Alaya's counter swing struck Sade's chin.

Sade drew back, momentarily dazed.

Alaya held up a hand and bent a few fingers, bending the limbs of the surrounding trees into her control. Their energy was supple and easy to warp. They hung in her command like arrows drawn back and ready to be released. "Get away from me," she warned.

"No."

"Get away *before I do something horrible to you, too.*"

Sade only stepped closer. "You can't just run away from those horrible things."

Alaya heaved for breath. Over and over, she inhaled as deeply as she could, but she never managed to truly catch that breath, and her voice cracked with the effort of it as she asked, "What else am I supposed to do?"

Sade took another step toward her, her gaze only briefly considering the tree limbs pointing their sharp fingers at her before she refocused on Alaya and said, "I don't know. But don't run. You *can't run.* Sylven will find you, or you'll go back to the Sun Kingdom yourself, and you'll—"

"I'm not going back there."

"Where else are you going to go?" Sade demanded.

"It doesn't matter."

"Yes, it *does!*"

Alaya's frustrations rose again, and the trees creaked and drew their limbs farther back, threatening to swing.

Sade tossed another wary glance at them, pursing her lips. "Stop being dramatic," she said.

A harsh laugh barked out of Alaya before she could stop it. "Everywhere we go, these dramatic things seem to follow us, don't they?"

As if to prove her point, the wind suddenly rose to a

howl, showering them both with the cold remnants of rain that had been clinging to the leaves.

Rue dropped down through the trees a moment later, her tail whipping and clearing a path, her claws catching branches and snapping them as if they were merely twigs and minor annoyances. Leaves and mud scattered in all directions as she landed.

Sade lifted an arm over her face to shield it from the debris, which gave Alaya the chance to move closer to the safety of her dragon.

The low rumbling in that dragon's throat was easy enough to interpret—*it would have been easier for me to land in that clearing in the distance*—but Rue still lowered her head and allowed Alaya to grasp one of the curved horns and swing onto her back.

As Alaya found her balance, bracing her hand between Rue's shoulder blades, her gaze leveled on Sade's once more. "You can't follow me this time," she told her.

Sade wiped mud from her cheek and narrowed her eyes. "Watch me and see if I don't."

They glared at each other for another moment, and then Rue was lifting, spinning, twisting free of the clutches of the trees and spiraling up into the clouds. Her scales shimmered to a hazy shade of dark grey, and soon, she and Alaya were both lost to the mist-swirled sky.

Alaya clenched the fine hairs that ran along Rue's neck, and she bowed her head and buried her face into that mane. "Don't let me go back to Idalia, Rue. No matter what I might say."

The dragon replied with a soft grunt, which Alaya took as agreement.

Not Idalia. Not back to Rykarra. She had no true home left to run to; so where was she going to go?

What did she have left?

She curled tighter into Rue, burying her face in the dragon's mane.

After an hour of trying not to think, she forced herself to lift her head and answer one of those questions by *counting* the things she had left. Touching them. Naming them. It was an old habit, something Madelaine Amani had taught her to do in those rare moments when she'd caught Alaya feeling sorry for herself as an orphaned child.

Focus on what you have, Ma would say, *and those things have a way of making you forget about what you've lost. At least, for a little while.*

She had her sword. Her magic. Her coat. The clothes on her body. The dragon beneath her. Her bags were gone, left at the inn—

But no, she wasn't focusing on the things that were *gone.*

Only on what she *had.*

She clenched her fists. Took a deep breath, and tried again, restarting her count by touching the latest item she had almost forgotten she'd acquired—that ring Emrys had given her. She traced it for a minute, lost in thought, before glancing down at it.

It was flecked with blood.

She almost vomited. Almost yanked the ring from her finger and crammed it into her pocket and out of sight—but stopped herself, because she was afraid she might end up losing it if she took it off. And besides, her hands were covered with even more blood, and she couldn't very well remove *those*.

She shoved her hand into the pocket of her coat and refused to look at the ring anymore.

Blood still blossomed in her vision every time she blinked. If not the blood-stained ring, then it was the image of blood blossoming across Emrys's chest, or the blood red shade of the wine she had poisoned.

"*Oh Dragon,*" she whispered to herself, recalling his words, his shock, his horror. "*What have you done?*"

Those words were agony enough to remember.

They were not as painful as *I love you,* though.

He had shown her that obviously enough over the past weeks, but he had never said it—not so clearly as he had hours ago.

He'd said it so clearly, and she had *heard it.*

But there had been other voices in her head at the time. Too many other voices, as there had been during her entire trip to Rykarra, and yet... As he'd said those words, she remembered hearing only his voice, just for a moment. It had cut through all of the other noise in her mind and *reached* her. Just three simple words.

And she had desperately wanted to say them back to him.

But she had ultimately remained a prisoner in her

own mind. He had reached her, but it hadn't brought her back, fully, hadn't broken the hold Sylven's magic had taken over her mind, and now...

Rue's voice purred through her thoughts. (*Sleep, Little Goddess.*)

"I don't think so."

(*Safe, for now.*)

She nodded absently, though she still had no intentions of closing her eyes, even though it was true: this *was* the only place she ever felt safe anymore, perched on Rue's back, high above the world and hidden from sight by the dragon's ability to control her appearance and blend with her surroundings.

And the more she thought about it, the more Alaya believed that it wasn't simply *physical* safety that the creature was providing. Something about Rue seemed to be protecting her mind, as well.

Alaya kept glancing at her palm, waiting for her mark to bleed black once more, and waiting for those voices in her head to return and drive her back to make certain she finished the job she'd been sent to do.

Yet each time, her mark stayed normal, and no voices came.

She leaned forward again and clung more tightly to Rue's neck. The possibility that their bond was strong enough to overrule her unwanted connection to Sylven and his controlling magic offered her a glimmer of hope against her dark thoughts.

But still her tears kept returning, no matter how many

times she wiped them away. Her face grew sticky and her throat became painfully hoarse. She *wanted* to sleep, as Rue had insisted. She wanted to forget what she'd done. But she couldn't.

They flew for another hour, and then another. Alaya felt no closer to falling asleep, no matter how much time passed, and so instead she watched the world sliding along beneath them.

They were moving in an easterly direction, it seemed, because soon the sparkling, foamy waves of the Belaric Sea were visible in the far-off distance. They glided along the coast for some time, occasionally swooping low enough that they frightened flocks of the sea-going *nargun* birds.

Finally, as Alaya heaved in great lungfuls of the salty air, the tears stopped. She closed her eyes for a while. She still didn't sleep as the briny breeze whipped her hair about, but she dreamed, at least—dreamed that they might fly like this forever, and that she would never have to land or look back on anything that had happened.

The sky began to ease toward the colors of morning. Rue was slowing, suddenly, gliding longer and lower between each mighty pump of her wings. At one point they sank so quickly toward the ground that Alaya was convinced the dragon had actually fallen asleep while flying. A couple of sharp nudges against her side sent the creature jerking upright again, snorting her irritation as she went.

They would have to land and properly rest, soon.

Hopefully, they could find a private place to do this—someplace where Alaya wouldn't have to distance herself from the dragon in any way—but what about after that?

She couldn't spend the rest of her life clinging to this dragon, even if Rue *was* the only thing that seemed to be able to keep her sane.

They turned inward, away from the sea, a short time later. Soon after, a river caught Alaya's eye. It snaked a narrow, twisted path through a sparse forest, and it looked like it was flowing with blood, owing to the red glow of a sun that was just peaking over the hills in the distance.

She guided Rue to the ground without another thought, then hopped from her back and commanded the dragon to stay in place. Though she was terrified of straying too far from the creature's presumed protective magic, Alaya knew she had to test her theory. If she wanted to have any hope of overcoming these things, she needed to understand what was really happening. Figure out her limits.

Rue made an uncertain noise deep in her throat, but Alaya ignored it and sprinted for the river. She knelt down and plunged her hands into it. The icy water bit painfully into her skin as she worked to scrub the blood from her hands, from the sleeves of her coat, from the ring that Emrys had given her.

She could still hear Rue in the distance. The dragon was pacing, snorting, and loudly swishing her tail through the leaves.

Alaya ran farther—as far as she could go without collapsing in exhaustion—following the river until she reached a wide, quiet bend of it that was densely sheltered by trees. She climbed onto a moss-carpeted rock and inched her way closer to the water.

She could no longer hear Rue. She couldn't see the dragon or anything beyond those trees packed so tightly around her. It made her feel as if she had stepped into a secret place, separated from the rest of the world. And the river seemed different here. Its flow had nearly stopped, and the pooling water was an odd shade of turquoise. Vines hung between the trees, their flowers delicate and withered; the faint breeze was enough to spill several of those brown-edged flowers onto the rock as she perched on it.

As Alaya reached for one of them, she felt a twitch in her palm. The same twitch that she had felt countless times over the past week. And she knew that if she looked down at that palm, she would see a Serpent mark that was shifting toward a poisoned shade of black—so she didn't look down.

But it was only seconds after that when the voice she was trying so desperately to escape slithered into her thoughts.

Voices in her head were nothing new. She'd started hearing them regularly after leaving the safety of her childhood home of Vanish; the voices of the exiled and lost members of the Serpent clan, in that case—whispers of the ones who had left curses upon the empire they'd been driven out of. Curses that were desperate to be awakened, and that had tried—sometimes successfully—to channel their way through Alaya and her semi-divine soul.

She had mostly learned to block them out, or to at least control them with a clear mind.

But this newest voice was different. It belonged to Sylven, not to those distant clan members she had never met. This voice was a danger that had burrowed itself deeply, more intimately, into her mind every time his magic had healed her, and now *she* was the curse that was in danger of being controlled.

It made her sick to even think of it. But she was determined to overcome it. She had managed to fight her way out of the grip of all of those other voices, after all.

So she would find a way to fight this one, too.

She still didn't look at her palm; instead, she gathered up more of the fallen flowers and picked off their petals, one-by-one. She piled them according to color, only to toss them all into the water a moment later, and then she used her magic to swirl circles of them together atop the river's gentle current. She didn't need Rue; she could distract herself well enough. And as long as she wasn't just sitting and *thinking*, she could keep the voice in her head to a whisper.

At least for a little while.

But it took only a moment of hesitation to ruin it.

She paused between distractions, and it was enough time to let her fears rise and send her thoughts tumbling.

She lost herself in those thoughts, and Sylven grabbed hold, his voice growing louder and more difficult to ignore. Soon, it seemed as if he was physically *there*, pressing a hand to either side of her head, whispering until she could no longer tell which thoughts were hers, and which were being planted by him.

And suddenly she was stuck in a memory she couldn't escape, sinking into it the way one sank into a muddy river that was deeper and more dangerous than it seemed from the shore—

She woke in the Sun Palace, rays of golden light assaulting her as they always did in that royal residence that didn't want to insult their Upper Goddess with shades that blocked out her gift. She was not alone. There were nurses surrounding her. The Sun Queen's personal attendant was overseeing them, along with the maids that were scurrying about.

And there was Mira, too, leaning against the wall, her head tilted away.

Alaya sat up.

Mira turned to her, revealing the other side of her face. Her eye on that side was puckered shut, the skin around it blistered and shining in various, gruesome shades of pink and red.

The words left Alaya without thought: "What happened to your face?"

"Don't you remember?" the older Serpent girl asked, coming to sit beside Alaya amongst the velvet and silk blankets. "The Rook King and his magic did this to me."

The blistered skin was horrible to look at; Alaya couldn't bring herself to stare at it for longer than a few seconds. She swallowed several times before she found her voice again. "But Haben is dead, at least. They told me—"

"Not Haben. His son."

"His..."

"Don't you remember?" came another voice, deeper and more pleasant than Mira's gravelly tone. Sylven's face was more pleasant to focus on, too, as he walked to Alaya's side and offered her a piece of fruit from the tray he carried. "Haben is indeed dead. You killed him. But his son lives. And his son may prove more powerful than his father ever did. Emrys already has magic—he was likely collecting it for some time without our knowledge—and he is already wielding it to rule over people. Mira will not be the last Serpent he burns. He plans to restart that vicious, empty war with our kind, to finish what his father couldn't."

"He would never..."

"Don't you understand? He used you to kill his father, as he had always planned to do. But the fear of our kind was only renewed by that assassination, and his subjects will not rest easy, nor fully support him, until that fear is dealt with. I've no doubt that he believes that eliminating you, and any other lingering Serpent-kind, will be the first great act of his reign."

The room seemed to spin. To violently crash to a stop. And then to start spinning again, faster this time, until Alaya finally buried her face in her hands to try and make it stop.

There had been signs of his magic use, hadn't there? Suspicious things that she had never confronted him about. There were more lies between them than truths, it felt like. And yet, for some reason, she had continued to trust him.

But now her mind saw only blackness every time she tried to think of the reason—or reasons—for it.

She felt a hand on her arm, and she peeked one eye open and saw Mira leaning closer to her. The burned side of her face was turned away, but now Alaya saw that the woman's arm was just as badly burned as her face.

And fury lashed through Alaya like a snake uncoiling to strike.

She lifted her head and asked, "What should I do?"

Sylven's eyes appeared brighter than usual as he turned to answer her. "We will burn his kingdom down before he has a chance to burn any more of us."

Most of the servants had dismissed themselves by this point, and the closest of those who remained were busy folding linens on the other side of the room. Still, Mira's voice was quiet as she added, "The Sun King has pledged his support to us, so long as you agree to fight."

"And you will fight," Sylven added.

It should have been a question. It wasn't. But Alaya still found herself nodding 'yes'.

"Yes. I will fight."

She inhaled deeply, as though coming up for air for the first time in minutes. She heard the gentle babble of the river, the soft breeze against her cheek, and she knew that she had briefly managed to escape the dark forest of her thoughts and mangled memories.

She didn't want to go back to that forest.

But more images were already clawing at her, sinking in and dragging her back into the deep and its darkness—

The brightness of the Sun Palace was gone.

She was riding a horse through a narrow mountain passage, heading north. The white stone walls rose tall on either side of her, splashed with scarlet sunlight at the very tops. Her horse's eyes were wide and white in the evening shadows; something had spooked him. Perhaps it had been Alaya herself that had done it. Her own eyes were unusually dark. Her palm ached, and she felt restless. The mountains occasionally groaned as she trotted past them, or else little hairline cracks appeared in the stone faces, or tiny pebbles beneath her horse's hooves lifted and fell and skittered across the dusty ground.

The suppression of her power made her shiver—because it was being restrained by someone else's command. She felt like a wolf, partially tamed by an irritating collar that she desperately wanted to break free of.

A whisper of Serpent-kind language twisted into her thoughts, replying to this complaint that she hadn't uttered aloud: "You will be free once he's dead."

And so she trotted on, thinking only of killing that fool of a Rook who wanted to start a war with her...

"No," she mumbled. To nobody, she thought, until she got a reply in the form of a warm puff of air—a breath from the dragon who was staring back at her when she blinked her eyes open.

Alaya didn't remember moving, but she had apparently crawled from the moss-covered rock by the river and curled against a tree instead.

Rue was crouched beside that tree as well, her snout

nudging Alaya's arm, her body curved in awkward angles to make her long body fit between the other trunks and bushes surrounding them. She had flattened a few of the smaller saplings beneath her claws, and her swishing tail was threatening to fell a couple more with repeated soft *thwacks.*

"I told you to stay back there," Alaya muttered, wrapping her arms as far as she could around the dragon's long face. Her fingertips barely reached to Rue's jawline.

(*Foolish.*)

Alaya sighed. "I know."

(*Do you. Truly?*)

"Yes. I was a fool to separate myself from you, because you seem to be the only thing that keeps me from losing myself here lately." She tapped her fingers in an absent-minded way against the dragon's head, trying to keep the frustrated tears from welling up in her eyes. "But what should I do? I can't bring you everywhere I go. You aren't exactly small and inconspicuous."

Rue arched her head away from Alaya's lap and twisted it toward her tail, as if to check her conspicuous size for herself. She didn't disagree with Alaya's assessment. She offered no other commentary. She only yawned and shuffled back a few steps to a more open spot—snapping several branches in the process—before turning in circles and then curling up and closing her eyes.

The dragon slept, and Alaya crawled closer to her, leaned against her scaly side, and tried to come up with a plan.

Pieces of that flashback from the palace were still replaying themselves in her mind, but they didn't consume her as they had before, now that Rue was close by. She could sort through them. She could safely let herself dwell on them, and on other events that had taken place in that palace, and she could search them for clues of what to do next.

For several minutes, Alaya tried and failed to find anything of significance in those thoughts.

But then she remembered the girl who had helped her escape the Sun Palace's prison chambers.

That girl—Hacari, wasn't it?—had given her the traveling cloak she was now wearing, and she had told her that there were letters from the Sun Queen hidden in one of its pockets; letters that would tell her where to go next.

Her head was almost clear, but Alaya still nearly convinced herself that she had made this memory up. Why should she trust anything her mind was telling her? And what were the odds that Sylven hadn't stolen the things from the pockets of her cloak, just as he had stolen away her ability to think and act freely?

Why reach into those pockets, only to be disappointed?

But she reached anyway, because she was stubborn, and her hand felt along the multiple pockets until she heard the tell-tale sound of crinkling parchment within one of them.

She pulled out several folded pieces of that parchment.

The first few that she opened contained information that had been intended to help her ill-fated attempt to escape Idalia. There were names, notes regarding people who could get her out of that city and on her way to Rykarra.

Nothing she needed *now*, in other words.

She kept searching anyhow, rummaging through the notes until she was down to the final folded scrap of paper.

She didn't want to open it. Clearly, Eliana had only planned on helping her escape Idalia, and then she expected Alaya to figure out the rest on her own. That was fair, wasn't it?

Alaya almost tossed the last letter aside at the thought.

But something stayed her hand, and after a moment of staring at the worn edges of that letter, she held her breath and unfolded it.

The first thing she noticed was a symbol that looked like a burst of light—the Star clan's symbol.

And underneath it were three neatly printed words:

Find the Spinner.

She exhaled slowly. Turned the paper over, hoping for more, but found only a few dots of ink that had bled through from the other side.

The clan who carried that light-burst symbol were mostly scattered throughout the southern kingdom, but there was one Lumerian village that had a higher concentration of them than anywhere else: Vespera.

And it made sense that Queen Eliana would send her to that village, to someone within it; the Star-kind were servants of the Sun in the hierarchy of their empire, and this 'Spinner' person would hopefully keep no secrets from his or her queen—or from anyone that queen sent to them for help.

It was a place to begin, at least.

Alaya refolded the note, tucked it back into her pocket, and lifted her eyes to the sky in thought.

A few of the brightest stars were still visible in that pale dawn sky. As she stared at them, another memory fell over her like raindrops into still water—and it began with three words, each one sending ripples of dread through her as they hit.

Death. Betrayal. Destruction.

This was the message that had been written in the stars on the night she was born.

The last time she had visited that Star-kind village, she had been confronted with this truth—and then later, one of the exiled Serpents she encountered had spoken this prophecy word-for-word. A prophecy that he'd been able to read because of knowledge given to him by the Star-kind.

The Star-kind were fortune tellers, sign readers, and so-called destiny revealers. Like all of the ones who carried magical gifts from the Marr and the lesser-spirits, their talents and skills were varied. But the general elements of that magic made Alaya uncomfortable, for obvious reasons, and she had left that village weeks ago with no desire to ever return to it.

She closed her eyes and leaned deeper into Rue's side, listening to the rhythmic, slow thumping of the dragon's heart. She tossed and turned with her thoughts, drifted in and out of sleep herself for several hours, and then finally fell into the deep, dreamless slumber of the deathly exhausted.

When next she blinked her eyes open, she found the sun was rising again. Her stomach ached with hunger, but her body felt well-rested, if stiff.

It seemed an entire day had passed, which caused a brief moment of panic. She had to get up. She could neither sleep nor debate with her thoughts any longer; she had already wasted too much time.

"Rue."

The dragon stretched her jaws wide in a yawn, and then she lifted and tilted her head toward Alaya. Something about being under the intelligent, scrutinizing gaze of the creature made Alaya feel small and briefly uncertain again, but she steeled herself, and she rose to her feet anyway.

She had made up her mind.

She could not go back to Rykarra. Or Idalia. She could not go home. But she would not stop moving. It was useless to sit around and ask what she should do—she had to keep going if she was ever going to figure that out.

"What I will do," she said to Rue, and as an affirmation to herself as well, "is go to Vespera and see if this so-called *Spinner* has anything that might be able to help me. Are you ready to fly?"

Rue purred in agreement, and she too rose to her feet, her claws kneading the dirt as she arched her back in a stretch. Then she lowered herself and allowed Alaya to climb on, and they flew out of the trees as the last of the stars twinkled out of the sky to make way for the new day.

CHAPTER 13

THE WORLD CAME BACK IN PIECES. LITTLE THREADS OF LIGHT. Brief snatches of sound and whispers and shadows that Emrys couldn't make sense of at first, but which eventually began to take on form and meaning.

He first recognized the heavily wrinkled face of Merric Ulondar, the Oak-kind doctor who had been employed by the Palace of Eyes since before Emrys had been born. Then there were familiar servants, familiar voices, and finally, a familiar, dark face with bright brown eyes that were wearing an expression of disapproval. An expression that was likely going to become permanent at the rate things were going.

This last face made him want to go back to sleep, but he powered through this desire and slowly tried to sit up instead.

"Careful, Your Highness," fretted Ulondar, reaching to better arrange the pillows at his back.

"I'm fine," Emrys assured him.

"You're awake, at least." It was difficult to tell whether Lady Isoni was relieved or annoyed as she lowered herself into the chair beside where he lay.

Pain sliced through Emrys's chest as he tried to move into a more comfortable position; he would have sworn for a moment that the fool of a doctor had forgotten to remove the daggers from his chest and abdomen. He glanced down, just to make certain that wasn't the case, but found only freshly closed scars where the daggers had pierced him.

"This should help with the soreness," Ulondar said, handing him a cup full of dark liquid that smelled suspiciously like pine needles and dirt. "And you should consider yourself extremely lucky that you escaped your ordeal with only a bit of soreness. And with some weakness, too, I assume? You lost a frightening amount of blood."

Emrys nodded; even the simple motion was enough to make him feel lightheaded and, yes, *weak*.

"There are few true remedies for that blood loss besides time and rest—or far more powerful magic than my own."

"Your magic is perfectly sufficient," Emrys said, sipping that earthy elixir he'd been given.

"Thank you for saying so," the doctor said, offhandedly, as he dabbed some sort of ointment across Emrys's chest. "I've managed to seal your wounds, at least; we'll need to watch for infection, but otherwise I think you're in the clear."

"Thank you."

"So you're finished, then?" Isoni asked.

The doctor nodded.

"Then leave us," she commanded, circling her gaze to the other servants in the room as well. "I'll send for you if his condition deteriorates again."

The doctor bowed and did as he was told, and the few lingering servants went with him. Isoni walked them out, making certain the door was shut tightly behind them before she turned and made her way back to the bed.

Emrys did not have the energy to try and get out of the impending lecture. So he sank back into the pillows, still clutching the cup of medicine, closed his eyes, and simply waited for Isoni to speak.

"So," she began. "You've managed to miss your own coronation, and the entire city is talking about how you were found lying in the mud, half-naked and covered in stab wounds. A fine start to your reign as the highest ruler of this empire. *Very* impressive."

"Thank you; I thought so too."

He didn't have to open his eyes to know she was scowling at him and his blithe tone.

"Go on, then," he encouraged with a weak cough, "tell me the rest. All of the terrible parts in all of their full, terrible glory and detail, please."

She breathed in deeply through her nose. Exhaled slowly. "You've been asleep for over two days now. A third of our guests have departed. The rest remain, content enough to attend a rescheduled coronation—but there is not a silent tongue amongst them. The...*official* story that we've told them all is that this attack was random, the work of a lone rebel who has since been dealt with, and that you were outside the palace walls for the simple, if foolish, reason of needing to breathe some fresh, unclouded air."

"A fine story." He cracked one eye open to see her scowl for himself. "But you don't believe it."

"Of course I don't. It's the least interesting version of events going around, after all. There are countless others."

His chest felt as if it might cave in from the sudden heaviness that overcame it. "Such as?"

"The ones hungry for war with the south are linking the attack to Levant and his followers. They're ready to march a full-scale army into Lumeria in retaliation."

"I see." He tried to keep his voice even. "You don't believe that one either, I presume?"

"I suspect it was connected to the Sun King in its own way." She fixed him with a withering look. "But it was no Sun-kind that attacked you, now, was it?"

He drained that medicine he'd been given in one long, slow sip, and then swirled the last drops of it around in the cup for a moment before he finally replied. "...I don't know who it was, to be honest," he said, quietly.

And it was the truth, wasn't it?

The woman who had attacked him...that had not been his Alaya.

"Well, I can think of only one reason why you would

have been foolish enough to leave the safety of your palace behind. Only one person who could have lured you out, in spite of all of the danger you *knew* it would put you in."

"You know me too well, don't you?" he asked, tonelessly.

"How many times has it been, now? How many times have I told you to forget about that Serpent girl and focus on your duties to this empire?"

"Might I remind you that you are the one that introduced us?"

"I need no reminder of that," she hissed. "I no longer sleep most nights because of it."

"But she killed my father, just as we'd hoped," he pointed out.

"And now, she's almost killed *you*."

"She was not herself, this time."

"Or perhaps she has finally shown her true self—that she is a true Serpent who has no real loyalty to anyone but her own kind, and certainly not to a *Rook*."

He reached to place the emptied medicine cup on the bedside table, wincing at the movement. The small effort of it was not only painful, but it also drained him enough that he nearly slipped back out of consciousness as his head hit the pillows once more.

But he had to stay awake.

He had to learn all of the details, however painful, and he had to figure out what he was going to *do* about these latest developments.

"Where is Sade?" he asked.

Isoni pursed her lips but didn't answer.

"Send for her." He lifted his head from the pillows and made his voice and his glare stern in spite of his pain. "Now."

Without a word, Isoni stood and went to the door. After a brief conversation with the guards outside of it, she returned and started to sort through and ration out the medicines he would be due to take, based on the instructions the doctor had left behind.

Emrys thought she was finished with her lecturing. But just as he was about to close his eyes and rest until Sade arrived, Isoni—looking unusually flustered—dropped a bottle of some sort of bubbly liquid. She cursed under her breath in her own clan's language, but she didn't bother to pick the bottle up. Instead, she gripped the edge of the bed and lifted her stare towards him once more.

"Let me make one thing clear to you," she said, "I never want to have to carry your lifeless body anywhere like that, ever again. I thought you were *dead* when we brought you into the palace lights and I got a good look at you. You looked like a corpse—and I have risen enough of those that I should know. I don't want to be able to work my magic over you any time soon. Do you hear me?"

He opened his mouth to speak, but he didn't manage to find words.

"I will *not* lose you."

There was more to this last declaration that they were

190

both aware of, though she didn't say it. He could read it in the silence, and in the way she was looking at him. He had eyes like his mother, and he had little doubt that it was his mother Isoni was thinking of as she stared into those eyes.

I will not lose you like I lost her.

That was what she meant.

And the only thing he could think to say was, "I'm sorry."

She nodded without meeting his eyes any longer; her gaze was glassy as she looked toward the window and wrapped her arms against her chest. After a moment, she turned back to the bed and the table beside it, and this time she busied herself with pouring a glass of water from the jade-colored pitcher that had been left there by the nurses.

She handed it to him and commanded him to drink.

He did, mostly because he was tired of arguing.

"I'm sorry," he repeated, after another long silence stretched between them. "But it doesn't change how I feel about her. She is the only one I would put on the throne beside me. What happened the other night was..." He couldn't think of a word to properly describe it, but he grimaced and settled on: "Horrible. But it was not her. I will find out what happened. I will—"

"It is pointless, Emrys." Her voice had softened—as much as it ever did; she was pleading with him now, her concern finally outweighing her irritation. "You understand this, don't you? Your kinds do not mix."

"Have you considered that the two of us might prove that assumption wrong? And how *else* could we better erase the damage my father did to this empire by waging that war against the Serpent-kind? He divided the three kingdoms with fear and prejudice. We could *unite* them by displaying the opposite."

Isoni's voice was cold. "You are being willfully, stupidly naive, Highness. There is no future with her that ends with anything other than endless bloodshed."

His teeth clenched, his temper threatening to erupt again. "Then it's a good thing I am willing to bleed," he snapped.

Before Isoni could reply, the door swung open and Sade rushed in. Isoni didn't seem to notice. "I'm finished arguing about this," she told Emrys. "And you should be resting." She stood, straightening her skirts. Her glare finally shifted to acknowledge Sade, and her next words fell like a threat from her lips: "Do not keep him awake for long."

Sade nodded, shrinking out of Isoni's path in a way that seemed uncharacteristic of her. She waited until the Bone lady was out of the room and clearly not coming back—holding her tongue for longer than she typically did, as well—before she turned to Emrys and said, "She looked like she was in an even more terrible mood than usual."

"Of course she was," he replied, taking another sip from the glass of water. "She knows the truth about what happened. About who I went to see."

"Ah. I had a feeling she would figure it out."

"And about what happened..." He let the words hang in the air for a moment, and was disappointed—if unsurprised—to see the corners of her mouth slowly turning downward.

"I wish I had good news to share."

"I want whatever news you have."

She took a deep breath before beginning. "It's been two days since...you know. I went after her that night, like you asked, and I caught up with her, and we fought, too, but then..."

"But then you lost her?" he guessed.

"I followed her as deep as I could into the Mosaic Forest, but she had a rather large advantage over me—in the form of a dragon."

He was quiet for a moment, thinking, before he muttered, "So not only did she disappear again, but now we've also reunited her with her dragon, which will make her impossible to catch."

"Yes. All in all, that night went rather poorly, I'd say." Sade dropped into the chair beside his bed and raked her hands through her hair, clenching the wavy strands so tightly that he wouldn't have been surprised to see her come away with fistfuls of red. "And I don't know what to do next. I've sent as many messages as I dared to send, trying to reach people who might have seen her. To her father; and Valla; and to the few contacts in Vanish that I still trust. Oh, and I also stole your seal and forged your signature on a few more messages that went to some of the masters of nearby cities."

He nearly choked on the water he'd just taken another sip of. "How did you obtain my seal?"

"I have many talents. Thievery is but one of them." She shrugged. "And I didn't know how long you were going to nap, so what else was I supposed to do?"

He accepted with a sigh. "It's fine. I'm glad you didn't wait. Just...make sure no one else in this palace finds out about that. About *any* of it, actually."

"Obviously. And obviously, I didn't tell any of these people I contacted all of the details about *why* we wanted to find Alaya, or why we wanted her kept alive. My wording was careful. Not that it looks like it's going to matter; I haven't heard back from everyone yet, but of the ones I have? No one has seen her. Rue is damn good at camouflaging herself, unfortunately. And I can't even think of where the two of them might go now."

Emrys sat up more fully, only wincing slightly as he did; that elixir the doctor had given him was beginning to smooth the edges of his many aches and pains, making movement possible, if not easy.

"They might not even be in this empire anymore," Sade continued with a wistful sigh. "The north border is likely, what? Two days by dragon flight, if that? And then less than another day over the Wildlands, and then she's..."

He could hear the panic rising in her voice, and he struggled not to mirror it. "She wouldn't find any safe place in the Kethran Empire," he said, quietly and calmly. "They are hostile to *anyone* with a mark and magic, these days. I know she and I had a discussion about that at least once before; I doubt she would have risked going there."

"Across the eastern sea, then? To Belaric?"

He closed his eyes against the thought. He didn't want to picture it—the woman he loved on the run for the rest of her life, forced to choose between one hostile place after another as she desperately tried to put more and more distance between herself and everything that had happened.

There was another way. Some way that she could stay in *this* empire, and the two of them could keep fighting together to fix Sundolia, just as they had promised each other they would.

There *had* to be another way.

He just couldn't see it yet.

But...there was a way to see. There were several kinds of magic that specialized in *seeing*, in fact, and he had already been working toward obtaining one of those kinds over the past weeks—practically since the moment he had first lost sight of her.

And trying out that new magic would be a start, at least.

"Give me tonight to work," he told Sade. "By morning, I will know where she is."

"How?"

He opened his eyes. Lifted his gaze, and stared expectantly at her for a moment, until realization dawned across her face.

"...Oh. It will be by way of some sort of magic that you've stolen, won't it?" Her expression was dubious, though her tone had shifted from slightly panicked to slightly hopeful.

He stayed quiet.

Sade's eyes glazed over in thought. She sank deeper into the chair and picked at the gold threads trimming its cushions for a moment before saying, "Wait. Are you sure you can manage to summon *any* magic in the condition you're in? I'm guessing it's not particularly easy to use magic that doesn't really belong to you, even when you're at your full strength—is it?"

He didn't answer her questions, because he wasn't entirely sure of the risks that would be involved in what was to come, and he didn't want to dwell on them either way. So he only said, "I'll get you the information you need about her whereabouts, along with whatever other help I can provide. But you'll need to be prepared to leave at sunrise to go after her."

She looked skeptical.

He knew he was going to have to more fully explain his thoughts to her, or else she'd never leave him alone. "The Air-kind's magic will make it possible," he added.

Possible.

He had to keep repeating that word to himself a lot here lately.

He still wasn't certain *he* believed in everything that

was running through his mind; but the skepticism slowly faded from Sade's eyes, at least, and though her brow remained creased with concern, she nodded. She knew as much about the respective clans and their powers as he did, and it was apparent that she knew what a person who carried the Air mark was capable of doing—whatever the risks.

They spent several more minutes discussing plans and possibilities, and then Sade left, and—after a brief check-in from one of the servants—Emrys was finally alone. He wanted to jump out of bed and immediately get to work. But it was mid-afternoon, and any move he attempted to make would not go unnoticed by the hordes of people who were no doubt circling as close as they could to his room, hoping to catch a glimpse of their mysteriously injured monarch.

He also had to admit to himself, however begrudgingly, that he still felt as if he'd been trampled on by a herd of antelope. The elixir had helped, but it was no cure. Rest would help more—and perhaps the combination of the two would keep him alive when he attempted that Air-kind magic later on.

So he tried to rest.

And he somewhat managed it.

When he drifted back into full awareness hours later, the shades had been pulled over his windows, and the shadows dancing across them were moonlight-made. There was only one other person in the room, as best he could tell through one partially opened eye; one of the

Oak-kind nurses who had been helping treat him earlier. She was whispering a spell as she came closer. He caught a glimpse of her clan mark beginning to glow before he closed his eyes tightly.

He pretended to sleep while the cool tingling of her spell settled over his scars. It did little to alleviate the dull aches that burned anew with every deep breath he took, but he didn't have to wait long for her to finish it, at least. Soon, he heard her gathering up objects from the bedside table, and then her footsteps heading out of the door that she shut softly behind her.

He waited to make sure no other visitors took her place before he quietly, slowly, *painfully* dragged himself from his bed. The stiffness of several days' worth of resting was almost as painful as his new scars. *Almost.* But he gritted his teeth and pushed through his discomfort, and he dressed as quickly as he could manage.

The guards outside were unavoidable, but he silenced their questioning with little more than a look, and they swore discretion—though he could tell they were uneasy about it.

"I'm not leaving the palace this time," he assured them. "And I won't be gone long."

That last part might have ended up being a lie, of course; he wasn't entirely sure *how* the night would go. He only knew that he had asked Sade to deliver a message on his behalf to Lord Feran, and that the old magic advisor should have been waiting for him in the queen's former study.

Now, Emrys simply had to get there, preferably without drawing too much attention to himself. A feat that seemed more and more impossible every time he turned a corner and found himself ambushed by people who insisted on having a conversation. There were far too many people out and about for such a late hour—and they all seemed to have been waiting around, preparing to compete with one another over who could show the most concern for him.

By the time he fought his way to a mostly empty corridor, his mouth was as sore as the rest of him after its vigorous workout of fake smiles and polite conversation. He took the longer route to the study from that point, ducking occasionally into servant corridors to avoid people.

He could have simply ordered those people to leave him be, he supposed. But it was easier to avoid them altogether. He had spent so much time avoiding things in this palace and...well, old habits, again.

The grand, Rook-adorned double doors of the study finally came into view, and Emrys was ready to sigh in relief when he heard a voice behind him.

CHAPTER 14

"A WORD, YOUR HIGHNESS?"

Lady Korva.

He held in his sigh. He'd hoped she was a part of that group of guests that Isoni had mentioned earlier—the group who had left.

But no; when he turned around, she was very much *there*, and her gaze was narrowed and her arms were crossed in a way that made her look smugly expectant.

He smiled politely.

She didn't return it.

"You're awake," she said. "And looking surprisingly lively."

"I'm far too stubborn to die, as it turns out."

She moved closer, circling him, and suddenly he felt like a wounded animal being singled out by a predator.

"Are you going to attack me? Should I be concerned that I left my knives in my room?"

She ignored the questions. Once she seemed satisfied that he was, in fact, solid and alive, her gaze became abruptly suspicious. "Another late night? What sort of trouble are you planning to get into this time? Or can you not tell me?"

He averted his gaze, pretending to adjust a button on the sleeve of his shirt. "I'm sorry if I disappointed you by not meeting you the other night, as I insisted I would—"

"Do you think I'm a fool?"

He was smart enough to know that there was no safe answer to that question, so he only said, "I beg your pardon?"

"You didn't *disappoint* me. I didn't expect you to come for me. Nor did I want you to. What did you think I was after, precisely?" She stepped uncomfortably close to him, just as she had outside the palace gates. That closeness bothered him. And it was obvious that she *knew* this, and that she was attempting to unsettle him by it—exactly as he'd done to her the other night.

He'd had this coming, he supposed.

He made a point of appearing as indifferent as he could to her nearness.

"Did you think I was going lose sleep over you?" she pressed, her voice low and a touch mocking. "That I was going to stand outside your door, *melting* just because you threw a smoldering glance in my direction? That I'm just another lovesick noblewoman who only cares about trying to win your attention and affection, and perhaps a crown while I'm at it?"

"I—"

"If you plan to be an effective king, you need to know that your silly attempts to be charming don't work on *everyone*; I actually find you terribly charmless."

"How rude," he said with a droll smile.

"I simply wanted to know the truth about where you were going the other night. I *still* want to know it, actually, as none of the rumors I've heard regarding it have satisfied me."

"I owe you no truth."

"You do if you want my allegiance."

His smile became razor thin. "Ah, but *do* I want your allegiance?"

"Perhaps not." She reflected that sharp smile back at him. "But then, it also means you don't have the allegiance of my army."

"*Your* army?"

"My father is not long for this world—did you not know? He has the *ostis-mortha*. The *bone sickness*." The words shook a tiny bit; a wavering vulnerability that was gone so quickly Emrys suspected he had imagined it. "The doctors say there is no cure. He made the journey here only thanks to his Oak-kind servant, whose magic is enough to keep him well enough to move—for now. But even the effects of that are beginning to lessen."

Perhaps *this* was why Lord Marius had seemed among the most eager to speak with Emrys at that pre-coronation banquet; there was perhaps no fear more motivating than the fear of time running out.

"*I* am essentially the steward of the Nyres Province these days," Lady Korva continued, "and of all of its many assets. Assets that you need on your side, whether you'd admit to it or not. So I am simply trying to decide whether you are going to be the sort of king that I should support or not."

He was in no mood for political games at the moment, and this made his reply curt. "Whether I need these things is rather beside the point," he said, "As I am not certain I would trust your allegiance—or your army's—whether you fully offered it to me or not, given that you already betrayed me once."

Her expression hardened, but she said nothing.

"Because I'm assuming it was *you* that alerted the palace to my last late-night excursion."

"Out of concern." Her tone lowered and turned harsh as a sudden, sharp crack through an iced-over river. "And you should be thanking me. Because *all* the rumors I've heard have agreed on one thing: You were nearly dead when they brought you back to this palace. What if they had taken longer to come after you?"

His smile brightened once more. "And here I thought you said you didn't care about me and my charmless self."

This drew a sour expression from the noblewoman—and then silence. A long, dark silence full of deep breaths and the biting beginnings of words that she ultimately swallowed back.

"Now," he began, stepping around her, "if you will excuse me, I once again have things to do."

"So you plan to be a king of secrets, then?"

He glanced back, though he didn't want to, as he knew she had a point; he could avoid people all he wanted to, but it would win him no favors from them—and he couldn't hope to lead a people who despised him, could he?

"I will tell you the truth, soon enough." He tried to make his voice sound more earnest for once. "But not tonight; I haven't the energy for it. Nearly dying is exhausting, you know."

A frustrated pause, but then: "Very well. But I will hold you to that promise, Rook Prince."

"King," he corrected automatically.

"We'll see if you make it to your official coronation, first."

"Too stubborn to die," he reminded her.

"We'll see," she repeated. "Good night, *prince*."

He turned quickly, so she couldn't see the scowl threatening to curve his lips. He walked to the doors of the study, pressed the Rook mark on his hand to the marble inset on the right door, and then whispered the words that made both that mark and that marble stone glow. The doors slowly swung open.

He stepped inside, and before even scanning the rest of the room, he pulled those doors shut and fortified them with the various manual locks on the inside.

"You don't trust the magical seal embedded in that door?" came Lord Feran's voice. "That was my own work, you know."

"I have nothing but respect for your work," Emrys replied, matching the dry tone of the older man's words. "But I don't trust my guests. They'll be trying to beat this door down, or burn it, or the gods only know what else. They are proving...relentless in their 'concern' for me."

Lord Feran regarded him with a bemused grin that quickly gave way to concern. "You *do* look tired, Your Highness."

Emrys waved him off; he'd spotted the wrapped knife on his desk, and he went to it before Feran could protest further.

Days ago, he had drawn blood with this same knife. A small sacrifice from an Air-kind. A *willing* Air-kind, though that willingness made little difference to Emrys; the memory of the blood-letting still made his stomach twist and his mouth taste sour.

But once the blade had been stained, he and Lord Feran had been able to take it to a Fire-kind on the outskirts of the city; the same Fire-kind who had sent Emrys that letter, along with the key to the address where he could obtain what he needed.

At this address, his blade had been washed in that dark, dangerous Fire magic that extracted the essence of the Air-kind's magic, and then that essence had been forged into something that Emrys could take and use for himself.

That something now rested within the blade itself, waiting for him to withdraw it and take it fully into his body.

He had waited for this last step, hoping that he wouldn't have to take it. Because once that magic became a part of him, there would be no going back. No getting rid of it. It would forever be entangled in his soul, and it would change him, just as the Fire magic he'd already stolen had changed him.

Those changes were still subtle—small, uncontrollable flares of magic, occasional thoughts that felt foreign and out-of-place—but delving into these shadowy rituals made him feel as if he was picking his way down a precariously steep slope.

He was waiting for the misstep that would send him tumbling, plunging down into a darkness that he couldn't climb out of. And at night he stayed awake wondering: How many thieving rituals had it taken before his father had fallen into that complete darkness?

But then he told himself that it had to have been dozens—perhaps hundreds—more than he himself had partaken in, or *planned* to partake in. And that Haben had been halfway down into that abyss before he'd even *started* such rituals, and so he hadn't needed to fall far before he became unreachable.

But then again...

"The knife, Highness," Feran prompted, pulling Emrys from his thoughts.

That knife was in his hands, he realized, though he didn't remember picking it up. He ignored the concerned look Feran was giving him, cleared his throat, and went to work.

He unwrapped the suede cloth protecting the blade's edges. Repeated the Fire-kind words that he'd memorized. That blade began to glow with a pale green light, and he touched a fingertip to that glow and breathed in deep.

The connection was nearly instantaneous—a jolt of energy lifting from the steel and twisting its way around his wrist and up his arm. The force of it was such that he found himself fumbling for the chair behind his desk, feeling his way into it and sinking down into the cushions. He gripped the armrests and clenched tightly as that energy continued to snake its way around his body. It swept over his skin, sending chills over his entire being, and then it dove deeper.

It felt as if that new magic was burrowing through him, trying to find a place to establish as its own. All of his aches and pains and wounds burned with the pressure of it for several agonizing moments—until finally, it settled.

The wound on his stomach remained irritated long after the Air magic had quieted; warmth seemed to be pooling around it. Concerned that it might have reopened, he pressed a hand to it, checking for blood—which drew another look of concern from Feran.

"I have to advise, at least once more, against this," Feran said. "Air magic is difficult to be precise with. In your condition—"

"I don't have time to wait." He pulled his hand away from his wound. There was no blood. He rose back to his feet, bracing his arms against the desk for support.

"Besides, that wasn't a particularly powerful bit of forging, was it? I can handle it."

Feran hesitated another moment before nodding and reluctantly advising him further. "You're correct; it was only a trace of blood that we used, and though our donor was exceptionally talented at his clan's magic, you still can only absorb so much from so little. The magic you've taken in isn't going to allow you to truly *reach* her, as more powerful Air-kind magic could. And there are other limitations—"

Emrys held up a hand, cutting him off. "A glimpse will do, for now. I only want to know where she's gone, and if she's safe. I have others who will reach her after I've collected the information I need."

Lord Feran still looked doubtful. But he was really a surprisingly sentimental old fool, and Emrys knew he could use this to his advantage.

"I need to see her, Tomas."

His advisor sucked in a slow breath, but then he gave the barest of nods. "Very well, then." He went to the table where he'd piled his cloak and other articles, and he retrieved a small, well-loved book from the pile. With nimble yet careful fingers, he flipped to a page marked by a feather. "Here are the words you need to speak to call forth this new magic. It will also help to have something of the person you're trying to reach—which you have, I hope?"

Emrys thought for a moment, and then he reached

into the drawer to his left, retrieved the red ribbon and offered it to Lord Feran in exchange for the book. "Will this do?"

"We'll see, I suppose," said Lord Feran, taking Emrys's hand—the unmarked one—spreading it flat, and stretching that ribbon across the lines of it. "The Air-kind serve the lesser-spirit of Cardea," he recited, "a being who once served as a messenger to Santi, the patron deity of the Sand clan and the middle-goddess of Time and Space.

"For her service, Santi and the Stone upper-god combined to grant her the power of moving freely through the very air we walk through and breathe in. The ones who carry the mark of this lesser-spirit all carry some facet of this power—as do you, now. So those are the deities you should be focusing on when you recite these words."

Emrys nodded.

"Go on, then. Just don't overdo it," his advisor said, hesitating for one last, concerned moment before he finally took a step back.

Emrys balanced the book in one hand, the ribbon in the other, and he recited the words Feran had provided.

Nothing happened.

He suddenly remembered the delayed emergence of his Fire-kind powers—how it had been days before he'd been able to really *command* that power after absorbing it.

He didn't *have* days.

Panic attempted to surge through him.

He pushed it down and tried again. Again. Again. *Again.* On the fourth try, Lord Feran made a motion toward him, as if to stop him, but Emrys still managed a fifth try before he was fully interrupted—

And suddenly, he felt the telltale pain in his marked hand, that twinge of resistance that seemed to come from the Rook God himself. As always, warnings accompanied it, whispers in his mind that he may or may not have been imagining.

This is unnatural.

This is wrong.

He pushed on, regardless. And soon there was a soft glow along the lines of his palm, the same celadon shade of that power he'd extracted from his blood-stained knife. It wrapped around Alaya's ribbon just as it had wrapped around his body, and then it began to stretch wider, taller, brighter.

Feran fell back and watched in silence as the glow became bright enough to illuminate every line on his tired face, every age spot on his skin— and then bright enough to blur all of these things from Emrys's sight.

Everything was illuminated.

All Emrys saw was that glowing, shifting shape of magic before him.

His eyes burned terribly from the brightness of it, tears pricking the corners. But he didn't dare blink, afraid that the spell might snap and take its power with it if he did.

He stared and stared—and eventually, that glow

began to subside and take on a more definite, rectangular shape that became darker in its center.

A portal.

And he stepped into it without hesitation, thinking of nothing except finding his way back to her.

CHAPTER 15

THE FIRST THING EMRYS NOTICED WAS THE SKY—DARK AND clear and swirling with more stars than he could count. *Outside.* He was outside. And a faint chill was brushing over his skin without truly sinking in, almost as if the Air spell had wrapped him in some sort of protective coating.

He looked behind him, expecting to see the other side of the portal he had stepped through, bracing himself for the pull of its magic.

It was gone.

The palace was gone. Lord Feran was gone. The city of Rykarra was gone.

He turned a slow circle, taking in the surroundings that had replaced it; he stood at a crossroads with four sandy white roads stretching in four different directions, and in the distance, he saw the tips of chimneys rising above gently sloping hills. There was a directional sign straight ahead, but he couldn't make out the words on it

—partly because the edges of everything appeared oddly blurred.

In spite of that blurriness, he had no doubt that this was not a dream. The scene before him was real, and a heady mixture of terror and euphoria overcame him as the reality of what he'd done sank in.

Air magic.

He had managed to perform Air-kind magic, and he had successfully transported himself through the air and to some place other than Rykarra. His mind raced, thinking of all the possible applications of this newfound ability. The places he could go, the things he could—

Focus, he commanded himself. *This spell will not last forever. And it has limitations, as Lord Feran said...*

"Focus," he repeated, out loud this time.

Where was she?

Where was *he?*

His surroundings felt oddly familiar the longer he studied them. But he was still confused, because he had expected the spell to take him directly to Alaya. Had the traces of her on that ribbon not been enough? Had it led him to someplace that only contained a recent *trace* of her?

He tried to remain positive. Perhaps she had been by this crossroads...

But where had she gone from here?

He wasn't overly knowledgeable of the Air-kind's language—particularly not of the ancient dialect that the spell had been written in—but he had recognized a few of those words in Feran's book. Loosely translated, the spell had ultimately meant something akin to *show me*.

He whispered those words once more, over and over, until their meaning and possibility consumed his thoughts.

Show me. Please, show me...

And the spell obeyed.

The lines of his palm glowed once more with grayish-green light, and when he reached his hand out, that light jumped down and pulsed faintly beneath the road, shimmering within the gritty bits of sand and showing him the way.

He followed it to the right, past the sign that was suddenly clearer. He didn't recognize the street names on that sign, but he recognized the clan symbol in its center, and he realized that this was Vespera, the City of Stars.

He continued down the faintly pulsing path. It led him over the hills and past the little huts with their smoking chimneys, through the closed marketplace with its shuttered windows and covered carts, and past the square with its statue of the middle-goddess Cepheid.

His steps felt light, almost as if he were floating past it all—much like the graceful Star-kind themselves seemed to do. He kept his eyes averted whenever he passed any of those kind, though he wasn't sure it was necessary; if they could see the strange magical path he was following, they gave no indication of it. They barely glanced his direction at all.

There was nothing so unusual about that, he

supposed; the Star-kind were famous for keeping to themselves. The vast majority of them never left this village, desperate as they were to avoid tangling themselves in the conflicts of the world outside.

Their magic would become too much of a burden, Isoni had told him once, *if they were constantly being bombarded by people who wished to know their futures. So they keep to themselves as a way of staying pure and not resentful of their power. Probably better for our empire, anyhow—could you imagine the trouble it would cause, if we all knew what was coming in our lives? That sort of knowledge changes people.*

No; it *haunted* people.

He had seen this firsthand, because the stars had supposedly screamed out Alaya's future on the night she was born—in the form of a prophecy written clearly enough for anyone who could read them.

Is that why she's returned to this village? he wondered. *To see if the stars have changed their minds?*

Personally, he didn't trust Star-kind magic; it had always seemed like the sort of power that was too easy to feign, or at least embellish for dramatic effect. Even his father had shown no interest in stealing any of Cepheid's power; supposedly, he had informed his advisors that he had no need to see his future through magic, because he was the only one who would control that future.

It was one of the only things the two of them had agreed on, at least in some form.

Emrys kept walking, and soon he came upon a place that he recognized more than anywhere else he'd seen since stepping through that portal; just ahead of him, a stone bridge stretched over a clear, softly trickling stream whose waters reflected a mountainous hill. Against the rocky face of that hill, boxes were affixed.

They contained ashes of deceased Star-kind.

It was the common practice in this village, to raise these boxes high enough that they might catch the Star Goddess's eye; the glittering designs painted against the sides of said boxes were meant to reflect her light and aid with this.

He'd lost track of how many weeks it had been since he'd sat by that stream, gazing up at those boxes for the first time, but he remembered every other detail of that night.

Midway through a funeral procession, Alaya had sat down beside him.

They had gazed at it all together, talking in soft voices, and her hand had eventually come to rest in the spaces between his. He'd pulled her close. It had been the first time he had honestly, truly held onto her without flinching. And though he hadn't realized it then, he was fairly certain now that this was the moment that had changed everything.

He hadn't seen it coming, and he sincerely doubted the stars had, either.

He stared at his reflection in the stream, more and more memories flooding in, threatening to distract him from his mission. He closed his eyes and repeated the words of the Air-kind spell several times before opening them again.

A quiet gasp escaped him at the sight of his reflection —because he was no longer alone.

Alaya was beside him, staring up at those shimmering boxes with the same awed expression she'd had the last time she looked at them.

He lifted his gaze from the water, and she was still there. Not in a reflection, not in a memory, but standing only a few feet away from him, as stunningly real and as stunningly beautiful as she had appeared all those weeks ago.

But she wasn't looking at him. She hadn't seen him.

He was so close—*how had she not seen him?*

As he stared at her, still stunned, a possible explanation came to him. A terrible explanation that he wanted to shake free from, that he didn't want to confirm, but which he had no choice but to test.

He steadied himself, and he stepped even closer to her, making a point of looking directly into her eyes. She didn't react.

She can't see me.

His fingers trembling slightly, he reached to brush his hand across her cheek. He felt cold air instead of soft skin.

She can't feel my touch.

A single word made it out on a shudder of breath: "Dragon."

She glanced around, warily, almost as if she'd sensed

something... But otherwise she didn't reply, and her eyes were soon drawn back to the Star-kind's coffins.

She can't hear me.

He drew his hand away from her and pressed it to the wound on his chest. He didn't feel the pain of it as sharply as he had when he was outside of the Air-kind spell, but it was still there. *He* was still there, and this was not a dream. It wasn't a trick of his mind, some hallucinatory side-effect of the many different medicines he'd been given...was it?

He studied Alaya more closely. Her eyes looked normal—clear and bright and splashed with gold. And her thoughts seemed clear, as well; she was kneeling in almost that exact spot where they had once sat together, and the pained expression on her face told him she was reliving that moment with the same clarity he had.

It was some relief, to see her calm and thinking clearly like this.

But she was so obviously upset by her coherent memories, and there was *nothing* he could do to comfort her, and so frustration quickly burned through his initial relief.

Alaya's eyes glazed over in thought as she knelt by the water. She took something from the inner pocket of her cloak—a slip of worn paper with a short note written on it—and absently flipped it around in her hands.

Curious, he sat beside her, just far enough away that they couldn't touch; he didn't want to accidentally brush against her and have to again feel the bitter cold where her warmth should have been. He tried to read the note, but she shoved it back into her pocket before he could.

She moved on to twisting the ring around her finger. The one he'd given her—so at least *some* connection between them remained.

He watched her studying it closer, and he had to stop himself from reaching and trying to touch her again when he noticed the few tears that had escaped and rolled down her cheek.

After a few minutes, she clenched her fist and stopped fiddling with the ring. She swept a gaze over her surroundings. Stood up. Took a deep, resolved breath, and then stepped directly toward him. Emrys leaned aside so they didn't brush as she passed by, and then he watched her walk back to the road that would carry her over a steep hill and back into the heart of the city. He was frozen in place for a moment, still overcome by the frustration, by the cruelty of it all.

So close, yet he couldn't reach her.

How many times did that make, now?

Was this really what they were destined to keep returning to, over and over again?

She made it nearly to the top of the hill before she glanced back. For just a moment, Emrys almost allowed himself to hope, to believe that she had realized she was leaving him behind. But then she returned to her path and picked up her pace.

He got the sense that his ghostly presence had unnerved her, and so he didn't follow immediately. And when he finally managed to make himself move, he trailed her at a distance. He still intended to find out as much information as he could; he might not have been able to physically reach her, but he had people in the area who could.

It would take Sade days to make her way to this village, but in the meantime, there were Valinesian soldiers stationed in the nearby towns of Orlyn and Belhurst, and along the coastal plains to the east of here. There were orders he could send them. He wasn't entirely sure *what* those orders would be—to capture her and bring her back to him? To watch over her? To make sure she didn't flee to somewhere else?

It doesn't matter at the moment, he thought, cresting the hill and finding her again, watching her hurry around the statue of Cepheid and take off to the right.

At the moment he only wanted to find out why she had come to Vespera in the first place.

He had to jog to catch up, to stay close enough to keep from losing sight of her. Her pace hadn't slowed. His spectral presence was still nowhere close to her, and yet it was obvious that *something* was catching her attention and driving her faster; she kept glancing furtively at her surroundings after every new road she turned down, and as they reached the edge of the city, she made an unusually abrupt turn into a narrow path between two houses, disappearing from sight.

A moment later, a shadowy figure darted out from behind a house on the opposite street. It traced the same steps Alaya had taken, closing some of the space between them before pressing close to another house and peering around the corner that Alaya had turned.

Emrys sucked in a sharp breath and drew abruptly to a stop.

Then he quickly decided that he would at least make use of his apparent invisibility. With only a few short sprints, he was close enough that he could have reached out and struck that shadowy figure stalking Alaya, if only he'd had a physical body.

He cleared his throat. "Excuse me."

The cloaked figure didn't respond in any way.

Good. So he *was* invisible to others besides Alaya.

He moved closer to his new target, and he quickly noticed two things: the mark of the Sun clan on what looked to be a slender, feminine hand, and the insignia of King Levant against the hilt of the knife that hand was casually gripping.

A Sun-kind soldier?

She wasn't wearing the typical, full regalia, if so. Plus, as far as he knew, the Vesperian leaders had a long-standing agreement with Levant that kept military forces out of their city.

A spy?

Before he could study her closer, she was already moving again. She slipped away, down that same narrow path Alaya had taken. She bounced from shadow to shadow, pausing occasionally to search and listen closer before dropping to a crouch and crawling onward.

Finally, she slowed completely to a stop at the sight of Alaya knocking on the black door of a small house with a domed roof.

The door opened.

Alaya stepped inside after only a moment of hesitation.

Emrys did not recognize this house. He only vaguely recognized the street they had ended up on, and the edges of things were starting to blur as they had when he'd first arrived in the village.

Was the spell fading?

He and the Sun-kind woman watched that closed door for several moments. Then, she straightened, took a few steps out of the shadows and moved toward the house. An uneasiness twisted through Emrys's stomach, shooting up along his spine and sending a prickling across the back of his neck. But that prickling felt vague and distant, much like the pain he'd felt when he'd pushed against his wounds earlier, leading him to question whether or not it was even real.

There was no need for that uneasiness, either way, because the Sun-kind kept moving. Her step became casual, and her hand left her knife and swung freely at her side as she strolled past the house with the black door. Apparently, she had seen what she needed to see for the moment.

Emrys watched her until she was out of sight, and then he watched the spot where she had disappeared for a minute more, making certain that she wasn't coming back.

Minutes later, he was still alone.

The clouds shifted, shrouding the stars and making the night suddenly darker, the edges of things even blurrier. Emrys could almost feel those things slipping away as he walked toward the black-doored house. The edges of his vision were turning dark. He repeated the Air-kind words to himself once more, trying to stretch the spell, trying to give himself just a little more time. He wasn't ready to leave her behind.

He was halfway to the door when he spotted another man approaching from the opposite direction.

His mouth paused and hung open, halfway through reciting the Air-kind spell.

He recognized this man, long before he spotted the Serpent-kind mark that was partially hidden by the slightly-too-long sleeves of his coat. And he was almost certain that this man was going to follow Alaya into that house—or else be waiting to ambush her when she stepped out of it.

There has to be a way I can warn her.

The thought rushed through his mind, and in the same instant he was running, desperately trying to get to that house before the Serpent-kind did.

The doorknob felt more solid beneath his touch than Alaya had, but it still gave more than it should have under the pressure of his hand; so much that he couldn't grip it.

But he didn't have to grip it. He didn't turn it, it simply *opened*—

He threw himself through it as quickly as he'd thrown himself through the portal that had led into this nightmare.

Only this time, he was met with no abrupt change of scenery. There was only blackness. An empty abyss, followed by pain that stabbed between his eyes and shot straight through the back of his skull.

The ground.

That pain in the back of his skull was from his head slamming into the ground, he realized dully. And he was still lying on that ground, staring up at the ceiling.

The ceiling of his study, with its elaborate molded edges and the symbols of his clan faintly pressed into each of the tin tiles.

"No." He shot upright. "No, *I wasn't finished.* I have to go back! I have to reach her, I have to warn her—"

Lord Feran placed a firm grip on either side of Emrys's face and held him until there was silence between them. Once Emrys stopped fighting, the old advisor took a deep breath and spoke. "Now," he began, slowly, "*calmly* tell me what happened, please."

Emrys jerked out of his grip, glaring at him, infuriated by his calmness. But, somehow, he managed to swallow that fury and speak. "I...I was in Vespera. I saw her, but she couldn't see me—though I thought for a moment that she might be able to *sense* me. I tried to follow her, but she went into a house, and as soon as *I* stepped into that house, I ended up back here."

"Did you recognize that house she walked into?"

He shook his head. "I've only been to Vespera twice, and both visits were brief. I don't know that house. I don't know why *she* would know it."

Lord Feran considered for a moment, and then he sighed, and he knelt down to pick up the book of spells that had at some point been knocked onto the floor along with Emrys. "One of those limitations that I tried to tell you about earlier," he said.

"What do you mean?"

"This particular spell we used tonight...it was really only in your mind, and it wasn't the sort that will let you go far beyond any place you haven't *personally* been to."

Emrys silently replayed things in his mind, nodding. "The edges of things began to blur even before I reached that house."

His advisor frowned. "The Air-kind who offered us his blood, his magic...apparently, he was less powerful than I believed. And it's possible we didn't perform the bloodletting as efficiently as we could have..."

"But there will be other Air-kind with stronger magic. Magic that's capable of *physically* transporting me. We could—"

"There certainly *are* others, but to extract more powerful magic requires..."

Emrys sighed, getting to his feet and straightening the

rumpled front of his shirt with quick, irate jerks of his hands. "...More potent sacrifice," he finished.

"Precisely." Feran hesitated, and then he added: "And using that more powerful magic would also require a strength that you don't currently possess, Your Highness."

Emrys stopped smoothing his shirt and shot him another glare.

"You were gravely injured," Lord Feran continued all the same. "It was irresponsible of me to even allow you to perform this simple spell tonight." He tucked that book of spells under his arm and fixed Emrys with a stern look. "And I hope you are not *seriously* considering trying to collect more powerful magic, anyhow."

Emrys averted his eyes.

"Shall I remind you? It is one thing to skim the magic of others. It is another thing entirely to take *all* of their life and magic. It is like the difference between drinking water and drowning in it, or between gaining the support of other people...and losing your soul completely to those other people. It makes you stronger up to a certain point, but without limits, it will crush you."

"I'm aware of the risks and consequences, thank you."

"I assumed. I only bring it up again because I gave your father the same advice, years ago, and I was nearly executed for my counsel—I likely would not be here if your mother had not intervened on my behalf. And I am simply hoping that you won't dismiss what I'm saying so violently as Haben did."

Emrys was quiet for a moment, the way he always

was when his parents were mentioned these days. Every one of those mentions was like a needle sliding into a wound that had only just started to scab over.

"No," he finally said. "No, of course not. I don't need deeper magic; I have others that can reach her, as I said before we started this little experiment..." He trailed off, his thoughts still racing dangerously.

He didn't want it to be *others* who reached her.

He wanted it to be himself.

But he also knew Lord Feran was right. There was a line between borrowing the talents of other clan-kinds and *terrorizing* those kinds. And he had sworn to himself that he would not cross it.

He tried to banish even the *thought* of crossing it as he finally met Feran's gaze. "Thank you for your help," he said. "And now, if you'll excuse me, I have orders I need to send."

He headed for the door. His knees threatened to buckle with every step, as if already anticipating and dreading having to climb the winding steps to the tower where their messenger birds were kept.

But he would climb it.

He would crawl up it, inch-by-inch, if he had to. He would see the keeper of those birds, and he would send those orders out tonight—and Sade would no doubt be ready to leave tonight, too, as soon as he told her what he had seen.

Would all of that be enough?

The fear that it wouldn't gripped tightly, making his

steps even more laborious and unsteady, because it was the sort of fear that he knew would drive him to do something foolish, if he didn't get control over it.

Banish the thought, he commanded himself once more.

But it only continued to twist and turn and drive itself deeper and deeper into his mind.

CHAPTER 16

ALAYA FELT AS IF SHE HAD STEPPED BACK IN TIME.

The house she had entered was lit with candles that flickered over cracked walls and faded paintings, over tiny statues whose edges were worn smooth and whose faces had weathered into mostly unrecognizable features. The floor was uneven, its wooden planks creaky and covered with dust. It was more like stepping into a forgotten temple than into the living space that she had been expecting.

And there was nothing warm or inviting about this space, as she'd hoped there might be. She heard no sounds of life in it, and after feeling her way down several hallways, and fighting her way out of various cobwebs, she decided that she must have made a mistake.

She was at the wrong house.

Or she had taken too long to arrive, and this Spinner person was dead or otherwise gone—so it was no wonder people had looked at her strangely when she had inquired about them, and no wonder that nobody had answered when she knocked. The door had opened on its own, but clearly its hinges were worn with age and that had only been a coincidence. A fluke.

Biting her lip in frustration, she turned around and started back to that door. Another cobweb assaulted her. She was swatting wildly at it—gods, she *hated* spiders—when a strange sound caught her attention.

She forced herself to be still and listen for a moment, and she heard it again: a soft *ting ting ting* that reminded her of raindrops falling hard against the roof of the orphanage back in Vanish. The memory of falling asleep to that sound washed over her and swept her into a trance.

A crawling sensation across the back of her neck snapped her out of that trance just as quickly—the Moraki and Marr both save her if that was *an actual spider* —and she twisted wildly and hit the wall with a loud *thump* that echoed through the dusty hallway.

Seconds later, she heard a voice. A quiet, mumbling voice that may or may not have been in response to her nearly elbowing a hole into the wall. But thanks to her ridiculous spider dance, the owner of that voice almost certainly knew she was here, now.

She gathered her courage and followed the mumbling, quietly but frantically swatting at the bits of web still clinging to her.

She came to a short corridor that led to two doors, one

open, the other partially ajar. It was so dark that she would have overlooked it all, but for the tiny bit of blue-tinted light shining through that half-opened door.

She moved toward the light and peered inside the dimly-lit room.

A man was sitting cross-legged on the floor in the center of this room, facing a low table that was covered in tiny, white stones.

She stood in the doorway a moment, watching him.

He gathered up the sparkling white stones and tossed them across the black table—just as Cepheid herself had first tossed stars across the night sky—and he studied the places where they had stopped, walking his fingers between them like he was mentally tracing out new constellations.

"A few weeks later than expected," he mumbled, "but then, what's a few weeks to the goddess that guides me? The stars are infinite, after all."

Alaya wasn't certain whether this man was talking to her, or to himself, but she felt as if she shouldn't inter-rupt, either way.

The man murmured softly to himself for a few more moments. Then he abruptly glanced up. His eyes were the milky-green color of scum over a stagnant pool of water, his wide stare a bit unsettling. But his smile was kind—and perhaps that was what gave her the courage to speak.

"Are you the...the Spinner?"

He glanced down at the stones he'd tossed, as if he needed to consult them for the answer. And apparently they informed him that the correct answer was *yes*, because he nodded. "The *Spinner of Stars*, yes. Yes, that is one of the names I go by."

She didn't ask about the others. She didn't have time. "The Queen of the Sun directed me to you. I was told you might be able to help me find my way?"

He consulted the stones again for a moment, and then: "Ah, yes, Ellie. I haven't heard from her recently— how is she?"

"I don't know," Alaya answered, honestly. She didn't like to think about what might have happened after the queen had attempted to help her escape. The attempt had been unsuccessful, but it didn't mean that Eliana's scheming against her husband had gone unnoticed.

Alaya gave her head a little shake, trying to focus on the things she could deal with at that moment. "The queen isn't the only one I'm concerned about, unfortunately. I have a..." She had rehearsed this conversation in her head a thousand times since the moment she'd decided to come to Vespera...why could she not put her request into words now?

"You have a...?" prompted the Star-Spinner.

"A problem," she finished, lamely. "A problem with my magic. And I don't know if there's anything you can do to help me. I don't know why Eliana wanted me to find you, but I'm desperate, so..."

He lifted those milky-green eyes to her, studying her with the same intense expression he'd studied his white stones with.

Then he stood, his joints creaking and popping as loudly as the wooden floors of his house had, and he beckoned her closer. "You're right. The hour is late, isn't it? So let's not waste time. Come here; I have something to give you."

She cautiously obeyed, crossing the room as he went to a desk in the corner and started rifling through its contents. She waited by the table, studying those stones scattered over it out of the corner of her vision, while still keeping an eye on the Spinner.

He returned quickly, clutching another stone—only this one was not white, but black, and it was larger and vaguely heart-shaped. There was nothing so very strange about that object itself—aside from the unusually bright, golden shade of the aura surrounding it.

It was brighter even than the faint gold light her sword gave off.

"Do you know what this is?" he asked.

Alaya shook her head, confused. "It's...it's a rock, isn't it? I don't see what..."

"Can you see its energy?"

She lifted her gaze to him, curious and eager for the explanation as to *why* it was giving off so much of that energy.

"You *can*, can't you? Ellie wrote to me of your adventures with the fire-soul—that power of the Serpent Goddess that you obtained, but which is too much for your partially mortal body to wield without serious side-effects."

"I..."

"*That* is the problem you spoke of before, correct?"

"...Yes." She had to swallow hard to keep her voice from cracking as she said, "I thought I could handle the power of that soul, but I was wrong. Using it makes me vulnerable to terrible things."

He nodded along in an understanding sort of way as she spoke, and his reply was quick: "Yes, but your mother could have taken that power in and made it stable; that is why she descended into this realm in the first place, isn't it?"

Alaya stared at him. His words stung in ways she didn't want to admit—why did he think it was necessary to compare her to her dead mother?

She breathed in deep and somehow managed to keep her voice even as she replied. "But my mother isn't here *now*."

He stretched out his hand to her, unclenching it and fully displaying the stone to her. "Take it," he encouraged.

Her curiosity quickly overcame her trepidation, and she reached for it. Took it and cradled it against her, focusing on the warmth and the buzz of its bright energy. And she heard a voice that nearly made her drop it to the dusty floor—

Carefully, my heart.

Alaya clenched the stone more tightly before lifting it up and shaking it at the Star-Spinner's pensive face.

"What *is* this?" she demanded, coldly. It felt like a trick; her mother's voice had sounded too clear, too real—

so real that it had to have been faked by some malicious kind of magic. Because her mother was gone. She was *dead*.

The Spinner was unmoved by the bitter tone of her voice; his was perfectly calm in comparison. "You came here for answers, did you not?"

She bit her lip to keep the sharp words inside of her.

"Trust me, then. Hold on to that object for a moment longer. Focus on its energy."

The back of her neck burned. She still was not convinced this wasn't a cruel prank, and she was torn between terror and longing when it came to the possibility of hearing her mother's voice again...

But she couldn't seem to let go of the heart-shaped stone, either way.

So she gripped it tighter, as the Star-Spinner had suggested.

She focused on the golden energy. And then her mouth was moving automatically, Serpent-kind words coming to her, unbidden, as they often did when she accessed the stronger shades of her power. The stone's aura glowed brighter and brighter, until bits of its golden energy were peeling away from it, floating like specks of dust in the air before drifting down toward the Serpent mark on her hand. They melted into that mark like snowflakes against warm earth.

She could do nothing except stare.

Within moments, the last specks of gold faded into her mark, and the stone she was holding was nothing more than an inanimate object with a dull, ash-colored aura.

"...What just happened?" Alaya could hear the fear creeping into her words, though she tried hard not to let it. The last time an object's energy had been fused with hers in a similar way, she had woken up with the fire-soul's dangerous power inside of her. She wasn't prepared for *more* power that she had no idea how to live with.

The Spinner watched her for a moment without speaking, and Alaya got the uncomfortable feeling that he was waiting to make sure that new power didn't make her do something terrible.

After what felt like an eternity, he spoke again: "Your mother was a temporary embodiment of the goddess Mairu—a caelestis, a *celestial shade*."

"I know that."

"But did you know that a shade can lose their divine essence after being in a realm such as this for too long? Or shed that essence *on purpose*, in some cases."

"I know that part of her power is in me... Are you saying that it was an intentional transfer of power? And that there are *other* pieces of this power lying around somewhere?"

"Precisely."

"And she lost them on purpose?"

"Mm. To avoid being recognized for what she was. To avoid drawing attention to *you*, whom she was trying so desperately to hide."

Alaya considered this for a moment, still staring at her

Serpent mark. It felt warm—pleasantly so. She also felt surprisingly *calm*. A feeling she hadn't felt in forever, it seemed. Her power was not threatening to rise or turn restless at all, despite the uncertainty and fear tingling through her body.

"She came here while trying to hide, correct?" she asked. "The last time I was here, I met a woman who told me my mother took refuge in this village while fleeing Amara."

"Yes."

"You met her when she stopped by?"

The Spinner shook his head. "No. But I've talked to plenty who did. And from what I've gathered, she was a different person—an entirely different being—when she left this village."

"What do you mean?"

"It was here that she realized she could still be recognized for what she was, and so it was here that she split her remaining power, as I mentioned, before moving on to another hiding place."

"But where did these split pieces of her *go*?"

"One of them stayed here for safe keeping; the shade of her power that you just extracted from that stone. Another, she transferred into you, as you've theorized. It would have been a weaker piece of herself, so it was still more or less untraceable—but also enough to help protect you in some small way, even in the event that the two of you were separated."

Alaya was silent for a moment, trying to fold these

things into what little she already knew and understood of her heritage.

"You recognized her voice just now, yes? Because I imagine you've heard it in your mind, even after she died, as something clearer, more potent than a memory."

Alaya could not deny this, so she simply continued to stare at her marked hand.

"Also," the Star-Spinner added, "If she *hadn't* bestowed a part of herself into you, then absorbing the fire-soul would likely have killed you."

"So I was given an extra piece of her power, and now, I've absorbed another. But what about the rest? Will gathering them all give me the strength to use the divine side of my power without losing myself?"

She was nearly breathless, suddenly, from the mere *possibility* of it. For what it could mean for her future, and the future of all the people and places tied to her.

For Emrys.

She shook his face from her thoughts; it was still too painful to think of their last meeting.

But she couldn't crush the hope inflating inside of her. For years, she had felt as if she didn't belong in this world. As if pieces of her were missing. Could these scattered shades of her mother's power really be the last key to unlocking her true self?

"I'm hopeful that gathering them will do exactly that," the Spinner told her. "As for the rest... Well, the good news is that there likely aren't more than a handful to find. These slivers of her soul and power could be dangerous in the wrong hands, much like the fire-soul; she would have wanted to limit how many she put out into the world, I suspect."

"And the bad news?"

"Is that they could be in anything, really. In other people. In other objects like that one." He pointed at the rock still clenched in Alaya's fist. "And maybe in places, or in creatures, in—oh, I don't know all the ways she split her power, though I wish I did." He pondered silently for a moment before jerking his attention back to her, his eyes wide and his mind clearly seized with a sudden idea. "But *you* likely know these things," he said, "even if you haven't been looking for them."

Alaya started to shake her head, still confused, but he continued in a rush—

"In the objects or places or people where these bits of divine power have taken up residence, a protective energy should exist. Something that you would have noticed."

Protective.

"Rue..." she whispered in sudden realization.

"Pardon?"

"Rue is a dragon that I...that I sort of freed when I escaped Amara. I've always felt a powerful connection to her; is it possible that my mother might have split off some of her power and left it in this creature before she left Amara with me?"

The Spinner looked thoughtful for a moment before nodding. "Very possible," he agreed.

"That might explain why I can sort of...talk to Rue.

And why being close to her helps to clear my mind and settle my magic."

"Yes, yes—good. But where else? *What* else? That makes three pieces accounted for, but there are likely more."

"I'm not sure, I..."

"*Think* child. Think of the times you've felt safe and protected throughout your life."

She thought.

And there were very few times she had felt *safe* in this empire, and so it took her only a minute to sort through them all and come up with another possibility. "My powers never overwhelmed me when I lived in Vanish," she said. "I believed it was simply because there were no Serpent curses there, but maybe..."

"Maybe there was something else there, something that contained your mother's essence, and thus, the divine power to keep you under control?"

Alaya frowned, not because she didn't think this was true—but because she felt that it *was*. It made too much sense. Which meant she was going to have to go back to that village and see what she could find for herself.

And that was a trip she'd been hoping to put off for at least a bit longer.

Perhaps the Star-Spinner sensed the sudden change in her mood, because his next words were much gentler: "There is your next stop, then, isn't it?"

She nodded, but avoided his gaze. Neither of them spoke for several minutes. He busied himself with flipping through a book, while Alaya lightly traced the feather-shaped scar on her arm and thought of the woman who would never see her son again.

The woman she would have to face if she returned to Vanish.

Her gaze shifted to the table beside her, to those white stones that had made her think of stars.

Death. Betrayal. Destruction.

She had told Kian that she was going to rewrite those stars, and she still remembered the exact response he had given her—she had played it over and over in her mind so many times that she knew she would never forget it.

If anybody could do it, it would be you.

He had been killed less than a day later. A death *and* a betrayal. And nothing but destruction had followed her ever since, it seemed like. She had kept moving all the same, convincing herself that she could outrun that prophecy if she only ran fast enough.

But somehow, the thought of having to go back to where it had all started stopped her in her tracks.

"Can I ask you something?" she heard herself say.

"I already know your question."

"Your stars told you to expect it, I'm assuming?" She cut her eyes sideways at the Spinner to find him watching her with a wistful little smile.

"I could have seen this question coming, even without their help." His smile wilted a bit in the corners. "You want to know about that prophecy they revealed on the night you were born, don't you?"

She hugged her arms against herself. Stared at those stones until her vision blurred, until she found the courage to press on with her questions, and then she cocked her head toward the Spinner of Stars once more. "Well?"

He nodded and, mumbling softly to himself, he gathered up those stones he'd tossed across the table. He held them in his cupped palms, and soon the language he was mumbling in changed—to the Star-kind language, Alaya guessed—and he once again flung them over the dark table.

"Give me your hand," he said to her, once the stones had all *ping ping pinged* to a stop, "and let's read some stars together, shall we?"

It was that insatiable, almost desperate curiosity that again made her obey. She reached forward and allowed him to guide her, to walk her fingers between the fallen stones as she'd seen him do earlier. She would have sworn she saw faint trails of light appearing along the paths her fingertips traced. It was mesmerizing. Her finger brushed against a particularly large stone in the corner of the table, and there was no way of denying the light that it emitted; it was a small explosion of it, and it startled her so much that she snatched her hand back to her chest.

"What are these things?" she asked, warily. "What does that light they're giving off mean?"

"These are the *monimos* stones," the Spinner explained. "They contain the blood and spells of powerful Star-kind, and that magical combination helps even those of us without much of Cepheid's power 'read' messages that the heavens are trying to send us."

She studied them for a moment before she quietly asked, "And what does this message say?"

He traced a large grouping of stones that had landed in a shape that resembled a crescent moon with an arrow shot through its center.

"This is the symbol of death." He pointed to the various small stones that had scattered away from that symbol. "The way it spreads suggests a great, cataclysmic death is coming, carried by the one symbolized here—" he nudged the stone that had brightened so violently at her touch.

"...Which is me?" she guessed in a whisper.

"Which is you."

She took a few steps away from the table. "It's the same as it was on the night I was born?"

He said nothing.

He didn't need to.

She paced the room, her heart pounding wildly in her chest. She didn't want to believe what he was saying. They were just stones on a table in a strange house in the middle of a secluded village, cast by this man she had never even met before tonight—why should she believe what he was telling her?

She *shouldn't* have.

But part of her still did.

"Then what is the point of my carrying on?" she asked, more to herself than him. "Of finding these...these *pieces* of my mother's power, of using them to gain full control of myself and my magic? What does it matter if it all ends in death, just the same?"

He didn't reply right away. He was busy shuffling that symbol of death, rearranging the pieces of it into a complete circle. And then, to her surprise and annoyance, he glanced up at her and smiled. "You've missed something."

"Oh, *have* I?" she couldn't help but snarl.

"Yes." He dropped the last of the stones into that newly-made circle. "Death is not always such a bad thing. Death means change, and sometimes change is painful—but also necessary and *good*. Sometimes things must burn out so that other things can turn to new. Do you understand?"

She glared at that circle he'd formed, still scowling a bit, but she held her tongue. She wasn't certain how to answer his question.

But now she couldn't stop thinking about it.

She thought of all of the changes that had befallen her and her world these past months. Some good. Some bad. Some that she feared she might never make sense of. And she felt dizzy, like when she and Sade and Kian used to spin around as children, playfully competing to see who could stay on their feet the longest.

But she didn't *want* to play now; she only wanted to find her balance and keep it.

"Change is inevitable," the Spinner said, "and so, too, is death. And life is full of betrayals and destructions. But what follows these things? That is the more important question."

"Can't you cast your star stones and *see* what follows? Look at the future of this empire—one season, two seasons, ten seasons from now, and tell me: what does it look like? Do we win the war against Levant and the Sun Kingdom?"

"Nobody wins wars."

"Do we *survive* it? What happens to the three kingdoms? To...to the ones ruling them?"

"I'm afraid I can't say—"

"Why *not*?"

He pursed his lips. It was more than reluctance or secrecy. The expression on his face was pained, almost— as if his goddess had suddenly stolen away his ability to speak.

"What aren't you telling me?"

"There is nothing to tell." He looked away, scooped the monimos stones from the table and deposited them into a small silk pouch. He was quiet for such a long time afterwards that Alaya thought he was just going to ignore her until she went away. But then he said: "There is nothing to tell, because there is nothing that any of my kind can see."

"...What?"

"Throughout our world's history, there have only been a few instances where even the most gifted of the Star-kind have not been able to read the future. Only a few moments of potential divergence so great that they destabilize our magical sight. And now another is coming. Following the nineteenth anniversary of your birth, our kind's visions simply...*end*. Countless numbers of us have tried to see what comes after that cataclysmic death that you and I read clearly enough minutes ago—but nothing beyond that moment is clear. You see, even the stars do not know what happens after that. It's dark to all of us."

"That...can't be a good sign, can it?"

He sighed, muttering something in his language.

"Oh. Right. Giant, obvious omens of darkness can be good *or* bad, huh? Much like death."

The Spinner either missed the hint of derision in her voice, or he chose to ignore it. "So you *were* listening to what I was trying to tell you," he said, and then he proceeded to place the stones onto a dusty shelf, as if the matter was settled.

Alaya frowned, but she said nothing else. The Spinner had been helpful and generous—if confusing—with his information; perhaps he didn't deserve her cynicism. Perhaps everything he'd said didn't *really* warrant that cynicism, anyhow. It was hard to say. Her mood was too foul. She was too tired, and hungry, and still unnerved by the people she'd sensed following her on her way through the village.

What awaited her when she left this place?

And if that prophecy of darkness was true...

Twenty-five days.

There were only twenty-five days until her nineteenth birthday, if she wasn't mistaken. And she was fairly certain she *wasn't* mistaken, even though all of her days were blurring together lately.

She wandered toward the room's lone window. A gust of wind rattled its pane, and she pulled her cloak tighter to ward off the chill it caused.

That same breeze was moving clouds and spilling starlight in patterns made strange by the layers of dust and cobwebs on the window. The Spinner stepped into those streams of light, lifted his hands and twisted them around, almost as if he was reading messages in them.

"There are people surrounding this house—and others surrounding this village—that mean you harm," he said after a moment. "But this house rests upon what was once an altar to Cepheid. It is a sacred space, and the middle-goddess of Stars and Sight will not allow anyone to pass into it while they harbor ill intentions. So rest here and stay safe tonight, if you like. But in the morning, you will have to move on."

Alaya nodded; she'd had no intentions of staying.

She was still no more certain about how this all would end. But she had her next step, and that was enough for now.

She took the heart-shaped stone that had contained her mother's essence, and she carried it with her into the room across the hall, where she found a reasonably clean and comfortable bed to rest in. She tucked the stone beneath the lumpy pillow and then laid back with her hands resting behind her head. There were skylights spaced evenly throughout this room, so that no matter which way she rolled in the tiny bed, she could still at least glimpse the stars.

It wasn't long before she grew tired of their twinkling. She curled onto her side and closed her eyes. Her hand found the ring Emrys had given her, and she fell into her recently-acquired habit of twisting it around her finger. It calmed her down, for some reason.

She fell asleep holding the ring close to her heart, imagining she was back at the Rook King's side, that all their wars had ended and they had become a force for good. *Together.*

But her dreams ended up being, not of Emrys, but of stars.

Countless stars that exploded across the sky, one after the other, until all the world below was covered in darkness.

CHAPTER 17

When Alaya awoke, the house was as quiet as a crypt. She reluctantly rolled her way from the bed, pulled on her boots, and walked the halls in a sleepy daze, searching for the Spinner and softly calling for him.

But he was gone.

Eventually, she gave up and gathered up her things, making her way to the door she'd entered through the night before. Beside it, she found supplies waiting for her —a bag filled to the brim with fresh fruits and cheeses, a blanket trimmed in silvery-blue thread, and other odds and ends including a knife whose blade was crisscrossed with white stripes of light, as though it had been used to slice up stars. She fastened the small knife and its ornate sheath to her belt, selected a particularly shiny looking apple from the pile of food, and called for the Spinner of Stars one last time.

Still no reply.

There was a note among that pile, too, but it was written in Star-kind language. She didn't recognize enough of the words to decipher it. She took it and tucked it into her cloak all the same, and then she closed the bag and shouldered it alongside her old one.

"Thank you," she called, although she was fairly certain there was nothing but dust and cobwebs to hear her.

As soon as she stepped outside, the first thing she did was attempt to catch Rue's attention.

Good morning, she thought.

She received no answer.

It wasn't entirely surprising; the dragon had stayed well outside of the city. She'd dropped Alaya in one of the towering pine forests outside of Vespera, and then, knowing her fondness for the sea, Rue had likely continued farther east, found herself a stretch of secluded beach, and slept by the sparkling teal waters of the Belaric.

It had seemed like the smart thing to do—to keep their distance from each other—given that Alaya wasn't trying to attract attention to herself. But it had meant walking several miles alone. And every step had been haunted by the fear of what might happen if she strayed too far from Rue.

She'd felt controlling magic hovering over her like a net ready to drop, the thoughts Sylven had planted trying to rise up and confuse her. The flashbacks and voices in her mind had nearly driven her racing out of the city to find Rue on more than one occasion.

But she'd stayed.

Instead of fleeing the city when she didn't immediately find the Spinner, she'd gone to the familiar riverside and stared up at the Star-kind's burial hill. There, she'd fought to grab hold of a memory—a *real* memory. One of her finding the prince sitting by the water as if he'd been waiting for her.

Most of what she and Emrys had spoken of that night was distorted and scattered in her mind, whether because of the passing of time or the pressing of Sylven's magic. But she distinctly remembered asking the prince if he thought they could bring peace. And the thoughtful way he'd looked at her...it had been the beginning of something. Of her thinking there might have been a chance that the two of them, together, could change the course of the empire's future.

That thought was still there. Even though she was so far from him, now, and so far from that night they'd sat together in this city, listening to the Star-kind sing their songs, watching solemnly as they went through their funeral rituals.

The thought of funerals sent her thoughts spiraling toward dark places. Places that involved the death rituals of the Rook-kind, an empire in mourning, and—

No.

Emrys *wasn't* dead.

If she had managed to kill him—as Levant and Sylven

had been hoping for—the news of such a disaster would surely have reached her, even in this reclusive village.

Still, she had no idea how badly she had injured him. Or if he would ever want to risk seeing her again. She wouldn't have blamed him if he wanted *her* dead; she had proven dangerous to him and his rule one too many times, maybe.

"I will not be dangerous when I return to him," she muttered, and then she forced away the nasty voice trying to tell her she *shouldn't* return to him, and she focused again on trying to hear the only voice she needed to worry about just then: Rue's.

She shielded her eyes against the early morning sun and looked to the open sky. She fixated on the image of that blue sky in her head, so that Rue might see it.

I'm coming to you, she thought. *I'm ready to move on. Or as ready as I'm going to be.*

She waited.

Still no reply.

She started to walk. The village seemed as deathly quiet as the Star-Spinner's house had been as she wound her way through it. Sunrise must have been at least an hour ago; where were the merchants setting up their shops? The animals waking and calling to be fed? The laughing children up far too early for their parents' liking? The only sounds were her own footsteps, along with the occasional bite she took from that apple, the crunches of which echoed eerily in the crisp morning air.

She palmed the handle of her sword and picked up

her pace, heading for the edge of the city as fast as she could. She didn't have to worry about drawing attention to herself by moving too quickly, at least; there were hardly any people around to notice her.

She tried not to panic at the continued silence from Rue.

She came to a fork in the road and paused, squinting into the distance. She could see the point where the neatly-kept houses of Vespera gave way to dry fields of golden grass swaying in the breeze. She tried to focus on every line and shape of this landscape, to hold the image of it in her head for a long, clear moment that Rue could share with her.

I believe I've found what I came for, she thought, picturing the dragon's face instead of her own surroundings, this time. *We need to move on.*

An unnerving possibility occurred to her in the continued silence; she didn't truly *know* all of the ways that her connection to Rue worked...

What if that supposedly divine essence she had absorbed last night had somehow ruined her connection to the dragon?

Panic swelled, making her breathing more difficult until finally, a reply: (*Scouting.*)

What did you see? Alaya wondered, still working to swallow that panic that had almost overtaken her.

Rue's reply was quick, this time. The dragon's vision slid over hers, and Alaya saw a piece of the world from high above: the dry, grassy fields giving way to that towering pine forest where Rue had left her the night before. There were shadows moving amongst the trees.

A small army's worth of shadows.

Rue drifted closer, and the vision she shared with Alaya became clearer, bringing that army into focus. At least a hundred or more were gathered around a camp that stretched through the forest. Their horses were dressed in armor of gold and white, and a few of the soldiers wore helmets with easily-recognizable symbols protruding from their peaks.

The Army of the Sun.

So many of them, Alaya thought. *Surely, they aren't all here looking for me?*

(*Do not go to the east,*) came Rue's response.

East was precisely the direction she had been heading in, so Alaya slowed and started back the other way. There were a few more people strolling about the village now. Far too many of them watched her as she walked past.

Why were they suddenly interested in her?

Heart pounding, she kept her head down and walked as quickly but casually as she could. Though she could still feel eyes watching her, nobody called out to her as she passed.

She made it to the main road that led west out of the city, towards the foothills of the Sinhara Mountains. The gatekeepers of the village grunted something at her in the Star-kind language as she left; she couldn't tell by their tone whether it was a blessing or a warning.

She kept walking, studying the landscape, pressing

the images deep into her mind so that Rue might see them as well.

The road carved through fields of golden grass to the west of the city, same as the roads that stretched east. But on this side those fields quickly became harder, drier, before giving way altogether to nothing but red dirt and rocks. The barren landscape made her feel uncomfortable, exposed, and within minutes, she had broken into a full-on jog while desperately scanning for a more protected route.

To her left, she finally saw a steep grouping of hills and valleys. She veered away from the flat and exposed path she was on and ran to the top of the tallest hill she could find. Once there, she spotted something that made the fear in her heart unclench a little: trees.

The once mighty River Indres was not far from here, she remembered; these trees were likely grouped around a tributary of that dried up river. Their scraggly branches and lack of leaves reflected the dried and supposedly cursed quality of Indres. But they were bunched tightly together, and in that moment, they looked like an army ready and waiting to surround and protect her.

She ran for them, weaving her way deeply into the maze of trunks before daring to stop and catch her breath.

A sudden fluttering of wings and squawking of birds startled her. She drew her sword and spun toward the sound, eyes wide and searching.

She saw nothing.

But she *sensed* an energy that felt out of place. Now

that she was outside of the village—away from all of the Star-kind and the steady and constant hum of their auras —to feel another person nearby was unexpected and unnerving.

Someone was following her.

And she had felt this same energy the evening prior, hadn't she? While on her way to the Spinner's house. It wasn't Star-kind energy, which was why she had briefly noticed it last night. But it had been faint, nearly lost among those Star-kind, and she had convinced herself that she had imagined it. That she was only being paranoid.

But apparently, I wasn't, because here it is trailing me again.

"Show yourself!" she called.

The woods were silent. Even the birds seemed to have disappeared after their startled show. She took a few steps toward the spot where she'd seen that flock of birds bursting up into the steely morning sky. Her eyes narrowed on the spaces between the trees, scanning the shadows and watching for a glimmer of that aura that didn't belong.

Then a horrible, sharply-pitched roar of pain distracted her from her search.

Rue.

A wild, rapid *whooshing* of her wings followed, and then a booming *thunk* and the cracking and splintering of branches—it sounded as if she had crashed.

Violently.

Alaya immediately twisted toward the sounds and started to run.

Seconds later she collided with that person she'd been searching the shadows for. His energy was obvious, over-whelming, and the force of their crash knocked her side-ways into a tree, slamming her head into the wood and leaving her vision spinning for several moments before it cleared.

He slid into focus slowly: An old man with dark, heavily scarred skin and cold blue eyes.

He said nothing.

She only managed one word at first: "*You.*"

This man before her was Kaladrius—the father of Sylven, and the head of the council of Serpent-kind that had attempted to kill Alaya not once, but twice. He had once been trapped, like all the others of his kind, in the hidden village of Amara. But she had destroyed the barrier keeping all of them inside. And she was not surprised to learn he had followed her out.

She was only surprised that it had taken him this long to find her.

"Get out of my way," she hissed. "And let me go to my dragon!"

"Never mind the dragon."

Another pained roar echoed through the forest.

"*What have you done to her?*"

"She is being properly subdued so that she doesn't interfere with what we need to do."

"*Subdued?*" Alaya lifted her sword and stepped closer to him.

His hand lifted, and an instant later, Alaya felt her blade attempting to jerk out of her grip. She clenched it more tightly, refusing to drop it, but the magic that had taken hold of it made it nearly impossible to swing.

"Subdued," Kaladrius repeated, his voice slightly strained with the effort of holding her sword in place. "The way she was for years before you came along—the way she *should* be. The way *you* should be. This empire has enough problems without a plague of dragons on top of them all."

Alaya glared—not at him, but at the ground beneath his feet. She locked onto the energy siphoning up from it, and she ripped it apart with a few savagely hissed words.

He leapt back, moving with surprising grace for someone who looked so ancient. He landed just outside of the collapsing ground.

But with his distraction came the release of her sword.

She sized up the cracks in the ground, preparing to leap them and send her sword crashing down into his skull, all in the same motion.

Before she could, however, she sensed new energies approaching.

Seconds later, she was surrounded by more Serpent-kind, all armed with bows and swords, in addition to whatever controlling magic they possessed.

She hesitated.

Kaladrius stepped around the crevices she'd made and

came closer to her once more. "I've been watching you," he said. "I know you came to Vespera hoping to find a Star-kind who might divine a different destiny for you. But you found it all unchanged, didn't you?"

"It can still change."

"Pitiful child," he tutted. "No it cannot."

The darkness and the coming day of prophecy that the Spinner had mentioned were still haunting her, but Alaya lifted her chin and refused to let Kaladrius see the torment in her eyes.

"My destiny isn't finished," she snapped.

"Well *I* am going to finish it, as I should have done nearly nineteen years ago."

"Finish *me*?" She glared at each of the Serpent-kind encircling her, and she held up the mark on her hand. "You know who I am, don't you? Essentially your very goddess in physical form—"

"*Blasphemy*." Kaladrius lunged toward her, snatched the front of her cloak, and jerked her face toward his. "You are a corrupted, nasty, torn little sliver of our goddess that should not exist."

Alaya grabbed him back—but with magic. With only an instant of concentration, she twisted his arms until he was forced to let her go or else hear the crack of his own bones.

"Do not *touch* me," she snarled.

He stumbled back, but her magic pursued; she was gripping the center of his aura, squeezing the brightest bit of it—the part that represented his very life force.

He reacted more calmly than most who found their breath being crushed away by her magic. He closed his eyes. He didn't struggle. He simply lifted a hand, and instantly, all of the other Serpent-kind were lifting their weapons, drawing bows and positioning knives to throw at Alaya.

So she released him.

For the moment.

He coughed for breath before continuing: "Twice, now, I was a fool for trusting that my own son would be able to see that truth about you. There will not be a third time. I know what my son plans to use you for, and I will not give him the chance. Our goddess will not suffer such a terrible corruption of her power and legacy."

Alaya saw a flicker of dismay in his expression—the wild, tragic resolve of a man desperate to redeem himself in the eyes of his gods. It was obvious he blamed himself for the disasters surrounding the Serpent-kind and that power they had stolen and misused. For the wars that had come about because of them—wars that were simmering toward explosion once more, at least partly because he had failed to kill her.

And it was strange to feel it, but she almost pitied him for it. *Almost.* Because she knew he was not going to accomplish what he so desperately believed he needed to do.

Because she was not dying today.

The arrows released from every direction.

She spun quickly, glimpsing each arrow-shaped sliver

of black aura just long enough to control it. Her hand swiping toward the sky made those projectiles curve upward as well, volleying them over her and sending them scattering harmlessly through the trees.

Kaladrius took several steps back from her, but then calmly continued to order his allies to attack.

Alaya heard footsteps pounding behind her. She twisted around, blade swinging. The first Serpent-kind ducked her attack, but her follow-up step was too fast for the second one trying to charge; her sword met the curve of a neck, and with a spray of blood and a choke that quickly turned to a drowning gurgle, the Serpent-kind dropped dead at Alaya's feet.

She stared at the corpse for only an instant—it was all the time she had before another rain of arrows was falling over her. She controlled them away from her as she had before, only this time, she took the one closest to her and flung it with enough precision and force that it impaled another Serpent-kind between the eyes.

The impaled Serpent-kind dropped to his knees, tripping another as he did. The one who had tripped managed only to lift his head and utter a single syllable of a battle-cry before Alaya was upon him, sword drawn. She ended him with a powerful blow to his head.

She stomped a boot onto his blood-splattered shoulder, and she was attempting to dislodge her sword from his skull when an arrow whizzed past, cutting cleanly through the side of her leg as it went. Not a deep wound, but enough to make her teeth clench and her steps burn with pain.

As she stumbled from that pain, she felt the tingling sensation of magic attempting to wrap around her sword once more. Her palms quickly started to itch with it. It was coming from too many directions at once; she could already feel her grip shaking loose.

Fine. If they wanted to fight with magic instead of swords, she would give them magic.

She sheathed her weapon, seeking the auras of the trees around her as she did. With a furious swipe of her arms and a whispered spell from her lips, three of those tallest trees were wrenched from the ground and sent hurtling in three separate directions. She managed to crush only one of her enemies directly, but several of the ones who avoided the initial falling were nonetheless caught up in the branches and roots of those felled trees.

And the roots were old and long and tangled, and Alaya focused her power on bringing those snaking roots to life, wrapping them around the ones trying to crawl out of them. It was easier to control a tree than a human. Easier to use those roots to hold them in place.

But those roots were just as effective at squeezing the breath from her enemies' lungs, it turned out.

Heaving for breath herself, Alaya watched the last bit of life shuddering away from each of them.

One, two, three, four.

Then she turned to find what remained of her enemies forming a loose circle around her. Only five remained, in addition to Kaladrius. And those five were looking to Kaladrius, waiting for instruction. Their stances were resolute, prepared to keep fighting. But even the slightest move she made now sent uncertainty and fear flickering through their expressions.

A twist of her hand, and they all winced, almost in unison.

It was thrilling.

She was tired, but her mind was clear and she still felt far away from her limit. Her mother's power had clearly been in that heart-shaped stone last night, and now it was clearly a part of her. It was obvious. And it was both exhilarating and terrifying to find that the edge of her magic had truly been expanded, and she had to take several deep breaths to calm herself down.

She had already killed six.

She knew she could kill the rest—for once, she had no doubts about her abilities. Only her conscience made her hesitate now, and it was only a quiet whisper in the back of her mind.

At what point does it become senseless slaughter?

She heard another roar, and then the thrashing and splintering sounds of Rue destroying more of whatever part of the forest she'd crashed into, and Alaya was reminded of *why* she had decided to fight in the first place —because she was not dying here, and neither was her dragon.

She narrowed her eyes at the Serpent-kind attempting to encircle her and cut her off from Rue.

And she ran straight through them.

They scattered as she'd suspected they might. She heard Kaladrius shouting at them, cursing and calling them cowards. She sprinted toward Rue without looking back, doing her best to ignore the pain that shot through her wounded leg with every too-hard step she took.

She found the dragon surrounded by broken trees and several mangled bodies. There were two women still standing amongst all the dead. One was scanning the woods, watching for anyone who might approach. The other had a sword in her hand, the tip of it pointing at Rue's closed eye, hovering just inches away from it.

Alaya swiftly tethered her magic to that sword and yanked, twisting it back and stabbing it through the chest of its owner.

The second woman turned quickly enough to put up a fight, at least; she rolled to avoid Alaya's swinging fist, and then she managed to summon enough magic to catch Alaya's sword as it was drawn.

Her sword hung in the air, held by that magic. Alaya briefly abandoned it and instead aimed a furious kick into the woman's stomach. As it connected, the woman buckled—and so, too, did her magic. Alaya heard her newly-released sword clatter against dirt and stone. She moved just as quickly, scooping it back into her hand and slicing upward into the woman as that woman attempted to regain her balance.

The woman fell, body hooking around the sword and bringing it to the ground with her. She uttered a breathy combination of prayers and curses as her body twitched and her blood stained the dirt, spreading slowly and turning it a deeper shade of red.

Within seconds, she was quiet.

Alaya left her sword on that stained ground, stumbled away from her latest kill, and dropped to her knees at Rue's side. She inspected the arrows protruding from the soft places in between the scales of the dragon's belly.

Those scales around the arrows were turning black, a shiny shade of obsidian that was a distinctly darker shade than the rest of her body, which were currently the same steely-blue shade as the sky.

What had they injected into her?

The memory of their first meeting dropped into her mind, though Alaya tried to keep it out; she didn't want to picture the dragon going still as stone, as she had been in that temple. She *wouldn't* picture it.

"You have to get up. We have to get out of here."

The dragon's eyes darted wildly beneath her closed lids. Her breaths were heavy, labored.

Frustrated tears squeezed out of Alaya's eyes and stained her cheeks. "Come *on*. We can't—"

The thud of footsteps cut her off.

She heard him, sensed who it was, but she still moved too slowly.

Fire. An explosion of it in the back of her thigh. Without even glancing back she knew that it was a knife that had caused it. She felt pain and blood welling up around the spot it had pierced, trickling warmth down her leg. She bit back a cry of pain and twisted to see Kaladrius looming over her.

She was nothing but rage and divine fury as she grabbed her sword with her magic and swept it in a deadly arc toward his chest.

He staggered backward, narrowly avoiding it. His expression was a terrible combination of determination and madness. He reached out a hand. A quick spell yanked the knife from her leg and then sent it hurtling toward her face.

She caught it with her own magic, but not before it pierced the skin of her cheek, reopening that almost-healed scratch she'd received in the dungeons of the Sun Palace.

Her pained cry awakened the dragon beneath her one last time.

Rue's body snapped suddenly to life and her tail struck low, lifting Kaladrius into the air and sending him flying up, up, up—and then back down into her waiting jaws. She snatched him with a sickening *crunch*. Opened her mouth once more, only to clamp down harder. Then she swung him viciously about several times before releasing him and sending him soaring through the air once again.

He struck one of the few trees still standing around them, and his horribly twisted and bleeding body slid down the trunk and into a broken heap at its base.

He didn't move.

Alaya crawled back to Rue's side as the dragon's eyes

started to flicker shut once more. She craned her neck and glanced back in the direction Kaladrius had come from. She saw no one else following him, but this offered her little comfort.

"They'll be back," she told Rue in a whisper.

And if not them, then others would come. An entire battalion of the Sun Army was only miles away, and if they knew she was here...

"We have to get up." She tried giving the massive creature a shove, which—unsurprisingly—accomplished nothing.

She rose to her feet, went to gather up her sword and the other supplies that had been strewn about while she'd battled. She returned quickly to the dragon, her body shaking as the scent of blood and the sudden still-ness of the forest threatened to overwhelm her.

"We're connected, you and I," she hissed at Rue. "You carry a piece of my mother's power inside of you. And I don't intend to leave you *or* that piece of her here to die. So *get up*. Please, *please* get up..."

A sudden, desperate idea occurred to her and Alaya dropped to her knees, held out her marked hand, and tried to find the same words she'd used last night, when she had absorbed the power from that heart-shaped stone. Only this time, she imagined the transfer of magic moving in the opposite direction.

"We're connected," she repeated, softly, just as her mark began to glow.

With a groan that was part pain, part irritation, one of

Rue's eyes blinked open. Its sapphire color seemed dulled, but it managed to *stay* open and to track Alaya's movement.

Alaya held in a hopeful, astonished gasp, and she immediately climbed onto Rue's back and situated herself in the familiar spot between the creature's shoulder blades. She didn't want to be harsh, but she didn't want to give the obstinate dragon a chance to quit on her again, either.

Rue managed little of her usual grace and speed as she rose into the air. More than once she clipped trees with her limply dangling tail and claws, and Alaya ended up with several more scratches on her skin to join her other wounds. But soon, they were clear of those trees, and the cold yet refreshing vapor of clouds swept over Alaya's skin.

They flew higher into the mountains, until Alaya saw a section of the red rocks that looked as if they might have caves of some sort that they could take refuge in.

Rue drifted downward at Alaya's command. But with every beat of her wings, Alaya could sense the dragon's strength slipping and her control over their descent growing shakier.

"Just a little farther," Alaya tried to encourage her. "You can do this."

For a moment, Rue seemed bolstered by the words. But then a sudden, fierce gust of wind slammed into them, and the dragon rocked so wildly back and forth that Alaya nearly tumbled off her back.

These were the distinctly warm Dravyn Winds that occasionally brought storms over to the east-facing slopes of the Sinharas. They were known to be wild. Rough. Difficult to predict.

And Rue was no match for them in her current state.

The dragon stretched her wings and flapped downward anyway, trying to push them above those winds. Then another gust battered them, twisting them violently through the air and sapping the last of Rue's resolve. Her wings drooped limply beneath her.

They dropped into a freefall.

Rue pulled up at the last moment, scarcely avoiding a full collision with the rocky ground. The violent motion threw Alaya to that ground, and she had to scramble to avoid being struck by Rue's tail as the dragon rolled to a stop.

The dust settled.

Once more, Alaya somehow found the strength to drag herself over to Rue's side, to try and nudge her into motion.

(*Sleep.*)

The familiar voice in her head was a welcome sound, but the faintness of it was alarming.

"Not here," Alaya told her, standing and beckoning the dragon to follow her. She had caught a glimpse of a promising shelter as they fell, and she was determined to reach it. She limped in the direction of it, keeping her eyes on Rue. She was nearly out of sight before the dragon rose with a huff and followed.

Bit by bit, they managed to cross the rocks together, to curl into a cave just large enough for the two of them. Rue collapsed immediately once she was inside, her shoulder scrapping the rock and sending pebbles and dust scattering as she did.

(*Sleep,*) she said again.

"Yes." Alaya's gaze found those blackened scales across Rue's stomach. The darkness was spreading, and the sight of it made Alaya's voice crack a bit as she added, "But you had better wake up afterwards. Don't leave me here alone, okay?"

Rue didn't reply. Her eyes were closed again.

Alaya huddled closer to her, and outside, the winds began to howl more loudly.

CHAPTER 18

THE DAYS PASSED IN A BLUR OF PAIN AND GROWING FEAR, WITH Alaya just barely able to keep track of them.

Five sunsets.

Six sunrises.

On that sixth morning, she started tallying each day, scratching a red-streak onto the cave wall by way of a muddy stone. At first, she had told herself there was no need to keep track like this; they wouldn't be staying in that cramped cave for long.

But now, she wasn't so sure.

Rue barely moved. She only occasionally opened her eyes, and her voice whispered into Alaya's head even less often than that. She refused to eat any of the animals that Alaya managed to find and kill—though she did drink eagerly from the water that was brought to her.

That water had to be collected from a small stream that was a steep, half-mile trek from their cave, and then carried back to Rue in the amounts that Alaya's canteens could hold—amounts that seemed pitifully small when one was trying to hydrate a dragon. It was not a particularly efficient method. But Alaya still trekked back and forth from the stream multiple times a day, every day, until the dragon's thirst was satisfied.

Thanks to these daily trips, Alaya's feet were covered in blisters, and the wounds on her legs hadn't healed properly, either. Luckily, she had found an ointment of some sort within the bag the Star-Spinner had given her, and it had helped to dull her pain. She had used it on Rue as well, which had earned her a response—a hiss and a thwack of a tail—if nothing else.

But she wasn't sure what that ointment was truly doing. Whether or not it was really *healing*. So whenever she ventured out for water and in search of something new to try and force the dragon to eat, she also kept an eye out for the few plants that she *knew* would aid even a dragon with her pain.

Of course, she knew of nothing that might stop the strange darkening of Rue's scales—a darkness that had continued spreading. Over these past six days, it had gone from Rue's belly down to her front legs, and now those legs seemed to have stiffened to the point that she couldn't move them.

Alaya was trying not to lose hope. She was constantly trying to come up with some sort of plan. She wasn't sure how long she could last in these mountains, but she didn't want to leave Rue; the dragon was the only creature in this empire that she knew for certain was still on her side.

She couldn't lose her.

She refused to.

But the chances of finding someone who would be willing and able to help her—and within walking distance of these desolate mountains—seemed infinitesimal.

And meanwhile, Alaya was only waiting for one of the many people hunting them to show up and finish them off.

She had slept little over the past five nights, as such. Her eyes burned with the same exhaustion as her limbs as she finished marking the sixth day on the cave wall, draped her canteens over her shoulders, and then started off toward the stream.

Rue's breathing had seemed less pained this morning, at least, and her sleep less tumultuous. Because of this, Alaya decided to chance going a greater distance from their cave before returning. Yesterday, she had spotted a section farther down the mountain where that stream she was drawing from appeared to widen. The increased moisture would mean increased vegetation, and she knew that spinnerflower grew along some river shores in this part of the empire—and it was a potent, albeit horrid tasting, pain-reliever.

She picked her way carefully down the mountain. The sun was only just peeking through the red rocks, but it was still hot. Beads of sweat soon dotted her forehead.

She kept glimpsing wider and bolder stretches of water between those sun-washed rocks, so she knew that she was heading in the right direction—but her target area ended up being much farther away than it had looked from above.

She finally reached a relatively flat slope of land, and there she heard the unmistakable rush of an impressive swath of water just ahead. She started toward it, limping a bit to avoid putting pressure on a particularly nasty blister on the back of her left heel. She rounded a corner and sighed in relief at the sight of the gentle rapids that greeted her; this section of the waterway was at least ten feet wide, and banked on either side by various types of vegetation that ran as far as she could see.

It hadn't been a mirage.

But her attention was almost immediately drawn away from it all by the sound of rocks skittering from a cliff somewhere above her.

She lifted her eyes toward the sound. Froze. Watched as a cloud of dust floated away from a ledge that over-looked the place where she stood.

She waited at least a minute, but the source of that dust never appeared.

Must have been an animal of some sort.

She cast a wary glance around her, but she continued toward the stream. She drank her fill of clear, cool water before starting her search for the spinnerflower, picking her way along the muddy shoreline and digging through clumps of weeds with the toe of her boot.

She found a shallow spot and waded across, and after that, it only took her a few moments to find what she *thought* was spinnerflower growing on the other side; the scalloped leaves were a slight variation of what she had grown up seeing around Vanish, but the color of those leaves seemed unmistakable—as did the purplish buds starting to bloom on some of the stalks.

She knelt, pulled the knife from the sheath at her ankle, cut several clumps of the flower free, and shoved it into one of her canteens. Then she filled both of those canteens with water before wading across and starting back up the path she had descended from.

Another sudden deluge of falling rocks caught her attention.

Her gaze snapped toward that same ledge as before. She was weary from her hike, but she still managed to focus her magic, her senses... And though she saw no physical body, she *did* see the faintest trace of white-colored energy hovering around that overhanging cliff.

She knew that energy.

Storm-kind.

She backed more quickly toward the trail she'd taken to this spot, ducking into a narrow passage between the rocks so that she was out of sight—but quickly decided that was pointless; they had almost certainly already seen her.

The ways back to her cave—to Rue—were limited. She might have been able to find a different path, to pick her way up steeper footing and avoid whomever had been watching her, but confronting them seemed like the better option. So she quietly took the canteens from her shoulder and leaned them against the rocks. Then she withdrew Suja and started up the path, pressing close to the cliff walls and creeping around corners while holding her breath.

She saw the shadow before she saw the man, so her sword was at the ready before he had even stepped into her path. His eyes widened a bit at the sight of her and that sword, clearly surprised that she had dared to come straight at him.

He hesitated only a moment—barely long enough for her to take in the sight of the Sun emblem on his coat and the Storm-kind symbol on his wrist—and then he ran away. Darted with incredible speed up and over a low ledge and scampered from sight, the sound of his footsteps bouncing off the rocks as he went.

And she had a sickening feeling she knew why.

A scout.

There were more of these soldiers close by. She would have bet her life on that—and it *was* her life at stake if she let that man get away. Both hers *and* Rue's.

Her aches and pains were forgotten, suddenly, and she sheathed her sword and bolted after the scout. She darted wildly from one precarious footing to another, occasionally using a quick burst of her magic to fling looser looking stones aside and open up a shorter path, allowing her to close the space between her and the scout quickly.

A minute later, she had him clearly back in her sights.

But they had reached an open plateau amongst the rocks, and he was gaining speed, racing toward a ridge of red stone that looked like jagged teeth. She knew the lay of this side of the mountain well enough by now to know what was over that jaw full of teeth; a steep incline that led down into a valley of more open land.

And she had a sickening feeling that a large segment of the Army of the Sun was gathering in that valley, waiting for her.

She stopped trying to catch the scout, and instead, she focused on the rocky walls lining the path ahead of him. She only needed a few of the larger ones to break free.

Easy enough.

A small avalanche was in her command a moment later, rushing down and blocking the scout's path—and ultimately crushing him as he tried to fight his way over it.

Alaya skidded to a stop as the last of his burial mound rolled into place, clutching her knees and doubling over to catch her breath.

Then she heard shouting.

"Damn it," she wheezed, glancing up. A small group of men and women were sliding down the steep paths that led into the plateau where she stood.

The group divided. Two of them picked up where their fallen accomplice had left off, climbing over the rubble that had buried him and continuing over the ledge and down to that valley on the other side.

The other two—a man and a woman wearing the

same Sun-marked coat as the fallen man—sprinted toward Alaya.

The man was faster; Alaya caught a glimpse of the symbol on his hand as he sprinted ahead and lifted that hand toward her.

Another Storm-kind.

His magic struck her before she had recovered enough to ready an attack of her own. Electricity leapt from his fingertips and sliced through the air like an overly long sword. It cut into her and made her body jerk uncontrollably for an instant, and as quick as that, she was on the ground, pebbles digging painfully into the scar on her cheek and dust flying into her eyes.

She was still on that ground, half-blinded by that dust, when the Storm-kind attempted a second attack. Her response was purely reflexive this time, a reaching of her magic that ignored how exhausted she was and came faster than she could blink. It wrapped around the Storm spell and curved it back toward its caster, burying the white bolt of energy into his chest. The countered magic didn't knock him to the ground as it had her, but it made him drop to one knee while he shuddered and tried to shake it off.

The woman who had charged alongside him slowed as well, casting a worried look between her partner and Alaya.

Alaya glanced behind her, quickly weighing her options.

She expected the Army of the Sun to come flooding

over the distant ridge at any second...but turning and running could lead them closer to Rue, who was obviously in no condition to fight.

So she stood and drew her sword.

This time, she was prepared when she saw the electric energy sizzling to life against the man's palm. She stepped and swung faster than he could finish summoning, driving her curved blade into his stomach as he lunged toward her.

The woman was upon her an instant later, forcing Alaya to twist awkwardly to avoid being tackled. She stumbled through the awkwardness and made it several steps—

But the woman caught her arm and jerked her back with a strength that felt supernatural.

Alaya couldn't see the woman's hand, but she suspected a Mountain-kind symbol graced it.

The woman managed a single word: "You—"

And then she was silenced by an arrow sliding cleanly into one cheek and out the other.

Alaya twisted her head and saw this first arrow just as a second followed it, striking the side of her captor's head this time. Alaya jerked free—causing the suddenly limp body holding her to collapse to the ground with a gruesome *thud*—and she turned to see a familiar person approaching her.

CHAPTER 19

"SADE?"

"Don't look so surprised. I told you I was going to follow you, didn't I? And so here I am, coming to your rescue, yet again."

Alaya started to reply, but in that instant, the first of the army she'd been anticipating ascended the ledge in the distance. More soldiers rapidly followed, filling in what had once seemed like a large expanse of open ground.

"Come with me!" Sade shouted. She snatched Alaya's hand before Alaya could protest, and she dragged her down a nearby path. One of the roan—the giant, mythical antelope beasts bred originally for Rook royalty—awaited them at a bend in this path.

"Get on," Sade instructed.

"I—"

"Trust me," Sade pressed, casting a harried look

toward that open space they'd ducked away from. The rocks trembled, vibrating under what must have been hundreds of feet and hooves. The sounds of shouting reverberated around them, growing louder and louder. The roan's black eyes were wide and darting, its ears flicking toward the sounds and its body twitching as Sade untied it from a gangly white tree that had sprouted sideways out of the mountain.

"Are you insane?" Alaya demanded. "We can't outrun them! There are too many, and we—"

"Obviously I'm insane, or I wouldn't have come after you like this in the first place. But that's not the point. We only need to get around them and outrun them for a short distance. Now *come on!*" She swung into the saddle and took up the reins in one hand while impatiently offering Alaya the other.

Alaya stared dubiously at that hand.

"*Trust me,*" Sade said again.

Alaya realized her other options were severely limited at this point, so she allowed herself to be pulled into the saddle behind Sade, and she wrapped her arms around Sade's waist and held on tight as they bounded into motion.

The roan were incredibly powerful, incredibly quick creatures. Even with the weight of two riders on its back, their steed managed to set off at a brisk pace, and it barely hesitated as Sade guided it up a sharply pitched, narrow path littered with loose pebbles and hedged with spiny vegetation. Overhanging rocks made the trail claustrophobic and dark, almost pitch black until they pulled closer to the top, at which point it flared open and the sun became blinding—like climbing out of a well they'd been trapped in for hours.

They reached the top of that well and, once her vision had adjusted, Alaya realized that they had climbed their way to that same jagged ridge that the Sun Army had flooded over. Much of that army was beside or behind them now.

The roan picked its way across the uneven rock until it came to a steep slope, where it pranced uncertainly to a stop. Sade snapped the reins and they rocketed down that slope, reached a ledge that stretched out over a deep ravine, and without another instant of hesitation, the roan leapt over it. Somehow, they landed gracefully on the other side, and the hardy antelope seemed no more worse for the wear.

They were spotted immediately.

A wave of soldiers curved after them and gave chase. Sade kicked the roan into a gallop. There was no turning around. Scores of soldiers were behind them—

But just as concerning were the soldiers that were rapidly moving to cut off the valley's exit, pinning them in while shouting and waving weapons that gleamed like diamonds in the daylight.

"You're going to have to clear a path!" Sade shouted.

Alaya wanted to protest, but there was no time. The only way out was through, so she focused on the line of horses racing out in front of the group that was converging to block their exit.

One-by-one her magic took hold of those horses. One-by-one their legs twisted beneath them until they fell. Most took several other horses and soldiers out with them as they crashed to the ground, and so the path was opened up—but still littered with bodies that they were forced to jump and dodge while Alaya continued to work her magic.

Finally, that crowd they were battling through began to thin. They reached the foot soldiers circling at the outskirts of the company, and Alaya drew her sword and used it to cut through the few who were brave enough to continue to try and stop them—or else too slow to get out of the way.

Then suddenly they were free, bursting through the last of the advancing line and into open space. Arrows whistled after them, but the roan seemed to have a sense for avoiding the projectiles; it weaved and ducked and dug its hooves harder into the ground, propelling them even faster toward the open foothills ahead.

They raced on for another mile at least before the roan's breathing became noticeably labored and its steps began to slow and occasionally stagger. Alaya clutched Sade more tightly, chancing a look behind them.

They were still being followed by no less than two hundred on horseback; most of those followers had not yet outrun the shadows cast by the mountains, so their details—and the true number of them—were dark and difficult to see.

Alaya pried her eyes away from their pursuers. She looked to the steeper hills ahead, hills that she was afraid would prove too much for the rapidly-tiring creature they rode. "How much longer do you think we can run?"

"Trust me!" Sade replied.

"You keep saying that," Alaya called back, "And it's *really* making me think you're just making this up as we go."

She felt Sade's stomach heave with a quick, silent laugh. Then Sade gave the roan a few more swift kicks. The creature bleated out a low-pitched complaint, but it quickly obeyed the next pull of the reins; it veered sharply to the right and fought its way up another hill. By the time they reached the top, its chest was nearly touching the ground, its legs shaking and threatening to crumple beneath them.

Once there, Sade commanded it to stop. She leapt from the roan's back and took the bow attached to its saddle, whipped an arrow from the quiver at her side, and quickly used it to shoot down their closest pursuer.

Alaya dropped to the ground as Sade nocked another arrow. She wrapped an arm around the sweat-dampened ruff of the antelope's neck, trying to support and soothe the creature as best she could. That creature's eyes were still as wide and panicked as they'd been back in the mountains. Alaya assumed hers appeared the same as she watched Sade drop another rider with another perfectly placed arrow.

Behind those two that Sade had shot, more were quickly closing the gap that the roan had managed to create. They were away from the mountains and easy to see, now.

Hundreds of them.

Alaya tried to keep her breathing steady. To keep her own panic from transferring into that creature she was trying to calm. But she couldn't keep the words from blurting out of her: "Why are we stopping? What exactly is the plan that I'm supposed to be trusting and..." she trailed off as she looked to where Sade had suddenly pointed.

Over the hill adjacent to where they stood, another army was climbing into view.

Only a trickle at first, so few that Alaya counted them. One, two...eight total soldiers who rode the same kind of giant antelope that she and Sade had ridden. They trotted out in a line until they were evenly spaced from one another. Then, several dozen more followed and filled in the spaces—most of these on horseback—and together they formed a row that stretched across the entirety of that wide hilltop.

Most of the ones who had been pursuing Sade and Alaya reared their horses to a stop. They turned to face the new threat that loomed above them.

The apparent leaders of that threat—the eight men and women perched on the backs of the roan—withdrew swords and lifted them high. With a shout, they charged down the hillside, throwing up clouds of red dust and dried grass as they came. The rest of their line soon followed. And then came a surge of other soldiers, at least as many as the number that had given chase to Alaya and Sade, if not more, rising up over the hill and sweeping down to engulf the Army of the Sun.

"The Valinesian Army?" Alaya guessed in a whisper. The roan leading the charge were indication enough. And the sheer number of them, as well as the silvery-black colors of their armor and banners confirmed it.

Sade nodded, confirming it as well. "And now *we* find a place to hide," she said, taking the antelope's reins and pulling it after her, "and we let them play their war games and forget about us for awhile."

Alaya followed for a few steps—until she was behind the hill and out of sight of the two armies—but the sounds of those armies colliding made her pause. The clanging of steel and the twanging of loosed arrows, the frantic whinnying of horses and the agonized screams of men and women meeting their violent fates...she was transfixed for a moment by all of these horrible sounds. It felt strange to be separated from the battle. To be standing in relative calm and safety after all the fighting she'd done this morning, after all the fighting she'd been doing these past weeks, months, years—forever.

After a minute, Sade grabbed her arm and started to drag her farther away from those sounds.

Alaya allowed herself to be hauled along to a better

hiding spot. They trudged on for what must have been close to a mile, and then they picked their way down an outcropping of rocks, until eventually, they found a slab of shiny red stone that was massive enough to serve as a main wall of protection. The rocks piled around it were plenty as well, and the various shapes and colors created a disorienting blend, such that anything hiding amongst them would have been difficult to pick out from a distance.

"We can't go far," Alaya said, cautiously peering around their stony shelter and looking back to the rugged outline of the Sinharas' peaks. "I have to get back to Rue. She's up in the mountains, hidden in a cave the two of us have been staying in."

"...You've been living in a *cave*?"

"Out of necessity. She's hurt. She can't fly—she can hardly move her front legs..." Alaya's voice was hushed, suddenly overcome with concern. How long had it been? Had Rue started to worry? What if the dragon came looking for her and instead found soldiers waiting?

"We'll go back to get her," Sade told her, warily, "but we need to at least wait until the Sun Army is drawn more fully out of those mountains. We can't risk sneaking back before then."

Alaya pursed her lips, but she could come up with no argument against this plan. "Since when did you become so logical?" she muttered.

"About the time you started to lose control of your

mind and magic on a regular basis." Sade cut her a sideways glance. "I figure we need to balance each other out."

They exchanged a grim smile. Alaya wanted to tell her about her latest plan to find control over those things, once and for all, but she didn't feel up to that conversation yet. But soon. Perhaps once they got away from this place, away from the sounds of battle cries and screams and the cloying scent of blood and death that the wind seemed to be carrying toward them.

How many would lie dead on that battlefield before nightfall?

Alaya shuddered and drew closer to the rocks, trying not think of it.

"What happened to Rue, exactly?" Sade asked, pulling a canteen from one of the small saddlebags. It took some coaxing to convince the exhausted antelope to open its mouth to drink; it looked as though it only wanted to sleep.

Alaya absently stroked that creature's coarse fur while she tried to recall the past days, starting with the moment she had left Vespera, and focusing particularly on the battle with Kaladrius and the strange blackness that had been spreading through Rue's scales ever since.

"Sounds like *oblesk* poisoning," Sade remarked once Alaya had finished.

"Oblesk?"

"Do you remember the varghest, and the Verlore Forest?"

"Hard to forget that beast that almost turned us to

stone, isn't it? I still have nightmares about your arm being petrified and then breaking off..."

"Well, after that whole stone-arm thing happened, Kian tried to make me feel better by telling me that he was fairly certain he knew of a remedy that would have healed it, even if killing the varghest hadn't undone the curse magic. Said that the whole turning to stone thing was similar to what he'd seen oblesk poison do—that is, poison that's derived from the petrified plants in the Verlore Forest."

"So you know of an antidote to this poison?" Alaya asked, cautiously hopeful.

Sade thought for a moment. "If I can remember all the ingredients, yes. No idea whether or not it will work on a dragon, though."

"It's worth a try."

Sade nodded, her eyes glazing over in thought once more as she presumably tried to remember those ingredients. She was quiet for a long time. Alaya didn't interrupt; she didn't want to interfere with whatever plan Sade was trying to come up with. Instead, she leaned back against the red stone and closed her eyes.

At some point, she drifted off and into a light, fitful sleep, and she stayed asleep until a sharp poke against her leg woke her up. She blinked her eyes open and found Sade tapping that leg with the blunt end of an arrow.

"It's bleeding," Sade said, making a rather obvious observation.

Most of the fabric across Alaya's thigh was slightly

damp with that blood—blood that was oozing from the stab wound that Kaladrius had left just before Rue had finished him off.

"Again," muttered Alaya.

"*Again?*"

"It happened when I was fighting Kaladrius. It's never really had a chance to heal."

"So, that happened several days ago?" Sade frowned. "It's going to get infected, if it isn't already."

"I know. But it's nothing compared to Rue's injuries, so I was, um..."

"Just going to ignore it and hope that your leg didn't fall off?"

Alaya rolled her eyes. "Yes. That."

Sade paused, considered for a moment, and then stood with a resolved sigh. "Okay," she began, dusting the dirt from her clothing and reaching for her bow. "You stay here, and stay off of that leg."

"I—"

"It's too soon to try heading back up the mountain, anyway; I can still hear them going at it over in the valley, can't you?"

Alaya had been trying to block out the distant sounds of that battlefield, but Sade was right; just a moment of quiet, of holding her breath and focusing, was enough to hear them. At least several hours had passed during her nap, judging by the sun's much higher position in the sky, but those horrible noises were still just as loud as before.

"Let's give them some more time to finish off those

Sun bastards," Sade suggested. "In the meantime, stay hidden. Nalia and I will head into Belhurst and see what ingredients I can find, and we'll take care of *that* —" she gave Alaya's leg another poke "—and then we'll sneak back up to your cave and take care of your dragon."

The antelope had lifted its head at what was apparently its name, and as Sade finished speaking, it rose stiffly to its feet and shook itself off with a grunt. It looked well-rested, at least.

Which left Alaya with no ready argument to make against Sade's plan, so she agreed with a nod. "Fine," she said.

"You think you can stay alive and hidden until I get back?" Sade asked.

"I've managed to stay alive without you before, haven't I?"

"Barely."

Alaya huffed out a laugh, as did Sade—but then Sade's expression quickly turned serious again. "No more running away. I'll just find you again if you do."

"Is that a threat?" Alaya asked with a wry smile.

"It's a promise."

"I'll be here," Alaya said, waving her off with that old Vanish goodbye: "Go well."

"Stay well," Sade replied.

As Sade disappeared into the distance, Alaya curled tighter amongst the rocks, wincing a bit at the burning pain in her thigh. She tried to ignore that pain in the same way that she had been ignoring it for days—by focusing instead on the pain that Rue was in.

I'm coming back, she thought, as clearly as she could. *Please stay where you are. Please don't worry.*

She received no response.

It was well after nightfall before Sade returned.

Alaya hadn't dared to sleep while alone, so she had watched the sunlight fade, bit by bit, through eyes that burned and watered with the effort of staying wide open. As the dark settled around her, paranoia had wrapped her up like a second skin, growing itchier with every odd shadow and each gust of wind that sent dried brush scratching across the rocks; Sade's sudden reappearance made her draw her sword in a hurry—and then curse under her breath when Sade stepped into a patch of moonlight that fully revealed her face.

"Please don't stab me," Sade said, lifting her hands.

Something painful twisted in Alaya's gut.

Sade's tone had been darkly humorous, as it often was, but there was an unspoken truth behind her pretend fear, wasn't there?

They had yet to speak of what had happened during Alaya's last night in Rykarra. Of what she'd done. Of the people she had hurt, and the risk she and her magic—and that magic's side effects—still posed. She was still hesitant to ask for the details of what she'd really done that night.

But Sade knew those details. She knew the aftermath of what had happened, and she had to have been thinking about it now. And yet she was still here. She had still followed.

"I found what I was looking for, mostly," Sade informed her. "And it seems like that particular battle we started is pretty well over with; I spotted a group of soldiers from the Sun Army retreating toward the coast. Plus, it's gone awfully quiet, hasn't it?"

Alaya nodded; aside from that occasionally gusty wind, it was eerily quiet.

They waited several more hours to be certain, passing them by tending to that wound on Alaya's leg, and then by mixing up the concoction that Sade hoped would be enough to heal Rue.

Finally, as the first light of a new day streaked into the sky, they decided to chance riding back toward the mountains.

They swung as wide as they could, not quite retracing the path they'd fled away on, but the Syndra Canyon to their south eventually pinched them closer to the battlefield than they wanted to go. Close enough that they saw occasional bodies; corpses that had crawled away from that main battlefield only to die alone on the fringes of it.

Alaya tried to keep her eyes on their distant destination. And she mostly managed it, until the sound of a cough, wet with blood, caught her attention. She found the source of the sound quickly; a man sprawled on the ground nearby, half-hidden in a dry patch of brambles.

"We should keep going, we—"

Alaya was off the roan's back before Sade could finish her sentence. She jogged to the man's side and knelt down, assessing him as she did. He wore Rook colors, and a ring on his finger bore the emblem of the royal family, but the clan mark on his bloodied palm told her he was Ice-kind.

He gasped out a plea: *"Help me."*

The pain in his voice was so wretched that she felt compelled to listen to him, though she had no idea how she could possibly help. The ground around him was already soaked with his blood. His skin was the color of ash.

"I'm sorry, I don't..."

He shifted his head toward her. Met her gaze. Stared hard at her for a moment before his trembling, colorless lips managed to push out a single sentence: "Your eyes are...strange."

She barely flinched at this comment; it wasn't the first time she'd heard it. And there was no point in hiding her strangeness from the dying.

He had clearly already recognized her, anyway.

She could see it in the way his own eyes abruptly widened and his body gave a violent, involuntary jerk. And as soon as that awareness came, his hand latched onto her wrist and he shakily lifted her hand to where he could see it, to where he could be certain of the mark that was on her skin.

"Goddess...of...Control." His eyes closed, and for a moment, Alaya thought it might have been for good, but then they flashed open and he stared, wide and unseeing, at the sky as he sputtered out a few more words: "Control the...the...the *end*..."

She understood what he was asking her to do.

The thought of doing it sent such a chill washing over her that she thought it might freeze her in place. But she swallowed hard and reached for her magic instead, and after a moment of concentrating, she saw the dying man's pale blue aura.

So faint.

"Please," he gasped.

Perhaps it was proof of her own growing and settling power that she managed to do it without violence. Without effort. Without any of the doubt or fear that had once accompanied her magic. It was only a simple wave of her hand that made that energy around the dying man shift and twist and then evaporate up towards the sky, taking his life force with it.

The man breathed in deeply. Exhaled. And then he was gone, and the world seemed strangely quiet, and Alaya felt heavy, as if that man's life-force had fallen back down and settled into her instead.

The ring glinted in a sudden burst of sunlight, as if trying to catch her attention. She wondered what this man's rank was, what his story was, and why he had carried the personal emblem of the royal family. Curiosity made her carefully slide that ring off his finger to carry with her, in hopes that she might be able to find out.

"Come on," Sade insisted, drawing Nalia up beside her.

Alaya stumbled away from them for only a few steps, her gaze sweeping across the landscape, searching for more bodies. She saw three others nearby; two were full of arrows, a third was crushed beneath his fallen horse.

None of them moved or cried out for help.

She still wanted to do something. To find more. To count them. She wanted to know the number. She also wanted to vomit. To scream. In the end, she staggered backwards toward Sade, not taking her eyes off the man she'd finished off as her back hit the roan's side and she slumped against it, breathing hard.

She turned that dead man's ring over and over in her hands, her gaze darting from its bloodied surface to the clean stone of the ring that Emrys had given her. And she couldn't stop them, now—all the thoughts and fears about what had become of her Rook, and of what was going to become of them as this war raged on.

"Sade."

"...Yes?"

"Tell me what happened after I fled Rykarra. What's become of Emrys?"

Sade shifted uncomfortably in the saddle; it was obvious that she had been dreading this. "He recovered well enough," she replied after a long pause. "Though you ruined the coronation party, I'm afraid. And things between him and his advisors and the foreign diplomats staying at the palace are...tense."

"I suspect he never wants to see me again."

"Are you serious?"

Alaya tilted her head back toward Sade.

"Who do you think sent that army to face off against the Sun King's? Did you think it was a *coincidence* that they showed up and intervened?"

An odd warmth tingled across Alaya's scalp, making her feel rather lightheaded and stupid. She pulled away from Sade and Nalia and walked on by herself for a few minutes. The warmth disappeared abruptly as she crested a hill and a sweeping view of the main battlefield came into sight.

There were so many bodies that they were hard to distinguish, both from one another and from the ground they rested upon—it almost looked as if they had always been there, nothing more than uneven bumps in the landscape. And yet, the occasional groan of pain and anguish reminded her that this was not natural at all.

Nobody wins wars.

Alaya shook the Star-Spinner's words from her head, peeled her gaze away from the carnage, and turned back to Sade.

"He knows you were in Vespera." Sade's voice was steady, though only through an obvious effort. She wasn't looking at that sea of dead bodies. "And he knew Kaladrius was as well. And then the reports of that battalion of the Sun Army came in... So he sent orders to his own soldiers, already stationed nearby, to confront them. I guess he rightly assumed that they would come after you if they realized you were nearby."

"But how did he know I was in Vespera?"

She had been careful not to leave a trail, she thought. She supposed it was *possible* that he'd employed a tracker that might have outsmarted her...but something in Sade's expression told her that wasn't the case.

"That is an excellent question." Sade trotted Nalia around in front of her, blocking her view of that valley of the dead. "One I think you should ask him when we get back to the palace."

"I can't go back to that palace."

Sade shot her a withering look.

"Not yet, anyway."

Again, Sade looked as if she were considering knocking some sense into her. But she shook her head, and instead she asked: "Why not?"

Alaya tucked that bloodied ring into her pocket. And as they trekked back to the cave where Rue was hopefully still resting and waiting, she tried to explain to Sade what she had learned in the Star-kind's village.

Sade listened without interrupting, until Alaya came to the part of her plan that centered around where she planned to go once Rue was able to fly again.

"...Back to Vanish," Sade repeated, her tone hollow with regret and tinged with something like fear.

Alaya didn't reply right away, because the mouth of

that cave they'd been climbing toward was suddenly visible, and now all she could think of was Rue.

She rushed inside to find the dragon sleeping. Crouched down and pressed her hands to the smoother scales on either side of Rue's face, and she whispered encouraging words until the dragon finally, sleepily blinked her eyes open.

Sade was slow to follow her inside. And she was silent as she worked, examining the dragon's wounds, taking the medicines from her bag and applying them all without comment.

Alaya already knew what Sade was thinking; because it was the same internal battle she herself had wrestled with over the past days, no doubt.

So she didn't force Sade to speak.

She sat cross-legged on the hard stone and simply watched. Part of Rue's head rested across her lap, still but for the occasional, irritable snort that came after Sade poked too hard or used some sort of concocted ointment that stung too sharply.

But once Sade seemed satisfied with the care she'd given, and she started to repack the leftover supplies, Alaya found that she could no longer hold her tongue.

"You don't have to come with me," she blurted out. "You found me, right? And I swear I plan on returning to Rykarra once this is finished, so you can go back to Emrys and tell him that, and then—"

"Of course I have to go with you, stupid."

Alaya opened her mouth to reply, but she could think of nothing to say.

Sade sighed. "It had to happen eventually anyway, didn't it?"

"...It's been a few months," Alaya said, softly. "And she knows...you know...I wrote to her soon after it happened, right before I got this." She held up that arm that had been purposely scarred, the skin on it marred into the shape of the Feather-clan's symbol. "A lot has changed. But Vanish was home once, wasn't it? Maybe we'll receive a warmer welcome this time than we did the last time."

Rue groaned as she rolled onto her side and closed her eyes. It almost sounded like she was vocalizing the doubt that Alaya had tried to keep out of her own tone.

"I will go with you," Sade reiterated, shoving the last of her supplies back into the bag. "But I'm not going to get my hopes up about a warm welcome."

CHAPTER 20

Five days later, the scales that had been stained black were once again the color of the sky that Rue was flying against.

It had taken two days for that antidote Sade had concocted to take effect. Two more days of rest had followed, and on the fifth day Alaya, had awakened to a dragon that adamantly refused to remain cooped up in their cave for a minute longer; to make her point, Rue had gently taken Alaya's leg in her jaws, and then rather unceremoniously dragged her out into the bright morning sunlight.

Sade had left Nalia on a farm at the base of the mountains. Though she was no fan of dragon riding, Alaya convinced her to endure it for the sake of traveling as quickly as possible—so quickly that by mid-afternoon on that fifth day, the white sand edges and swaying sea-grass plains of the Greybank Peninsula were sweeping into view below them.

The sight of tiny huts and the cramped streets of the village of Vanish soon followed, and Alaya's heart promptly leapt into her throat.

She had spent the beginning of their flight frantically rehearsing all of the things she wanted to say to Kian's mother, only to give up and attempt to not think about it all instead.

Because how could she possibly prepare for a home-coming like this?

I'll just have to do it, prepared or not, she told herself, repeatedly, as she guided the dragon to the ground miles outside of that village, just as she had done when visiting Vespera. If she was honest with herself, she still didn't believe a warm welcome was in store for them here in her childhood home, regardless of what she'd told Sade. And again: Descending on the back of a dragon likely wouldn't help with that.

She waited for the cover of darkness as well, and then she traveled the few remaining miles on foot. Sade stayed behind, setting up camp on the edge of the Clearsight Plains that encircled the small village. She had muttered something about needing to guard their supplies, and Alaya didn't object. Five days was not enough time for Sade to have come to terms with returning to what remained of home, she supposed, and she understood it.

So Alaya walked the quiet streets of Vanish alone.

The journey felt shorter than it should have, and in no

time at all, she found the familiar silhouette of the orphanage coming into view. She slowed her steps, and she checked the windows out of habit, still searching for the light that Kian used to leave burning for her on nights when she was out fighting her battles with her fellow rebels.

But there were no candles burning in any of those windows, of course.

A good thing, she told herself, *because the darkness makes me harder to see.*

She drew her hood more tightly around herself and slipped around to the back of the house. The back door still didn't lock properly. Even after everything that had happened, it still hadn't been fixed, and the small shrine to the lesser-spirit of Security was still there doing whatever it could to keep intruders out.

"Ever the optimist," Alaya mused, thinking of the way Kian's mother had never missed a night of praying to that shrine. It looked as if she had offered it flowers tonight, as well.

But that shrine couldn't keep Alaya out. She knew precisely how to twist that broken lock. And she had snuck into this house late at night a thousand times, creeping quietly in from missions with Sade and Auric and the rest of that rebel group. She knew every creaking place in the floor boards, every patch of light and shadow, and every angle to take to avoid being sighted from every different room.

So it was relatively easy to make her way through that

house, even in the dark, and to find her way to her old room.

She paused outside that room. The door was cracked partially open, so she braced a hand against the frame and peered inside to find that her bed had been taken over by someone. She squinted, and she quickly recognized the small face nearly engulfed by the blanket.

Gavin.

Her sweet, mischievous Gavi with his wild curls—curls that were plastered to his forehead with sweat, and long enough now that they nearly covered eyes that were clenched unusually tightly together; he looked as if he might have been having a nightmare.

Alaya's throat felt as if it was closing in, suddenly, and her knees threatened to buckle beneath her as memories rushed over her.

A hot day turned abruptly cool.

A company of the high king's monsters surrounding the orphanage.

One of those monsters holding Gavi.

And then a choice, a single choice to run or to interfere and draw the monsters to her by revealing her mark...

She had never regretted saving him, but it was impossible not to think about how her life had been cleaved in two at that moment. How things might have turned out differently if she had decided to keep still.

"Don't wake him," came a gruff voice from the other end of the hallway. "Takes me forever to get him to sleep these days."

Alaya recognized the voice without turning toward the speaker. She didn't trust herself to be able to reply quietly, nor without her own voice breaking. So she kept her hand braced against the doorway and her eyes on Gavi for a moment more.

But she had no plans to wake him. The thought of talking to him again was somehow more intimidating than facing any other person in this orphanage—including the person sharing the hallway with her now—so eventually, she forced herself to turn and walk away from her old room, still taking care not to step on any of the squeak-prone floorboards.

Madelaine—no, Ma, because she would always be *Ma* in Alaya's mind—looked her over as she approached, appraising her the way she so often had after she'd caught Alaya shirking her chores or sneaking extra dessert. The eventual assessment she decided on this time was blunt: "You look like you haven't had a proper meal in weeks."

Alaya released the breath she'd been holding, and she was relieved when nothing resembling a sob escaped along with it. "I...I haven't."

Without another word, Ma turned and beckoned for her to follow.

Alaya hesitated, thinking of turning once more to her room; as much as she didn't want to face Gavi, she had come here with a mission, hadn't she? Her magic rose at the thought, searching, bringing dull colors to life around all of the objects within sight. Her old room seemed like the most obvious place to search for that particular aura that she was looking for, and she almost took a step back toward it...

But then she caught a glimpse of golden light—or *thought* she glimpsed it, at least—in the direction that Ma had disappeared.

Curious, she turned and followed that trace of light and the sound of the old woman's footsteps, eventually catching up with her in the kitchen at the back of the house.

"Sit," Ma insisted, waving her toward the well-loved table in the corner.

Alaya obeyed—knowing better than to argue—sinking into the chair that had always been her favorite: a wide seat with ornately carved armrests and velvet-trimmed cushions. Despite the multiple patches sewed into those overstuffed cushions, it had always made her feel like she was sitting on a throne.

She stared at Ma and tried to focus, tried to make that gold-colored energy return. But she couldn't see it anymore.

Perhaps I'm trying too hard.

Frustrated, she sank deeper into the worn-out throne and tried to relax instead.

The room seemed smaller, darker, dingier than she remembered. Perhaps because it had always been so full of life in her past; the chairs overflowing with squabbling children; the walls vibrating with the raucous laughter of Ma's many friends and helpers; the games of cards and

Teran dice almost always growing heated in a friendly but passionate way.

The entire village of Vanish had eaten at this table at least once, Alaya was fairly certain, but now she felt as if she were preparing to dine with their ghosts.

Ma kept her back to that table, muttering softly to herself as she lit a fire and quietly hung a pot over it. Then she was dicing vegetables and digging through the spice cabinet, then through the bread box, humming a tune that grew softer as the moments pressed on.

After several minutes, she shuffled over and dropped an iron bowl in front of Alaya, sloshing bits of stew onto the table as she did. It smelled strongly of onion and salt, as the vast majority of Ma's cooking did.

"Eat," she instructed.

Alaya's stomach churned, reluctant to obey, though she had told the truth; the hunting had been poor during their final days spent in the mountains, and she no longer remembered the last time she'd eaten a proper meal.

She stared at the steaming bowl without really seeing it, swallowing the dryness from her throat several times before she managed to start the speech that she'd been rehearsing on her flight here: "I know we haven't really talked since I left all those months ago. And I don't know if you received the letters I sent, or if..."

"I got them." Ma was staring at the spoon that still rested, unused, beside the iron bowl.

Alaya hastily picked it up. She clenched it firmly to keep it from shaking, but she still didn't eat more than the few polite bites that she could make herself stomach. "I didn't tell you everything in those letters," she said after those bites had settled, "but I assume you've managed to guess at the other truths about me. The things I was hiding. The, um, the—"

"Guess?"

Alaya lifted her gaze toward her.

"Child, I did not have to *guess* at anything. I never did." Ma laughed softly, and the sound was not entirely bitter, hardly the attack that Alaya had been bracing herself for. "Did you really think I had no idea what you were, even long before you revealed yourself?"

Alaya stiffened—both from shock, and because she was still waiting for the rest of that statement. For the harsh words that she was almost certain would follow.

I knew what you were, so I should have gotten rid of you when I had the chance.

Because how many times had she heard some variation of those words?

But all Ma said was, "Now: Are you going to eat the rest of that stew, or just sit and watch it go cold? Because you know I'm still going to make you eat it even if it goes rotten and cold."

Alaya stomached a few more bites, and then she asked, "What *do* you know?"

Ma raised an eyebrow. She went to the door that led into the side yard, propping it open while she fiddled with the water pump just outside. She filled a bucket and returned to the kitchen, and then she set to work washing the dishes she'd just dirtied. That much hadn't changed; her hands always had to be busy with *something*.

"I know where you went the night before those monsters came for the children," she said as she scrubbed. "Maybe not the specifics, but I knew enough about what you did with Auric and Sade and the rest of them on that night, and on all the nights before that."

"Kian told you?" Alaya guessed.

"He is—" Her hand slipped, sloshing water down the front of her night dress. But she carried on quickly, as if nothing had happened. "—*Was* a terrible liar," she corrected. "He knew what you were doing with Auric and all of his followers, and therefore so did I."

Alaya breathed a wistful sigh. He hadn't kept her secrets as closely as she'd believed, after all. But she couldn't find it in her heart to be annoyed by it, particularly since now she wondered how often Ma had aided her without her even knowing it.

"We still keep to ourselves as much as possible here," Ma said after a long pause. "I don't even go to the market myself, anymore, because I don't care to hear the gossip. But I still heard that High King Haben is dead. And there are talks of more wars, of battles that have already left hundreds upon hundreds dead—the kind of stuff that is impossible not to hear about, you know. So much turmoil, and it makes me curious, whether I want to be or not..." She placed the last of the cleaned dishes on the shelf. Stared blankly at that shelf for a moment before giving her head a small shake, then dried her hands on a ragged cloth, tossed it aside, and grabbed a cup from the windowsill.

She took several sips from that cup before walking closer to Alaya once more. "So tell me, my heart, did you really finish that fight you started all those years ago?"

Alaya stared at Ma's wrinkled hands, at the strong grasp they had on her drink, as she said, "Not yet."

"Then why are you here? You've not come back to hide, I hope?"

"No. I'm done hiding."

Ma nodded as though she believed this statement entirely—and suddenly, for the first time, Alaya realized that she did, too.

"I came here in search of something," she said.

Ma settled down in a chair and listened as Alaya explained, as succinctly as she could, what she had learned of herself, of her power and the prophecy that surrounded it.

After she was finished, the two of them sat quietly for several minutes, both lost in thought.

"Growing up, Kian didn't know that I was Serpent-kind," Alaya finally said, breaking both the silence and Ma's stoic expression.

"No."

"But you said *you* knew, even before I revealed myself. How?"

Ma placed her emptied cup down on the table between them, and her head stayed slightly bowed toward it as she said, "The night your mother died..." She paused. Considered. Cleared her throat and tried again: "Your mother knew the high king's soldiers were coming for her, days before they actually arrived. She knew she wasn't going to make it through that night, and she made me swear that I would protect you after she was gone. So yes—she told me the truth about you."

"So for nine years..."

"I knew."

"And you told no one."

Ma shrugged. "People didn't need to know. Because people... Well, they can be cruel toward things they don't understand."

"But not all people. Not you."

"I understand you better than most, don't I? Better than you understood yourself, at times."

Alaya found herself speechless.

"As for the pieces of yourself that you've come in search of, *those* I'm not sure I understand entirely. But I do know that your mother gave me something that night, when she asked me to protect you after she was gone. It came with a command: *Keep her close.* And that something...it was magic unlike anything I'd ever witnessed. Terrifying magic, to be frank. But she told me that just having it, that occasionally letting its influence wash over you, would keep *your* power from overwhelming you before you were ready to handle it. So I accepted it.

"And some nights, while you slept, I watched over you and I recited the words she'd given me to say. I watched that magic work a wall of protection around you, and I was always glad that I had taken it in, even if I didn't understand it."

Alaya still couldn't speak. Because she hadn't imagined that light in the hallway earlier, she realized. It was obvious, now: Here was the fourth piece of her mother's splintered power.

"*Keep her close,*" Ma repeated, her voice breaking slightly as she stood and started to pace the room.

Alaya stood as well, and she closed the space between them and wrapped her arms around Ma and held her still.

"I failed to do it, though, didn't I?" Ma whispered.

Alaya shook her head, and suddenly Ma was hugging her back. It was a bit startling, that returned squeeze; because hers had always been a rough-edged warmth, not the type that made her quick to shower people in kisses and compliments or to wrap them in embraces like this.

But she was holding her so tightly now that Alaya could scarcely breathe.

And it was back—that golden-colored energy. Alaya closed her eyes as it swirled around them, as a vision dropped into her head...one so clear it might as well have been from her own memory: An image of two mothers, huddled together in this very room, their hands interlocked as a light passed between them.

When Alaya opened her eyes again, that same light was on the move once more, circling her own hand and diving into the mark on it, setting it ablaze.

And just as before, she felt a rush of strength as the

light settled into her, followed by an overwhelming sense of calm. She wanted to melt into that sea of calm and float in it forever.

"You don't need me anymore, it seems," Ma whispered after a moment, "but I hope you know that you can always come back here all the same."

Alaya nodded, but she couldn't bring herself to pull away just yet. She might not have needed her childhood protector anymore, but in that moment, she felt smaller, younger, ready to be held and kept safe as she had been so many times in the past. The two of them needed each other. A mother who had lost her child, and a child who had lost her mother. It didn't matter how much time, or how many terrible things, had transpired since they had last been together—they still needed each other.

When they finally pulled away moments later, Ma kept one hand on Alaya's arm, while the other reached to brush away the tears on her cheek, "Now, promise me you won't stop until you set it all as right as you can, yes?"

Alaya breathed in deeply, forcing herself to resurface from that sea of calmness, reminding herself of all she had left to do.

"I promise," she said.

A BRIEF TIME LATER, after allowing herself to be fussed over and fed some more, and after gathering all of the advice Ma had to give about where she should go next, Alaya left the orphanage and stole her way back through the silent streets of Vanish.

She was nearly to the edge of the village when she saw the familiar silhouette of Sade approaching.

"I...I changed my mind," Sade told her, not quite meeting Alaya's curious gaze. "I think I should just, you know, say hello. Because it *has* been a while, like you said."

An unspoken understanding passed between them, and Alaya nodded and simply told her: "I'll wait for you."

While she waited, she spent the pre-dawn hours hunting and replenishing their water supply in the familiar streams outside the village, picking and eating the same fresh berries, and climbing the same hills and taking in the same views she had as a child. Anything to keep herself busy, because she could keep her thoughts clearer if she kept herself moving. Which was something *else* she had inherited from Ma, now that she thought about it.

Eventually, her busyness turned into practicing magic. By the time Sade returned, Alaya was in particularly good spirits; she had just successfully managed to temporarily change the direction of a swiftly-flowing stream, and her mind was only the tiniest bit foggy from the effort—a fogginess that went away after they returned to the campsite and reunited with Rue.

Sade didn't offer to share the details of her reunion with Ma. Alaya didn't pressure her for them; they told each other everything in time, anyway, and there were more pressing things that needed discussing at the moment.

"So," Sade began, packing up her bedroll and securing it with its leather strap. "You were just practicing magic, and you actually looked *happy* about it—so I take it that your search for that piece of your mother's magic or whatever was successful?"

"Yes."

"So how many does that leave to find?"

"I'm not sure. But not many; the Star-Spinner said there were likely only a handful. And I already feel incredibly...*stable*, for once. Although I *do* still feel like something is missing... I can't quite explain why, but I've been thinking about another possible piece, and..."

"You think you know what that piece is contained in?"

"Maybe." Her good spirits deflated a bit, the reality of having to move on—of facing the next challenge— settling in. "There's only one problem."

"Only *one*? Well, that's an improvement for us, isn't it?"

Alaya tried to mirror the wry grin Sade gave her, but her frown proved more stubborn. "The problem is that this piece—this *last* piece, hopefully—is in that bracelet that used to belong to my mother. The one that I used to keep hidden, along with my father's book and all of those other things?"

"Yes; I remember you wearing that bracelet. So, why is that a problem?"

"Because that bracelet is now in the Sun Palace. I was

wearing it on the day I killed the high king. But it was taken off of me after that, obviously, because otherwise I don't think my mind could have been so overpowered by Sylven's magic."

"Taken off? You think he..."

Alaya nodded. "And that's just more evidence that it holds some part of my mother's power. I think Sylven might have taken it *because* he realized there was power in it. And who knows what he did with it. If it's really filled with divine magic, I don't think he'll be able to destroy it, but..."

Sade cursed under her breath, and narrowed her eyes toward the sky, as if glaring at the gods themselves. "If I let you go back to the Sun Palace, Emrys will kill me. That is not an exaggeration. I'm actually a little surprised that he hasn't *already* sent someone to assassinate me for taking so long to bring you back."

"You're right."

"...I am?"

"For once."

Sade snorted.

Alaya finally managed to return that crooked grin her friend was giving her, and then she went to work packing up the rest of their camp while she ran through plans in her mind. She was eager to collect what she hoped was that last piece of her power, but now that her thoughts were clear and she felt safer than she had in months, she very clearly saw the place she wanted to go—the person she wanted to be beside when she faced whatever came next.

"I've been away from him for far too long," she told Sade. "And we didn't exactly part on the best of terms last time."

"Understatement," Sade deadpanned.

"But we're supposed to face the end of all this together, I think."

Sade looked relieved. "I have a feeling he's going to agree with you about that."

"Back to Rykarra, then?"

"I can't believe I'm actually somewhat *eager* to go back to that horrible city."

Rue stood and stretched out her wings, and that seemed to finalize the decision. Alaya took a deep breath, and then she started to situate the few bags and belongings they carried onto the dragon's back.

Her past felt more resolved now; she could finally turn away from Vanish and everything it represented without feeling like she needed to constantly be looking over her shoulder, waiting for it to sneak up and attack her.

Her present felt equally settled, her power as stable and calm as it had ever been in that moment.

And now, she thought as she climbed onto Rue's back, *I only need to secure the future.*

CHAPTER 21

THE OLD SWORD HAD BEEN RECENTLY POLISHED, AND ITS BLACK obsidian blade gleamed in the torchlight. A rook bird held each of the two torches providing that light—two menacing creatures carved into the stone wall on either side of the blade's pedestal, their wings stretched wide and their hollow eyes glaring.

Emrys had been staring at that sword for nearly five minutes now. He had taken its belt and sheath and fixed them around himself, but he hadn't yet summoned the courage to pick up the sword itself.

He would have to do so, eventually.

It might start a rumor of yet another of his weaknesses, otherwise, if any of the people in this palace learned that he couldn't stomach the simple act of brandishing this ceremonial sword—a sword that had belonged to his father, and to his grandfather before that. It was the very sword that had blinded them both—in accordance with Rook tradition—and it was an integral part of making their leaders into kings.

He was rewriting that tradition of blinding, yes. But there were grumblings of opposition to this revision already, and so he and his advisors had agreed to a compromise: The sword would still play a part. It did not have to blind, but it would still pierce his skin and draw a sacrifice of his blood on the night of his coronation.

Which, barring another disaster, would be tonight.

Tonight, he would have to carry that sword, heavy as it was with tradition and with memories of his father that he would have preferred to bury in a deep pit and never think of again.

Tonight, he would have to endure it all without any sign of his doubts or personal misgivings.

No more signs of weakness, no more signs of weakness...

That disastrous meeting with Alaya—and the wounds and days of bedrest that had resulted from it—had done enough damage to his reputation as it was. Physically, he was nearly healed, but he had spent the past weeks trying to mend the more abstract wounds that had come about as a result of that attempt on his life.

People were concerned about the high throne and its presumptive heir. And they had a right to that concern, he supposed. So his head was constantly spinning from the number of personal meetings he'd held with his foreign guests. From the number of times he'd had to silence people uttering fears and raising rumors. From the aggressive orders he had given and the decisions he had made to prove to his doubters that he was perfectly capable of doing so...

All of these things were slowly solidifying the ground he stood on once more, his advisors assured him.

But it still didn't feel like enough.

He snatched the sword from its marble pedestal and sheathed it at his hip. He was due for a meeting—and then there were countless more preparations to be made for tonight's coronation after that. He couldn't be late.

Without so much as a glance back at the pedestal or the torch-bearing birds around it, he set off at a brisk pace for the throne room.

***

HIS ADVISORS, Captain Helder among them, rose from their chairs as he entered the small war room that was connected to the throne room by a narrow, dark hallway.

"Another report from the soldiers stationed in Tera's southeastern quadrant," Helder said, handing Emrys a loosely rolled letter. While the others finished bowing and retook their seats, the captain remained standing, his arms folded across his broad chest while he watched Emrys unroll and scan that letter.

The scroll contained numbers, mostly—a tally of the dead.

The careless scribbles of math in the margins made Emrys uneasy, though he didn't show it.

"The soldiers of the Sun have overtaken Alderstone,"

Helder explained. "The people of Alderstone are being held inside their homes, being executed for merely stepping into their own yards. And Levant has made it clear that he doesn't intend to stop these brutal demonstrations until you comply with his wishes. He still demands a personal audience with you, to discuss the...how did he put it...*the validity of your rule*."

"He wants the Rook throne abolished in the most violent way possible," muttered the woman to Emrys's left—Lady Korva. She was attending this meeting on behalf of her father, whose illness had apparently flared overnight and kept him in bed that morning. "Why not just say it?" she demanded. "No sense in skirting around what we're dealing with."

Captain Helder unfolded his arms and clasped his hands behind his back. "That abolishment is...one of the demands he's made, yes."

"Let him demand it all he wants," countered another advisor. "If we simply ignore him, he will get tired of throwing his weight around eventually."

"Nearly fifty dead in Alderstone already," Helder replied in a grim tone. "Which adds to the already worrisome total we've collected after the battles in the Sinharian foothills. The exact number is..." He shuffled through more papers on the table before him, all of them similar reports to the one he'd handed Emrys.

"The exact number is seven hundred and eighty-six," Emrys interjected, his voice calm despite the storm starting to build inside of him.

It wasn't entirely an emotional storm, either. It was electricity of the most literal sense; because two nights ago, he had convinced Lord Feran to accompany him to the house of the same Fire-kind who had helped him fuse that Air-kind magic into his body. And this time, he had carried a blade stained with Storm-kind blood along with him.

Now, that Storm-kind magic twisted through his own veins, joining the magic of the Fire and Air-kinds.

He was finding it more complex than the Air-kind magic; he hadn't managed to do much with it yet, aside from creating a few sparks and making his own hair stand on end from the aftershocks. But that was how the Fire-kind magic had started, too—as a restless tingling, a whisper of power that had taken time to *acquaint* itself with him before it became truly usable.

It was better to take it slow, anyway, he kept telling himself. It made it easier to hold on to himself, to not cross the lines he'd mentally drawn for himself at the beginning of all of this. He still clearly remembered the words of advice that he'd been given when he first started acquiring magic in this dangerous way: *To remain unchanged in the heart even as your abilities change...that is the most difficult part of any magic.*

And it was proving difficult, indeed.

He finally took his seat at the head of the table, partly because he was concerned by the tingling of electricity in his fingertips. This was hardly the time or place for a demonstration of new, barely-controlled magic—particularly since most of the ones seated at this table still had no idea about the dangerous powers their leader was dealing with.

"Right—seven hundred and eighty-six," Helder repeated, obeying as Emrys motioned for him to be seated as well. "A concerning number, as I said. And we can't ignore this latest siege any longer; if the ports in Alderstone are damaged, we'll end up with trouble from Belaric as well. You all know as well as I do that we have trade agreements that must be honored to keep the peace with that eastern empire, regardless of our own internal conflicts."

"Let Belaric send help, then," muttered Lady Korva.

"I wouldn't ignore this even if Alderstone *wasn't* an important trade hub," Emrys said. "Innocent people are dying."

Captain Helder opened his mouth to reply, but then seemed to think better of it. He didn't need to speak; Emrys suspected he already knew what the old man was thinking. What almost *everyone* in the room was likely thinking.

There was little chance of avoiding more innocent people dying at this point.

Seven hundred and eighty-six...

Emrys held his tongue for the moment, but the voices continued to rise around him.

"Levant was never so bold in his objections to Rook rule before now," said one. "It's that Serpent-kind he has hissing in his ear, no doubt. Can you imagine what will happen if that hissing monster ends up on a throne, as the Sun King has suggested?"

"What are you proposing we do?" asked another. "Plan an assassination of said monster? As though *that* would not cause a disastrous retaliation?"

"At least that would be doing *something* calculated, rather than letting our army sweep aimlessly from one corner of the empire to the other, accruing dreadful losses as it goes."

"The battle in the foothills was not *aimless*, it was—"

"There are other Serpent-kind that have sworn no allegiance, not to the Sun king or any other," Lady Korva pointed out. "They once fought alongside Rook-kind and helped them onto the high throne, didn't they? Why not seek them out and strike a deal with them? They have already reinfected our empire at this point, so we may as well fight dragons with dragons..."

This last suggestion, predictably, caused an uproarious disagreement, and all hope of rational and even-tempered discussion was momentarily lost.

Emrys sighed, leaning back in his chair and absently reaching into one of the pockets of his coat. His hand brushed a slip of parchment deep in that left pocket. It was folded over several times, such that no one in the room had any chance of glimpsing what was written on it, but he clenched it tightly in his fist all the same, completely crushing the contents of it from sight.

It was a list of names. And one had already been marked off: *Tavon Silver, of the Storm Clan.*

But there were dozens more.

All of them were targets. People to siphon more magic from, as needed. It was mostly comprised of criminals in the kingdom who had been sentenced to death; those who were being held in the dungeons in his own palace, along with a few scattered through the prisons of neighboring towns.

The one he had taken his Storm magic from was the only one crossed off thus far. But for the past several days —beginning after that Air-kind spell he'd employed to track Alaya—he had been studying the rest of the names on that list. Studying the information beside those names, the facts so meticulously collected by Lord Feran and his other magic advisors... That information told him who these people were, what clans they belonged to, and the extent of the magic they had been blessed with.

It was how his father had initially started his collections: They had all been criminals in the beginning, not willing sacrificers, and his theft of their magic had been considered a just punishment by most.

Then the definition of *criminal* had shifted as Haben had grown hungrier.

But these names that Emrys had were all guilty of their crimes; he had made certain of it. And he had memorized those crimes along with their names, repeated them over and over to himself until he had no hope of forgetting them. He wondered if his father had ever bothered to do that, even in the beginning.

But did it make a difference?

Did it make you any less a murderer, if you knew the person you were killing?

The answer came to him quickly, every time he asked it of himself: *No. It doesn't.*

But there were other dead that he had to be concerned with, and he feared that dealing with that concern would require a strength and magic that he did not yet possess —but one which he still intended to gain, however he had to do it.

Seven hundred and eighty-six...

That number was only a conservative estimate.

He would ascend to the throne tonight, officially, and after that, he would not be ripped from it without a fight. There were too many things he needed to accomplish from that seat of power; stopping Levant's rampage would only be the beginning.

The arguments continued to build around him, while Emrys accepted a glass of wine poured for him by Lady Korva. She said nothing, nor added anything else to those arguments—because she understood what Emrys himself had recently learned: That it was easier to let his courtiers wear themselves out with their arguing. Let them feel heard, and then they would be more likely to sit quietly and listen to whatever he had to say. He could silence them with a command, but it was a far less efficient use of his energy.

On this occasion, it took at least ten minutes before the group around him trailed into a silence that was punctured only occasionally by quiet grumbles—enough time to allow him to gather his thoughts *and* finish his glass of wine.

He cleared his throat and the grumbling ceased entirely. "We will move the soldiers stationed in Erimarsh and Termarth toward the Gate of the Sun," he informed them. "If necessary, we'll be prepared to battle and secure the border, but that will not be the goal. That gate has seen plenty of amicable meetings between the leaders of Valin and Lumeria before; I will go there myself and give Levant the meeting he desires, and we'll see what comes of it."

That 'gate' was not a manmade gateway, but a natural passage through the middle of the Sinhara Mountains— one that stretched across the Valin Kingdom's southern border and trailed deep into Lumeria. For decades, no wall or fence or other barrier had been erected over this opening, serving as a sign of trust and peace between the two kingdoms.

"You should send an emissary, Highness," urged Captain Helder. "We have no reason to believe that *this* would be an amicable meeting; it's too much of a risk to go yourself."

"I can take care of myself, thank you, Captain." He clenched that list of names in his pocket more tightly.

The room fell momentarily quiet, the group of them clearly wrestling with whether or not they dared to disagree. When the objections finally came, they were directed not at Emrys but at each other, and an entirely new debate roared to life regarding how to prepare for such a summit at the gate.

Then a sudden commotion in the adjacent throne room cut those debates short.

The men and women around the table leapt to their feet. Emrys's personal guards moved from the edges of the room and surrounded him in an instant, preparing to whisk him away to safety. And he was prepared to go with them without argument—until he heard a familiar voice arguing with the guards in the throne room.

Sade.

He was moving an instant later, heading not for the hidden passage in the corner of the room, but for the main exit. And despite the objections lifting behind him, he threw open that main door and rushed through the hallway on the other side, emerging into the throne room with Captain Helder, Lady Korva, and a host of others at his heels.

Sade was there, standing before his throne; he hadn't misheard. But he barely exchanged a glance with her.

Because beside her, being detained by three separate guards, was his Dragon.

After shock came fury at the way those guards were handling her so roughly, and it was fury that finally pushed him to speak: "Unhand her, immediately."

"Highness—"

"*Immediately.*"

The guards loosened their grip. She ripped the rest of the way free, taking a few steps toward him. Their eyes met. She stared at him as though she'd already forgotten the ones who had just been holding her so tightly, and then she was stumbling a few more steps forward, and it happened in an instant—before anyone else could intervene—her arms around his neck, her lips against his, her body curving to him, pressing closer as he instinctively wrapped his arms around her waist.

It wasn't that recently-acquired Storm magic sparking his nerves to life and making his blood run hot, suddenly.

They would pay for this later. In rumors. In lectures. In hostile, disapproving whispers. But at the moment, he didn't care. He only wanted to kiss her. To hold her for as long as he could get away with. And he kept his forehead pressed to hers even when their lips parted, his hands cupping against her face and his gaze locked onto hers.

Footsteps. He closed his eyes against the sound, and when he opened them, he found more guards swarming toward them, led by a furious-looking Lady Isoni who was impossible not to see in his peripheral vision.

He reluctantly lowered his hands back to his sides, sliding his gaze toward Isoni and choosing his words very carefully. "We appear to have gained another guest for the day's upcoming celebrations."

Isoni would refrain from disagreeing with him in front of so many others, he knew.

Later, though, there would be hell to pay.

But for now, her features fell into a much calmer mask, and her voice was as unaffected as his own as she said, "I will personally escort her to a guest room, if you'd like."

Emrys tensed at the suggestion—the thought of Isoni *personally escorting* her was worrying—but Alaya took a step back and gave a subtle bow of her head. It finished shattering the ethereal quality of the moment; Emrys was suddenly, painfully reminded of the meeting he had fled from. He still had important decisions to make and orders to give. Duty was already calling him back.

Again.

And in the meantime, Alaya could handle herself well enough. He knew this to be true, even if he didn't want to spend another second away from her.

"One of the guest rooms on my personal wing," he told Isoni, taking his eyes from Alaya's only for a moment.

Foolish, perhaps, to have her so close when he couldn't be certain that she was really herself. But they had been pushing the narrative that Alaya had had nothing to do with that attack weeks ago, and what better way to convince people that they actually *believed* this?

Perhaps Isoni was thinking this exact thing, because there was surprisingly little venom in her gaze as she said, "Of course."

"And she *will* be a guest at the coronation. See to it that she has everything she needs to prepare for this, and I will be up to meet with her before it begins. We have... much to discuss before then."

A barely-suppressed twitch moved her lips, but the

Bone lady did not object. She gave a low bow, and then she turned and led Alaya from the room.

"Sade. A word," he said, before she could turn to follow Isoni and Alaya.

Sade paused, her gaze darting uncertainly toward the group that had followed Emrys into the throne room.

"As for the rest of you, our discussion is not finished," he said, motioning that group back toward the meeting place they'd charged away from. "I will be back in shortly, after I have a moment of privacy with Lady Sade..."

After a bit of hesitation, they filed away as ordered, the more reluctant driven by cross words and stern glares from Captain Helder. Emrys waited until he heard their distant voices rising in that other room before he spoke again; they were already arguing amongst themselves once more, which hopefully meant that none of them were trying to overhear him.

But he still kept his voice lowered as he stepped toward Sade and asked, "You really could not have found a more *subtle* way to bring her back into this palace?"

"When have we ever been subtle?"

He nearly smiled in spite of himself, but refrained. He should have disapproved of the whole display; he should have been angry at Alaya for the foolish, reckless way she'd kissed him in front of so many.

He *wasn't*.

But he should have been.

"I did what you asked." Sade shrugged. "She's here, and she's safe."

"Safe..."

Sade nodded, though her frown was uncertain. "It's a long, complicated story. A lot for you two to *discuss,* as you said. But in short? Yes. I think *you're* safe from any attacks, this time. And I assume that's what you wanted to have a word about?"

"Yes," he said. And then he forced himself to add: "That will be all, for now. I have to get back to this meeting."

For once, Sade looked sympathetic toward him, instead of gleeful over being able to slip away from those political obligations that weighed him down. "I'll go help protect her from Isoni's wrath. And I'll tell her that you'll be along soon."

He nodded. Thanked her, and walked back to those obligations, wishing that *soon* didn't feel so far away.

CHAPTER 22

ALAYA KEPT HER EYES ON THE PATH BEFORE HER AS SHE CLIMBED staircase after staircase, avoiding the steady stream of gazes that turned her way as she passed people.

So many people.

Sade had warned her that the impending coronation had brought nobles from all corners of the empire to Rykarra, and that most of them likely wouldn't be thrilled to see a Serpent-kind within their midst. Her attack on Emrys weeks ago had been smoothed over, blamed on independent rebels who had supposedly since disappeared, but this had apparently not stopped the rumors that she had been involved. She had already slain one king, after all. Her reputation preceded her.

But she kept marching through the palace all the same. She was finished with running away and hiding, as she had told Ma the day before. Tonight, she was a guest in this palace. She was staying on the same level as its soon-to-be high king. And she was slowly but surely beginning to accept that she might eventually take her place as his queen.

After what felt like an impossibly long trek, Isoni finally stopped next to a door that, unlike many of the magic-sealed doors in this palace, had a proper lock. The rattle and clink of a key and the slight creak of the door's hinge pulled Alaya from her thoughts of future kings and crowns and back to the present moment.

Isoni had not spoken to Alaya during the entire walk to this room, and she did not speak now; she only moved stiffly from one side of the room to the other, taking blankets from trunks, yanking back curtains, and tilting open windows.

The light that flooded in through those windows revealed a room so beautiful that it nearly took Alaya's breath away. She'd half-expected Isoni to try and lock her in a dungeon cell despite Emrys's orders. The marble floors, silk wallpaper, and priceless artwork that instead greeted her made her head spin; it had been some time since she had walked the floors of this residence—not including its dungeons—and she'd forgotten how overly-extravagant most of the upper rooms in this palace were.

As Isoni turned away and started to unfold and inspect linens, Alaya couldn't help running her fingers along one of the room's two polished and shining dressing tables. She wasn't sure what sort of wood it was made out of, she only knew that it looked expensive.

She was reaching for the silver tin on the dresser's center, curious about its contents, when Isoni suddenly snatched her wrist and stopped her.

"Why have you come back here?" Isoni demanded.

Alaya had expected to be attacked by such questions, so her response was quick and fierce: "Because I am going to help Emrys stabilize this empire and put an end to its wars."

"You?" Isoni laughed. "You and your power are some of the most *unstable* atrocities I've ever encountered in the three kingdoms."

"That power may be the only thing that can stop the Sun King and the ones working alongside him." She jerked free of Isoni's grip. "So I suggest you make sure you're on the right side of that power before it's too late."

"Are you *threatening* me, little Serpent girl?"

"Don't act shocked," Alaya said, squaring her shoulders and refusing to step back, even as Isoni moved uncomfortably close to her, "or as if you haven't been threatening *me* from the very beginning. Did you think I had *forgotten* about that night when you threatened to raze my home village to the ground if I did not cooperate with you?"

"And yet your village still stands," Isoni said. "Even though you failed to do as I asked you to. So it seems we're *both* full of hollow threats."

"You don't know if mine are hollow or not. Not yet."

"I have a feeling," Isoni replied, drily.

"I didn't fail, either," Alaya snapped. "I killed the high king, didn't I?"

Isoni studied her for a moment, her lip curling, before yielding with a huff: "Yes. I suppose you did manage it in the end. But not under the circumstances we had agreed upon."

"Details," Alaya snarled.

"Rather *important* details, I'd say."

For the moment, it seemed as if the two of them had reached an impasse, as Isoni turned away once more and busied herself with reorganizing the glass bottles of perfume and the tin containers on the closest dressing table. But after a minute, she paused, staring blankly down at the bottle in her hand, and she said, "Because it was not supposed to end up this way, you know. Emrys was not supposed to have taken the throne so soon. It should have been his mother, first. He should have been older before..." She trailed off, shaking her head. There had been something odd in her voice toward the end.

A...*vulnerability*, almost.

Alaya was certain she had imagined it. All the same, she softened a bit of the snarl from her own voice as she replied: "Well, *I* believe he is more than capable of handling that throne. I'm sorry you don't feel that way."

Isoni sat the bottle back down with a loud *thud* and braced both hands against the table, still not looking at her. "Don't assume you understand my feelings."

It was there again—that vulnerability edging the

words as they seethed from Isoni's mouth. Alaya was certain of it this time.

A sudden pounding on the door interrupted them. Isoni went over and yanked it open to find Sade waiting on the other side.

"You're needed downstairs," Sade informed her.

Alaya still couldn't see Isoni's face, but now she assumed it was scowling.

Sade squeezed her way inside, maneuvering well outside of Isoni's reach before nodding back toward the door. "A certain Lord Graylock is requesting to speak with whomever is in charge of what he referred to as *'the dreadful servants running this palace'*. That would be you, wouldn't it?"

"It would." There was a hint of suspicion in Isoni's words. But ultimately, she didn't question Sade's message; she only turned back to Alaya one final time and said, "The ceremony is only a few hours away, now. Emrys insists that you attend, so you *will* attend, but first, let's establish a few rules, shall we?"

"Rules?"

"You will not make a scene. You will be on your best behavior. You will do nothing to fuel the rumors already rampant in this palace, and you will not even *speak* to the high king unless he speaks to you first."

Alaya glared at her, but she managed to swallow her protests.

Just nod. Just agree...

"Lord Graylock seemed very adamant that you hurry down to him," Sade said, loudly.

Isoni kept her gaze leveled on Alaya's and her voice low as she asked, "Do we have an understanding?"

Alaya inhaled slowly through her nose. Exhaled even slower. She managed a nod—mostly because she wanted the uncomfortable conversation to be over with.

"Very good. I will send servants to deal with..." She paused, glancing up and down at Alaya's travel-worn attire and the tangled strands of hair framing her face. "*This*," she concluded, gesturing over the entirety of her. And then she left without another word, locking the door behind her.

"There is no Lord Graylock." Sade grinned, flopping down onto the bed.

"I had a feeling," Alaya said, returning that grin.

"It's turning into my favorite way to pass the time in this palace—finding new ways to make her mad."

"I'm glad you've found an amusing way to occupy yourself while you're here."

"She's deserved every bit of it," Sade insisted, crossing her arms behind her head and making herself comfortable against the mountain of pillows. "Actually, she deserves worse." Her tone remained light and amused, but her eyes closed, and the way they clenched made Alaya wonder what her friend was truly thinking about. There were plenty of unpleasant memories of Isoni that could have been making Sade's brow furrow the way it was.

Alaya wandered toward the table where Isoni had only just stood. She picked up the same bottle that the Bone-kind lady had held, running her fingers along its flower-shaped stopper while she lost herself in thought. When she set it down a minute later, her hands came away smelling of soft powder and roses. "I want to agree," she said, "but then again, I don't know. I want to hate her, but..."

"But?"

"It's not going to help anything, creating more division between us and the high-ranking people in this palace."

"I'm not going to forgive her for the lies she told and the awful magic she worked over my father."

"I don't—"

"She's done terrible things."

"So have I," Alaya said, gently. "And so have you. And I forgave you."

"Yes, but you're a stronger person than me," Sade said with a shrug.

Alaya made a face. "That's debatable."

Sade rolled over onto her side and drew her knees to her chest.

The silence that stretched on from that point was long and uncomfortable, until Alaya could no longer take it. "Anyway," she blurted out, "it's tricky however we look at it, isn't it? She and Emrys are close, however complicated their relationship... He once referred to her as his 'grumpy old aunt'." There had actually been a few more colorful descriptors sprinkled into Emrys's assessment of the woman, but Alaya didn't repeat them now. "Family, in other words," she said, "and the only 'family' that he really has left."

"Yeah. Good luck marrying into that."

Her cheeks burned, and a half-lie muttered through her lips: "I haven't made plans to marry anybody."

"No? I thought it was more or less a given, at this point."

Alaya rolled her eyes at the teasing tone of her friend's voice. "There are a few more pressing matters to attend to first, I think."

"...Good point," Sade conceded, rolling onto her back once more. "Such as the trip you're planning to the Sun Palace. Which, when are you planning on bringing *that* up with him?"

"Not until this coronation ceremony is over with, at least. I believe bringing it up before then might count as *causing a scene*. And I'm not allowed to do that this evening, if you remember."

Sade nodded in agreement before closing her eyes and appearing, at least for the moment, as if she were considering taking a nap. "This bed is ridiculously comfortable," she yawned. "I shouldn't be enjoying it so much, or looking forward to attending this extravagant evening as a *guest*." She opened her eyes and stared thoughtfully at the coffered ceiling for a moment before adding, "I remember the last time we were here together, and how disgusted I was by the wealth they flaunted over us..."

"It's jarring, after having gone back to Vanish just a day ago," Alaya agreed. "But it will be different in the future. We'll see to it that villages like Vanish don't go hungry while the royalty grows fat in this palace, won't we?"

Sade nodded. Neither of them said what Alaya was certain they were both thinking: That all of this was assuming that a future—*any* future—actually came to pass.

There were now only twelve days left until her nineteenth year. Until the darkness that even the Stars could not see beyond would supposedly descend. She felt oddly separated from the prophecy in this room, surrounded by all of these fineries and towering high above the city in the distance.

But in her heart, she knew that it was only a matter of time before they would have to face the darkness.

It was at least two hours more before servants arrived to 'deal' with her appearance. At this point, Sade left to go to her own room and prepare, and Alaya was ushered into the adjoining washroom by five different maidservants.

The bath was pleasant. Warm water scented with flower petals and blended with scrubbing salts, just soothing enough that she managed not to think about the torture that she knew she was being ushered into next; a dress had been procured for her, but there were alterations that needed to be made, and then there was the matter of her hair...

By this point, she had been through enough similar ordeals to know that it was easiest just to relax and accept the way they poked and prodded her, wrestling her wild waves into an elegant crown of braids. That she shouldn't complain about the paint they used on her eyes and lips, or the stiff undergarments that limited her weapon-swinging abilities, or the powders they perfumed her with. It wasn't as if she hadn't endured worse things.

The servants were much kinder than Isoni had been, at least, if still a bit stand-offish. It was the same brand of initial uncertainty and fear that she was used to enduring. Alaya tried to be as friendly as possible, and after a few minutes, they at least stopped flinching whenever she shifted her stance.

One of them—a young girl with shockingly blue eyes and a violet streak dyed into her black hair—even met her gaze a few times; usually to kindly ask her to be still, lest she accidentally stab her with one of the needles or pins she was using to make alterations. This girl was Jewel-kind. And Alaya recognized her, she believed, from the last time she had been in this palace.

How *different* this moment was, compared to back then.

But the end result was similar; she ended up staring into a tall, ornate mirror, hardly recognizing herself at first, while the servants gathered around her and admired their work.

Her accessories were much simpler than the jewelry they had decorated her with that last time she was here, when Haben had intended to sacrifice her; there was only a necklace with a tear-drop diamond hanging from its silver chain and two small, similarly-shaped earrings. They left the ring that Emrys had given her as well, though only after cleaning it several times more than what Alaya felt was necessary; they were studying it, she suspected. And judging by the whispered Jewel-kind words and occasional giggles, they recognized it, and they knew who it had once belonged to.

They didn't seem to be against him giving her this gift, as Isoni was; their gossipy tones did not sound unkind, merely curious. Or perhaps even a bit excited. Which made Alaya feel embarrassed—albeit warmly so.

She kept her gaze on her reflection.

The strapless gown looked deceptively plain until she moved, at which point the subtle colors shimmered and the different shades of them became more visible. What appeared to be an ivory dress at first glance actually consisted of various threads of white and grey that became gradually darker towards the floor-sweeping hem. The soft colors shouldn't have been so boldly beautiful, but they were; those bottom waves of fabric made her think of grey rain clouds, with each curve warmly edged in the light from a sun they were covering.

The servants watched as she lifted the sides of the dress and twirled it about, admiring the way the fabric moved and fell back to elegantly hug her body.

"It's lovely," Alaya assured them, which caused a few genuine smiles to break out.

"His Majesty picked out the gown."

"Did he?" Alaya felt her face growing hot again.

"Excellent taste," one of the servants said.

"And on such short notice," chirped another.

"Our young king can get anything he wants, can't he?"

The blue-eyed girl shushed them and swatted them away, then turned back and made a few more tiny alterations before declaring the job finished. "It suits you well," she told Alaya, straightening and sticking her pins into the cushion she'd balanced on the dressing table.

Alaya felt a sudden kinship with this young girl that she couldn't readily explain. She wanted to ask her name —to ask more than that. She could almost envision it: a future spent as a queen, with young women such as this keeping her company. And she wanted to get to know that woman. But a soft knock on the door interrupted before they could get any better acquainted; the girl went to the door and opened it.

Emrys was waiting on the other side. He spoke no orders. He didn't need to; a single, meaningful glance in Alaya's direction, and the servants bowed low and then filed out quickly, leaving the two of them alone.

He wasted no time in picking up where they had left off in the throne room. His arms wrapped around her and pulled her close, and his lips crashed over hers. It was not the same sort of shocked, somewhat reserved kiss they had shared in that throne room. It was deep and full of a demanding, starved passion.

But there was still a desperation clinging to it; a sense that it couldn't last as long as they wanted it to.

It lasted long enough that Alaya felt a bit dizzy when he finally pulled away. She took his hand and tried to calm her breathing enough to casually ask: "Well? How do I look?"

He lifted that hand he held and stepped around her, studying her, moving almost as if they had begun a slow, graceful dance. "Like a queen," he concluded.

She had *felt* like a queen while those servants stood around her, but for some reason, hearing him say it so earnestly made her resolve wither a bit, and her voice was quieter as she asked: "You would still call me your queen, even after what I did to you?"

"Yes." There was no hesitation in the reply. But when he spoke again after a moment, he was frowning. "But Dragon, you know I have to ask..." He let go of her hand, and a troubled expression briefly darkened his face. "What happened that night at the inn? And what happens now? With you, and with..."

"I can explain that. I *will* explain that. It's just..." She glanced toward the window, to the sight of the sun setting and turning the palace roofs a fiery shade of orange.

He nodded slowly, reluctant but understanding, and he finished the thought for her: "It's going to take more time than we have at the moment."

"Yes. But I swear I've found answers, and I don't want to keep any of these things a secret from you. Not anymore."

"Nor stab me anymore, I hope?"

She grimaced. "Nor do I want to stab you," she agreed. "So, after the ceremony tonight...no more secrets."

"And no more stabbing."

"Correct."

"Those seem like good rules for a relationship."

"We should have established them earlier, really."

"Would have saved us a lot of trouble."

"Precisely what I was thinking." She smiled, and she allowed herself to exhale the tension that had been gathering in her shoulders. She let her eyes roam as well, fully taking in the sight of the man standing before her.

The elegant clothing he wore had been made for no one except him; it was finely tailored to every muscular line of his tall frame. There were marks painted across his face, indicating his status and the clan he came from. A silver circlet sat atop his soft, dark waves of hair—a smaller, temporary symbol of power until the real one took its place. The hardships of the past months had carved a certain darkness into his expression that made him look older, but his eyes were still the same brilliant shade of forest green, and still shining with the same youthful curiosity they'd held when he'd first met her gaze all those months ago.

And there was no doubt, staring at him now, that he was meant to be a ruler of this empire.

A corner of his lips curved upward as she stared at him, and in that moment, Alaya was quite certain he could have ruled over anything he wanted to.

"Well? How do *I* look?" he asked.

She swallowed hard, hoping the flush in her cheeks was not as obvious as it felt. "Like a king," she said.

"Excellent. Hopefully I'll fool everyone downstairs, too."

She sighed softly at this, a wistful smile playing at her lips as she turned back to her reflection. "*You* don't have to worry about fooling anybody. As for me...say what you will, but I think I look a bit...strange. Particularly after weeks of sleeping in the dirt and huddling away in caves. And it always feels like a bit of a betrayal to the places I came from, when I play dress up like this."

"If it makes you feel any better, I made certain the seamstress was paid very handsomely for that dress."

"It...does. Somewhat."

He took her hand and tugged her back around to face him. "I can't promise you peace," he said. "I can't promise you that this evening is going to go smoothly for you, without any objections from my court. So at least let me lavish you with gifts—in exchange for you not keeping secrets or stabbing me anymore, let's say."

"Bribery." She glanced up at him from underneath raised brows. "I think what you're suggesting is called *bribery*."

"Of course. Isn't that the most effective way to get someone to love you?"

"Or to not stab you, at least."

He laughed softly, and then planted a kiss on her forehead. "I have to go. I'll see you downstairs."

She nodded, trying to smile in return—but the weight of everything she was keeping from him made this nearly impossible.

It seemed he misunderstood her frown, assuming she was nervous only about the upcoming evening and the objections she would surely be walking into, because he squeezed her hand and added, "It will be fine. Just...try to blend."

"Oh, I've been very good at that recently, so no problem there."

He laughed again, taking her face in his hands and kissing her one last time on her lips—a slow, lingering kiss that caused a shiver that lasted even once he had left the room.

She stood alone for a long time after, eventually turning to stare into the mirror once more.

Twelve days.

After the ceremony, she truly did intend to tell him everything. About the prophecy. The darkness. The pieces of herself that were still scattered, and the things she would have to do to finish gathering them. Things that made her a questionable choice for a queen, at best— while meanwhile, he seemed so confident, so certain, so unshakable in his new role as high king that it was almost intimidating.

Was she fooling herself, thinking she could truly reign at his side?

"Either way, I will not hide," she muttered to her reflection. "I will not hide."

She backed away from the mirror and started for the ballroom, repeating these words silently to herself as she went.

CHAPTER 23

Alaya had lost track of time.

It was tradition for the passing of the Rook crown to take place in front of *only* Rook eyes—in a private ceremony. One that lasted hours, apparently. Too long for Alaya to keep counting the minutes, as she had started to do when she first walked into this ballroom and joined the host of others who were waiting, preparing themselves for the eventual arrival of their new high king.

The party in that ballroom had not started in earnest yet—it wouldn't until the king arrived—but there was still plenty of food and drink to be had.

Sade passed the time by sampling most of it. She fit in surprisingly well amongst the other partygoers, smiling and drawing them toward her with the more outlandish stories they'd grown up hearing around Vanish's campfires. It made Alaya glad to see it.

At least one of them was adjusting to life in this palace.

The temptation to join Sade, to drink until she felt as if she *was* adjusting, was very real. But for the moment, Alaya accepted only a single glass of a dry, bitter-tasting wine. She clutched it tightly as she walked the room and studied the artwork and other decor around her.

People moved out of her path as she came close to them, but it was more subtle than the way they had tripped over themselves to get away from her the last time she was here; she couldn't help but wonder if the new king had anything to do with that—if he had warned people about mistreating her. A few of them even offered a slight bow as they stepped aside, which suggested that they at least partially believed the rumors that she was destined to be his queen.

But the reverence didn't feel particularly genuine, and soon, she found herself wishing she could disappear, if only for a moment.

After wandering for a bit, she remembered the place she had disappeared to before—that quiet, tucked-away alcove where Emrys had first talked to her. They had studied a painting together; a depiction of a dragon being thrown from the heavens, hurtling toward ground that was covered in writhing snakes.

But when she made her way to the spot where that painting should have been, she found that it was gone.

Her chest felt tight, suddenly, her heart swelling as she stared up at the painting of a starlight-drenched mountain that had taken its place. She swept her gaze around the tiny alcove, briefly wondering if she was mistaken, if she had somehow gotten confused and ended up in the wrong place. But no; because there was the image of Amara, the Gateway to the Middle-Heavens, that they had studied after that portrayal of the dragon's fall...

She looked back to that newly-hung mountain painting. But before she could inspect it closer, the sound of drums, and of a voice rising with a declaration, drew her attention.

She stepped out from the tucked-away corner and moved toward the sound along with the rest of the room. Most of that room had trained their eyes on the set of doors at the top of a winding staircase.

Those doors opened, revealing Emrys and several of his closest advisors, and Alaya froze.

A new memory slid into the front of her mind—yet another one of that last night she had spent in this room; she distinctly remembered the sight of High King Haben walking through those same doors. Descending those same steps. She remembered how he had glittered with all of his jewels, and how he had paused before reaching the bottom—so that he towered above his subjects and could more easily offer his rings for them to kiss.

But Emrys did not flash his jewelry, and he did not stop above anyone; he stepped all the way down to the floor, moving easily through the crowd even as they all clamored to be the first to greet him, to speak with him.

Alaya felt her breaths growing tighter once more, her

heart thudding in its deeper, expanding rhythm as she watched over him. He was swarmed with people, yet he somehow seemed aware of every single one of them. He turned no one away. It was another moment of peace, of certainty about some things, at least: She had no doubt that Emrys would make a better king than his father had.

And she had absolutely no doubt that she was in love with him.

But after a few moments, she turned away, trying not to look in his direction any more than she had to. Because every time she caught a glimpse of him, it seemed as if he was more firmly entrenched in conversation with yet another noble-looking audience. As if he was sinking more and more deeply into this world that she didn't belong to.

It was strange.

She had helped put him on the throne, and he was so close to her...and yet, it felt as if the two of them were on separate islands, each aware of the other but unable to cross the monster-infested waters to reunite.

Her mind raced with uncertainty and fear about their future, but she refused to let it show.

She did not approach Emrys, did not join that crowd of people eager to offer their well-wishes and bow at his feet, but she would not cower in the corner anymore, either. Instead, she decided to move through the crowded ballroom with all the grace and authority of someone who belonged there.

People continued to step aside for her. And she turned

more and more heads in her direction—whether because of those rumors about her, or the dress she wore and that new confidence she moved with, or maybe some combination of all three—and soon a few of the bravest and most intrigued among the guests approached her and made small talk. A few of the more intoxicated ones even asked her to dance. As the night wore on—and the wine began to flow more freely and Alaya slowly sipped away her inhibitions—she accepted more than one of those dances.

Hours later, she was not *drunk*, but she was growing careless. Careless enough that she made the mistake of letting her eyes wander in the direction of the high king. And once they landed on him, she couldn't bring herself to immediately look away.

He eventually tilted his face in her direction, as if sensing her eyes on him, and Alaya quickly averted her gaze. She could still feel his stare burning towards her as she turned and strode purposefully toward a table against the far wall. She settled into a chair at that table, and it was several minutes later before she chanced a quick search for him. She spotted him dancing with a beautiful woman in a stunning green dress.

Sade promptly sat down in the chair directly across from her, blocking Alaya's view of the woman in the green dress. On purpose, it felt like. "First of all," Sade said, in between sips from the silver goblet in her hand, "you're prettier than she is."

"Are you drunk?"

"No. I'm smart."

Alaya scoffed.

"Smart enough to see that you're doubting your place in this room. In this palace. And that you fully expect Emrys to run off with some other woman by the end of the night."

"I wasn't worried about that. I wasn't even thinking about such ridiculous things."

Sade arched an eyebrow.

Alaya took another sip from the goblet of wine, concentrating for a minute on the feel of it burning a bitter path down her throat. "She's not exactly horrible to look at though, is she?"

"*Second* of all," Sade continued, ignoring Alaya's question, "I don't think you need to worry. For all of the misgivings I've had about your Rook, I don't doubt his loyalty to you."

"I'm not worried." Alaya sighed, picking silently at the setting that held the stone of her ring. "But just out of curiosity...who is she?"

"Lady Korva," Sade said after a reluctant pause. "Her father is Lord Marius, the ruler of the Nyres Province—though she's apparently very close to taking over as ruler in his stead. They're Ice-kind, and they command a very impressive army of those kind... She's been cozying up to Emrys these past weeks, yes, but I honestly think it's more political than anything. She wants to make certain her province—and all that it's done for Rook-kind—isn't forgotten in this new reign. But she doesn't strike me as the king-stealing type."

Alaya was unconvinced. "But she makes more sense, doesn't she? Her—or any of those other noblewomen he's been dancing with all night. Women with armies and power and status at least similar to his own."

"Why do you care if it makes sense? There isn't much about the last few months that has 'made sense' for us," Sade pointed out.

"No. But let's be honest: I am out of place here. It would be selfish for me to insist on staying by his side and making *him* appear out of place for this role he's taken on."

"You have more power than any of the women in this room. Or the men, for that matter."

"But not the sort of power the people in this room worship. Do you honestly believe they will ever accept me as their queen?"

Sade exhaled a frustrated sigh, but she didn't seem able to come up with an immediate argument against this. She sipped her drink in silence.

"I thought it might be different," Alaya mused, "if I could gain control over myself and my powers. But I forgot about that hierarchy of clans. It's still in place, and I am still very much at the bottom, particularly in this palace." Her voice threatened to crack with the words, but she swallowed hard and continued: "But I can still work with him, can't I? I can still help him from a distance. That's all that matters, in the end. We can still do what we set out to do. And once it's done, maybe I can disappear. Perhaps I'll go north; I've heard the Kethran Empire is much kinder to the unmarked, and I can still pass for one of those. You can come with me."

Sade frowned at the suggestion, but she still didn't speak.

"It's only one possibility, of course—and it's assuming we can actually make it through all of the uncertainty and bloodshed, and that we can stop all of *this* empire's wars first." Alaya shrugged and angled her chair so she wouldn't accidentally glance in the direction where Emrys was still dancing.

She didn't want to let it bother her. He was merely playing his role, as expected. There was nothing more than politics between him and that woman—between him and *any* of the other women he'd danced with. She believed that. And yet...

Sade turned her chair as well, keeping her company. A silent, thoughtful sort of company that didn't question even the more ridiculous parts of Alaya's ramblings and uncertainties.

Alaya stared at the glass in her hands, occasionally swirling its sparkling contents and studying its bubbles as she forced away the tears burning the corners of her eyes. Once she finally felt confident that she could make it across the room without those tears escaping, she cleared her throat and said, "I think I'm going up to my room. I want to sleep."

Sade didn't object, though she looked like she

wanted to.

Alaya stood, not giving her a chance to speak, and she was straightening her skirts and preparing to make a dignified exit when she felt a hand on her arm. She turned. A sudden weakness struck her knees, but she didn't lose her balance, not even for an instant—because the High King of Sundolia did not let go of her arm.

"Dance with me," he said.

No. The rejection sounded adamant enough in her mind. *No, I can't. We shouldn't.* But it was always harder to follow that logical voice in her thoughts when Emrys was looking at her the way he was doing now.

She swallowed several times to clear the lump building in her throat, before she said: "People might find it...distasteful."

"I didn't care about that on the night we met, and I certainly don't care about it now."

"You should care."

"But I don't." He reached out his free hand to her.

She stared at it. For all the changes that had occurred since their last dance, this still felt dangerous in so many of the same ways. Still taboo. Impossible. And yet, she still handed her emptied glass to Sade, her gaze remaining fixed on the prince's—no, *the king's.*

And then she reached back.

He pulled her toward the middle of the room. The crowd parted for them, and Alaya tried not to let their stares bother her.

"I have to be honest with you," Emrys said, his voice

just above a whisper, "I've been hoping you would rush over to me, throw your arms around my neck, and kiss me again, like you did in the throne room earlier."

"I was told not to make a scene."

"Isoni told you that?" He phrased it as a question, but the irritation that flickered through his eyes made it obvious that he already knew the answer.

Alaya gave a noncommittal shrug.

"She'll...come around."

Alaya stared past him, at the tapestry on the wall behind him, at the gilded staircase he'd descended, at the statue of the Rook God, Anga, at the bottom of that staircase—at *anything* she could find aside from his face. "But what if she doesn't? And it isn't just her; we are asking a *lot* of people to come around to the idea of us dancing together, aren't we? I want us to unite people; but what if all we're doing is tearing them further apart?"

He considered her words for a moment as he swept her along, spinning her effortlessly away before drawing her back to face him and lacing his fingers through hers. "And what *else* do you want?" he asked. "What if you stripped away all of the politics? All of the nonsense about destinies and clans and everything else, and you were just left with *us*?"

"I..."

"What do you want, Dragon? Right now?"

Right now, she wanted to kiss him.

And she could tell he wanted to kiss her. He was very close, suddenly, his interlocked fingers squeezing her hand and pulling her nearer, inch by inch, until their noses almost touched. She willed her gaze to slide out of focus, to blur away the tempting way his lips parted as he awaited her reply.

"It doesn't matter what I want," she whispered.

"It matters to me."

"...I should go." She tried, very hard, to keep away the bitterness that threatened to overwhelm her words. "I think it might have been a mistake, coming back to this palace so soon."

"No it wasn't."

"It was certainly a mistake, dancing with you like this—"

"*We are not a mistake.*" His voice had become too harsh, too loud, and he realized it immediately, judging by the way his expression soured. He drew her closer to him—as if he could protect her from the stares that were suddenly growing bolder, and the whispers that were growing louder—and then he pulled her away from the center of the floor. He didn't stop until they reached the very edge of the room.

They were much more secluded now, but Alaya still heard someone hissing the word *Serpent*, along with what she was all but certain were insults in the Rook-kind language. Her face burned with embarrassment. Emrys started toward the speaker, but Alaya grabbed the sleeve of his coat and held him until he managed to take a calming breath and turn back to her.

"The night was going perfectly," she muttered.

"Everyone in this room was clearly in love with you, thrilled at your taking the throne, *why* did you have to ruin it by insisting on dancing with the likes of me? *Why?*"

"Everyone in this room is in love with me," he repeated. "Everyone?"

He was no longer looking at any of those other people.

He was only looking at her, his gaze narrowed in a way that temporarily stole her breath and made lying feel impossible.

"Everyone." She had meant to angrily snap out the word, but it came out sounding pained and breathless. She had her pounding heart to thank for that, she supposed.

Stupid, stupid heart.

"I should go," she said again. "I'm tired, I—"

"You owe me explanations," he said, snatching her by the wrist before she could step away. "We agreed to that much, didn't we? And I don't care if you are second-guessing your decision to return here; you will not leave this palace until you have *given* me those explanations."

It was a testament to her growing control over her power, that the wall behind him did not begin to shiver and crack with her irritation. "Is that an *order?*" she asked.

"Yes. It is." His teeth clenched with the words. "And from the high king, no less."

Their standoff lasted only a moment more before she caved beneath his smoldering glare. "Fine," she said. "But I *am* finished with this party."

She jerked her arm from his grip. He let her go

without protest. A calm mask had slid over his face—but she knew him well enough to recognize the irritation still simmering just beneath the surface, twisting his lips and twitching his jaw just enough to set this expression apart from his truly calm one.

He summoned a servant with a wave of his hand, and he spoke a few clipped sentences in the Rook-kind language before pushing that servant toward her. "An escort for you."

Did he not trust her to walk the halls of this palace on her own?

To not *stay,* after she had promised she would?

The thought irritated her—though not nearly as much as the people who were closing in around them now. The woman in the green dress was among them, and Alaya did not miss the concerned expression that flitted over this *Lady Korva's* face as she drew near.

"I will be up to speak with you as soon as I am able to get away," Emrys said, his gaze locking on Alaya's once more.

"No need to rush," she replied, coldly. "It would appear that you have plenty of people to keep you company in the meantime."

He looked as though he desperately wanted to reply to this, but, after a quick glance at all the subjects surrounding him, he held his tongue.

She turned and headed for the nearest exit, walking too quickly for the tears shimmering in her eyes to have a chance to fall.

CHAPTER 24

Alaya's escort insisted on bringing her to Emrys's chambers to wait, instead of to her own guest room. She protested, but her complaints fell on deaf ears; the high king's dwelling was much better guarded, the escort insisted. Much quieter. Much safer.

It also would be a considerably more difficult room for her to sneak out of—and she strongly suspected that this was the *real* reason she had been taken to his room, despite his servant's denials about the matter.

It was infuriating at first. But as the minutes ticked by, the spikes of her anger smoothed and eventually became only a low hum of irritation in the back of her mind. And soon she wondered if even *that* was being fair; because she had escaped him last time—bolted away and left him with nothing except questions and bleeding wounds.

So could she truly blame him for wanting to keep her under his strongest lock and key, this time?

And as prisons went, this one was comfortable, at least. Servants filed in and out constantly, to 'check on her'—to forever keep her in their sights and make sneaking away impossible, in other words.

But at least some of them brought cakes and pastries and wine with them.

She ate and drank her fill of those delicacies, and she made herself at home, reclining first on the overstuffed settee that cradled her so deeply she thought she might never be able to climb out, before moving to the bed that was large enough to essentially warrant its own ruling council. She stayed on top of the neatly-drawn covers, but made a fortress around herself using the ample amount of pillows piled at the head of that bed. Those pillows felt silky and cool as she buried herself amongst them.

She had only been in his room once before, and only because she had broken in. On that night, they had fought, and then she fled through the window and across the rooftops. She hadn't really had time to take in the scenery. So she did it now; she counted the books on the shelves—five different shelves—until her eyes blurred and lost track. Many of those books had little slips of paper or other makeshift page-markers in them.

She noted the painting of his mother holding him, hanging in the center of the far wall; he couldn't have been more than five-years-old when he posed for that picture. His face was far rounder—downright chubby, honestly—but his eyes were easily recognizable. They really did look exactly like his mother's.

In one corner of the room was a small desk, messy with opened books and scraps of parchment and pens. In the opposite corner, a table that held a much neater assortment of objects was set up. It was an odd grouping of things that she assumed he'd been studying—everything from flowers in small dishes, to a small-scale model of a dragon's skeleton, to what appeared to be an ancient instrument of some sort.

Her eyelids were growing heavy. Her thoughts were oddly peaceful, nudging her toward rest. She couldn't remember the last time she had been relaxed enough to *want* to sleep, rather than simply so exhausted that she *needed* to sleep. And then she realized...

It was because she felt safe here.

Here, of all places; inside this palace full of the ones who should have been her enemy. The palace whose former ruler had burned and ravaged so much of her life. But it didn't smell of smoke or blood or anything else that made her think of the fallen king; it smelled of *Emrys*. Of a subtle warm and earthy scent that, she now saw, at least partly came from the incense burning in a tray by the washroom door. The pillows surrounding her were scented with something that she had breathed in from him before, as well; something that reminded her of rain-soaked moss.

She didn't remember drifting off as she breathed in these peaceful things, but then a sudden *thud* startled her awake. Her eyes snapped open to find the light in the room had been dimmed, and that somebody had draped a thick wool blanket over her. She sat up, rubbing her eyes as they adjusted, and she saw Emrys standing in front of the armoire on the other side of the room.

"Sorry I woke you," he said, keeping his back to her as he fought with the buttons on his coat.

"Sorry I fell asleep. It's been some time since I slept in an actual bed, and this one is more comfortable than it has any right to be."

He nodded. Gave up on the coat's fastenings with a soft, frustrated sigh, and then walked to the hall door, opened it, and summoned a few of the guards patrolling the hallway. He spoke to them in the Rook-kind language, and those guards glanced in Alaya's direction more than once before the conversation ended. Then they bowed and set off down the hall.

"What did you say to them?" she asked, after he had closed the door.

He undid the last buttons of his coat and then slid it off, tossing it onto the nearby chair and not bothering to pick it up when it slid off onto the floor. It was oddly endearing, the messy, careless act from this man who was now officially the most powerful person in the entire empire. "I told them you were staying with me tonight, and to collect some things from your guest room. Unless you'd rather go back to that other room?"

She kept her eyes on that fallen coat. "No. Here is good, I suppose."

"You suppose?" He huffed out a laugh that didn't sound amused in the slightest.

"I wasn't really given a choice about coming here; I assumed I didn't have any real choice about leaving."

"You always have a choice. I'm not in the business of holding hostages." His gaze burned into hers for a moment before he jerked his head toward the door. "Leave if you want."

She breathed in deep, inhaling that earth and rain scent and trying to get back to that safe place she'd fallen asleep in. "I don't want to leave," she said softly.

He studied her for a moment, as if waiting for her to change her mind. Then he walked away without comment, disappearing into the washroom for several minutes.

She stayed on the bed. She could hear him rattling through cabinets, splashing water—and rearranging everything he could to avoid coming out and talking to her, it seemed like.

"And I didn't want to leave you earlier, either," she called, after she finally heard him go still and silent. "It's... it's not *you* that I want to leave. It's just everything else. It's..."

He reappeared, a towel in hand, wiping at what remained of the marks that had been painted on his face. The ties of his shirt were undone. It hung loosely open, and some of that water she'd heard him splashing had soaked the front of it.

So messy.

She kept her gaze on the relative safety of his face— not his partially-soaked chest—as he walked over and sat on the edge of the bed. He still didn't speak. He only balanced his elbows against his knees and leaned forward in a more relaxed position, his head bowed in thought. He was waiting for her to explain, she could tell.

But she wasn't sure where to start.

She decided on the easiest truth first: "I feel out of place here. I'm afraid I'll always feel out of place here. And I suppose in the grand scheme of things, it doesn't matter much—I should be focusing on the bigger wars around us. On bigger problems."

He looked back at her, his lips parting several times as he clearly tried to find words.

A knock at the door interrupted them; the servants who had been sent to fetch her things had returned.

While Emrys sat at his desk and flipped distractedly through a book, she went and changed out of her dress in the privacy of the adjoining room. The night gown she'd been provided with was nearly as luxurious as the dress; it was simpler, and shorter, but the material felt equally expensive—soft as velvet but a much lighter, more comfortable weight that hugged her just tightly enough to hint at the curves underneath.

When she reemerged into the bedroom, Emrys had changed as well. He wore only a pair of casual, loosely-fitting pants, and he was reclining amongst the pillows she'd piled up on the bed. He'd brought the book with him. He was still studying it, the tip of a pen poised against one of its pages and his eyes narrowed in concentration.

She stood in the doorway, watching him. She waited until the servants had all left before she spoke again. "Do you want to know why I really left the party earlier?"

He slowly closed the book and glanced up at her without a word.

"Because I was jealous."

"...Jealous?"

She hugged her arms against herself, wandering closer to the bed. "I'm not usually the jealous type, I just..."

"*Jealous.*" He looked as though he was about to laugh.

"Is it really so funny? Given your status, your wealth, your...well, *everything you have.* Everything that so many of the ones in that party had, and I have almost *none* of those things, and I—"

He was honestly laughing at her now, chuckling softly to himself as he crawled to the edge of the bed and took her hand before she had a chance to storm away from him again.

"It is *not* funny."

"Yes. It is." He pulled her closer, taking the hand he held and pressing it to his chest. "Because you nearly killed me, just a few weeks ago."

Her hand splayed across his bare chest, and numbness tingled through her as her fingertips brushed the latest scars she'd left on him. "I'm sorry about that. I'm so, so sorry, but I don't understand how that..."

"Let me finish," he interrupted, his tone a bit softer, a bit more serious. "You nearly killed me—and I still insisted on letting you sleep in my bed. I still *want* you to sleep in this bed. With me. To be tangled in the same sheets, sharing the same pillows." He glanced at the makeshift fortress that she'd built. "Which, I like that you've made a fort out of those pillows, by the way. It's very cozy."

She managed a slight smile. "I'm glad you're enjoying it."

He shifted from his place on his knees and swung his legs over the edge of the bed, planting a foot on either side of her and drawing her even closer to him. Her hands draped around his neck and slid their way down, her fingertips following the strong lines of his back. Her mouth tilted toward his. He met it eagerly, his tongue parting her lips, pushing its way inside and exploring for a moment before slowly, teasingly pulling away.

She kept her eyes closed for a moment afterwards, still dizzy with the taste and the sensations he'd left behind.

"Jealous," he said again, this time with a sigh of disbelief.

"Yes," she said, blinking her eyes open. "Because how many other beautiful women did you dance with tonight? How many women of status and power and wealth?"

"I've no interest in those women."

"No?"

"No. Only in Dragons."

"I see. Well, I'll be sure to inform Rue of your interest in her, then."

Then he was laughing again—a deeper, richer sound than before. One that vibrated through her and pushed away the uncertainty that had tried to take up so much space inside of her.

She leaned in to kiss him again, her hands pushing into his hair and clutching, pulling his lips up to hers. They pressed together, the kiss slow and long and hard, until she finally came up for air, to catch her balance and breathe out a single plea: "I just want you to tell me how this all ends, Rook."

"I don't know." He kissed a trail along her throat, making her close her eyes, and she started to tilt her head back, until he said, "I'm not Star-kind."

Her eyes opened. The hum of pleasure building in her throat abruptly died. And though she wanted him to keep going, she heard herself say, "They don't know, either."

A pause, and then: "What do you mean?"

She didn't want to tell him. *Gods*, how she wanted to keep kissing him and forget about all of the mess. But she had made a promise. Had told him that there would be explanations tonight—and if she didn't hurry and spit those explanations out, she feared she would never manage to do it.

He leaned back so he could better see her face.

"I recently met with one of the Star-kind. That's... that's one of the places I went." The words trembled from her lips. She took a step back from him so that she could focus, breathed in a deep breath, and then launched into an explanation of at least *some* of what she had learned.

371

She had told this story twice, now—first to Sade, and then to Ma—so at least the words rushed from her without tripping together on their way out. It was quick, concise, clear...

All the way up until she came to the worst part of what the Star-Spinner had told her.

Emrys was watching her very closely by this point, his elbows resting once more upon his knees and his chin upon his clasped hands. "And then what?" he prompted.

"And then the prophecies all apparently just...*end*." She lowered her head, staring at the Serpent curled upon her palm. "It's all darkness, no matter how hard even the most gifted Star-kind tries to read things. And *this* is why even my own kind want me dead."

Emrys was quiet for a long moment, and then he said, "How many days left until it supposedly all goes dark?"

"Twelve."

"Twelve days."

"Yes." She somehow found the courage to lift her head and meet his eyes once more. "And before it comes, I feel like you should also know that I..."

He stared directly back at her, expectant, his face remarkably stoic in spite of all he had just heard.

Remarkably kinglike, she thought to herself, and her breath fluttered and faltered a few times before she managed to settle it, and then to finish what she had started to say: "I love you. I wanted to say it so badly in the same moment you did, at that inn, before I...I..." Her gaze fell to those scars on his chest.

"You heard me that night? You...I mean, you remember it?"

"Yes. It's one of the only clear things I remember from that awful night." Her eyes stayed on his scars. She couldn't pry them away—not until he sat up, reached for her hand, and pulled her close once more. Close enough that she could no longer see those terrible marks.

He cupped her chin and lifted her gaze back to his.

"Say it again," he commanded.

She didn't have to ask what part he wanted her to repeat.

"I love you," she whispered, tilting even closer, so that her lips nearly brushed against his as she spoke. "And I know I don't fit in here, in this palace, but I still want it to be you and me in the end."

"You and me," he repeated.

"Even if it all goes dark."

He leaned forward another inch, letting his lips briefly linger against hers before he whispered back, "I love you too."

They kept still, foreheads pressed together, fully breathing in those words and letting them sink more deeply in. Finally, *finally* they could truly sink in. They could settle, and the world was stable enough to hold them, if only for a moment. Just for a moment, there was no fire, no blood, no magic—only her and her king and those four words echoing in Alaya's mind, flooding warmth through her body.

"It's late," Emrys eventually said. "Maybe we should try sorting all of those other things out in the morning?"

A brief pang of guilt struck her—because she wasn't really finished speaking; there was at least one more thing she needed to tell him. She couldn't keep her plans to return to the Sun Palace a secret from him for much longer.

No more secrets...

Wasn't that what they'd agreed to?

But now he was looking at her with a very obvious, very different sort of plan in mind. He no longer wanted to talk. And so all of those other details...

Well, they could wait for the morning, she decided.

"And in the meantime, you want to sleep?" she asked, grinning slightly.

"That's one option, yes." He smiled back, a sinful curve that, coupled with the low tone of his voice, sent a pleasant shiver over her body.

She started to teasingly ask what the other options might be, but he silenced her—first with a kiss, and then with his hands, which slid between the soft skin of her thighs and the silky fabric of her gown. She inhaled sharply as one of those hands moved to the suddenly aching warmth between her legs, and the words she'd been planning to tease him with left her completely.

While that hand moved against her ache, the other found the small of her back, and he guided her closer, more flush against his body. Both of his hands moved to her hips. She sank deeper into his lap, letting him pull her in, feeling his need for her throbbing against her sensitive area. It was nearly enough to send her crashing toward a beautiful edge; it had been too long since they had been together this way.

And perhaps, she thought, they'd never *truly* been together like this.

Because he had seen every inch of her, it was true, and he had explored most of those inches with his hands, his lips, his tongue—but never with whispers of *I love you* slipping in between the caresses. And he had never looked at her with quite the same admiration or devotion as he was doing now, as he wrapped her legs around him and lifted her with ease, holding her for a moment before claiming her lips with his once more.

He kissed her without pause or mercy, until she was nearly gasping from her need to breathe, and then he laid her gently back on the bed. She stretched out beneath him. He murmured a few words in the Rook language— words she didn't understand—but then followed them up with common ones she did: "My Dragon. My *queen*."

His hands traced the outline of her body against the silky blankets, then roved across her stomach, up over the hard peaks of her breasts that were pressing through the thin fabric of her nightgown. She closed her eyes. Lost herself in the feel of his fingertips, in the rasp of his breathing, in the low rumble of his voice in her ear as he pulled her gown and everything else out of his way.

They eased more deeply together, and for the first

time since she'd arrived in this palace, she felt as if she truly *belonged* in it.

She fit with him, and he with her. It was a bit messy, a bit painful, but ultimately, they moved together in perfect rhythm, and so—at least for the next few hours—she would not be concerned about the stars, or about any darkness that might lie beyond them.

ALAYA WOKE EARLY the next morning, long before Emrys did. She kept very still, not wanting to wake him, and she stared at the rays of sun spreading across the ceiling.

She lost herself in thought, resurfacing only when she felt his body moving beside her, curling closer, brushing against her naked body and sending electricity rippling from her scalp down to the tips of her toes.

"Finally," he mumbled.

"Finally?"

"This is how it's supposed to be: You, in my room, beside me in my bed whenever I wake up."

She smiled as he slid an arm underneath her and rolled her towards him, but inside she was wilting, dreading the conversation that was about to happen.

Because this *was* how it was supposed to be—the two of them side-by-side like this. They were supposed to face the day together. She had let herself believe in this fantasy, and it had brought her back to this palace, temporarily, and then she had let herself fall for the same lie again last night.

But the truth was, this couldn't be their reality. Not yet. She still had personal battles to fight, and she couldn't drag the High King of Sundolia into them, she had decided—this empire needed him here, safe and alive and not caught up in her wars. He had too many other wars to focus on.

"I left out something important last night," she said quietly.

"Oh?"

"Not really on purpose, I just...I got distracted before I got around to telling you this...something."

"You should probably say it quickly." He brushed a hand across her cheek, tucked a strand of hair behind her ear, and let his fingers fall along the curve of her jaw and down across her neck. "Before I start distracting you again."

She knew she wasn't strong enough to *not* get distracted again, so she pulled away from him and sat up, clutching a pillow against her bare chest. And then she blurted out her thoughts, word for word: "I am going back to the Palace of the Sun. Those pieces of my mother's power that I told you about last night...what I *didn't* tell you is that I'm fairly certain one of the last pieces, if not *the* last piece, is in that southern palace. In Sylven's possession. And I need to go—"

"Absolutely not."

She exhaled a slow breath.

"I won't allow it."

She moved to stand, but he grabbed her arm and pulled her back—more roughly than he'd meant to, judging by the way he released her just as quickly. He tossed a frustrated glare at his hand, as though it had betrayed some deeper, darker side of him that he didn't particularly like, and he clenched it into a fist as she rose to her feet.

"I thought you weren't in the business of holding people hostage," she muttered, reaching for a throw blanket to wrap around herself. At some point during the night, her dressing gown had ended up on a chair on the other side of the room. She strode toward it with as much casualness as she could muster. "I overheard some talk at the party, regarding the Sun King wanting to speak personally with you, and a mention of you sending an emissary, so I thought—"

"I am not sending *you*."

"Why not? I am more powerful than any soldier in your army. And closer to you than any of those soldiers, aren't I? Levant knows this; so perhaps he would accept your queen in place of you. I am capable of holding the same political conversations you are. I could do this, if you would just give me the information I need, and then trust me to be able to think on my feet—which I've more than proven capable of doing, haven't I?"

He glared at her, his fist still clenched tightly, but he didn't answer.

Because he couldn't disagree, could he?

After a moment, he reached for the pants on the floor and yanked them on. He walked to his wardrobe next, still without speaking. Pulled out a shirt, and finished dressing in still more silence. She started to believe that she might actually win this argument.

"Besides," she said, pulling her gown back over her head, still trying to keep her movements and her tone as casual and matter-of-fact as she could, "my life does not mean any more than the lives of whatever other person you might send as your emissary, does it? As a high king, you should—"

"Enough."

His tone was harsh—more harsh than she had ever heard it—and it startled her into a long silence. She couldn't seem to make herself move, either, even as he closed the space between them with furious steps. She flinched, thinking he was going to grab her again, but he only knelt and snatched up that coat that had slipped from the chair the night before.

"*Enough*," he repeated. "Because you know I don't think of you as just some other person. And your life means *everything*."

She managed to catch her breath and find her voice, though it was considerably shakier than before as she said: "It's not entirely my life until I collect all of its pieces. I don't want you to have only part of me. If I am going to be your queen, then I will be your whole queen and nothing less than that. You have to let me go. You have to let me do this."

"No, I don't."

"Then I will go without your permission. I don't actually *need* your permission, you know."

He slipped the coat on slowly. Smoothed its collar with tense, precise flicks of his hand. Adjusted one buttoned cuff, and then the other. The fury was gone from his eyes, but now they held that familiar stubbornness, that challenge that seemed to say *just try me, Dragon.*

So she did.

She lifted her chin and said, "You know as well as I do that the walls of this palace cannot hold me."

"You are not running off by yourself again," he said, simply.

"I—"

"Because I am going with you this time. And that is the end of the discussion."

CHAPTER 25

"How are you enjoying the Storm-kind magic, Majesty?"

"Even just the traces of it are impressive." Emrys closed the heavy metal door behind him, and he turned and met Lord Feran's gaze. "But we both know that I am not here to discuss that kind of magic."

Lord Feran shifted his weight from one foot to the other. Brushed at some invisible fleck on the collar of his robe. It was the closest the old man ever came to showing discomfort.

Emrys paid it no mind; he had already spent the morning steeling his resolve and coming to terms with what he was about to do, and no argument that Lord Feran might have made could have changed his mind. They were out of time for arguments.

It had been three days since his coronation. And he had received three more messages from the southern king, each one regarding the desire he had for a meeting

—a meeting that was going to be granted, Emrys had assured him in a letter sent just hours after he and Alaya had fought about it.

It was official, now, this summit at the Gate of the Sun.

Levant's acceptance of this compromise for their meeting spot had been cordial, even. And he had agreed to bring all of Alaya's belongings from the Sun Palace as well, with no arguments or questions about any of it.

All of which made Emrys suspicious, of course.

Because this had all the makings of a trap.

He knew this. His advisors knew this. Alaya knew this, and she had pointed this out to him no less than twenty times over the past days; she still was not pleased at his decision to go with her.

She was also not pleased at the three days that had already passed. For all the ways she'd changed since they'd first met, she was still terribly impatient. If she'd had her way, she would have been on Rue's back and already to Lumeria by now, ready to take on the entire Army of the Sun by herself if need be.

For her own sake, she was not getting her way this time.

Instead, they would go together, as he'd told her they would. A company was being assembled to travel south with them—at least a hundred and fifty strong, with more to join them, if need be, from those he already had stationed near the border.

He had also been communicating with more of Alaya's clan—with her father, who knew more Serpent-kind who might trust and follow his lead. Emrys hadn't received any return correspondence from that man, and he didn't hold much hope that they would aid them in the end. But the idea was intriguing. Lady Korva had raised a decent point in that last meeting he'd attended as the heir apparent to the high throne: Why shouldn't they fight Dragons with Dragons?

If he could convince more of this clan to fight alongside him, as Levant had managed to do, it might warm his own subjects to the idea of a Dragon *Queen*, if nothing else.

At any rate, they needed to be prepared for a full-scale battle at the gate.

He hoped it wouldn't come to that. But he was preparing as if this was all but a certainty. He knew that he needed to have a reliable means of escaping if this all turned out to be a trap—and magic could provide such an escape.

Which was why he was meeting Lord Feran deep in the belly of the palace, in the most desolate and dark of its dungeons.

Because he had a target.

An Air-kind—but a much stronger one, this time. This particular target had been blessed—*very* blessed—by that lesser-spirit. He was capable of what only a few of their kind were; actual, physical travel through time and space.

Air-kind such as this were notoriously difficult to imprison. And this particular one had a history of escaping; he'd managed it three times when he was younger, during the first stretch of his near twenty-year stint in the palace dungeons. There was now a rotation of Sky-kind constantly working a special barrier around him, and he was shackled with Storm-magic-infused cuffs that numbed his muscles, and he was frequently drugged with *sultas* elixir—all to keep him from using the very same magic that Emrys sought to take from him.

The guards on either side of the lone, tiny cell bowed low as Emrys approached. The Sky-kind on duty did the same, drawing her magic back to her as she did. The barrier she'd been creating fizzled, falling away into nothing but a fine mist that rained down and melted into the dirt floor the prisoner was kneeling on.

The guards opened the door.

The Air-kind lifted his eyes without lifting his head, and Emrys noted the milky blue shade of the right one. He wondered if the man could see out of either of them; the light from the torches carried by himself and Lord Feran must have been disorienting, at the very least, after twenty years of almost constant near-darkness.

Emrys handed that torch off to the Sky-kind and motioned for her to back away. He reached into the inner pocket of his coat. Steadied his hand, and then he withdrew the slip of paper that he'd written notes on hours ago.

"Silas Fellmir," he read—by memory more than sight. "Charged and found guilty of murder. You killed two men who allegedly trespassed on your land. The judgement handed down by the high king before me was imprisonment for life, but I am reconsidering things. So...do you have anything that you would like to add to your testimony?"

Silence for a long, heavy moment, and then came a voice that sounded as if it was choking through twenty years' worth of grit and dust: "Would it matter?"

Emrys arched a brow, but he said nothing.

"I have something you want, don't I? And Rooks are *scavengers*, bloody, hungry—"

The guards moved to silence him, but Emrys held up his hand and brought them to a halt.

He said nothing to the accusations the prisoner had made against the Rook clan; accusations which continued even as he stepped closer to the man. They sounded like the ramblings of a mostly-gone mind. Unsettling—but then again, Emrys had not come down here to have a pleasant chat.

Lord Feran stood off to the side, murmuring prayers to the Fire Goddess, Moto. Those prayers would turn to spells, soon. Different spells, depending on what level of magic harvesting they decided to orchestrate.

They had discussed the possibility of both a sacrifice and a stealing. It looked as though it was going to require theft, this time; this prisoner clearly was not going to willingly give his magic. As to the level of thievery...

A minor blood-letting of such a powerful Air-kind might be enough to give Emrys the sort of magic he sought.

Might.

But if he wanted to guarantee the strength of these new powers, it would require more than that.

He stared at the prisoner. *Silas Fellmir.* He had a wife and a daughter, according to the record-keeper's book. But, according to those same records, neither of those women had ever petitioned for his freedom nor attempted to visit him. Were they even still alive?

What of this man's legacy existed outside of these prison walls?

It seemed important to wonder about these things. To see all of his life, and not just the gaunt face and dead eyes that he had been reduced to. To see more than the sunken in stomach, clearly visible through the ragged shirt he wore. More than the Air clan symbol on his withered hand.

But seeing him as more than these things would also make it more difficult to kill him.

If a target was killed during an extraction, there was no life-force for its magic to cling to anymore. That magic, as a result, released more fully, and it could be drawn from spilled blood more completely. It would latch onto its new host without complications. It would be more powerful.

Twenty years, Emrys thought.

And the man looked as though he had suffered every second of those years. It was a mercy to let him die at this point, wasn't it?

Emrys let a slow, ragged breath escape him, and the prisoner's lips curled into an odd little smile—almost as if this Air-kind's twisted, murderous mind could read another potential killer's thoughts.

Mercy.

It frightened Emrys, that word. The idea of deciding who should receive mercy, and who should not—and what that word even *meant*, now that he had the power to show mercy to everyone...

Or to no one at all.

Hadn't his father used that very word, far too often, when making his declarations and collecting his victims? Hadn't he convinced half an empire that his actions were ultimately merciful, and not monstrous?

Alaya had accused him of being a monster like his father, once. On the very first night they'd met. And he'd smiled and told her, *I am a very different sort of monster.*

But maybe all monsters were the same in the end.

The end.

The end was coming. His thoughts rushed through the fears that kept him up at night, exploded with images of stars and the battles and destruction and darkness they had foretold for his empire. For his people. For the woman he loved.

He gave his head a small shake, forcing himself away from those thoughts and into action.

"Speak, son of the Air spirit," he commanded quietly, "if you have any reason to give as to why I should not change your sentence to death."

The Air-kind did not speak.

The cell grew quiet enough to hear heartbeats. Lord

Feran stopped his prayers. Held his breath, perhaps waiting for Emrys to change his mind. Then slowly, one carefully measured word after another, he began to recite one of the Fire-kind's spells of forging.

Emrys drew his sword. *Aetherus.* The noble blade he'd been given as a child, which was already stained with the deaths of others—though none who he'd slain in this manner. He would not stain it with many more of these slayings, he promised himself.

And he repeated this promise to himself, over and over—*I am not the same, I am not the same*—even as he plunged the blade deep into the prisoner's stomach and twisted it.

AN HOUR LATER, the transfer was complete, and Emrys found himself stable enough to walk again—at least for a short distance. He managed to climb back into the brighter places of his palace, and he very nearly made it to the second floor before he had to stop and lean his back against the wall while he caught his breath.

The new magic twisted around him like the undercurrent of a mighty sea, threatening to rip his feet out from underneath him. It was terribly heavy and strong; Lord Feran had warned him it would be. It could take days to properly acclimate to such a great amount of magic, he'd said. Days before he could even practice it, much less wield it with anything like grace or precision.

To which Emrys had stubbornly replied, *Then I will be setting the record for such feats, it looks like.* He had also told Lord Feran that he felt perfectly fine shortly after the actual harvesting spell was finished, and to leave him be.

And now he was very close to cursing his own hubris as he braced himself against the wall behind him and tried not to faint.

"Your Majesty?"

He lifted his head away from the wall, reluctantly.

"A word, my king?"

My king.

He still wasn't used to hearing himself referred to as such, and with a hint of reverence attached to it, at that—a reverence that was even more surprising, given that the speaker was Lady Korva.

She was still here because her father's illness would have made travel too precarious—particularly since there were recent reports of attacks close to the city of Frost-climb, where they hailed from. No substantial losses had occurred from those attacks, yet, but it was clear that Levant's forces were attempting to intimidate the Ice-kind, Lord Marius, and his army. Likely trying to make them think twice about coming to the aid of the new Rook King.

And if this final...*darkness* that Alaya had spoken of was truly going to come to pass, then Emrys was likely going to need that Ice-kind army to be ready to answer his call. So for this reason, he once again smiled and greeted Lady Korva as though they themselves were personal, longtime allies.

"Why is it that every time I stumble upon you, you look as though you've just been up to something?" she asked.

"Perhaps because I'm *always* up to something? What do you expect of a king? For him to sit and twiddle his thumbs and grow fat while sitting uselessly on his throne?"

She lifted her eyes to the ceiling, muttering something under her breath.

"What are you doing? Trying to picture me as fat?" He managed a grin even through a sudden, agonizing twist of that settling Air magic.

She lowered her gaze and glowered at him. "No. I wasn't imagining anything. I was sent to find you—to inform you that Captain Helder has finished the tasks you assigned him, and that your company awaits only your command to march south. But now I am wondering if you are actually *capable* of having a serious conversation... And also questioning what that is on your coat." Her gaze had fallen to the cuff of his right sleeve—to the few threads that had been stained with the Air-kind's blood.

He grimaced. This was yet another conversation he didn't have time for. But he suspected that the quickest and least offensive way to end it was to tell Lady Korva some scraps of the truth. So he summoned his strength, pushed away from the wall, and then—after making certain no potential gossipers were watching them—he beckoned her to follow him into a nearby room.

"It's blood," he told her, once they were safely inside.

"Blood?" She sounded only mildly curious.

"Yes. Because I've spent the morning harvesting magic from a criminal who wasn't particularly cooperative about the whole thing."

If this revelation pushed her beyond *mildly curious*, she did a fine job of not showing it. "Like father, like son?" she commented.

"If I had the time, I would explain, in painstaking detail, all of the reasons why that assumption is wrong."

She folded her arms across her chest, puffed a strand of her pale hair from her eyes, and said, "But you don't have the time."

"But I don't have the time," he repeated. "I do, however, have a favor to ask of you."

"And why should I do you any favors?"

"Because I am the high king. Because your clan and its warriors have a history of serving mine. Because I have shown nothing except hospitality to you, your sick father, and all of the countless people who traveled with you to my palace. There are three reasons—pick one."

Her lips pursed, but she didn't object to any of these things. "What is this *favor* you need?"

"I've reason to believe that a catastrophic battle is about to befall us. And I need to know that the fabled Sword of Winter—the army that you yourself recently reminded me was perhaps one of the Rook-kind's greatest weapons—will be ready to rise against whatever threat comes crashing down on me and my other allies."

Her expression finally cracked, rearranging into a hardened expression that was more befitting of a woman who had been raised by a clan of warriors. "And why do you believe this latest catastrophe is coming?"

He had always been skeptical of Star-kind magic before, and he was loath to speak of their prophecies as fact now. But the more he replayed the conversation with Alaya in his mind, the more he relived that moment when he'd seen the fear and uncertainty in her eyes...and the more his skepticism faded.

She clearly believed that this darkness was a very real and possible thing.

So he did too.

And he told Lady Korva as much, and he was somewhat surprised at the way she listened quietly until he was finished giving her an abbreviated version of things.

"So," he concluded, "now I suppose the question is... what can you and your army do for me and my empire?"

She fixed him with a stare. Her eyes betrayed nothing of what she thought, but he could almost sense the wheels turning behind them, and he watched those wheels part her lips and close them several times before she finally said, "You've told me the truth about what you were doing, despite the questionable morality of it all..."

Because I actually care very little about what you think of me and my morals, he thought.

But for once he managed to keep this smart comment

trapped safely inside of him, where it couldn't irritate his potential ally.

"...And I suppose I appreciate the honesty," she continued. "So, I will see what I can do. What preparations I might be able to make, even with the distance currently between myself and my *fabled* army. But I promise nothing for certain."

"And I expect little."

"Good. Then we have an understanding."

"It seems we do." Her eyes flickered toward that blood on his sleeve once more, perhaps betraying just a hint of her true curiosity, before her eyes darted back to his. "Shall I go tell Captain Helder that you'll be with him shortly?"

"Please do."

"Are you sure you're not going to faint when I walk away? You look ill."

"I've felt worse."

He was fairly certain she rolled her eyes at this; but he didn't actually see it, because she'd turned and walked away too quickly, leaving him alone in this room that was private and dimly lit—and that would have served as the perfect place to curl up and rest until the new magic burning through him didn't seem so heavy.

But he couldn't rest. He needed to move. He had brought this magic upon himself, and now he would have to deal with it in stride; they couldn't delay leaving because he had suddenly taken ill.

"I'm *not* ill," he muttered. Perhaps if he just saying it,

it would eventually become true. With this strategy in mind, he took a deep breath and left the room.

The gods save me from anymore distractions as I go, he thought, stepping through the doorway.

The second he thought this, he looked up and saw Alaya standing on the other end of the hall.

Of course.

She appeared to be waiting on him, but she did not look especially happy to see him.

"Thank you for nothing, gods," he muttered with a cross, upward glance.

Under normal circumstances, he would never have considered Alaya a *distraction*—or at least, not an unwelcome one—but he could feel another wave of his new, unsettled magic rising, and he was sorely tempted to keep moving before it crashed over him.

He couldn't bring himself to walk away from her, though.

He'd never truly been able to.

"Did you tell Sade she had to stay here?" she asked, her eyes narrowing on him as he approached her.

"I didn't *tell* her so much as ask her. Commanding her to do things usually works about as well as commanding *you* to do things. Which is to say, it doesn't work at all, and it usually leads to a terrible headache for me."

"Why did you ask her to stay?" she demanded. "She's far less of a liability than you."

"I'm a liability, now?" He tried to make the words

sound incredulous, even though that weighty, new magic made him feel *exactly* like a liability.

"If you die, the entire empire will suffer for it," she said. "So *yes*. You are. And I know at least some of your advisors—even the more dimwitted ones—have told you as much. *I* have told you this, too. Several times, in fact."

He sighed.

"Now, answer my question: Why did you ask Sade to stay?"

"Because I need somebody in this palace that I can reliably receive updates and communications from while we're away. Captain Helder will be accompanying us to the south, and Lady Isoni...well, I need somebody to balance her out."

Alaya frowned, and she looked to be trying to come up with the best possible argument against his points.

"You're stuck with just me, I'm afraid," he said, before she could. "Well, me and a few hundred or so of our closest soldier friends."

"I'd actually be better off just going alone," she told him.

Again.

He reached and brushed a hand across her cheek. He couldn't help wanting to touch her, to try and soothe some of the irritation from her. And to steady himself maybe, too; the warmth and softness of her skin had a way of making him forget about whatever heaviness he was carrying, magical or otherwise. He made certain to reach with the hand not edged by the blood-stained sleeve, and he kept those drops of blood tucked against his body and out of sight—though he felt guilty about it.

No more secrets.

Hadn't they agreed on that?

And now he had told Lady Korva one of his greatest secrets while continuing to leave Alaya in the dark about it. It was wrong, he realized this—but he hadn't thought of it as sharing meaningful moments or secrets with the foreign noblewoman; it had merely been a strategic move in the increasingly complicated game of war they were playing.

Sharing the truth about his stolen magic with Alaya would be...different.

Because he actually cared about her opinion of him. And he was terrified of losing her. Of giving her another reason to run.

She hadn't drawn away from his touch, he realized.

They had slept in separate beds since their argument the other morning, and they had scarcely seen each other between the preparations and meetings he'd had to attend to... She had clearly missed his touch, judging by the way her face relaxed into it and her eyes gently closed.

He had certainly missed touching her.

And now he was thinking of something far more invigorating than taking a nap in that dimly-lit room he'd just left.

Her brow furrowed. She wanted to be irritated, he could tell, but when he leaned his mouth closer to hers, she hesitated only a moment before meeting it with her own. The kiss was long and slow, and she tasted like sun berries—a tart fruit that he knew she was fond of, which was why he had made a point of making sure it was included in the breakfast tray delivered to her each morning.

Her eyes stayed closed even after he pulled back, lingering in that peaceful moment for as long as she could.

He didn't want to shatter that peace, but he had to keep moving. "I've received countless, increasingly threatening messages from the Sun King," he told her. "Levant wants to see *me* at this summit; the easiest way to keep the peace is to go myself and deal with this. Or else... what would you have me tell him instead?"

She was quiet for a long moment, and he almost breathed a soft sigh of relief.

But then her eyes flashed open, and in a perfectly flat voice she said: "My thoughts on the matter have not changed. You could have told him that your future queen is equal in status to you, and that she would have been happy to meet on your behalf." And with that, she brushed past him and disappeared down the hall.

He sighed again, watching her go.

Four days to the Gate of the Sun.

It was going to be a long four days, from the looks of things.

CHAPTER 26

FOR THREE DAYS, THE MOOD BETWEEN EMRYS AND ALAYA remained tense. They spoke of nothing but the route ahead of them and their potential strategies for dealing with their enemies, and though they shared a tent, they slept on opposite sides of it.

During the day, she flew overhead on Rue, refusing to land even when the rest of their party stopped to rest. So they made a scout out of her and that dragon, entrusting her to search for any danger that might be awaiting them —or stalking them; it was the only reason she hadn't taken off and left them entirely, Emrys suspected. She wouldn't leave him or their group vulnerable to possible attack, despite her grumblings about that group having come along with her.

Her refusal to spend any more time with him than necessary had one advantage, at least: It made it easier for him to slip away and practice his recently acquired Air-kind magic.

He went every morning, leaving before she awoke, and she was usually on her way out to find Rue when he returned. She never asked where he'd been. He never offered an explanation—partly because he was in no state to talk immediately after any of these practice sessions.

The stronger shades of this Air-kind magic were interesting. Disorienting. Terrifying. The first time he had managed to use a proper part of it—transporting his body from one side of a small stream to another—he'd been almost certain that he'd left part of that body behind. For hours afterward, he had felt as if he was in pieces, unable to find his balance, and it had been a miracle that no one in his company had noticed.

After several dozen more attempts, this disorientation became somewhat less horrifying; more like a spell of drunkenness than an actual out-of-body experience. And by the fourth day, he managed to do it without feeling intoxicated afterwards, even—though it was still not without side-effects.

He did not feel drunk, but he felt beyond exhausted as he made his way back to their shared tent. And it must have been more obvious this morning than in the mornings before, because when he passed Alaya on his way back into that tent, her eyes actually met his and held them for a moment. They widened in concern, and then narrowed in suspicion as she watched him collapse onto his pile of blankets.

She left, as usual—but minutes later she returned with two steaming tin cups full of *kuzca* tea.

"Here," she said, handing one to him. "You look like you need something to warm you."

"...A peace offering?"

She sat back on her bedroll, crossing her legs in front of her and swirling the contents of her own cup. "Just drink it," she commanded.

He sipped the scalding tea without protest, though he couldn't help wrinkling his nose at the smoky, bitter taste. Captain Helder swore by this wretched stuff—it could revive a dead man, he claimed—but Emrys suspected that some might find death the preferred option over drinking it.

"This is refreshing," he commented after a minute, "but you know, if you *truly* wanted to help warm me..."

"Do not push your luck, Rook," Alaya warned.

He grinned.

It took her a moment, but eventually she gave in and offered a slight grin in return. "...I'm sorry," she said. "I know I've been in a terrible mood these past days. I just want this over with. I want all of my pieces—"

"As do I."

"*And* I don't want anybody else to get hurt during this latest adventure I'm on," she pressed. "Least of all you."

"I'm fine," he assured her. "And I will continue to be fine."

"And the hundreds of others out there?" she asked, lowering her voice and nodding toward the sliver of camp that could be seen through the tent's partially-opened flap.

Emrys moved to more tightly seal that opening. "The Valinesian Army is not compulsory; I've made that far more clear than my father ever did. These men and women are here because they decided to be of service to my crown and purpose—whatever that purpose might be."

"Yes. But be honest with me... Your current purpose is not *really* about meeting Levant or playing politics; it's mostly because you did not want me to go back to the Sun Kingdom alone. Otherwise, you wouldn't have risked this trip."

He settled back onto the bedroll opposite of her, and his grin faded a bit as he said, "Guilty as charged, I suppose."

"And most of that army of volunteers wants nothing to do with *me*. If they realized the truth..."

He shrugged. "Don't think of it as them helping you, then, but as aiding the greater purpose of serving our empire. You are potentially the most powerful person in that empire. They should want to help you, shouldn't they? So that you are, in turn, able to help them."

She sipped her drink without comment, her expression vacant. After a moment she said, "This tea is awful."

"It really is," he laughed.

She stared into the cup, her eyes glazing over in thought once more. But whatever she was truly thinking about, she still didn't seem to be able to put it into words. The silence stretched for several more minutes.

"It will be fine," he said. "We will finish this business of sorting out your powers, and then face whatever comes next, whenever it comes."

He could tell she was about to ask him how he could be certain things would be *fine*—but he was saved by the voice of Captain Helder filtering in from outside, requesting his company.

"I should go." His balance swayed a bit as he stood, drawing another concerned look from Alaya.

"Are you sure you're alright?"

His smile was a bit forced as he fought off another rush of dizziness. "Better," he told her, "now that you're actually speaking to me again." And then he hurried out before she could question him further.

Several curious pairs of eyes turned his direction as he stepped out into the camp.

Captain Helder muttered something under his breath that Emrys didn't catch, and then he turned and suggested they take a walk.

Emrys nodded, and he followed him into the surrounding woods, waiting until they were well out of earshot of anyone else before he quietly said, "You have news that you didn't want the rest of the camp to overhear, I presume?"

"I'm afraid so."

He tossed a worried glance back toward that camp. "Out with it, then."

"I received a message from the general stationed in Kavus. There's a Sun-aligned army that's gathered to Rykarra's northwestern borders. They appear ready to march on the capital any day now."

"How many?"

"Three thousand strong, at least."

"Three *thousand*?" He thought that he'd misheard, surely, but Helder confirmed it with a solemn nod. "And are they aware that the high king they have such a problem with is not even home at the moment?"

Captain Helder gave him an expectant look.

"Oh. They are," Emrys said slowly, realization dawning on him. "Of course they are."

"...This way, even if they don't manage to kill you at this border summit—which, for the record, I still believe is a trap—then they can still slander you and weaken your hold over the throne; you left your city, in the company of a Serpent no less, and that city was attacked in the meantime. So how does that look to your subjects?"

"But *how did this happen*? How have they moved an army of several thousand strong so close to our center city without us noticing it before now?"

"Some kind of magic?" the captain guessed. "Such as Air-kind, for example?"

Emrys tensed.

The captain continued to speak, his voice measured: "The strongest Air-kind can transport objects, and even people, through the use of the gateways they create. Very useful for the transfer of goods on an ordinary day, but they also used portals like these to great effect during the Battle of the Wild Northlands, for example. My father told me many stories about that infamous battle...of course, that battle was a long time ago, and the Air-kind with that sort of power are rare these days. But they say there's a cluster of this clan near Sira. So, not far from our friend Levant." He cut Emrys a sideways glance. "You're aware of Air-kind magic, aren't you?"

Emrys kept his gaze on the leafy undergrowth they were trudging through. His hands were folded casually behind his back, and in a voice as evenly measured as the captain's he said, "You've been talking to Lord Feran, I suspect."

"I can't properly protect my young king if I don't know all of the different kinds of trouble he's wrapping himself in, now can I?" The captain's tone was droll. Unapologetic.

They walked on in silence, until they came to the banks of a river that was swollen with the prior night's rainfall.

"Three-thousand strong." Repeating it nearly took Emrys's breath away all over again.

"Judging by those numbers, they don't intend to leave anyone alive. I suspect Levant wanted to draw you to this summit at the gate—to this *trap*—with the intention of demanding that you, once and for all, surrender your claim to the high throne. And if you don't..."

"He has his other hand ready to demolish it."

"And every person within a hundred-mile radius of it."

"Just to *start*."

"Yes," Helder agreed. "I imagine it will escalate quickly from that point."

Emrys tried to massage away a sudden pounding in his temple as he asked, "What sort of time do we have?"

He had a terrible, gut-wrenching feeling that he already knew what his captain was going to say, but he listened all the same.

"They marched across the desert just this morning. They'll be at the province border by nightfall, and at Rykarra's gates in five days or less, I'd wager."

Five days.

Which would bring them there on the eve of Alaya's nineteenth year in this world, because of course it would.

Damn the Stars and all of their prophecies.

"This is assuming, of course, that they don't employ some sort of magic to get them there even faster."

"So. What do you propose we do, Captain?"

"If Rykarra falls, we lose your most important foothold, and the slide from that point could be devastating. They need a high king in command more than ever. So if your magic can take you back to that city quickly, my advice is that you should use that magic. Whatever that advice is worth to you."

"Your advice is worth plenty..."

"Thank you for saying so."

"But I need time to think."

"Of course." The captain gave a slight bow of his head. "I'll prepare us to move, either way."

Emrys nodded, and he trailed a bit behind him as they returned to camp, thinking as he walked.

If he decided to return to Rykarra, he would have to tell Alaya *how* he planned to return. He couldn't just disappear into thin air and expect her not to have questions. And if she asked him, he wouldn't lie to her. So it was better to just tell her the truth before it happened.

No more secrets.

Yes; whichever direction he went from this point, this particular secret ended today.

He moved quickly once he reached the edge of camp, both to avoid conversation and to avoid giving himself time to second-guess his decision. He ducked into the tent, intending only to grab his sword, and then he would be off in whatever direction Alaya and Rue had flown toward...

But Alaya remained in that tent.

And she was asleep.

Strange.

Her foul mood was likely to start all over again if he woke her, but the discussion he needed to have with her couldn't wait. So he knelt beside her, grabbed her shoulder, and gently shook her.

She didn't wake.

He shook her harder, and still...nothing. He brushed his fingers across her cheek. Her skin was ice cold. At his touch, her eyes fluttered beneath her closed lids, but they didn't open.

The tent spun around him as he leapt back to his feet and ran outside. *A healer.* He needed a *healer—*

The sight of dozens of his soldiers lying on the ground, as still and lifeless as Alaya was, made him stumble.

He gazed frantically around. Watched as two, three, four more people close to him froze in place and then fell down, rolled into awkward positions, and then no longer moved. A fifth and a sixth person appeared to be running in slow motion, their faces twisting in horror as though they were being pursued by invisible demons that were dragging them back, inch by inch.

Then he felt an odd, gritty, brushing sensation over his skin, as though he was being buried in dirt.

No, not dirt—*sand*

MOVE! shouted a voice in his head.

Because it was Sand magic dropping these soldiers left and right, freezing them in time—and it was coming for him now.

He turned once more to the tent where he'd left Alaya, sprinting so quickly back to it that he nearly tripped and fell headlong through the opening. As he stumbled inside, he tried to dart to her side. But it felt as if that Sand magic falling over him was beginning to bury him, rooting his feet to the ground, making them too heavy to properly direct.

He had to keep moving.

He had to get to her, to use his Air magic to get them both out of this place.

The sand piled thicker, heavier, brought him to his knees.

He kept crawling, the Air-kind spell choking out of him as he went. He lifted his hand as he fell forward. His fingertips brushed Alaya's lifeless body. He felt the Air magic surging to life inside of him, and he braced himself, refusing to think about the dangers of trying to spirit away *two* different bodies at once. Was he even capable of such a thing? No; it didn't matter. He wouldn't think. He would find out.

The last of the spell's words were on his tongue.

But his mouth felt as if it was filling with sand, suddenly. It buried the words in his throat. He was *choking*. He was *sinking*—

Everything went still.

CHAPTER 27

Alaya woke because of a voice whispering in her ear.

But when she jerked upright in the tent, nobody was beside her. Nobody was speaking. The only other person she saw was Emrys, and he was asleep.

It was still daylight, and she didn't remember him coming back, nor did she remember falling back to sleep herself. Her head felt strangely fuzzy. Her mouth, oddly dry.

She slowly sat up, calling Emrys's name.

He didn't reply.

She crawled over to him. He wasn't breathing. His body was stiff. Frozen, though she saw no sign of Ice magic, and his skin was only slightly chilled. His hand was stretched toward where she'd been resting. His eyes were tightly shut and his face clenched, as though he'd been struck by something just before freezing in place.

She shook him over and over, shouting his name, to

no response. And then, in a numb panic, she crawled out of the tent and into the blinding light of what she guessed was mid-day.

Her eyes adjusted, and she saw Sylven waiting for her outside of that tent.

He was standing before an entire camp full of bodies that were frozen, contorted strangely, several of them staring at nothing with their open, unblinking eyes.

Her mind flashed back to the last battlefield she had walked across. To that man she'd killed and the ring she'd taken from him, and to all the other dead and all their blind gazes. She clenched her own eyes shut for a moment and tried to squeeze the memory away. Swallowed down the bile in her throat. Slowly, she rose to her feet.

Her heart pounded so hard that it made her voice shake as she asked, "What have you done?"

"I've come to see you," he replied, simply. "It's been too long, hasn't it?"

She recoiled. "What is going on?"

"Let's go for a stroll." It sounded less like a suggestion, more like a command. He turned and started to walk.

Alaya remained rooted in place, determined not to fall under his control so easily.

She was stronger than the last time they had met— strong enough that she was not going to let him use his magic against her, and she would not be overwhelmed by her *own* magic, either. She was stronger than the terror coursing through her, stronger than any magic, stronger than the stars and that darkness beyond them.

I am stronger, I am stronger...

But Sylven didn't resort to magic. He only tilted his face back to her and said, "If you want any of them to wake up again, I would come with me."

She forgot to breathe for a moment as she tried to come up with a plan. Her gaze slid back toward her tent, to the sheath resting next to her bedroll.

"No swords," Sylven called without looking back. "This is going to be a friendly stroll."

She exhaled. Then inhaled slowly. Steeled herself and started to walk. If he didn't want her to arm herself, then fine.

She didn't need a sword.

She wasn't yet convinced that this camp they were strolling through was truly real, anyhow. The world around her seemed to have the same blurry quality of her flashbacks, of the planted thoughts and memories that Sylven's magic had been plaguing her with these past weeks.

This could have been yet another attempt to control her mind and body.

She could wake up from this, if only she focused. She was stronger...

Rue? she tried thinking.

"Your dragon is asleep as well."

The words sent chills creeping down her spine.

Was he reading her thoughts?

She kept her walk steady, her words and fears buried deep inside, where hopefully he wouldn't be able to find them.

They kept walking, leaving the campsite behind and climbing the largest of the hills that overlooked it. There were two watchmen collapsed against each other on top of this hill. Alaya stared at the Rook symbols on their hands as she asked, "What do you want from me?"

Sylven didn't answer immediately, distracting himself by controlling a few scattered leaves into a tightly-spinning whirlwind. "You've made it obvious that you don't support a Serpent-kind on a throne—"

"Oh, the throne in Rykarra *will* see a Serpent on it before the end of this. It just won't be you."

"Ah, yes...I've heard those rumors," he sneered. "The ones that have more or less proven that you are a traitor to your own kind, tripping over yourself to become a Rook's *queen*." He crushed his fingers back into a fist, and the swirling leaves dropped back to the ground. "Or his weapon, more like."

"Isn't that what you wanted to make of me, more or less?"

"Yes, but at least I'm upfront about the matter. I never claimed to love you, like he does; only that you and I might make a formidable pair on that throne that the Rook-kind have overstayed their welcome on. A pair that could right the wrongs that said kind have wrought upon this empire."

"I can right those wrongs with him, too. It doesn't have to be us versus them."

"Yes. It *does*." His eyes were suddenly wild, blind with

412

a righteous indignation as he stormed forward, stopping just short of grabbing hold of her.

She didn't flinch. She didn't step back. She wasn't certain *why* she was trying to reason with him now; there was no reason left in the darkness of his eyes. She could clearly see that. And it was unnerving to look into that darkness. It was...

"How sad that you actually believe that," she said, quietly.

He laughed. "Spare me your pity; I don't need it. And I don't actually *need* you, either. I can rule without you. I will make a fine solitary king, I believe."

"You will have to kill me first."

"I can do that, too."

"Not likely."

"Why? Because you've gotten stronger? Strong enough to get rid of me, you think?"

She opened her mouth to snap out a response, but something in his expression made her hesitate. He knew something she didn't. She wanted to know what it was.

He leaned away from her, and he reached into the pocket of his coat.

She tensed but still didn't run.

"I know what you came here to find," he said, withdrawing, not a weapon, but that bracelet that had once belonged to her mother.

She stared at the round beads, speechless for a moment before she managed to choke out a single question: "...How did you know I was coming for that?"

"I have sources everywhere. I'm also very good at making people talk. And I also have a very potent connection to *you*, don't I?"

"Oh, I promise you that you *don't*," she hissed.

His smile twisted up in one corner. "But I do. I have, for nearly nineteen years. I've just been working through the finer details of that bond, here lately."

"Nineteen years…"

"Yes—because I helped you the night you were born. You and your mother would not have escaped that prison for the exiled Serpents if not for *me*. And for my troubles, that *caelestis* of Mairu blessed me with a piece of the same kind of magic you've set about collecting."

She was speechless again.

"That's right; I know about the ability she had to fracture her power. I know you initially only had one piece of that divine power, but you've been gaining more… And every time you've merged with another piece of it over these past weeks, I've felt it. I've seen it. I've been watching you, and it's been tantalizing, really—and maddening, having to wait so long for you to find your way back to me like this."

"You protected me that night of my birth, so she thought…" She shook her head, trying to make sense of it all, while at the same time wishing she didn't have to see it all so clearly.

"I could still protect you," he said with a shrug. "She gifted it to me for a reason, and you could prove her decision right."

"Nothing about this is *right*."

"Either way, you and I are even *more* connected, now, by these shared pieces. I have two. You have three now, I believe? And the dragon still has one, I noticed."

Horror was rapidly tightening her throat, but somehow, she managed to keep speaking. "You have two..."

"You were looking for this because of the piece it held, weren't you?" He reached forward and placed the bracelet into her Serpent-marked palm. She braced herself automatically, ready to feel the same surge of her mother's power as before.

But nothing happened.

Sylven kept his hand against hers until she jerked it away. And then she tried to focus her senses, tried to find that aura that she'd seen around the Star-kind's stone, and around Ma, but...

"It's power, it's essence is..."

"Is gone."

She clenched the bracelet more tightly, as though she could squeeze the last drops of her mother's power from it if only she held it fiercely enough.

"Because I already took it," Sylven said.

Alaya suddenly felt, of all things...grief. As if she was living through her mother's death all over again. Because part of the connection she had finally found to that woman had been taken. Tainted.

The thief was still talking.

"You see," he said, "that initial gift your mother gave me increased my power that was already greater than most Serpent-kind's. It also made me able to absorb *more* of her gifts, just as you've been trying to do. So, thank you, for doing the work of gathering those pieces and drawing them neatly inside of yourself. Now I can simply take them all at once when I kill you. And *that*, to answer your question from before, is what I want from you. I will—"

"Be quiet."

He lifted an eyebrow.

"You thief. You *bastard*."

"Such foul language. Not really befitting of a supposed queen, is it?"

Her lungs heaved. The world swayed. Her eyes darted in search of a plan, and she spied strange movement—the faintest shaking of leaves—in one of the trees edging the campsite below. She immediately averted her eyes from that movement before Sylven noticed what *she* had noticed.

But the instant he started to talk again, to circle around her now, she let her gaze drift briefly back to those trees. She focused her magical senses.

And she saw a shimmer of bronze-colored energy in those trees.

This is not a nightmare.

It wasn't a trick. It *was* magic that had twisted the campsite into that horrible scene of frozen bodies—it simply wasn't Sylven's magic. He had helpers.

Her gaze returned to the hilltop they stood on. One of those collapsed lookouts had a bow resting beside him. Alaya kept her senses focused, and she found the faint aura pulsing around that weapon. At the same time, she was focused on pushing Sylven's voice from her mind, on trying to keep him from reading the plan that was forming in her thoughts.

"Trying to block me out, are we?"

"I *will* block you out."

"To what end? Your precious king and all of his soldiers will pay for your stubbornness. Keep refusing me—drawing this out—and I told you: They will all die."

He stepped closer to her once more.

She kept her eyes on his, but she could now feel the energy of that fallen lookout's weapon. Could feel her magic writhing to life, wrapping around that energy.

Sylven reached his hand back toward that bracelet he'd given her. "Why don't you just submit to me and end this without any more unnecessary death?"

She wrapped her control completely around the lookout's bow and quiver, and an instant later, both that bow and an arrow were flying through the air and into her hands.

Sylven stopped reaching for her.

She nocked the arrow and aimed her newly-caught weapon at his chest.

"You really think I can't stop anything you fire at me?"

"I know you can." She drew the arrow back all the same. And a moment before she loosed it, she moved its aim just inches to the left; it sailed past Sylven's head and hurtled toward the tree far below.

He realized what she was doing, and he twisted and struck his hand toward the flying arrow.

But she was prepared for this. Her magic was faster. Her control caught the projectile before his power did, and she guided it directly into her target, pushing it faster, sinking it more deeply into the magic user hiding in the trees. A cry rang through the eerily still camp. A body tumbled from the branches, sending a flock of birds into flight as it hit the ground.

She watched as the bronze-energy around that body faded from sight.

Moments later, there was movement among the camp. Spells coming undone, bodies unfreezing, groans escaping as mouths fell open.

But far too many of those soldiers remained on the ground. And there was no movement, at least none that she could see, coming from the tent that she and Emrys had been sharing.

"There's more than one Sand-kind," she breathed in realization.

Of course there's more than one.

She ran.

She raced back down to the camp, jerking the few waking soldiers to their feet, orders bellowing out of her: "IT'S SAND MAGIC! WAKE UP! FIND THE SAND-KIND AND KILL THEM! *WAKE UP*—"

She was struck from behind; Sylven's fist drove into her spine and sent sharp pain roaring through her. She stumbled. Fell to the dirt. Rolled to face him—just as he pulled a sword through the air and into his grip.

He stabbed downward.

She twisted, and he impaled only earth. She took that earth into her magic's control and broke it open, swallowing his stolen blade and trying to bury it completely.

As he stumbled back to avoid being buried himself, she leapt to her feet and backed away from him. He used magic to wrench his sword free of the dirt and back into his hands.

The camp thundered to life around them. More of the Sand-kind fell, taking their magic with them, and in exchange, more of the spelled Valinesian soldiers shook free of that magic that had frozen them in time. There were Sun soldiers flooding in from all directions, too. A fierce wind howled, and the horses and roan stamped and neighed and bellowed, and soon it all turned to a cacophony of indistinguishable noise and havoc.

Alaya ignored the noise. She reached out a hand to steal a sword of her own from one of those enemy soldiers. She caught it, balanced it, and readied herself just in time to meet the sweep of Sylven's blade. Her teeth clenched as the collision of their strength vibrated through her. They shoved against one another, both digging into their stances and refusing to yield.

But then came an abrupt movement—he whisked his blade down and away from hers— and as Alaya winced from the screech of steel sliding away from steel, Sylven aimed his hand at the ground.

The dirt beneath Alaya's feet grew unsteady. She danced away from the destruction he was trying to cause and countered with her own, grabbing hold of a second enemy sword and sending it flying, end over end, toward his head.

He gained control over it and sent it ricocheting away at the last second, slicing it into a nearby soldier. That soldier twisted in such a gruesome way that Alaya nearly closed her eyes against the sight and fell to her knees. But she kept them open and stayed standing, and she watched as the soldier dropped and a puddle of red oozed into the dust around his body.

The effort of catching the hurtling sword had momentarily slowed Sylven. While he tried to catch his breath, Alaya raced for a less-crowded area. She sprinted through more fallen bodies. Ran her sword through a Sand-kind that attempted to stop her. Wrenched that sword out and then kept moving, darting around sparring matches, knocking away wayward strands of Ice and Storm and Fire magic with her own controlling magic.

She saw the mountains rising in the distance, and the various narrow, rock-lined gaps that led deep into those mountains.

If she could lure Sylven into one of those gaps...

A vision of her closing the gap on top of him, of burying him in an avalanche of boulders and dirt, flashed in her mind. She ran faster. Sprinted until she could no longer feel her feet, and then farther still—until she found her path blocked by the dozens of horses and roan tied along the edge of their encampment.

She hesitated only a moment, looking for the easiest way around or through the floundering, panicking animals, and then she heard someone shouting her name—

She looked back.

She *shouldn't* have, but she did.

And she was frozen in place for a moment, struck by the sight of Sylven walking calmly through the battle to reach her.

His sword swung easily at his side. His lips were forming spells. His free hand reached toward that herd of animals behind her, and several of the largest antelope and horses ripped free of their ties and stampeded toward her.

She spun to avoid being gored by a pair of wickedly sharp and twisted horns, but ended up crashing against the flank of another roan. It bucked wildly about at her touch, nearly crushing her between its body and the sweat-drenched flank of the closest horse. Alaya ducked and rolled to avoid being squashed—but then she was on her back, on the ground, and the roan was rearing and preparing to stomp her into that ground.

She dropped her sword and thrusted both hands upward. The roan's energy was easy enough to find, but it was still intertwined with Sylven's magic. She had to push both of them away at once. Her body felt as if it might break in half from the effort, but she managed to send the antelope prancing back several steps, tossing its head irritably as it went.

With one hand still outstretched toward it, Alaya scrambled to her knees and then tripped her way back to her feet. The roan lowered its head and attempted to charge her again.

But she was more prepared this time.

Her magic caught it, twisted its head away and then shoved its entire body back. It let out several terrible, guttural bellows as it struggled, caught in the center of their combined magic until Alaya finally managed to overpower Sylven's. The rush of her strength lifted the creature momentarily off its feet before sending it careening across the ground, digging a trench as it went.

Sylven glared at it. He released his control over the other creatures, and they scattered as he rushed at her himself. He and Alaya circled through the camp, creating a deadly vortex of flying objects controlled by their magic. Anything that was not tightly secured could be thrown— and most of it was. Rocks, arrows, swords, the bodies of the fallen and the stakes of the pitched tents.

Everything was a weapon.

Alaya spotted a knife, limply grasped in the hand of a fallen soldier of the Sun. She wrapped her magic around it and flung it with all the strength and speed she could muster.

It struck Sylven's chest. She drove it deeper, twisting it in with a twist of her hand and a concentration that made her face break out in a cold sweat. Scarlet blossomed across his shirt. He dropped to one knee as he tried to rip the blade out. She pushed it deeper still, determined to crush him as one crushed a bug beneath a stone, twisting the weight back and forth until nothing of his life remained.

Then she saw something she did not expect—a dark golden light spilling from his bloodied chest.

She gasped, and her controlling magic slipped, and Sylven immediately jerked the blade from his chest before she could do any more damage with it.

It wasn't a fatal wound—within moments he was already staggering back to his feet—but she had drawn blood, and she had somehow drawn out his aura.

His *life-force.*

That's what that dark light was.

She had never been able to focus her senses enough to find it before. But now, a grim yet hopeful thought occurred to her: That same connection he'd been gloating about earlier could be the very thing that would allow her to kill him.

She could still see the faint glow of his energy. It was nearly the same golden shade as what she had seen around Ma, and around that stone the Star-Spinner had given her, and around Rue. So it felt familiar. She could connect herself to it, even amongst the chaos. It was still faint—he was controlling it, still suppressing it somehow —but she managed to grasp it, however weak her hold.

And when she attempted to wrap her own magic around it, he felt it.

She *knew* he'd felt it.

Because suddenly she saw something she had never seen in his eyes before: *Fear.*

It was quickly replaced by fury, and then his gaze was darting, calculating his next move. He backed away from her, shouting orders at someone in the distance as he went. Then he lifted an entire quiver full of arrows from a nearby Sun soldier, and he heaved them all at Alaya, all at once.

She batted the arrows down and chased after him—

But she was intercepted by a familiar Serpent-kind: *Mira.*

Yet another helper, along with the Sand-kind, and how many others who were waiting to charge into the fray?

She had no way of knowing the true toll this battle might have been taking on the ones she'd allied herself with.

She also didn't care. Not at the moment. The questions skipped out of her mind as quickly as they'd come. Because she had seen fear, she had drawn blood, she had proven that Sylven had weaknesses, and now her power rose like a starving, unstoppable beast that was capable of thinking of *nothing* except finishing the kill.

Her vision tunneled in the direction that Sylven had fled. "Get out of my way," she snarled at Mira.

Mira drew her sword and pointed it toward Alaya. "*Traitor,*" she snapped back in the language of Serpent-kind. Two more of those kind stepped to either side of her as she spoke, brandishing weapons of their own.

Alaya's thoughts narrowed as her vision had, and in her mind, she saw one single, clear image after another, all of them a testament to that rising power inside of her: the earth, broken; beasts, tamed; monsters, slain. She had been through fire and devastation and loss, and she had survived it all and kept fighting, and she would *not* be stopped now.

I am stronger, I am stronger—

That strength rushed through her and became an explosion of magic that took hold of every spark of energy around her. She clutched them all into her command.

And then she lost herself in commanding them.

Bodies convulsed, swords danced, dirt and stone lifted and spun around her and everything became a blur of death and destruction.

When it settled, she stood in a small crater of that destruction, and all three of the Serpent-kind lay dead at her feet.

Everyone still standing anywhere close—ally and enemy alike—scrambled to put as much distance between themselves and her as possible. The human side of her returned, briefly, as Alaya felt the all-too familiar sting of their fearful gazes.

While swallowing great lungfuls of air and trying to settle the trembling in her hands, she stood for a moment over Mira's body. The burn scars on the woman's face were splattered with her blood. Her own sword had sliced through her neck, it looked like. It was a horrid sight.

Alaya had once felt something of a kin-ship with this woman—one of her own clan, and one of the few who had actually bothered to try and relate to her, however short that relationship had been.

Now she had killed her.

It all felt so senseless. Infuriatingly senseless. She briefly felt like the traitor that she had been accused of being—but then she was simply more *angry*, this time with herself, for even dwelling on those poisonous claims.

That odd, furious grief from earlier was suddenly back. And she couldn't make sense of it, either. She only wanted, again, to kill the person she felt was most responsible for it, and everything else fell away once more as she rocketed through the camp, searching for him, throwing aside every person who tried to stop her, paying no attention to whether they were friend or foe.

And then suddenly—*there he was.* Standing in the mouth of one of those passages she'd planned on luring him into, his face hidden in the shadows of the rocks.

He appeared calm as she approached. Prepared for her assault. Had been expecting it, maybe, patiently waiting for it—perhaps he'd used their connection to read her thoughts and thus had seen her coming long before now.

That wouldn't save him.

She sought that connection again, and she found the faint light shimmering around him. But something in her resisted as she tried to grab hold of his energy this time;

every twist of her hand, every attempt to crush his life away felt as if it was crushing *her* life with the same effort.

It didn't matter, she quickly decided. She only wanted him dead. If it caused her pain as well, then so be it.

She didn't care if it killed her.

She grasped her power more tightly.

His knees buckled, and so did hers. Soon she couldn't move from the pain, couldn't focus on anything except trying not to lose her hold on that faint pulse of his life. But then she vaguely registered the sight of his mouth moving, and the sound of the stone walls cracking and shifting, echoing through the passage.

She lifted her eyes to the rocks. It all became a dream; a slow-moving nightmare where she saw pieces of those rocks breaking apart and tumbling down—one-by-one at first, and then building rapidly into a sliding mass of stone and mud that gained speed as it hurtled toward her.

She closed her eyes so that she could concentrate on keeping Sylven's life in her hands.

I am stronger.

She *was* stronger. Not strong enough to survive everything collapsing in on her, but strong enough to drag that monster down with her on her way out. A strange peace overwhelmed her at the thought. The pain of their twisted-together magic faded. She felt as if she was floating for a moment, and then sinking slowly into an oblivion that she did not intend to swim out of.

Then for some reason, she decided to open her eyes

one last time, and she looked back to the passage's opening.

And she saw something far worse than the rocks falling over her: *Emrys.*

He was sprinting into the passage, running straight toward her, seemingly unaware of those rocks that were about to crush them both.

She tried to find her voice, to scream at him to get away. When she didn't manage that, she stopped trying to kill Sylven and instead redirected her magic toward the avalanche of stone. But her arms shook. Her magic was unstable from the sudden shift in her focus. She couldn't stop those rocks, could barely slow them down—

Emrys reached her and threw his arms around her, ignoring her shouting.

He was saying something, a string of words she didn't understand.

She felt an odd itch against her scalp, a terrible pressure against her insides, and then all of the world shifted and spun away from them.

CHAPTER 28

A MIGHTY *CRACK!* ECHOED THROUGH THE AIR, AND ALAYA'S back slammed into the ground hard enough to knock her breath away. She blinked her eyes open to blue sky, and she sat up slowly, groaning at the pain buzzing through her spine.

Emrys was several feet away from her, already sitting up. "I'm really glad that worked," he muttered, massaging a cramp from his hand.

She rolled over and pushed herself to her feet, her balance swaying a bit from her pain—and from the realization that was settling over her like a numbing, icy rain. "That was..."

He sighed, getting to his feet as well, and wiping the dust and dried grass from his knees. "Air magic."

"*I knew it.*"

He started toward her. "Dragon, I can explain—"

"How long have you been doing this?" She backed out of his reach.

He curled his outstretched hand into a fist and slowly lowered it. "Since our stay at the Bay of Sinking Souls. Valla took me to a friend of hers, and she explained to me how it works, and there are...others in my city who have helped me, too."

"I told myself it wasn't true." She took another step back, slowly shaking her head. "That I had misremembered, that it was just another lie that Sylven had planted into my head. But you *did* use stolen magic that night at the inn, didn't you? And you've used it before, too. You burned Mira's face. How many others have you hurt?"

"It had to be done."

"*How many?*"

"It doesn't matter right now."

"It's *stolen*. It's stolen magic, just like your—"

"*That stolen magic just saved your life.*"

"At what cost to *your* life?" she roared back, loud enough that she shocked even herself, and for a moment, the two of them could do nothing except stare at one another. She had been angry with him before—so angry that she couldn't breathe—but she had never yelled at him like this.

And yet the sound was nowhere near as deafening as the sounds of that battle they'd fled.

Emrys narrowed his eyes in the direction of that battlefield for a moment, and then he said, "We will talk about this back at the palace. We need to get away from here."

"No. No, I wasn't finished fighting. I—"

"There is a bigger fight descending towards Rykarra as we speak."

She had shoved her way past him and started back toward the camp, but his words made her pause.

"Another arm of Levant's forces threatens to surround and crush my palace, my city, and any allies that might try to stand with us," he said. "And the expected time of their arrival lines up with the prophecy the Star-kind gave you."

She slowly turned back to face him.

"Three thousand strong, I've been told."

Fear ignited like fire in her gut. "Sade. And..."

"And all of the innocent citizens still reeling from the *last* attack on that capital city—not to mention the additional lives that will be at risk if we fall, and the Army of the Sun can then continue to run rampant and unchecked through the empire."

She held her breath, trying to slow down that fiery terror spreading through her by starving it of air.

"Levant never intended to meet me here, I'm guessing. This was a decoy. And perhaps also a plot orchestrated by Sylven to try and kill you. Which he very nearly did."

"I would have killed *him* if you'd just left me alone."

"And killed yourself in the process. Which, we've been

over this, haven't we? What part of *I am not okay with you dying* do you not understand?"

She exhaled in a huff, but otherwise didn't respond right away. The distant roar of her dragon suddenly drew their attention, and her gaze scanned the skies, looking for Rue but not finding her.

"So we're going to run away from this battle?" she asked.

"Yes. It's called regrouping and living to fight another day. Captain Helder is already aware that I was considering going back—he insisted upon it, actually. He can handle this. Once the Sun Army realizes that you and I are gone, they're likely to retreat anyways, if they haven't already lost by that point."

"And if they *don't* retreat? If more come and overwhelm our forces?"

"Then our forces will lose. Such is war."

She glared at him.

He was unmoved by it.

"Call Rue," he said. "We're going back. And I'd rather travel by dragon flight than by magic."

"I can't leave. Sylven is still—"

"We're leaving."

His commanding tone, in addition to everything else she was still fuming about, annoyed her to the point that she couldn't swallow her angry words down anymore. "Or *what?*" she snapped. "What sort of magic are you going to use against me if I refuse to obey you?"

His expression flashed between hurt and fury. It

settled on fury, and he stepped closer to her, snatching her by the arm when she attempted to turn away from him. "Call. Your. Dragon."

She was not finished with their argument. But she was also worried about Sade, and about the implications of Rykarra being overtaken. There was no clear path to that piece of her mother's essence that she had come for, either, and though she felt powerful—more powerful than ever—Sylven apparently was, too.

She needed time to think.

To *regroup,* as Emrys had put it, as much as she didn't want to.

So as she pushed away from him, she looked to the skies once more, and then she closed her eyes and focused on projecting an image of her surroundings to Rue.

I need you, she thought.

After a moment, the familiar voice purred through her thoughts: (*You sound upset, Little Goddess.*)

Just hurry up.

A great shadow overtook them minutes later, and Rue landed with a graceful *thump* and intertwined her long body around them both.

And without another glance at that battle they'd escaped, they climbed onto the dragon's back and soared for the greater battle that lay just ahead.

WHAT HAD TAKEN three days with their company of soldiers took less than one with only the two of them on the back of a dragon; by that evening, they were crossing into the familiar plains that soon sloped towards Rykarra.

She and Emrys had barely spoken during the flight. The unfortunate side-effect of this was that the quiet made it difficult for Alaya to stay awake—but trying to rest was a poor option; every time her eyes fluttered shut, she had to suffer the sound of Sylven's voice and his thoughts intruding upon hers.

Their brief reconnection seemed to have given him a renewed ability to attack her.

He could not control her anymore—her magic use had not left her as vulnerable as it had in the past. She *was* stronger, now, just as she'd told herself. Strong enough to not mistake these images he was forcing upon her as truth. But he still managed to torture her with his voice, with his disgustingly cruel thoughts that she couldn't escape. It was like a terrible ache in her head, a painful twinge in her teeth; it would not break her, but it was still agony as she waited for it to pass.

She came very close to falling asleep just as the flames of the Palace of Eyes came into view—but, once again, Sylven's voice caught her just before she tumbled over the edge of slumber.

Soon, he promised her. *I'll see you again very soon.*

She jolted awake.

"What's wrong?" Emrys asked.

She curled more tightly against Rue's back.

"Alaya?"

She still did not answer, partly because she was still furious with him, but mostly because she couldn't think clearly enough to form words.

Emrys sighed, but he left her alone after that.

When they landed in one of the palace courtyards a short time later, Emrys was immediately swarmed by his anxious courtiers. Immediately pulled away from her. Again. And she was still too angry and hurt by the secret he'd kept from her to try and stop it from happening.

Instead, she let him be dragged away, and then—after a brief trip to her room to change and wash away the grime of her travels—she went to find Sade.

Her search led her to the wide balcony that wrapped around the second floor of the palace, where she found Sade situated in a hammock stretched between two marble columns.

"You look comfortable," Alaya commented.

Sade leapt from her perch and threw her arms around Alaya's neck. "What are you doing back so soon?" she asked as she pulled away.

Alaya walked to the edge of the balcony, hugging her arms against herself as she peered out over a city that seemed strangely quiet. Its chimneys were devoid of their usual smoke, its winding streets all but empty.

Did that city know what was coming?

"We had a slight change in plans," she told Sade. "We were attacked before we even properly made it to the Gate of the Sun...and then *His Majesty* insisted we return."

"But you returned for good reason, right? You know about the threat marching toward this city? The palace has been in an uproar about it since soon after you two left. They've started calling for the city folk to volunteer to fight if they're able, and they've evacuated most of the ones who won't fight to the fortress at Hollowforge."

That explained some of the quiet.

Alaya nodded stiffly. "Our return was for good reason."

"But you still seem upset."

"Yes."

"Because...?"

"Because the only reason he and I escaped that ill-fated battle was because Emrys used magic. Air-kind magic."

Sade did not look nearly as shocked or upset about this as she should have, which sent a fresh shudder of irritation burning through Alaya.

"...But you already knew that he was experimenting with that magic, didn't you?" she guessed, flatly.

Sade rubbed a hand along the back of her neck, looking uncomfortable, as she settled back into the hammock. "I'm sorry. I...I thought it would be better if you heard it from him. I would have told you soon, if he hadn't."

Alaya scowled, but she didn't have time to properly fight about the matter before they were interrupted; that Ice-kind noblewoman—*Lady Korva, wasn't it?*—that she had watched Emrys dance with on the night of his coronation had just stepped out onto the balcony.

She looked shocked to see Alaya. And Alaya was shocked to see *her*, but apparently Sade had been in the middle of a discussion with her before Alaya had shown up; they had recessed only so that Lady Korva could go and find drinks for the two of them.

It was the first time Alaya had been so close to her, and Lady Korva looked every bit as beautiful and regal up close as she had from across the room. The tiniest bit of jealousy spasmed through Alaya once more, but she quickly pushed it down; there were more important things to worry about, weren't there?

"Sorry," Lady Korva said, nodding to the two cups in her hands. "I didn't know you would be here as well, or I would have brought you something."

Alaya distractedly waved off the apology. She tried to go back to gazing out toward the city, but she felt Lady Korva staring at her still. She glanced back to find the Icekind offering one of the cups to her.

"Take mine. You look as though you need a drink more than I do."

Alaya stared at that cup, suddenly uncertain of what to say.

"It's not poisoned, I swear. I've seen how irrational your king becomes over you, and believe me: I have no desire to deal with the fallout of giving you so much as an upset stomach." Lady Korva hesitated, drawing the cup back slightly. "Though, if you can't hold your alcohol, this might do just that; it's Kemarian ale. Not exactly for the faint of heart or stomach."

"I can hold it just fine," Alaya said, working to smooth the crossness from her tone as she took the drink. "Thank you."

"You're welcome."

Alaya sipped it, still unsure of what else to do; she still had plenty to learn about interacting with these kinds of people. She couldn't help feeling that everything nobles gave—even a simple cup of ale—came with threads attached to it, and that those threads would trip her if she wasn't constantly watching for them.

That ale was oddly sweet, with hardly any of the bite that accompanied most alcohol, and yet, she could already feel a pleasant tingling starting to spread through her mind. Delicious and potent. *The most dangerous kind of drink*, she mused to herself.

The three of them made idle chatter for several minutes while she sipped at that drink—safe, pointless chatter, until finally Lady Korva said, "It's good that you're back. Hopefully having their king here once more will calm some of the nerves in this place."

"He never should have left in the first place," Alaya muttered, more to herself than anyone.

"He left to accompany you, did he not?"

Alaya cut her eyes sideways at the prying woman.

"Well?"

"The king and I were not exactly on speaking terms when we left, nor are we at the moment."

"Why not?"

The ale made Alaya less reserved than usual. "Because he is too fond of secrets," she said. "Not that it's any business of yours."

Lady Korva rolled her eyes. "Oh, do get over it already."

"...Pardon?"

"Forgive my boldness, but I now understand why my father warned me about the dramatics of this court; most of my encounters with Rook-kind and the palace dwellers here have led me to believe that they are masters of theater—not governing, not war, not anything useful. How have they held onto the high throne for as long as they have?"

"I—"

"I want to climb to the highest tower of this palace and start shouting orders of my own."

"Orders?"

"To stop all of the bickering—and yes, the secret keeping—and just *fight* for the things that actually matter. Is that really so difficult?"

"Things are not so black and white. It isn't that easy."

"It is to *me*. And thank the Moraki my army is on the way to show all of you how to fight with something resembling focus, or else we'd all be doomed."

"We're likely all doomed anyways," Sade put in, rather unhelpfully.

"Not if *I* can help it," Lady Korva countered.

"Well, let's all hope that you can save the day for us," Alaya said with a tightly-clenched smile.

The lady quirked a grin that suggested she planned to do exactly that, and then she dismissed herself, muttering something about needing a drink of her own after all.

Alaya watched her go, then downed the rest of her own drink and slammed the cup onto the balcony railing. "*Somebody* thinks very highly of her clan and their role in this war, don't they?"

Sade grinned. "Sorry, but I like her. I like her a lot, actually."

Alaya was tired of arguing, though she did manage a mildly vexed look. "Whose side are you on, anyway?" she muttered.

Sade rocked upright, swinging her long legs over the side of the hammock and wobbling for a moment before successfully planting her feet. "Yours," she said, standing and stretching. "In the end, it's always going to be yours. And no, I don't think Lady Korva is entirely right; it's more complicated than that, as you said. And yet...as someone on your side, I *do* have to insist that you go fix this thing with your king—before the war arrives at our doorstep, and you find yourself too distracted by the drama to survive the battle."

"This new, full-of-logical-advice version of you is kind of...*annoying*."

"I've always lived to annoy you; nothing has changed about that."

"That's true enough."

"But on a serious note? People make mistakes." Sade stepped closer, wrapped her arms around her and gave another light squeeze. "It doesn't mean they don't love you."

"...I know," Alaya said, as she reluctantly sighed, relaxed, and hugged Sade back.

And then she promptly pretended to gag at the show of affection, which earned her a swat from Sade, and for a moment they were laughing—as relaxed and fearless as they had been once upon a time.

The fearlessness faded as Alaya gazed out toward the city again and an ominous sight caught her eye: the outer gates to the palace grounds were opening, and several scores worth of soldiers were marching inside.

"More allies...?" Sade commented, her laughter abruptly ending and her voice dropping to a whisper.

They stared silently at those ranks of soldiers filing in. The air felt heavier, suddenly, sticky with a humidity that Alaya hadn't noticed until just now.

"I should go talk to Emrys," she said after a minute.

"Yes," Sade agreed. "But maybe you should have another drink first."

CHAPTER 29

HOURS LATER, ALAYA LEFT SADE AND THE PILE OF EMPTY CUPS they'd collected between the two of them, and she headed towards the throne room, where she knew Emrys was likely still deeply entrenched in meetings.

She was not drunk enough to consider another interruption with a kiss, so she was mulling over her other options as she walked. Less *dramatic* options. She could be calm. Dignified. Queenlike. And the guards would likely yield to her, anyhow, if she simply asked them to; she was not *officially* the queen, no. But turning her away would anger their king.

Wouldn't it?

Her standing in this palace felt odd, in-between, and it didn't help settle the surreal disconnect she'd been feeling after staring at that city empty of everything but soldiers.

But when she arrived in the hallway outside that

throne room, her feelings and plans ultimately didn't matter—because she was distracted from them by the last face she expected to see just then.

"...Father?"

"Oh. Hello." He turned to her, and his expression was strange at first—briefly pained, briefly uncertain—before he managed to twist it into something almost-normal as he said, "I was hoping I might run into you soon."

"What are you doing here?"

He stepped away from the group surrounding him—a group of no less than ten other Serpent-kind, some of whom she vaguely recognized from her brief interactions with them in Amara. "I'm here for an audience with the high king," her father said, once they were a private enough distance away—though the eyes of those Serpent-kind continued to occasionally dart in her direction.

"An audience?" she repeated. "Regarding what?"

"He has sent me so many letters..." He trailed off with a slight shrug. "I suppose I decided it was time to answer them."

"Letters?"

"About you. And about our clan and the recent...*events* they've been involved in throughout the empire. In short, he's insisting that the time has come for us to set aside our differences and fight alongside one another. He's convinced that the stigma against our kind can be reversed, the past undone in some ways..." He trailed off once more, that uncertainty briefly flashing across his face again before he pulled his gaze back to hers and offered her a small smile. "I'm not certain he's right, but...there are more of us waiting in the city outside, all the same. We'll see what happens, won't we? It does feel like we're on the edge of something. A great change, for better or worse."

She thought again of the Star-kinds' prophecy, of the day of reckoning that was coming and all the death—the *change*—that the empire was lurching towards. But she didn't want to talk to him about it. So she only nodded. "It does feel that way."

She understood why Emrys had sent for him. Because he had seen her father heal her in the past, and the magic that all the Serpent-kind possessed would be useful in all the battles pressing toward them. So she wasn't *angry* to see him...

But their relationship still felt odd. Raw. Tender, as if the slightest wrong move might cause the pain to flare again.

They shared blood, and memories, and a connection to the same goddess.

But that alone did not make them family.

Maybe it could change, assuming they all survived the coming days.

We'll see what happens.

The crowd outside Emrys's throne room was greater than she'd expected. It wasn't only her father and his companions that were awaiting an audience with the king, but a host of others from all different clans, most of them leaders representing the forces who had answered the king's call to fight.

As she stared at them all, her anger suddenly seemed...well, *foolish*. And interrupting his meetings seemed even more foolish.

So instead, she went outside and wandered the court-yards, breathing the muggy air in as deeply as she could. There were no clear stars tonight; only hazy pinpricks of light that seemed to be disappearing even as she watched them. It was nothing more than a light shower moving in, just clouds covering up those lights, but it was still eerie to see the darkness sweeping like an omen across the sky.

And as she was looking up, searching for more light, she heard that familiar voice slithering through her distracted thoughts once more—

Soon.

The mark on her hand pulsed. She imagined warmth oozing over it. *Blood.* There was nothing there when she looked, of course—but the voice in her mind was relent-less, along with Sylven's tricks: *Very soon, now,* he said. *And I'm looking forward to seeing you again. To finishing this.*

She pressed her hand against a nearby statue, both to steady herself and to hide her mark from sight. The thought of smashing her forehead into the stone, of trying to brutally knock the terrible voice from her head, briefly occurred to her. But she managed to stagger away from the statue. To think clearly enough to keep walking. She was *determined* to keep walking. To appear normal to the few people that she passed on her way to finding Rue.

The dragon was curled up at the very edge of the courtyard, resting. As Alaya approached, she blinked one eye open and exhaled a breath that shook a patch of nearby flowers, nearly uprooting several of them.

(*Sleeping?*) It was a grumpy accusation, the translation—*you should be sleeping, not bothering me.*

"I can't," Alaya told her, slumping down into the crease between the dragon's side and her wing. It felt a bit like a hug, pressing under that wing joint. "I needed another voice in my head. Aside from mine. And aside from Sylven's."

(*...Stay close?*) the dragon suggested, breathing out another slow, powerful breath and wrapping her tail towards her snout, creating a circle of protection around Alaya. That tail flicked up and down, tapping a beat against the dirt that was hypnotizing, almost; Alaya wondered if the dragon was doing it on purpose, a more primitive version of controlling 'magic' that was intended to lull her target to sleep. She welcomed it, if so.

And though she never actually slept—the beast's rumbly breathing and occasional startling, booming snores helped make certain of that—she did manage to rest for a while.

WHEN THE SUDDEN sound of nearby voices jolted her fully awake after what must have been hours later, her head was silent. Her powers, combined with the shade of that same power that Rue carried, seemed to have effectively driven Sylven away.

At least for the time being.

She didn't know how long it would last. But her thoughts were clear and she suddenly felt wide awake, and all she could think about was how badly she wanted to see and talk to her Rook.

It was late; she realized just *how* late when she noticed how quiet the palace had become. There were no longer people milling about outside the throne room, or outside of Emrys's study, or around any of his other regular meeting rooms. She expected he was in his own private chambers by now, preparing for bed—if not already asleep—and so she quickly headed to that floor.

She was practically sprinting by the time she reached the top of the stairs to it, slowing down only once she caught sight of the guards pacing in front of his room. She took a deep breath, preparing to order them to move aside and let her in. But before she reached those guards, she heard a familiar voice calling after her.

"He isn't in his room."

"...Where is he?"

Predictably, Isoni didn't answer her question. Instead, the lady climbed the last few stairs up to the floor with slow, deliberate steps, and then she walked toward Alaya in the same manner, her eyes narrowed and studying as she came.

"Well?" Alaya said, impatiently.

"He's spent the entire day catching up on things..."

Alaya bit the inside of her lip to keep from snapping out a response.

"...because, once again, he followed you into trouble outside of his palace. And now we are—or rather, *he* is—ill-prepared for the battle marching toward said palace, and for the troubles that he is *truly* responsible for. Are you pleased to have commanded his attention for the past few days?"

Months ago, Alaya might have simply lowered her gaze and did her best to escape this woman's ire. For so many years, she had hidden her mark and averted her eyes, doing her best to disappear when people started throwing stones and calling her a curse.

Tonight, she kept her head lifted and her gaze locked on Isoni's as she walked back to her.

"Well?" Isoni prompted. "What do have to say for yourself?"

"A few things, actually."

Isoni did a poor job of masking her surprise as Alaya stepped even closer, bringing their faces only inches apart.

"First of all," Alaya began in a low, dangerous voice, "I *tried* to talk him out of going to the Gate of the Sun with me—we've argued about it for days—but he insisted on coming. And do you know why?"

Isoni's lip curled into a snarl, but she didn't speak.

"It's because he's in love with me," Alaya answered for her. "Which brings me to the second thing I need to say: I am not the curse you accused me of being when you and I first met. I am going to be a queen of this empire, whether you like it or not. And I love him, whether you like *that* or not. So I don't care if you don't want to tell me where he is; I will just go and find him myself." She paused for breath, and then continued in that same dark voice: "Now, get out of my way, or else I am going to remind you of why most of this empire has been terrified of me at one point or another."

A muscle in her jaw twitched, but still Isoni was silent. She slowly stepped aside, glaring as Alaya walked past her.

But as she reached the stairs, Alaya finally heard her moving, and then clearing her throat.

"Alaya."

She stopped, only because part of her was shocked to hear this woman use her actual name, instead of referring to her as *Serpent* or by some derogatory variation of that word. She masked the shock from her face and turned back to face Isoni.

"He is in the Hall of Smoke. The stairs to the right of the Tower of Anga's entrance will take you down to it."

"...Thank you."

"You're welcome." Isoni gave a slight bow of her head. Alaya thought she might have seen the beginnings of a very slight smile on the Bone-kind's face before she turned, walked to the guards outside of Emrys's door, and began a conversation with them.

Alaya followed Isoni's directions. She eventually found her way to that tower, and to the guarded doorway that she assumed led to the Hall of Smoke. The walls on either side of that doorway were inset with white marble, and a depiction of the Rook God, Anga, had been carved into the stone, his head facing the door, inquisitive eyes watching over everyone who went in and out of it.

The guards let her pass without hesitation, pressing the Rook symbols on their hands against panels in the frame until the door opened and revealed a spiraling staircase.

She quietly thanked them and stepped inside. She wondered if Emrys had ordered them to let her in without so much as a question. If he'd been expecting her to come. Or at least *hoping* she would come...

The thought that he'd been hoping to see her wrapped her in a layer of warmth, protecting her against the chill of the space she was descending into.

She had heard stories about this place. Some called it a monument, others referred to it as a crypt. Either way, it was sacred space that she doubted many outside of Rook royalty had ever seen in person.

At the bottom of the stairs, she found herself facing a long, wide hallway with evenly placed, partially open rooms branching off from it. Each of those recessed spaces held artifacts specific to a fallen Rook of seemingly great importance; their possessions, including jewelry and pottery and books; paintings and other likenesses of them; a few even had life-size statues, or reliefs carved into the walls with the same intricate detail as the Rook gods she'd seen upstairs.

And in the center of each of these alcoves was a pedestal with a glowing, smoke-filled stone resting upon it.

She didn't have to go far to find Emrys.

He was standing in one of these spaces, surrounded by his mother's artifacts. The jewel in the center of this particular space was pulsing with a faint purplish color, and in the light of that glowing stone, he was flipping through an old book.

And he was...beautiful. Clearly tired, his normally bright eyes appearing darker than she knew them to be. But her stomach still fluttered at the soft parting of his lips, at the thoughtful furrow of his brow, and at the way he had lost himself so completely in whatever was inside that book. She wondered if she would ever stop feeling that fluttering when she looked at him—*really* looked at him—as she was doing now.

I hope not, she thought.

She was still frustrated with him.

But it was now impossible to deny that she was also very much in love with him, and all she wanted right then was to irritably stand beside him. So this is what she did; as he sat that book down and glanced her way, she moved without speaking to his side.

"These are the *mortha* stones," he explained to her, his voice low as he motioned toward the glowing rock, which was their only real source of light in the tucked away space.

"Mortha?"

"We burn the dead, and we discard the ashes, but we catch the smoke in these special crystals, which are then magically sealed in such a way that this smoke continues to tumble and fall for eternity."

She pulled her cloak more tightly against a sudden chill, but she couldn't deny the morbid fascination she felt as she stared into the smoky glow.

"I always thought it was less sad than an outright burial of some kind," he continued. "The smoke seems more...*alive*, doesn't it? And people even say that properly sealed-in wisps of this smoke will also hold the true energy of the deceased person themselves—the energy they carried in life, that is."

She stared at it as he spoke, watched as it rose and fell, the tendrils of it swinging back and forth in a steady arc that was oddly soothing to watch.

They were quiet for a long time after that. Eventually, she released the tight grip she had on her cloak, and he reached for her hand, lacing his fingers through hers. She didn't pull away.

He absently ran his thumb along the curve of her hand, still looking at that smoky light when he said, "I should have told you about my magic a long time ago."

"Yes. You should have told me the day you gained the very first of it."

His hand went still against hers.

"But it doesn't matter, now, does it?" she said, softer.

"It doesn't?"

"No."

"Even though it's stolen, precisely as my father used to steal it?" His tone was odd. Quiet. Hard. Difficult to read.

"I...I shouldn't have said that before. I didn't actually *believe* it." She started to pull away, suddenly embarrassed by the memory of her outburst, but he squeezed her hand more tightly and pulled her around to face him.

"Good." His eyes were more serious than she had ever seen them. "Because I would *never* hurt you—not with this magic or anything else—and you need to understand that."

"I do."

"Gods, Dragon, the main reason I wanted it in the first place was because I was desperate to *protect you*, so that you didn't have to fight alone, and so you wouldn't..." He trailed off, shaking his head in frustration.

"I know," she whispered.

It was so she wouldn't end up as nothing more than smoke trapped in a stone.

She turned her gaze away from that smoking stone as she said, "You were right, anyways."

"About...?"

"I'm not sure I could have defeated Sylven alone, even if you'd let me go back to the fight."

He tilted his face toward her.

"Partly because he has what I believe are the last pieces of that power I've been trying to collect."

"He does?"

"I didn't realize it until we fought at the camp. But my

mother gave one of those pieces to him, nearly nineteen years ago, when he helped us escape Amara. And then he figured out that I was tracking down the other pieces... He was able to figure it out enough that he extracted the power that *I* intended to take from my mother's bracelet —power that belongs to *me*. It's why I couldn't kill him. And why I believe he still haunts my thoughts, even now. We're still...connected. I've already heard his voice several times since we came back to the city. I'm going to keep hearing it, I think, until one of us is dead."

Emrys inhaled deeply—clearly infuriated by the thought of Sylven's voice in her mind, but trying to stay calm for her sake. "But he isn't *controlling* you with that voice, correct?"

"No. Not anymore."

"So...that's an improvement, isn't it?"

"I suppose it is. I've gone from accidentally tearing up cities, to being prone to murderous rages, to just hearing voices in my head."

He drew her closer and kissed her forehead, laughing softly. "You're practically a normal person. How boring."

She gave him a wry smile, and then she let herself relax against his chest. He wrapped her up more tightly, and she felt safe enough to close her eyes and not think, for just a moment, about anything other than the sound of his heartbeat.

"He keeps telling me *soon*," she eventually continued. "He's going to join any force that's marching against this city, I'm sure."

"Let him join them." The words rumbled in her king's chest, a quiet, dark threat that sent a shiver over her skin.

As it settled, she drew back, and he took her hand once more. They left the Hall of Smoke and its dead, and she let him lead the way back to the upper levels of the palace. He stopped short of delivering her to her room, however, instead pausing at the top of the stairs and peering back down to what they could see of the floors below.

The hall on either side of them was eerily quiet. Nothing except the painted faces of faded portraits, and those few distant guards hovering around Emrys's door, kept them company.

But down below, the palace still showed signs of life. Not as many as earlier in the day, but...

"There are more people up than I would have expected for this time of night," she commented.

Emrys let go of her hand and leaned against the railing that wound away from the stairs, staring down at those people. "They're all afraid, I'd guess. Anxious and unable to sleep. Terrified that their young king will let their city fall. That yet another age of endless wars is beginning." He braced his arms against the railing and bowed his head. "Say what you will about my father, but this palace believed it was invincible while he was ruling it. Most Rook-kind felt that way. And I...I almost...understand why he wanted magic. Or why he did at first, anyways. I don't want to understand it. It *horrifies* me that

I understand it. That I feel that same need to gain strength, however I can. But..."

"You can be strong in other ways besides magic," she insisted. "You *are* strong in other ways."

He didn't reply right away, though he did lift his head and breathe in several deep, calming breaths.

And after a long pause he said, "Tell me how this all ends, Dragon."

She smiled a bit at the memory of standing before him in his room, asking that same question only days ago.

"I don't know," she said, stealing his answer. But it didn't feel like enough of a response, so she thought for a moment, and then she added, "But I know what comes first."

"Well, how does it start, then?"

"First, we fight. We stop the army that's marching against us. We kill Sylven. We neutralize Levant. The empire shifts because of these things, and then it all goes very dark for awhile, I imagine—just as the Stars said it would. Because sometimes change means death, and sometimes change means darkness, but then..."

He turned away from the people below so that he could face her, folding his arms across his chest and leaning back against the railing as he did. "But then?"

"But then we come out on the other side, and we rebuild."

"And we rebuild it better."

"And brighter," she agreed. "So we hold on..."

"Even if it all goes dark?"

"Exactly." She took his hand again. He pulled her to him once more, and she splayed her hands across his chest while his arms draped loosely around her waist.

He sighed deeply, almost contentedly. But it only lasted a few moments before she felt him turning to look at the space below them again.

"You're thinking of going back down there?" she guessed. "To do what? Meet with more people? Discuss more strategy? At this hour?"

"...Four days," he reminded her, frowning. "Maybe less, if the latest reports of movement on the border of our province are accurate."

"You still have to sleep at some point before then."

He considered this, tracing his fingers up and down her arm. It was an absentminded, innocent motion, but it still made the muscles in her core clench and her entire body flush hot. And then he said, "Fair point. But I have one other concern."

"Which is what?"

"I need you in my arms if I am going to sleep tonight. No more of this sleeping in other beds and in opposite corners of tents and nonsense like that—I hate it."

She swallowed the small lump in her throat, and she tried to manage a teasing, composed tone. "Fine. For the sake of the empire, and because the high king needs his rest, I will share a bed with him."

"How charitable." His grin was her undoing, as it had been over and over again during these past months.

She gave in to that burning in her skin, and she lifted

on to her tiptoes to press her lips against his. Her voice was low as she pulled away and said, "It isn't *entirely* charity. I'll expect payment of some kind."

"I'm sure we can work something out," he said, his hands moving to grasp her hips and his voice raspy with sudden need. "But we should probably get to that bed sooner rather than later. I'm very...*tired*."

She smiled before slowly leaning back and taking hold of his hands. And this time, she led the way, pulling him down the hall, into his room, and shutting them away from the wars one last time.

CHAPTER 30

THREE DAYS PASSED IN A FLURRY OF MEETINGS AND preparations, with Emrys pouring endlessly over reports, studying potential battle strategies, and settling arguments between subjects who were growing increasingly tense as the battle drew closer to their capital city.

The fourth day dawned accompanied by thunder, which woke him from a fitful sleep that he'd only fallen into an hour ago.

Alaya was already awake. She was sitting on the bench tucked beneath the room's tallest window, bathed in the pinkish-golden light of the sunrise.

He rubbed the sleep from his eyes. She slowly came into sharper focus. She was twisting the ring he'd given her around on her finger, humming softly to herself; he'd heard her humming notes of that song before—it was one of the ones her mother used to sing to her when she couldn't sleep, she'd told him once.

"Dragon? What's wrong?"

She stopped humming. Exhaled a slow, shuddering breath, and without looking at him she said: "His voice woke me up."

An uneasy, violent shiver coursed through him. That voice and the visions in her head had been silent and still over the past days of preparation, as far as he knew.

He tried to keep his own voice composed as he stood and started to dress. "And what did he say?"

It took her a moment to answer. "The prophecy," she finally said. "He keeps mentioning it. The darkness, the death, the destruction. *Today is the day the stars burn out*, he said, and now I can't get those words out of my mind."

Emrys's jaw clenched. He pulled a shirt over his head with a swift jerk. Snatched up his belt and daggers and the most recent report that had been delivered to him; he'd fallen asleep with it in his hand, and the rolled parchment had ended up on the floor.

"I suspected before that it has gotten to the point where we're connected enough that he can read my thoughts," Alaya continued as he rerolled that parchment. "And it seems I was right; because my thoughts have been about nothing other than that prophecy all night, really. So, of course, he's trying to use that against me."

"He's a coward playing tricks to try and frighten you; nothing more."

She stood, slowly, and she turned to face him. She didn't look afraid. She looked fierce, determined, and ready to face whatever fate the day might hold for them.

He took her hand, pulled her in and held her tightly to his chest for a minute. "And I am looking forward to today, suddenly."

"You are?"

"Or at least the part of today where he dies a violent, painful death at the end of my sword."

She tilted her head back enough to see his face. "Your sword will have to be quicker than mine."

"Or perhaps they can fall at the same time," he suggested.

"I could live with that."

A sudden pounding against the door rattled the paintings on the far wall. It didn't make him jump. He had gotten used to being jolted awake at all hours of the night, to being summoned at all hours of the day, called to that door to meet the demands and questions of his frantic council and courtiers.

When he flung open the door this time, Captain Helder was standing there, returned from the Gate of the Sun and bursting with more news regarding the battles roaring toward them—grim news.

They were almost out of time.

The captain had already started to mobilize their collected forces. The day would end with bloodshed, with a battle that was imminent now, and then after that...

Even the Stars don't know.

Emrys pushed this last thought from his mind as he dismissed Helder, and then he washed up and finished dressing in a rush. He kissed Alaya before turning to leave, that violence he'd felt toward Sylven earlier resurfacing as he did. He would have given anything to be able to silence the noise in her head before they marched into battle.

He kissed her harder, reluctant to leave her side, even though he knew he had no choice.

"I'll tell the armory to be expecting you soon," he said, letting his hand lingered against her palm for as long as he could before he pulled away, "and I will see you and your dragon outside the city."

That was his first stop—the armory. While the servants of the armory outfitted him, he listened to the remainder of Captain Helder's reports. Then the two of them gathered the rest of the king's guard, and all of their horses, and they began a long, quiet march through the city—a city that was partly evacuated, but that still seemed to be crawling with more people than it should have been for this time of morning.

Eyes peered out from every other window he passed. The still air— mist-laden now that the rain had stopped —was frequently interrupted by footsteps following them, cautiously but curiously close, and by whispers that echoed through the fog. Emrys kept his head high and his grip on the reins loose. The city bristled with fear and uncertainty; he felt it like a second pulse beating erratically beneath his skin. He would not add to the doubt by looking uncertain of his path.

They crossed the Red River and continued to the open Etherin Fields beyond it. This was the weakest stretch of border around Rykarra; here, that river that surrounded the city was at its narrowest. There had once been a great wall erected around the perimeter instead, but his father had torn much of it down, insisting that his power was great enough to protect the city. He hadn't needed walls.

Fool, Emrys couldn't help thinking as he took in the disturbing openness around him.

Any enemy that wanted to crush this city would most likely strike here first—so this was where they were concentrating most of their numbers.

One of the few parts of the once-great wall that remained was the Watchtower of Ander, perched on top of a hill taller than even the one the Palace of Eyes sat upon. As that watchtower came into focus, so too did the legions of soldiers who had been organizing since before dawn broke. The sounds of swords being sharpened, of men and women rallying each other with stories of past battles, and of armor clanking and chainmail slinking into place—all of it drowned out the foggy echoes of the city behind them. The air still hummed with uncertainty. But there was a sharper edge to it here, a bold promise of movement in spite of that fear.

As the morning pressed on, more soldiers filed in after Emrys's party. Still more came up over the hills beyond the city. Fire-kind, along with a smattering of Ice-kind and Bone-kind, made up most of their army outside of the Rooks. So some of the old allegiances remained, even as the crown had shifted.

And the fourth allegiance was mending; after making several rounds through the soldiers in the fields, Emrys headed back to the watchtower to find Alaya's father, Orion, standing at the base of it, along with dozens of other Serpent-kind who were outfitted for battle, their faces grim but resigned. Both Captain Helder and Emrys offered a slight nod in their direction, which was returned —an unspoken understanding passing between them.

They weren't here to protect the city. They were fighting only because Alaya was fighting.

But it was the beginning of what Emrys hoped was a positive change, at least.

He had started to dismount, planning to summit the tower, when a group of approaching soldiers caught his attention: No less than three hundred cloaked figures moved in rows of ten, all holding what appeared to be identical swords across their chests. The swords were unnaturally white, with a bluish hint to their edges that appeared to be glowing, as if Ice magic had been embedded in the steel.

Which was likely the case, he realized after a moment.

"So it's true: Some of the fabled Sword of Winter *has* decided to join us after all," the captain commented.

Emrys nodded, still staring. They moved with such synchronization that it seemed as if they had frozen the ground along their path, and they were gliding seamlessly along it with no need to lift their feet. White gloves covered their hands and grey masks covered their faces which, combined with the drawn hoods of their pale blue cloaks, left no part of their skin showing.

They reminded him of the grey-faced thorn-reapers

he'd read about in books—mostly in books that were about the beasts that resided in the Wild Northlands that separated his empire from the northern Kethran Empire. His mother had tried to hide those books from him, afraid that the stories might give him nightmares. But even as a small child, he had not been afraid. Not of storybooks, anyway.

And these particular monsters were on his side, so they didn't scare him either.

He spotted Lady Korva just ahead, sitting astride a white horse that was standing still enough to pass for a statue. She was welcoming her Ice-kind allies in with occasional cold nods of approval, her face as expressionless as the masks they wore.

He guided his horse over to hers. "They look intimidating, at least," he remarked.

"I am going to take that as a *thank you for your service* —in which case, you're welcome," she said, briefly glancing at him and giving a quick wink.

"I'll be sure to thank them heartily when and if they help us survive the day," he replied with wry look.

"Only time will tell if we manage that."

He breathed in deeply to steady himself against the thought that they might *not* manage it. "The bridge and the river itself need securing," he told her. "We cannot let them be crossed."

"Then we will see it secured," she said with a slight bow of her head.

He left her and climbed to the top of the watchtower,

where Captain Helder already stood taking in the sight below them, counting and muttering under his breath. All told, they estimated that they had perhaps a thousand forming ranks around the fields.

"Less than a third of what we *know* our enemy to be bringing," the captain said. "Three thousand marched across the Mirkrand Dunes this morning. But there are *also* reports of battalions forming in Silverbane and Mistwilde to join what I suppose they believe is the final march to topple the Rook throne."

"More could come to *our* aid before the day is over with as well," Emrys pointed out. "Not everyone wants us toppled. We sent summons far and wide. It's possible their replies were struck down by our enemies; it doesn't mean they won't show up soon."

Before the captain could say anything to this, they were interrupted by a messenger from the palace. His face was a flaming shade of red, streaked with sweat, and his chest heaved for breath as he knelt and informed them of the latest correspondence that had reached the palace.

"Condense it for us, boy," said Captain Helder, impatiently. "What's the worst of it, first off?"

The messenger lifted his gaze and said, "They've broken through the barriers in the shadow valleys."

Emrys exhaled a soft curse. Those valleys were one of the places where they had stationed soldiers as a sort of preliminary shield, hoping to thin the numbers of the Sun King's marching army before they drew too close to Rykarra.

"Numbers?" Captain Helder demanded.

The messenger looked as if he didn't want to answer, but he dutifully stammered on all the same: "Still in the thousands, my captain. With a great host of Sky-kind and Storm-kind among them—they number at least as many as the Sun-kind themselves. Very few of them fell in the valleys."

"Lovely," the captain grumbled.

Emrys kept his face impassive, though he shared the sentiment. The presence of Sky and Storm-kind was not unexpected; the Sun had their ancient allegiances, too, after all. But an abundance of Sky magic meant an abundance of annoyingly tricky shields to deal with. And Storm-kind magic... Well, he knew firsthand how deadly that could be.

Emrys discreetly pressed his fingertips together, feeling the spark of that magic rising inside of him at the mere mention of the Storm. A literal bolt of it appeared for a brief instant, a jagged line of bluish-white running up across the back of his hand before disintegrating in the air.

Captain Helder saw it, but he said nothing. It was clear, now, that he'd had several discussions with Lord Feran regarding the harvesting of magic that was occurring. He knew of his king's magic, at least to an extent.

After today, far more would likely know—after seeing it with their own eyes. But that was a problem for another day. If they *reached* another day.

When we reach it, he corrected himself.

The messenger was dismissed, and Captain Helder

turned back to the field and finished his job of sizing up their situation. "We destroyed many of the Sand-kind that were aiding them in the battle at the Gate of the Sun," he said, his tone offering a bit of cautious optimism, though his expression was still bleak. "And I have credible informants that tell me the leaders among that clan are starting to rebel against their alliance with Levant, at least in part because of how many they've already lost— so I doubt we'll have to deal with much of that kind of magic this time."

"The Sky and Storm magic will be plenty to deal with on its own."

"Agreed." A pause, and then: "Not everyone expects their young king to stay and fight, you know." He kept his eyes trained on the far-off hills. "You could join the legions that have fled to the fortress at Hollowforge. They need a leader there as much as this army does here. And your experience is likely better suited to leading the people at that fortress."

"Did Lady Isoni bribe you into saying these things?" he asked drily.

"You should know that I cannot be bribed, Your Majesty."

"Well, I am not *fleeing* to anywhere. And this city needs to know that. This *empire* needs to know that." He gripped the rough edge of the parapet before him and leaned over it a bit, more closely watching the soldiers scurrying about. "And besides, there is at least one person on his way to this city that I need to have a personal meeting with."

The captain considered this for a moment before quietly saying, "We are outnumbered. Grievously."

"I'm aware."

"They have more magic in their ranks than we do."

A sudden roar rumbled across the fields, and Emrys couldn't help the slight smile spreading across his face as the people below them pointed up at Rue's sudden appearance. "But *we* have a dragon, at least," he said.

Captain Helder's expression remained unchanged, but Emrys simply clapped him on the shoulder and walked away, moving to the other side of the tower and staring instead at the city behind them.

He watched as the Sword of Winter swept their magic over and around the Red River, freezing both that narrow band of water and the banks on either side of it. They stood at the edge of the created ice carpet that was closest to the city; the frozen ground they had made didn't seem to be affecting *their* ability to walk, but he suspected it would be disastrous to any enemy attempting to cross it.

Clever, he had to admit.

He pulled his eyes away from the mesmerizing shimmer of that Ice magic, and next he watched Rue soaring overhead with Alaya on her back. The two of them occasionally swooped out wider than he could see, scouting far into the hills and forests in the distance, creating a knot of anxiety in his stomach that wouldn't dissolve until they flew back into sight minutes, or some-times nearly an hour, later.

He watched the soldiers forming tighter ranks. The flares of magic popping up as the anxious users loosened themselves up for the imminent battle.

He watched the company of archers that Sade was organizing and shouting orders at, alongside one of his official generals.

He watched everything around him, and he waited.

An hour passed, and then another, and another—he lost count of the hours—and still no sign of their enemy appeared.

He saw Alaya returning from one of her extended scouting missions, and he found himself anxious to talk to her. There was no easy place for the dragon to land on the tower, so Emrys and Captain Helder left their posts and went below once more.

Their horses waited in the care of two young soldiers. Sybell, the old mare who had first faithfully served his mother, and now served him, lifted her head and snorted as Emrys approached. Her armor glistened. Her mane and tail had been braided and dyed blood-red, and there were patterns of the same shade painted across what little parts of her weren't covered by that armor—in keeping with one of the oldest battle traditions of Rook-kind. The roan that most of his soldiers rode had the same patterns. Any actual blood that an enemy might draw would be lost amongst the paint.

He gave Bell an affectionate pat before hoisting

himself into her saddle, nudging her away from the stone tower, and galloping toward the open field with his eyes trained above him.

Alaya caught sight of him and guided Rue lower. They were circling just above the ground, Alaya crouched between the dragon's shoulder blades and prepared to leap from her back and jog the rest of the distance to him. As steady as Bell was, she was not a fan of that dragon coming any closer than necessary.

But just before Alaya leapt from Rue's back, a shout from the watchtower distracted them all.

The source of that shout was pointing toward a person who had appeared on the crest of one of those distant hills, perhaps a half-mile from the edge of their outermost ranks.

This person was walking slowly toward the city.

Then came another.

And another.

But that was all. Three men walking toward an entire army, slowly and casually, with no others following them.

Emrys galloped closer, until he could see the men's faces more clearly, before he slowed to a stop.

Captain Helder drew his horse up beside Bell and muttered, "What sort of trickery is this?"

The three men advancing toward them stopped as well, and the center one called out: "If there is truly a high king amongst you, let him come forth!"

"You don't have to go," Captain Helder said. "This is not the Wild Age of our distant ancestors; we do not need to give in to foolish demands for the sake of tradition."

"Keep the lines organized behind me, and be prepared to counter whatever *trick* this is," Emrys told him, spurring Bell into a quick trot.

He was tired of waiting.

If today was truly the day the stars burned out and the darkness came for them, then he would meet that darkness head on, without flinching.

He did not charge toward that darkness alone; he had trotted Bell only half the distance to the three men when Rue's shadow overtook him and his horse once more. She glided ahead, her feathered tail sweeping back and forth, trimming the tips of grass just beyond Bell's step.

To their credit, the three enemy soldiers hardly shuddered at the sight—even as the dragon landed, dragging the grass and dirt up with her claws as she slid to a stop only a few dozen feet away from them. She arched her body like a snake prepared to strike, and she held that pose, lifting Alaya high above them.

Alaya drew her sword and rose to her feet, all while remaining perfectly balanced on the dragon's back, causing one of the men to briefly lose his balance at the sight.

The other two kept still, their gazes locked on Emrys, as if they could actually ignore that dragon and his queen.

Fools.

It was the middle one who spoke once more: "We are here on behalf of the Sun King," he said. "We were instructed to grant you a final chance to step down and let the high throne pass peacefully from your Rook claws."

"A final chance? How gracious." Emrys let the Storm magic inside of him spark to life once more, and he withdrew his sword as well; during the limited practice he'd had with this magic, he'd found that it was easier to draw out and 'conduct' it through the use of either sword or dagger. "And if I refuse?"

The soldiers visibly tensed, but otherwise didn't reply.

The silence stretched tight, each second a little more tense than the last until Alaya suddenly demanded: "Why are you three hiding your marks?"

The middle soldier remained motionless. But the other two took a partial step back at the question, and one of them instinctively moved to grip the black glove that reached midway up his forearm.

Alaya was summoning her magic a breath later, directing it toward the left glove of the man closest to her. That glove was ripped off, caught up in a whirlwind of her magic, and tossed aside. He snatched for it, but it was too late; the symbol on his wrist was plain to see—

A symbol that looked like a broken shard of a mirror.

Mimic-kind.

Emrys's blood turned to ice as he stared at that mark. He breathed out a realization just loud enough for Alaya to hear him: "They're combining Sky shields with Mimic trickery."

A volley of arrows flew toward them the instant the

words left his mouth, appearing to materialize from thin air.

Alaya brought them into her control with another quick Serpent spell, snatching the first of the projectiles away just before it struck Emrys in the shoulder. She threw all of them to the ground, save for one, which she retargeted toward the nearest Mimic-kind and hurled with incredible force—enough force that it drove through his thin chainmail, pierced his chest and dropped him to his knees. As he fell, she hooked a second arrow upwards, driving it into his throat.

He slumped forward onto the ground.

As that Mimic's pulse grew fainter, his breathing more labored, the air far behind him began to shimmer and separate, revealing what his magic had been hiding.

The other two Mimic-kind moved to block the view of that revelation.

Emrys pointed his sword toward them. With a whisper of Storm-kind words, he sent electricity wrapping around the blade and striking out from its tip. Bell reared at the sudden explosion of magic, but Emrys managed to pull her under control with one hand. The other hand kept his sword pointed at his enemies, and electricity tangled around those Mimic-kind and sent them convulsing toward the ground.

It was not enough to kill them. But it was enough to keep them in place. And while they were nearly paralyzed, fighting to shake free of the lightning he'd summoned, Rue lashed forward, spearing one with her claws and breaking the second's body with a snap of her long, powerful tail.

The air behind the bloodied and broken Mimic-kind shimmered and pulsed more violently. More of it shifted, and more of what was hidden by their power was revealed. There was still a shield of Sky-kind magic, but it was no longer mimicking a scene of an empty field—he could see through its pulsating face.

And he saw only a small part of the army on the other side.

"Can you break their shield?" he shouted to Alaya.

Her hand was already raised toward it, and she nodded. "I can see its magical energy, now that the Mimic's energy is gone!" she called back.

Emrys sheathed his sword, and he spun Bell back towards his own army and pushed her into a gallop, shouting orders as he went. "They're hiding the shields! Aim first for any Mimic-kind you see! Reveal the shields!"

He twisted back to see more of those shields appearing as the last bits of life faded from the already slain Mimic-kind. But there were still more Mimics at work, clearly still hiding other shields and creating an odd, patchwork wall across the landscape. It made it impossible to discern the true number of people marching toward them.

But the number that he already *could* see left him momentarily stunned and breathless.

Alaya was high above that number now. Rue circled, weaving and ducking the occasional shower of arrows while her rider summoned her power and overtook those shields that she could sense. Emrys could feel the force of her power, even from a distance. It twisted more completely into the revealed shields below Alaya, and suddenly, the air was filled with sparks—not the same as the Storm-kind he'd summoned, but a flashing of the two magics colliding, fighting for dominance.

Alaya's magic quickly crushed the Sky-kind's. A ripple of displaced energy raced out from each of those crushed magical shields, flattening the grass as it rushed toward Rykarra and the army around it.

By the time the waves of energy fully washed over Emrys, they had diffused to a point that they did little more than raise a slight chill across his skin.

But then, with their protection and concealing trickery now gone, the first band of the enemy army began their true charge.

Hundreds funneled through the openings where the shields had been, coming both on foot and on horseback, their swords and spears and arrows flashing in the sun and magic lighting in some of their palms.

Emrys called out to one of the nearby leaders of his Fire-kind forces. He raced across the front of his army, summoning fire himself and drawing a line of it into the beginnings of a barrier. The soldiers seemed momentarily stunned to see his magic use, but there was no time to question it. They performed their duties despite their shock, galloping in his wake and reinforcing the flames with their own magic, until a wall of those flames rose taller than he could see over.

Through the twisting fire, he could still see the faces of the ones charging toward him.

His archers would be able to see them, too.

Emrys circled back behind the wall of fire. He found Sade and the archers she stood in front of. She didn't need him to shout any orders; the moment their eyes met, she nodded, and she started shouting orders of her own.

To the right of Sade and her group, Captain Helder had initiated a similar strategy. The walls of flames were rising higher, while the archers directly behind those walls nocked arrows and drew back, holding as the enemies rushed closer, and closer—

Hundreds of arrows soared. Some volleyed over the flames, others shot straight through and caught that magic fire before piercing targets on the other side.

The Sky-kind countered by wrapping themselves and their fellow soldiers in shields and pressing forward.

The fire burned away many of those shields, but not quickly enough to keep the shielded ones from passing through the barrier. They pushed their way through the flames, first one-by-one, but then in greater numbers as the magic behind the fires faltered and extinguished.

Arrows met the first ones before they could manage even a few steps, but soon they were coming far too quickly to fully stop them.

Emrys drew Bell in a circle, eyes darting and seeking

his next strategy, when suddenly a familiar face appeared beside him.

Alaya's father walked calmly alongside a long line of other Serpent-kind, and they stepped in front of the archery line and began to work their magic.

Some took hold of the flames themselves and stretched them higher, wider, reigniting the magic that had started to die out. Others aimed for the ground beneath the charging army, splitting it open and swallowing entire swaths of the enemy. Several of the charging horses were overtaken as well, controlled into stumbling and crashing into each other.

The disruption gave the Fire-kind a chance to reinforce and rebuild their wall, and the two sides remained separated, at least for the moment.

Archers continued to pick off the charging enemies.

The greater numbers of that enemy hadn't overwhelmed them.

Not yet.

But in the distance, more Mimic-kind were being killed off, more shields were being revealed, and the impossible numbers that they faced grew more and more evident.

Emrys swerved and ducked his way back behind the lines of his archers.

He spotted a group of Sun-kind soldiers that had crept their way past the wall of fire; they were sweeping wide outside the center of the battle, heading toward the city, clearly trying to sneak their way into it. The Ice magic that had frozen the river reached far, but this group was racing toward the very edge of it. The ones farthest ahead were already attempting to break through that Ice with the use of Storm magic—and having some success with it.

He considered both Fire and Storm spells of his own, but hesitated to do either; he could feel his reserves of that magic already weakening a bit. He could only manage so many spells at once—and the greatest of their enemies had yet to reveal himself. He would need magic to face Sylven, to burn and shatter him beyond recognition.

So, instead, he opted to save that magic and rely on his sword, withdrawing it as he charged toward that sneaking line. He called for support as he galloped, and along with the small group that fell in alongside him, he hacked a bloody path through their enemies and brought their magic-breaking to an abrupt halt.

While his soldiers continued to engage the others in battle, Emrys spun and raced back for the bridge—the only section connected to the river that wasn't frozen with magic. He caught sight of Lady Korva on the other side, and he shouted to her, alerting her to the enemies attempting to thaw and ford that river.

With only a few wordless signals from her, several dozen of those strange Ice soldiers peeled silently away from the main group of them and slid toward the potential breaching of their barricade.

He was back in the shadows of the watchtower now. So he leapt from Bell's back with the intentions of climbing it and seeing the shape of the battle, of making his next decisions after taking in the view of it all from high above. He made it to the first of the tower's steps—

He sensed someone lunging toward him.

He pushed off the step and curved around, sword sweeping as he went. His blade clanged against the blade of a white-haired woman, the metallic crash echoing louder because of the rock tower walls that partially enclosed them. Their swords briefly locked together. He stepped into the deadlock, shoved and twisted free of it, and in the next instant, he was bringing his sword down upon her head.

The woman parried at the last instant and danced back and away. She had a Sun mark on her hand and two rays of gold above the pocket of her coat, he noticed—a higher-ranking member of the Army of the Sun.

He was surprised to see her so deep into his territory already.

He glanced to the fields beyond the tower. The wall of fire was burning out, and the enemy was indeed pouring in more deeply now, slaughtering mercilessly as they came.

He saw one of his soldiers impaled by a spear and slammed against the tower wall just before he yanked his gaze back to the woman before him. The soldier's dying cry echoed through Emrys's skull as he darted toward the Sun-kind and resumed their battle. They circled and crashed and fell away over and over in a dizzying exchange of swings and parries.

Then a pained cross between a roar and a shriek—a noise that could have come from nothing other than a dragon—made Emrys stumble mid-swing. His opponent took advantage of this and stabbed forward, catching his side with the tip of her sword. It was only a glancing blow, and the chainmail he wore protected him from the worst of it. But he could already feel the beginning of a bruise. All movement now caused a teeth-clenching, throbbing pain to fire through him.

Another roar shook the air.

It pulsed through Emrys like the beat of a war drum, the fear of what that roar could mean awakening his full strength, and with a vicious lunge, he managed to thrust his sword into the Sun-kind's side. He wedged it into a thin opening in her armor, pushed deep, and twisted it deeper still.

She dropped to one knee. He jerked his sword free as hers clattered to the ground, and his boot stomped onto her wrist as she reached for that fallen sword.

He finished immobilizing her with a streak of Storm-kind magic, no longer caring about conserving it. As she convulsed against the ground, he ran from under the tower, searching the skies...

He spotted Rue in the distance, wrapped in magic. She was ablaze with the white-blue energy and streaking toward the earth like a falling star.

He whistled for Bell, pulling himself into the saddle before the horse had even slowed to a complete stop. He kicked her into a hard gallop. They raced through the battlefield, dodging and leaping over fallen bodies, cutting a path through the living with a combination of sword and magic. Bell was old, but she was still fast and nimble, fast and nimble enough to give even the roan a good chase—

But they were still too slow.

The dragon struck the ground just as he reached them, throwing Alaya from her back and rattling the earth so violently that Bell's knees buckled and caused her to throw her rider as well.

Emrys hit the ground and rolled violently to a stop. Pain blossomed from every inch of his body. He pushed onto his knees, holding his bruised side and trying to catch his breath, searching.

Rue was flailing under the effects of the Storm magic, desperately lashing out with her claws and tail.

Alaya was crumpled in the grass a few feet away, not moving.

And their enemies circled around them, closing them off from the rest of their allies.

CHAPTER 31

ALAYA SENSED FOOTSTEPS...AND THEN A BODY LOOMING over her.

She heard Emrys calling her name.

Her eyes popped open and she moved, rolling under the swing of a sword and settling into a crouch a few feet away from the person wielding it. She found that person's energy—*Sun-kind*. He charged her with a violent cry, and the yellow-white light of his aura expanded and rose along with his fervor.

The sword was easier to catch and control, so Alaya took it and turned it against its owner, impaling him and turning his battle-cry into a gurgling, ultimately fruitless attempt to merely breathe.

Rue thrashed behind her, her serpentine body rising and falling to crush more of the soldiers trying to encircle them. Her hisses were part fury, part pain, her movements jerky from the Storm magic still sizzling through her.

Alaya fought her way past the two soldiers separating her from her dragon, and she swiftly inspected the damage the magic had done.

Electricity still sparked along Rue's scales. But the larger, mightier bolts of it that had wrapped her up and made them crash were dissipating. The dragon's movements grew steadily less twitchy as the seconds passed— though they were clearly still more labored than before that crash.

"Get away from here!" Alaya shouted, pushing the beast and urging her to her feet.

The dragon bellowed out her resistance, but Alaya insisted. Because Rue could likely fly, however unsteadily, now that she had shaken off the bulk of the spell that had knocked her from the skies. She could take off and land somewhere outside of the battle, and pause there until the debilitating effects of the Storm-kind magic more completely left her.

"*Go!* So I don't have to worry about you!"

Rue twisted wildly about, snapping a limb from one of their enemies, then stomping a second one into the ground and squeezing the last of his life away within a cage of her claws.

But then her intelligent eyes briefly locked with Alaya's pleading ones, and she paused.

"*Go,*" Alaya urged once more, almost begging now.

With a snort and a pained groan, the dragon lifted

shakily into the air and soared up above the battlefield once more.

And Alaya could have sworn she felt power slipping from Rue as she went—those warm, familiar-by-now shades of her mother's magic winding down to her and sinking in. She didn't have time to fully focus on them, but she felt them twisting through her body and settling like an extra layer of armor around her heart.

She turned back to the battle. Emrys reached her in the same instant, catching an enemy sword falling toward her and knocking it away with his own. He pivoted expertly around her latest attacker and finished them off with a slicing blow into their lower back.

Sade appeared shortly after that, her arrows preceding her, striking two men dead and sending them pitching face-forward onto the ground at Alaya's feet.

Alaya stepped over the dead bodies, withdrew her sword, and braced herself as more enemies rushed toward them.

She stood with Emrys and Sade at her back, and she felt almost invincible with them there, and with whatever extra power Rue had passed to her—untouchable enough that she could lose herself in the ebb and flow of her magic. It became a deadly, effortless extension of her attack. As easy as the steps she took and the sword she swung.

She found herself staring down the tip of an arrow that a Sky-kind had drawn and pointed at her. She snapped the arrow after swiftly wrapping its energy into her control and merely snapping it between her fingers, and then she ripped the life-force from her would-be assassin just as quickly.

So easy.

They paved a road of death through the field. She felled most of their enemies with her magic, while her companions picked off the few who managed to dodge the reach of that deadly control of hers.

And very soon, the number of those enemies who were brave enough to attack them had dwindled. A wide circle opened around them. As they finished off the last of their attackers within that circle, someone shouted Captain Helder's name. Alaya and Emrys both turned toward the sound, and they spotted the captain on his knees, holding his stomach.

Emrys was off in an instant, cutting a path toward the captain to aid him.

Alaya and Sade went back to the few scattered enemies around them, and minutes later, their immediate surroundings consisted of nothing more than scorched grass, blood-soaked earth, and still bodies.

The battle still raged, just outside of that immediate space. But for an instant, at least, they were able to pause and catch their breath.

Sade gazed at the destruction around them, kicking one of those seemingly lifeless bodies only to have it groan back at her. She finished it with an arrow as she backed her way toward Alaya.

"And I find myself asking that same question that first

occurred to me months ago," Sade muttered. "Which is, of course: *How the hell are we still alive?*"

Alaya inhaled deeply, regretting it instantly as the cloying scent of blood and other bodily fluids flooded her mouth. "No idea," she said, "but I wouldn't bet against us at this point—isn't that what we decided a while ago?"

She turned to offer Sade a grim smile.

But that smile never materialized.

Because what caught and held Alaya's attention was not the dark, bitter amusement in Sade's eyes, but the flash of a crossbow rising in the setting sun's light and being pointed at Sade's head.

Alaya managed to see the bolt's faint energy just as it was loosed from the bow. She tried to control it. To veer it away from Sade. But the one who'd shot it was otherwise armed—he was Fire-kind. And his magic was rising in the same instant, the aura of it powerful and threatening and distracting—

The bolt struck Sade in her throat.

Alaya froze.

Only for a second.

It seemed much longer than that as the world shifted and tipped, and she felt her stomach lurching with it.

Her retaliation was a swift reflex; she was blind with rage and she didn't even remember seeking that fiery life-force of her target. But when the haze lifted away from her vision, the wielder of the bow was lying on the ground, his body contorted in gruesomely unnatural ways and his weapon lying uselessly beside him.

She dropped to her knees and crawled to Sade's side. Shakily brushed away the hair that was matted to Sade's throat by blood. Her chest fluttered and caved, fluttered and caved. She couldn't breathe. *She couldn't breathe.*

But Sade breathed out a surprisingly slow, normal breath. "You...you really did forgive me for everything, didn't you?"

Alaya slipped a hand underneath Sade's head, cradling it, trying to keep it off the sharp rocks on the ground. Her lips parted and a whisper slipped from them, though it bared only the slightest resemblance to the words she was attempting to say: *Yes. Yes, I forgave you.*

"Good," Sade replied, exhaling one last long, slow breath before going frighteningly still.

"Wait—no." Alaya carefully gathered Sade closer to her, gasping at the amount of blood that quickly spread over her hands and made her grip dangerously slippery. "No. You know what? *No.* You aren't forgiven, actually, I— *look at me.* You aren't forgiven. And if you die, I swear I am never, ever, *ever* forgiving you. Do you understand me?"

"It's all even now, right?" Sade whispered, shutting her eyes tightly.

"Oh, don't be *stupid,*" Alaya said through clenched teeth. "We don't have to make things *even.* We...we..." Tears burned in her eyes. There was too much blood on her hands to try and wipe them away, so she just let them fall.

Enemies were converging around them once more.

Alaya struck the first several of them dead with her

magic before they were within sword's reach of her and Sade. But there were too many more arriving, too fast. Their opponent's greatest weapon had collapsed into a weakened, weeping puddle on the ground, and word of this spread quickly. So quickly that Alaya stopped trying to pick out their individual energies as they charged her; she simply attacked them all, ripped them indiscriminately apart and quickly lost track of how many bodies fell around her.

Eventually, they would stop coming.

Eventually, she would rip them all apart, and they would stop hurting her.

She would rip the entire *world* apart if that was what it took.

This last thought numbed her magic for a moment, because she knew that it was all wrong; she was a force for *good* in this world. This was why they'd gone to battle, wasn't it?

She wouldn't rip it all apart, no matter how badly she wanted to.

Her second of hesitation was all it took—a sword broke through that brief pause in the whirlwind of her magic. She saw it coming before it was properly swung at her. She tried to grab it, but she was shaking too hard, both from the effort of so much magic at once, and from her grief, and just as she had been too slow and distracted to catch that crossbow's bolt, she failed to stop this attack, too.

The sword sliced toward them.

She covered Sade's body with hers as best she could to protect it from the sharpness.

But the bite of steel never came.

Instead, Alaya heard a sudden metallic *pinging* and *cracking*—an odd sound that reminded her of tree limbs breaking off in an ice storm.

She lifted her gaze and saw that sword paused above her, and that ice was indeed sweeping across its surface and shattering it as if it *were* a mere tree limb.

Its wielder tried to drop it, but he was too slow; that Ice magic shot from the handle of his shattering sword and raced up his arm, freezing it and causing him to scream in pain before tumbling back and falling to the ground.

Cloaked figures in grey masks swept in around Alaya, and they drove her enemies back with frigid magic that flew both from their fingertips and from the enchanted white blades they carried. She had heard about those magic-infused blades, she remembered vaguely. Lady Korva had mentioned them when discussing the army that hailed from her province.

And Lady Korva herself galloped into sight seconds later. She took one look at Sade's bloody, lifeless figure, and then she was leaping from her horse's back and kneeling beside Alaya.

"I'm sorry," she said.

Alaya ignored the apology, because she refused to believe that there was anything to be sorry *for*.

Sade was not dead.

She was *not dead*.

"Take her back to the city," she commanded. "There are Oak-kind and Bone-kind along the edge of it, a whole host of them waiting to heal and stave off death; we stationed them there to help the wounded. To...to..."

"I know we have them there, but she is already—"

"Take her!"

Lady Korva drew back, resolve and understanding slowly settling over her face. She nodded and slowly rose back to her feet. At a click of her tongue, her horse trotted to her and knelt down, allowing her rider to load Sade into the saddle before she climbed into it herself. Sade slumped against the horse's neck, her blood flowing freely out from her wound for a moment, until Lady Korva managed to apply pressure to it.

That blood appeared startlingly bright against the horse's white body.

And that brightness was the last thing Alaya saw before she picked up her sword, turned, and saw Sylven walking toward her with a smile on his face.

CHAPTER 32

THE WORLD TILTED UNDER HER FEET AGAIN, AND EVERY STEP Sylven took toward her made it angle more sharply, threatening to knock her off balance.

But she would not fall.

She steadied her grip on her sword, and she mirrored his calmness as she strode forward to meet him. People ran at the sight of them coming together, as if fleeing at the sight of a building tidal wave, desperate as they were to get away before the powerful collision of sea and shore. By the time they reached one another, Alaya saw almost no others in her peripheral vision—though the sounds of those others battling still battered the air and made the earth beneath her tremble.

Sylven tilted his head and peered around her, staring in the direction that Sade had been carried off to. "That didn't have to happen, you know."

"Be quiet," Alaya snarled, lifting her own sword while seeking out the energy of the one he carried.

"You have quite the collection of dead friends and family now, don't you?"

"She's not dead."

"You can sense energies, can you not?"

Alaya didn't reply; he already knew the answer was *yes*.

"Well? Can you still sense hers? Does it still feel *alive*?"

Alaya refused to try, one way or the other, because she would not be distracted from the fight that now stood directly in front of her.

The sky was darkening. The day was ending. The moment of prophecy was arriving. Her magic was focused, now seeking that faint light of Sylven's aura that she had managed to see when last they'd fought. She knew she could find it again.

And this time, she would rip it out of him, and it would take his breath with it.

A thousand times, she had played out this battle in her mind, and now her body moved forward as if bursting into a rehearsed dance.

Last time, it had taken drawing blood to make that golden light spill out of him, so this was her main focus now. She circled him and caught his sword in a web of her magic. While he struggled to free his weapon, she sliced hers toward his legs.

He dropped the sword so he could dodge her more

easily. As it hit the ground, he leapt away from her swing and landed gracefully several feet away.

She abandoned her hold on his sword and thought only of stabbing him with her own—

A mistake.

He grabbed his weapon the instant she released it, not with his hands but with his magic, and he jerked it through the air. She dove aside as it streamed toward her. The sword passed close enough to her face that she felt the breeze it stirred up; she was surprised it didn't cut the strands from her hair that were flying more freely, increasingly disheveled from her battles.

Her dive ended in a roll across the pebbly ground. She sprang instantly back to her feet, and with a vicious cry, she spun toward him; he parried at the last possible second, meeting her sword clumsily and only just managing to push it away from his face.

Closer, this time.

She was getting closer to drawing blood.

She kept up her assault, yanking her sword away, causing a screech of steel sliding down steel that was still echoing in her ears as she swung again.

Again, again, *again*, she swung, and she pivoted, and she darted around him in a blur of fury and power.

Several times, she tried to take his sword in her magic's grasp and twist it, trying to throw off his ability to counter her. It was a strategy that had served her well in most of her battles on this field today—but one that he quickly circumvented by employing the same trick against her. Soon her sword was constantly being knocked off course by his magic. He stopped trying to attack her with any real earnest, and instead he focused on simply disrupting *her* attacks. Those disruptions threw off her balance and rhythm, frustrating her.

It felt like he was toying with her.

After several minutes of this, her arms were growing sore. Her steps were slowing. Then, out of the corner of her eye, she spied one of the countless dead who were strewn over the field; one of the cloaked Ice soldiers that answered to Lady Korva. His sword rested on the ground beside him. It still glittered with pale blue shades of Ice-kind magic, and if she could strike Sylven with it, then perhaps...

She dropped her sword and focused on that fallen one instead, lifting it and attempting to impale him in the back with it.

But he heard it coming. He whirled around, struck it down, and then in a single fluid motion he was swiveling back around and striking for her.

Without her sword to parry his, she was forced to jump back to avoid the attack. She lost her balance. She caught herself with one hand against the ground and shoved herself back up, reaching out for her sword as she did.

Before she could possess it, Sylven's hand caught her throat and slammed her back down.

His grip stayed around her throat, crushing her windpipe, while he brought the tip of his sword down to hover just above her chest and whispered, "After I kill you, I am going to take all those other pieces of that divine magic inside of you, and I will become so much more powerful than the mere supplanter king you were all so concerned about. So much more *dangerous*."

A rock had lodged itself into the back of Alaya's head as she'd slammed against the ground, and pain carved a very clear and brightly burning path through her skull as she fought to breathe.

"You would have been better off just working alongside me, if you *truly* cared about shaping this empire, as you claim. I hope you realize that. Because I want you to die thinking about it."

There was a weakness in her armor, an opening under her arm to allow for a freer range of movement. The tip of Sylven's sword found it and twisted in, causing her to cry out in pain.

"We could have been a beautiful pair," he said. "But you chose the wrong king. Oh well."

"You...you are not...a...*king*." She nearly fainted from the effort of forcing out the words with the tiny amount of breath she had left. "Never...will...be..."

"No, perhaps not. But I *am* about to be a god, so I think I'll manage just fine."

She didn't reply.

She needed to save her breath for the plan that was surfacing, fighting its way into her fading mind.

There was a knife sheathed against her ankle. Just an old hunting knife that was neither large nor sharp. But she knew its energy well, and it was easy to grab it, even as dark spots started to swim into her vision.

She focused on that energy. Cupped her hand. Beckoned. And suddenly, that knife was wrenching free of its casing and flying up toward her, then arcing upwards to slash across his neck.

Blood showered over her, and then his grip on her throat faltered enough that she managed to twist, to find enough leverage to slam a knee into his side. His body buckled. She rolled out from underneath it, called the knife into her hand, and braced her other hand against the ground while she inhaled several deep breaths and fought her way back from the faintness that had almost overtaken her.

Sylven was doubled over from her kick. One hand was pressed against his neck, and it was covered in blood.

Blood.

And with it came a dark golden light, just as before. Not only from the wound itself, but from all over his body; he couldn't hide his energy when he was injured and bleeding like this. It roiled off of him like smoke.

She reached out with her own magic, and just as before, she saw the flicker of fear and fury cross his face.

He grabbed his sword and leapt back into action before she could take hold of him completely.

But drawing blood and energy from him had reignited her drive, helping her push past her own injuries. She easily skirted around his attack, wrenching his weapon out of his grasp as she did.

He tried to catch it.

The sword was suspended in mid-air for a moment, both of them attempting to overcome the other's hold.

She had more magic than he did.

But he had spent more time *mastering* his magic—mastering it with this one end goal in mind, it seemed, and now he pushed into that goal with a ruthless strength that made her stumble and awkwardly twist her ankle as she tried to keep her equilibrium.

She attempted to shift her weight to her other foot, but that instant of unbalance was all he'd needed.

He momentarily gained complete control of the sword, and he pushed it forward instead of pulling it back to him as she'd expected. The sword struck that same small opening under her arm as before, only now it plunged deeper. Pain erupted through her. She gritted her teeth and bit back a cry as he yanked that sword back out with the same ferocity.

She dropped to one knee and pressed a fist to the wound, trying to put pressure on the frightening amount of blood she could already feel oozing out and sliding down beneath her armor.

He stepped toward her.

She found the energy of the stones littering the ground, and she clung to each individual sliver of it, wrapped those slivers into her control and then flung them as hard as she could.

All trace of his usual cruel smile disappeared as he

knocked the stones aside and came closer and closer, and then he reached out a hand over her.

He didn't touch her.

And yet her throat felt dry and hollow, as if he was choking her again, and she couldn't inhale a true breath no matter how hard she tried.

It took her only a moment to realize what was happening; because how many times had she performed this same spell?

He was controlling the breath from her lungs.

And she should have seen this coming. She should have realized that his connection to her life and power, and that the latest divine magic he'd collected, might allow him to work such divine and dangerous control over her. But it still shot panic straight into her core, that inability to breathe, and all of her strength was suddenly focused on not collapsing into a mire of that panic.

She kept her eyes open. She tried to hang on. *This is not how it ends,* she told herself, over and over. *This is not how it ends, I promised I wouldn't stop until I set it all right—*

"This is not how it ends," she said, loud enough for Sylven to hear this time.

And this time, she took more than a stone into her command; she grabbed the earth beneath it as well, and she ripped a massive strip of it up into the air. Still wheezing for breath, she hurled it like a javelin into his chest.

His hold on her breathing slipped as he was struck.

The aura around him flared again. Alaya staggered back to her feet. Centered her sight on that flaring glow.

And then she began to draw it out.

Words fell into her head and she whispered them without pausing to think—the same words that she had spoken when she had drawn her mother's magic out of everything else.

She would take that magic first, and then he would be nothing but a shell that would be easy to crush.

"If you take it from me, it will kill you," he coughed.

She hesitated—though she'd tried not to—and she immediately hated herself for doing so.

Because he was smiling again...that same cruel smile that he always had when he sensed her fear. "You think you were meant to have *all* of this power?" he asked. "There's a reason your mother did not give it all to you—because you aren't strong enough to hold it all. You are not her. You are not *divine*. You will absorb this magic and yes, you will burn fierce and bright for a moment with it —but then you will flicker out just as quickly."

"I don't care."

His lips parted, but she cut him off—

"I don't care, as long as I burn long enough to finish killing *you*."

She reached again for that magic.

But the light he carried was no longer billowing out like smoke from a suddenly-doused fire; there were only wisps of it that she could see, now. She swayed from the effort of attempting to keep pulling those wisps from him.

She could feel him fighting back, holding on to that power as he had held onto that sword between them earlier.

She needed to draw more blood.

To weaken him further.

Her balance swayed again at the mere thought. She briefly squeezed her eyes shut and forced herself to breathe. And when she opened them again, she saw something that made her heart leap. Perhaps the only sight that could have kept her on her feet just then—

The High King of Sundolia was walking toward them.

Blood covered the right side of his face, his hands, his shoulder.

But his steps were still steady, and so was his grip on his sword. Fire ignited around his hands as he came closer, and the tendrils of it wrapped down around that blade at his side.

Alaya exhaled slowly. She forced her eyes to Sylven's, holding them with a fierce gaze that kept his attention on her. She only needed to keep it for a moment.

It happened that quickly.

Sylven turned too slowly.

A Fire-kind spell roared from Emrys's mouth, causing the magic to blaze brighter around his sword as he stabbed it into Sylven's chest.

That magic burned right through the chainmail Sylven was wearing; Alaya could smell it in an instant, a tangy, acrid twist of melting metal and burning flesh that grew nauseatingly intense as Emrys shoved his blade deeper.

She held her breath, caught that sword with her magic, and pulled it the rest of the way through.

Sylven's face contorted in agony. His mouth fell open, but no sound beyond a breathy grunt escaped him, even as he collapsed to the ground. His body bled streams of red into the dirt around him. It twitched and it smoldered with the remnants of Fire magic.

And then it began to radiate with a vivid, golden light.

As Alaya stepped over him, his eyes blinked open, and words trickled out alongside the blood from his mouth: "If you take it, *it will kill you.*"

Alaya knew there was a chance he was telling the truth.

But she was not afraid. She wasn't certain whether it was her mother's voice, or her own thoughts; all she knew was that the last pieces of her power were rising in front of her, and now the whispers she heard were very clear—

This power was meant to save you.

It belongs to you.

And so she took it.

Her body twisted with it, and her knees buckled.

Emrys was by her side a breath later, catching her and laying her gently back against the ground. His hand then went immediately to the deep wound beneath her arm, and he moved her clothing and armor aside by only inches before drawing his hand back in alarm and twisting around to call for help.

As he turned back to her, she reached up and pressed a hand to his beautiful, panicked, bloodied face. She felt her breaths slowing. Her vision fading. Heard a roaring in her ears that was somehow both frightening and peaceful at the same time.

Emrys reached back, trailing his fingers over her cheek.

She focused on his touch with every ounce of strength she had left.

And then it all went dark.

CHAPTER 33

Wake up, my heart.

She felt a hand squeezing hers.

Wake up.

A warm breeze tousled her blood-soaked hair.

Wake up and finish things.

Alaya opened her eyes to a sky full of the brightest stars she had ever seen.

Emrys was still beside her, holding one of her hands. In front of them stood Captain Helder and a dozen others, shielding them both from their enemies. An Oak-kind knelt beside her as well. And because of that Oak-kind, her wound had stopped bleeding, it seemed like; it was only sore, and sticky with dried blood that pulled painfully at her skin when she moved.

"FALL BACK!" the captain was roaring. "Fall back and protect the city!"

Emrys glanced down at Alaya, noticed her eyes were

504

open, and he gently started to help her sit up. "Come on, we need to—"

"No." The authority in her own voice surprised her.

"...No?"

"I can stop them. I can finish things."

"There are too many, we need to try and regroup, to..." he trailed off, a sudden, unmistakable expression of awe overtaking him as he lifted his eyes and fully took in the sight of her.

She had no way of knowing what she looked like. But she felt as if she were glowing, burning brighter than any of those stars above her.

She felt steady.

She felt alive.

She felt *whole*.

Emrys let go of her and took a step back, and she rose to her feet on her own and took a few steps toward their approaching enemies.

"What is she doing?" she heard Captain Helder demand.

Out of the corner of her vision, she saw Emrys watching her, a bit of uncertainty creeping in amongst his awe.

Forever the skeptic, she thought with a slight smile.

But however skeptical he was, he still held up a hand and brought the captain to a halt, and he and his soldiers simply watched as Alaya moved across the field.

She walked alone to that enemy army. They were reforming their ranks, preparing for one last march to finish off the ones who were currently fleeing back toward the city.

Finish things, whispered that voice in her head once more.

For once, she didn't question whether or not she could do this.

She let her magic flow through her and take over her vision. She no longer saw individual people. She saw a multitude of colors, a great ribbon of them moving in a wave across the field.

And she pushed that wave back.

She was not killing them. She did not *want* to kill them, to pull their breaths away; instead, she was the breath herself—a great, divine breeze blowing over them, taking hold of every body on that front line and forcing their limbs to tremble and their feet to stop and then ultimately step back.

The second wave stopped on their own. Their stares alternated between those controlled ones and the small, solitary figure that was doing the controlling. Some cried out. Some turned and raced away. Some fell to their knees, convinced they were witnessing one of the Marr themselves, reincarnated into flesh and come to put an end to their empty wars.

A few tried to fight their way past Alaya's control, and they were quickly dealt with.

And in the end, all that remained of their enemy's army turned and fled beyond the hills and out of sight.

A hush fell over the battlefield, interrupted at first by

only the occasional groan of the injured and dying.

Then the whispers began. They grew louder and louder. Loud enough that she could make out individual words, at which point she braced herself out of habit, waiting for the fearful curses to fly at her.

But that was not what she heard.

She was certain she was mistaken about what she was hearing, because they were not cursing her name...they were hailing it, and some were even using a new title along with it.

The Dragon Queen brings victory!

She turned around and found Emrys walking toward her, while the crowds behind him grew louder still.

Hail the king!

Hail the queen!

We have victory!

Her king took her hand, and she lifted her eyes to the dark sky, to the stars, to the light of a weary half-moon that was only just peeking out behind the clouds.

Victory!

She wanted to smile at those distant cheers. But the scent of death around her was too strong. Her head tucked to her chest as she tried not to let sickness overtake her. Her eyes stayed open through sheer force of will. She noticed the blood on her hands, the blood staining her boots, and she thought of the brightness that had stained Lady Korva's horse.

"Victory..." she heard herself mutter.

They had victory, but not without its costs.

EPILOGUE

Two Weeks Later

THREE DAYS AFTER LEAVING FOR A POLITICAL VISIT TO THE CITY of the Sun, Alaya was soaring once more over the familiar streets of Rykarra.

Rue touched down lightly in the largest of the palace courtyards. The guards strolling the paths in that yard only jumped slightly at the sight of her...and then they sighed in relief as they realized they were not actually in danger of being eaten.

Alaya leapt from Rue's back, pressed her forehead to the dragon's, and gave her a quick squeeze. Then she stepped back and watched as Rue took flight again, staring until the dragon was nothing more than a silhouette against the early evening sky. She was likely headed off to find someplace cozy to nap.

Alaya could only guess at this, of course; in the two weeks since the battle in the Etherin Fields, she had not been able to hear Rue's voice in her head, and she no longer shared the beast's sight, either. She suspected it had to do with the last moment she'd spent with Rue on that battlefield, when she had felt what seemed to be more of mother's power passing from the dragon and into her.

So she didn't know where Rue was going. But she hoped the dragon was sleeping well, wherever she went —she had earned this much, at least.

And she might have lost her ability to fully communicate with the creature, but at least she hadn't lost her entirely.

In the end, she had been extraordinarily fortunate when it came to loss—a fact that she reminded herself of once again as she turned and headed for the nearest palace door.

She still had Rue.

She still had Emrys.

And by some miracle that she still didn't quite believe in, she still had Sade, too.

The courtyard guards bowed a proper welcome as Alaya passed them, as did the guards that opened that door for her. From there, she took the steps to the second floor in leaps and bounds, quickly making her way to the room that had become Sade's permanent residence.

Sade was awake, sitting up in her bed with a tray of food in her lap.

"Still not dead," Alaya commented, smiling.

Sade smiled back. "No betting against us."

"I brought a gift from the Sun Queen," she told her, withdrawing a necklace from the bag slung across her body. "It was made by the Star-kind; they say the light in it helps calm even the worst pains and anxieties."

"I thought we were done trusting the word of Stars?"

Alaya's grin brightened at this, and she shrugged. "It's a pretty necklace, at least."

"Very true," Sade agreed, holding out her hand.

She handed it over, and as Sade lifted it by its golden chain and studied it closer, Alaya's gaze lingered, just for a moment, on the marks running along Sade's forearm.

Sade's body was still covered in these marks, in faint scars that would likely become permanent. The patterns they made across her skin were not unlike the patterns that frost etched onto window panes. They were the result of an old Ice-kind trick, as Lady Korva had explained to them; a sudden coating of Ice magic sent the body into a shock that could keep it alive for a short time, until other healing methods were available.

Alaya owed the Ice-kind her best friend's life, and she wasn't sure she would ever be able to repay her.

But even though Sade had lived, her days following that battle had been spent perilously teetering on the edge between life and death. And she had been bedridden for most of these past weeks, even as her strength slowly returned.

So Alaya had gone without her to the Kingdom of the Sun—though not entirely alone, of course. She had her own personal guard now, just as the king did, and she had been accompanied by her father and several other Serpent-kind, as well.

She could have had an entire army following her, if she'd asked for it.

But it wasn't necessary, now; word had spread of her power, of Sylven's death, and of her victory on the Fields of Etherin. She and her group had faced little opposition when they arrived in Idalia for a second attempt at that summit that should have taken place at the Gate of the Sun.

She had gone to that city with a goal, and she had achieved it: Levant was now a prisoner in his own palace dungeons. The Sun Queen that had helped Alaya escape those very same dungeons now helped her by taking over the southern crown and its duties.

And the seemingly endless battles between the kingdoms had stopped, at least for the time being.

She was still haunted by the battles that had already taken place. She likely always would be, because they could not be undone. All the blood could not be unspilled. And every night, she still heard Ma's voice in her head, asking her that same question—*did you really finish that fight you started all those years ago?*

But she had also accepted the fact that she would always have to keep fighting in some way. Because peace, she had decided, was not so much a destination to reach or a thing to be obtained, but a thing to be planted. Watered. Protected. Maintained.

So day after day, she woke and tended to that fragile peace alongside the Rook King, and she had hope that their efforts would soon begin to bloom into something that was both beautiful and lasting.

A knock at the door brought Alaya to her feet, and she answered it to find Lady Isoni standing there holding a stoppered bottle and a bag of medicinal herbs that she could smell even though that bag was tied.

"Oh. You're back." It was either mild relief or resolved indifference in Lady Isoni's voice—it was impossible to say which, really.

Alaya decided to offer her a friendly smile, regardless. "You've brought her medicine?"

"Clearly."

"You're delivering it? Couldn't you have sent a servant?"

"I could have."

"Ah. But you're personally worried about her, I suppose."

"Yes," Isoni deadpanned. "I'm personally worried that she's dragging this out, overreacting just to get attention —and wasting my servants' time in the process."

"I can hear you," Sade called.

"I know," Lady Isoni called back before shoving the door open with her shoulder and disappearing inside.

Alaya laughed softly to herself, and she stepped out of the room; Sade would fuss at her for leaving her to face Isoni alone, but there was at least one other person who would be eager to know that she was home.

She found him on the roof of one of the library towers, tucked into the corner and reclining in a hammock.

The top of this tower was accessible only by way of a tall, narrow metal ladder—one that always made her heart race as she climbed it—and it was a beautiful place to watch a sunset, she'd discovered. But Emrys didn't seem to be aware of the sunset; he was too focused on reading the letter in his hands. An entire pile of letters, along with several books, rested on the ground beside the hammock.

Alaya cleared her throat and said, "Hello, Rook-King."

He looked up. A slow smile stretched over his face as he rose to his feet. "Hello, Dragon-Queen," he replied, crossing the roof and taking her into his arms.

She held tightly to him, her fingers clenching his shirt as she breathed in his familiar scent. It was at least a full minute before she pulled away and gave him a brief account of her time spent in Idalia.

He listened dutifully to her report, but by the time she had finished, he was wearing a slightly sheepish smile, and she could tell that his mind had drifted to other things.

"I missed you," he said, tilting her chin up and sweeping a soft kiss across her lips.

She couldn't help smiling back when he looked at her —and kissed her—like that, and all thoughts of politics and peace talks briefly vanished from her mind as she stood on her toes to kiss him again. "I missed you too," she said.

"Also, I expected you'd be back tonight, so I have something for you here..." He went back to the hammock he'd been reclining in, reached behind the pile of books beside it, and pulled out a small parcel wrapped in a velvety cloth. He walked slowly back to her, handing it to her with a look she couldn't quite decipher on his face. "I had it made while you were away."

She unwrapped the cloth to find a crown inside.

"It's...it's beautiful," she whispered.

And it was. The polished silver glistened even in the shadows where they stood. It was light, but it felt sturdy and unyielding in her grasp. The sides of it were twisted and shaped into what resembled an artful entanglement of dragon and bird wings, and they elegantly wrapped around to the front and center of the piece, where they weaved between a trio of embedded diamonds—one for each of the three kingdoms.

She turned it over and around in her hands for a minute, and then she said, "I suppose this makes it official, then."

"Well, not *officially* official. There's the matter of a

proper betrothal. And a wedding—the people in this palace always insist upon a wedding, for some reason."

"Oh, right. We never actually had one of those, did we?"

"A wedding? No. But in our defense, we've been distracted."

"And the betrothal? You never properly *asked* me to be your queen, either, did you?"

"I don't suppose I have."

She tilted her head expectantly.

His eyes danced with laughter as he asked, "Well? Shall we, then?"

She stared at that beautiful crown for another moment, marveling again at how light it felt in her grasp. And then she plopped it, rather unceremoniously, onto her head.

"I'll take that as a yes," he said, laughing as he wrapped her into his arms and held her tight against him once more.

Over the sound of his heartbeat, Alaya soon heard music playing from somewhere in the city; a soft melody of strings on the wind, accompanied by the occasional warble of drums and the hopeful high notes of a flute.

Neither of them had to ask the other to dance this time.

They simply began to move together in the same instant, gliding apart and then back together, twirling and stepping with a rhythm they both seemed to know by heart. They kept dancing even after that music had stopped, and long after the darkness of night had fallen...

And not once did they bother to glance at the stars above them.

THE END

Made in United States
Troutdale, OR
12/23/2024

27224187R00322